continued . . .

"Stirling is a perfect master of keep-them-up-all-night pacing, possibly the best in American SF, quite capable of sweeping readers all the way to the end."

—*Booklist* (starred review)

"I liked this book. . . . Stirling is a master of world building. This series has gone a long way from its point of departure, but still keeps a horde of fans wanting more."

—SFRevu

"Stirling has crafted a complex follow-up to *The Sunrise Lands* that vividly describes the political landscape."

—Monsters and Critics

The Sunrise Lands

"Combines vigorous military adventure with cleverly packaged political idealism. . . . Stirling's narrative deftly balances sharply contrasting ideologies. . . . The thought-provoking and engaging storytelling should please Stirling's many fans." —*Publishers Weekly*

"Brilliant action." —*Booklist*

"Fast-paced." —*Futures Mystery Anthology Magazine*

"A master of speculative fiction and alternate history, Stirling delivers another chapter in an epic of survival and rebirth." —*Library Journal*

A Meeting at Corvallis

"[A] richly realized story of swordplay and intrigue."
—*Entertainment Weekly*

"Stirling concludes his alternative-history trilogy in high style. . . . [The story] resembles one of the cavalry charges the novel describes—gorgeous, stirring, and gathering such earth-pounding momentum that it's difficult to resist."

—*Publishers Weekly*

"A fascinating glimpse into a future transformed by the lack of easy solutions to both human and technological dilemmas."   —*Library Journal*

The Protector's War

"Absorbing."   —*The San Diego Union-Tribune*

"[A] vivid portrait of a world gone insane . . . it also has human warmth and courage. . . . It is full of bloody action, exposition that expands character, and telling detail that makes it all seem very real. . . . It is the determination of its major characters to create a safe and loving world that makes the book so affecting."

—*Statesman Journal* (Salem, OR)

"Reminds me of Poul Anderson at his best."

—David Drake, author of *What Distant Deeps*

"Rousing. . . . Without a doubt [*The Protector's War*] will raise the bar for alternate-universe fiction."

—John Ringo, *New York Times* bestselling author of *Citadel*

Dies the Fire

"*Dies the Fire* kept me reading till five in the morning so I could finish at one great gulp. . . . Don't miss it."

—Harry Turtledove

"Gritty, realistic, apocalyptic, yet a grim hopefulness pervades it like a fog of light. The characters are multidimensional, unusual, and so very human. Buy *Dies the Fire*. Sell your house; sell your soul; get the book. You won't be sorry."   —John Ringo

"A stunning speculative vision of a near-future bereft of modern conveniences but filled with human hope and determination. Highly recommended."   —*Library Journal*

The
High King of
Montival

A NOVEL OF THE CHANGE

S. M. STIRLING

A ROC BOOK

ROC
Published by New American Library, a division of
Penguin Group (USA) Inc., 375 Hudson Street,
New York, New York 10014, USA
Penguin Group (Canada), 90 Eglinton Avenue East, Suite 700, Toronto,
Ontario M4P 2Y3, Canada (a division of Pearson Penguin Canada Inc.)
Penguin Books Ltd., 80 Strand, London WC2R 0RL, England
Penguin Ireland, 25 St. Stephen's Green, Dublin 2,
Ireland (a division of Penguin Books Ltd.)
Penguin Group (Australia), 250 Camberwell Road, Camberwell, Victoria 3124,
Australia (a division of Pearson Australia Group Pty. Ltd.)
Penguin Books India Pvt. Ltd., 11 Community Centre, Panchsheel Park,
New Delhi - 110 017, India
Penguin Group (NZ), 67 Apollo Drive, Rosedale, Auckland 0632,
New Zealand (a division of Pearson New Zealand Ltd.)
Penguin Books (South Africa) (Pty.) Ltd., 24 Sturdee Avenue,
Rosebank, Johannesburg 2196, South Africa

Penguin Books Ltd., Registered Offices:
80 Strand, London WC2R 0RL, England

Published by Roc, an imprint of New American Library, a division of Penguin
Group (USA) Inc. Previously published in a Roc hardcover edition.

First Roc Mass Market Printing, September 2011
10 9 8 7 6 5 4 3 2 1

Copyright © Steven M. Stirling, 2010
Map by Cortney Skinner
All rights reserved

To Diana Paxson, fellow bard

Acknowledgments

Yet more!

Thanks to my friends who are also first readers:

To Steve Brady, for assistance with dialects and British background, and also natural history of all sorts.

Thanks also to Kier Salmon, for once again helping with the beautiful complexities of the Old Religion, and with . . . well, all sorts of stuff!

To Diana L. Paxson, for help and advice, and for writing the beautiful Westria books, among many others. If you like the Change novels, you'll probably enjoy the hell out of the Westria books—I certainly did, and they were one of the inspirations for this series; and her *Essential Asatru* and recommendation of *Our Troth* were extremely helpful . . . and fascinating reading.

To Dale Price, for help with Catholic organization, theology and praxis; and for his entertaining blog, Dyspeptic Mutterings, which can be read at http://dprice.blogspot.com/.

To Brenda Sutton, for multitudinous advice.

To Melinda Snodgrass, Emily Mah, Terry England, George R. R. Martin, Walter Jon Williams, Vic Milan, Jan

Stirling and Ian Tregellis of Critical Mass, for constant help and advice as the book was under construction.

Thanks to John Miller, good friend, writer and scholar, for many useful discussions, for loaning me some great books, and for some really, really cool old movies.

Special thanks to Heather Alexander, bard and balladeer, for permission to use the lyrics from her beautiful songs, which can be—and should be!—ordered at www.heath -erlands.com. Run, do not walk, to do so.

Thanks again to William Pint and Felicia Dale for permission to use their music, which can be found at http:// members.aol.com/pintndale/, and should be, for anyone with an ear and salt water in their veins.

And to Three Weird Sisters—Gwen Knighton, Mary Crowell, Brenda Sutton and Teresa Powell—whose alternately funny and beautiful music can be found at www.threeweirdsisters.com.

And to Heather Dale for permission to quote the lyrics of her songs, whose beautiful (and strangely appropriate!) music can be found at www.HeatherDale.com and is highly recommended. The lyrics are wonderful and the tunes make it even better.

Thanks to S. J. "Sooj" Tucker for permission to use the lyrics of her beautiful songs, which can be found at www .skinnywhitechick.com, and should be.

Thanks again to Russell Galen, my agent, who has been an invaluable help and friend for a decade now, and never more than in these difficult times.

All mistakes, infelicities and errors are of course my own.

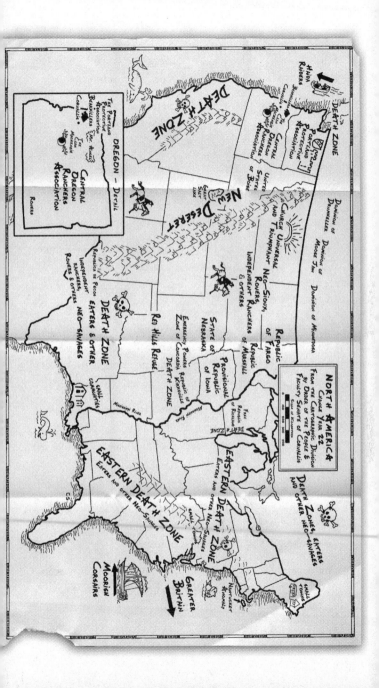

CHAPTER ONE

"**W**here did it all *go*?" Mathilda Arminger said. "There were roads and houses! Now it's just trees. They're *old* trees too; you can see that, even if the sea-wind has stunted them."

"Why are you asking me?" Rudi Mackenzie said, with studied reason in his tones.

The which always drives you crazy and makes your eyes sparkle fetchingly, anamchara mine, he thought.

"You're the one with the magic sword!"

Mathilda caught the twinkle in his own eye and stuck out her tongue at him. They laughed, a quiet, relieved sound; it was *good* to have nothing but a mystery troubling them, as opposed to homicidal strangers. Rudi let his hand fall to the hilt of the weapon slung at his right hip. The pommel shaped of moon-crystal held in antlers gave him a slight cool shock as his calloused palm touched it, less a physical sensation than a mental one . . . or possibly spiritual.

"What does it feel like?" Mathilda asked, subdued again.

"To hold it?"

She nodded, and he went on: "It's . . . hard to describe; that it is. Not as much of a shock as the first time; I grow used to it, but . . . It's as if my thoughts themselves were faster somehow. More sure. More *themselves.* You know how you think, *If I do a certain thing, that might happen, or the other thing, or, then again, perhaps this*? And your wit and experience give you an idea of each, and how likely they are? Well, when I do that now it's as if little mummers were making a play of it in my head, and I *know* what's most likely. It's . . . disconcerting; that it is."

"It would be," she said seriously. "Useful! But, well, Rudi, if you could really see what would happen whenever you did something, would you have any freedom of choice at all? After all, you'd always know the best thing to do!"

He laughed a little, but there was less amusement in it this time.

"Sure. Don't folk choose to do things even if they know it's folly and the result will be black disaster? And don't they do that all the time?"

She snorted and elbowed him in the side. In armor it was more heard than felt, but he took the point.

"So, bearer of the Sword of the Lady, what does its power tell you about this island? What and where and what is it, now?" she said.

"It's not visions I'm receiving," he said. "And there's no printed list of directions on the scabbard!" He could feel her shift.

"You'll probably spend a lot of time learning what it can do," she said.

Rudi smiled at the winter ocean. *Nobody's fool, my*

Matti! he thought. Aloud: "That I will! So far it's like the sharpening of my own thoughts. And I think . . ." He hesitated for an instant. "I think that this island has been a . . . a patchwork since the Change ended the old world; that it has. Not quite the place it was before that day. Not quite the island of another time, or many other times. Now it's all of one thing—and that thing is the Nantucket Island that was before men first cut down its trees for cornfields. As if a thing started the year we were born has now been completed."

"Then what happened to the island from our time? Or at least from the time of the Change? There were thousands of people here according to the books."

"I *suspect*—not know, mind, but suspect—that the island that lay here twenty-four years ago was switched for the one we've gotten. And so began the Change Years."

She frowned. "But wouldn't that have made things different? Changed the past, I mean. When the English came here they didn't find men *speaking* English, or riding horses, or forging iron swords."

The vision that had come with the Sword's finding was slipping away, as such things did. Flickers of a forest far grander than this, grander even than the Douglas fir woods of his homeland. Trees that towered towards a crescent moon. Three Ladies—Maiden, Mother, Crone—had spoken with him, and he could still grasp at shattered fragments of what they told, at vistas of time and space vaster than a human mind could ever hold, of universes born and dying and reborn again.

He touched the hilt, and Mathilda shivered against him. Rudi was tempted to do likewise.

"You've the right of that. There's something . . . something about what the Ladies said to me—spirals of time, and each different yet partly the same . . . As to how the one is linked to the other, well, don't ask me, for I can't do more than babble of wondrous things seen in dreams."

Then he worked his shoulders and returned to practicalities: "From the sky, the weather and the way our wounds have healed, I'd say we lost about a month since we arrived . . . in an instant or so," he said. "And to be sure, we've lost that . . . town too. If it was altogether here to begin with . . . the strangeness and dark bewilderment of it. I kept seeing it *different* while we were running through it."

"Me too," Mathilda said, and crossed herself. "Then . . . it was as if someone was *talking* to me."

"Who?" Rudi said, and tightened his arm as she shivered.

"A . . . a woman in blue? Ignatius saw her in the mountains, but . . . or was she in armor? There's Saint Joan . . . I don't know. And they were the most important words I'd ever heard but now they're gone, mostly. Then you were back, and I didn't care anymore where we were."

She took his arm. "Now . . . now, like you said, it's all of a piece. And, more important, it looks like it isn't going to change on us again." There was as much question as certainty in her voice.

He nodded. "It *feels* that way to me, as well."

Now there was a thick, low forest of leafless brown oak and chestnut, and green pine behind; ahead lay beach, and salt marsh full of dead brown reeds, and the ruffled gray surface of a broad inlet of the winter-season Atlantic. It still seemed a little unnatural for the glow of *sunrise* to be over the eastern waters; the only ocean he'd ever seen until a month ago had been the Pacific, which beat on the shores of Montival—what the old world had called Oregon and Washington.

It's still the Mother's sea, he thought.

The wind came off it, damp and chill under a sky the color of frosted lead, blowing his shoulder-length red-blond hair around his face and smelling of salt and seawrack; it brought out the gray in his changeable eyes as well, overshadowing the blue and green. Mathilda's brown locks were in two practical braids bound with leather thongs, framing her strong-boned, slightly irregular young face. She leaned against him and he put his chin on her head; she was taller than most women, but his height of six-two made the action easy. A few stray locks tickled his nose. He shut his eyes, letting the scents of sea and woman fill his nostrils, and the rushing-retreating *shshshsshs* of waves on sand and the raucous cries of gulls fill his ears.

She sighed deeply. "I feel . . . I feel like all the way from home to here I've been running down a set of tower stairs in Castle Todenangst, the way we did when we were kids and you were visiting? And it's dark and I don't notice I am at the bottom and my feet keep trying to run down after I've hit the floor."

He nodded—she could feel the pressure of his chin, even if she was looking into the green leather surface of his brigandine. Between that, with its inner layer of little riveted steel plates, and her titanium-alloy mail hauberk and the stiff coat of padding beneath, the embrace was more theoretical than real, but comforting nonetheless.

"I know what you mean! Near two years we've been after the Sword, from sunset to sunrise, from Montival to

Nantucket . . . and now we've *got* it, the creature. What next?"

"Home," she said, and there was longing in the word, a feeling he could taste in his own mouth.

"Home. Though that walk is likely to be *upstairs*, as it were."

Then she went on: "You said to walk towards the Sword was to walk towards your own death. Now we've got it—and you're still alive, by Father, Son and Holy Ghost!"

"And I'm *still* walking towards death," he said. At her scowl: "Though to be sure, we all are! At the rate of a day for every day, so to speak."

Then she sighed, and he nodded. It was cold, if bleakly beautiful, and the damp chill penetrated their grimy wools and leathers and padding. More, there was work to be done. They turned and walked hand in hand back towards the spot where the . . . town . . . had been.

The Nantucket where the Change had begun a generation before was gone. So was the *Bou el-Mogdad*, the captured Moorish corsair vessel they'd run ashore as it burned beneath them, and the wharf it had struck with multiton violence. Slightly charred, the long, slender shape of her sister-ship lay canted on the shore. Even awkwardly stranded on the sandy mud by the retreating tide, the pirate schooner *Gisandu* still had the graceful menace of her namesake—the word meant *Shark* in the Wolof tongue. Beaching her hadn't done any harm; ships of that breed were built for longshore work.

Three groups stood there under the shadow of its bowsprit, edging apart. Rudi's friends and kin and the followers picked up along the way, thirty altogether, stood around a crackling driftwood fire that spat sparks blue and green. The surviving dark-faced corsairs from the two Saloum rovers were a bit farther away with their heels to the waves that hissed up the sand, forty of them . . . and not *quite* enemies anymore. And the High Seeker of the Church Universal and Triumphant was farther away still, with the ten men left to him glaring helplessly at *both* the other groups.

Only Rudi's own folk were armed; they'd awoken to find the others still groggy and helpless. The Cutters and corsairs were looking uneasily at the cold steel glint of sword blades and spearheads and the points of nocked arrows. Father Ignatius of the Order of the Shield of St. Benedict nodded to Rudi, a short, brisk gesture. His hands rested on the pommel of his own sheathed longsword; his tilted dark eyes were calm, and his armor showed through the battle rents in his kirted-up black robe. Their injuries had healed, but not the damage to their gear.

"We had best settle matters here soon, Your Majesty. Our food supplies are very low. The *Gisandu*'s stores were exhausted bringing both her crew and the Cutters here. Also we do not have so much of an advantage over them that we can long delay," he said.

There was a limit to the number of men you could hold at the point of a blade, and it wasn't very high if they were brave and knew their business. Which described everyone here quite well.

"That's the truth. It's past time to . . . settle . . . these Cutter fellows, Chief," Edain Aylward Mackenzie said grimly. "Settle them in the Mother's earth, and send the souls of them off to the Summerlands for a talking-to from Herself."

Edain was a few years younger than his chieftain, but

he was no longer the carefree youth who'd crossed the Cascades.

He came because I asked him; because I was his friend, and his chief . . . I'd feel guiltier about that if things were any better back home.

They weren't; from the little they'd heard, the war against the Cutters and their allies wasn't going well at all.

"It's tired and weary and plain buggering *annoyed* with them I am, and that's a fact," Edain went on.

The cold wind tousled the other clansman's mop of oak-brown curls. Usually his gray eyes were calm and friendly, but now they were as bleak as the ocean waves. The long yellow stave of his yew longbow twitched slightly in his grip. The Mackenzies were a people of the bow, and even in that company his friend was Aylward the Archer, as his father had been before him.

Rudi nodded thoughtfully; the Sword of the Prophet and the magi in the bloodred robes had been on their heels all the way from Montival—though nobody had known that was the land's name when they left. They'd killed and injured friends and kinfolk and sworn men of his, and if the questers weren't *all* dead it wasn't for want of the men out of Corwin trying. Their Prophet himself had set them on his trail, and they'd followed it with bulldog tenacity.

"*Hain dago,*" his half sister Mary said—they shared a father. "Kill them."

She touched her eye patch and scowled at them with the one cornflower-blue orb left her; the other had been cut out of her head by another red-robed magus of the Corwinite cult back in the mountains of what had once been Montana. Her twin, Ritva Havel, nodded vigorously and spoke as her thick yellow fighting-braid bobbed on her shoulder.

"Aunt Astrid has a standard order for situations like this," she said.

She fell into Sindarin again for a moment, the pretty-sounding liquid trills of the language the Dúnedain Rangers used among themselves—for secrecy, because few others knew it, and because their founders were devoted to a set of tales of the ancient world they called the Histories.

Then she translated: "*Behead them every one, and that instantly.*"

Rudi's mouth quirked. That was actually from a different set of writings. But Astrid Havel, the *Hiril Dúnedain*—the Lady of the Rangers—did have a rather straightforward approach to such matters.

When he replied, it was in the tone you used to quote from a holy book: "*Do not be too eager to deal out death in judgment. Even the very wise cannot see all ends.*"

He spoke with malice aforethought from the actual Histories; the Rangers weren't the only ones who liked to read old tales by the fireside in the Black Months. His own mother had told that one aloud in Dun Juniper's hall many times when he was a child. It was a grand story of battle and adventure, and it had songs she'd rendered in her fine bard's voice.

The twins gave an identical wince; they'd been too similar even for close kin to tell them apart, before Mary lost the eye. Rangers took their Histories *seriously*. You could do worse as a guide to life, though he didn't really think they were as close to fact as most of the Dúnedain imagined. Still, who could tell? The world before the Change had been very strange by all accounts, and it was difficult to tell fancy from truth in those tales. Dragons and Rings of Power were no odder than flying ships and weapons that burned whole cities.

Or stranger than some things I've met myself, he reminded himself, his hand on the moonstone pommel.

"I don't think any of them is Gollum material," Ritva said, a trace of sulkiness in her tone.

"Though I wouldn't put it past them to bite off a finger if they got within snapping range," Mary added.

Her husband, Ingolf, nodded. "Me neither, Rudi," he said in his flat Wisconsin rasp. "Kill 'em and be damned to them."

He was a big man, as tall as Rudi and a little broader, with a battered face beneath his cropped brown beard that showed all thirty of his years. Normally it was good-natured, despite hard times spent as a hired soldier and salvager, but now it clenched like a fist. He'd been a prisoner of the Church Universal and Triumphant in Corwin itself. The wounds on his body had healed, though the marks were there. The ones in his mind and soul had taken longer to knit, and scars remained there too, visible sometimes in his dark blue eyes.

"Matti?" Rudi asked.

"Kill them," she said firmly, though with a slight undertone of regret. "You didn't promise them quarter the way you did the pirates, and they're not knightly foes who are protected by the laws of chivalry. As *Ard Rí* you certainly command the High Justice, and as your principal vassals and tenants-in-chief, we're a sufficient court under feudal law. Also we just don't have the people or attention to spare to guard them, or the food to keep them."

Her parents had been founders of the Portland Protective Association, and before that in the Society for Creative Anachronism—a fellowship dedicated to the preservation of ancient ways and skills. When the Change set them free to live out their dreams, they'd also turned out to be the two most pellucidly ruthless human beings Rudi had ever met. Her long-dead father, Norman, had wrought in sheer throttled rage at anything that thwarted him, and from a vicious relish at the power to deal out death. Sandra Arminger was very much alive, still Regent of the Association; unlike her dreadful spouse she was a cold killer rather than a hot one. Her daughter was neither, tenderhearted if anything, but she'd still been raised to the stern necessities of kingcraft.

So had he, if on the smaller and gentler scale of the Clan Mackenzie. His mother had condemned men to death when she had to, though never without regret.

"Fred?"

Frederick Thurston's brown, blunt-featured face scowled. "They were behind my father's murder. Kill them."

Actually that was your elder brother, Rudi thought. *He wanted to be President in Boise too, and to hell with old customs like elections, which your father wanted to preserve.*

Though the Cutters might have planted the seeds of that bit of murderous treachery, at that. Virginia Thurston nodded vigorously; the CUT had overrun her family's ranch in the Powder River country out west in what had once been Wyoming, and killed *her* father. She'd brought her own feud to add to the balance when she met Fred on the journey east and joined the quest.

"Father Ignatius?"

The knight-brother frowned; his Order trained as scholars as well as in the warlike arts, and often acted as de facto judges in the wild places where they did much of their work.

"This is certainly *terrae nullius*, land without sovereign or law," he said. "Certainly the Cutters are heretics, murderers, oppressors and wagers of unjust war, and their adept is an open diabolist. In which, I think, he merely represents the whole hierarchy of the cult. And you, Your Majesty, are a King—if not yet an anointed one. You may therefore judge them at your discretion."

Rudi's mouth quirked a little; that "anointed" bit *was* going to be awkward when they got back home. He was of the Old Religion, like nearly all Mackenzies, and wouldn't object to a Catholic ceremony—his faith taught that all paths to the Divine were valid. Christians tended to be a little more exclusive.

"In other words, I must do as I think best?" he asked. "And take the burden of it for good or ill?"

Ignatius inclined his tonsured head; he was so grave usually that you forgot he was only a few years older than Rudi's twenty-four.

"Precisely, Your Majesty. We must each bear the cross that God gives us, carry it up to Heaven's Gate, and that is the one He has given you."

I'm a well-loved man, Rudi thought, glancing to meet Mathilda's grave regard.

And I've true friends and comrades here at hand, who'll never fear to speak their minds to me. But at seventh and last to be King is to be alone, alone in the narrow passage where there is neither brother nor friend. Kingship is to stand for your folk before the Powers, and before necessity.

"Something new has come into the world," he said quietly, just loud enough to be heard above the wind. "I was given the Sword to use, as well as to bear. And not only for the chopping of heads; plain steel would do near as well for that."

A smile. "Like the fine sword you gave me, which saved my life many a time."

"Which just disappeared," she said, frustrated.

He drew the blade forged in the World beyond the world. It had the form of a knight's weapon, long and double-edged and tapered to a savage point. It felt lighter in his hand than he would have expected from the thirty-eight inches of the blade. Or perhaps it felt *alive*, rather than light in any physical sense. The metal *looked* like steel at first glance, pattern-welded in intricate, waving layers. Then if you looked more closely the patterns seemed to disappear into untouchable depths, shape within shape, a soft endless *pull* at the eyes that repeated . . .

All the way down, he thought. *It doesn't glow. Not precisely. Not to the body's eye, at least.*

The High Seeker took a step back as Rudi approached; he didn't think there was the slightest physical fear in it.

Major Graber stepped between them. His angular face had the look of a man ready to die, but then he'd always been like that. His fists were clenched and held in a position that Rudi recognized; his tutors in unarmed combat had used it sometimes. The other troopers of the Sword of the Prophet moved to flank him; behind, Rudi could hear the rustle and clink of his folk making ready.

"Don't begin anything without my word," he said, looking over his shoulder for an instant. "That's an order, mind."

Graber swallowed and met Rudi's eyes. "High Seeker!" he said, managing to throw his voice over his shoulder *without* turning his head. "What are your orders?"

The Cutter magus ignored him, his eyes fixed on Rudi. The expression in them was not quite fear, and he paid as much attention to the Sword as to the man bearing it.

Not enough is left of the man to fear the body's death, Rudi thought, meeting the empty eyes and a snarl like malice distilled. *What was it that Abbot Dorje said, back in the Valley of the Sun? Yes:* Men who sell their souls invariably make a very bad bargain. *Whatever dwells there where the man once was fears this blade, with a terror that has little to do with the fate of the mortal shell it inhabits.*

"High Seeker!" Graber said desperately, but the magus stayed in his slight crouch, snarling silently.

A shock ran up Rudi's hand; the Sword seemed to *twitch.* Then he reversed it in a single fluid tossing snap, holding it by the hilt with the blade down.

"Major Graber," Rudi said briskly. "You're a soldier, and a good one. I've fought you often enough to know, and for you to know me somewhat. Believe me, then: stand aside, and your men will be unharmed, nor will anything happen harmful to your honor or your oaths. On that you have *my* oath."

Graber gave one last look at the High Seeker and then jerked his head, as if using the tuft of chin-beard that marked the center of his rock-formed jaw as a pointer. He and the troopers stood aside, but they were tensed to spring if they must.

Rudi raised the Sword until the crystal pommel was level with his own eyes . . . and then pressed it to the High Seeker's forehead.

He'd expected a scream. Instead the Cutter adept seemed to *stop.* The thin-lipped grimace on his face died away, and then the rigid inner tension that had made it a thing of slabs and angles. Then the hazel eyes blinked at him, and suddenly they were just eyes once more, not the bars of a cage where something looked out and hungered.

Silence stretched; there was a sheen of sweat on Graber's face, and a fear that had nothing to do with his own danger. The High Seeker blinked again and looked around him.

"Mom?" he said uncertainly, in a wavering voice, as if the harsh gravel tones weren't *his*. "Mom? I'm scared, Mom. Dad said I have to be brave when the Church men come, but I'm scared. Where are you?"

He patted himself, and then looked at his hands. An expression of horror crumpled his face then, and tears leaked down his cheeks. He stumbled forward, the empty sheath of his shete banging awkwardly against his leg, as if he'd forgotten how to walk with it. Forgotten how to walk with the body of a man of thirty-odd years, too.

"Lady?" he blurted out to Mathilda. "I feel funny, lady. You seen my mom, ma'am? She looks a little like you."

Mathilda's face was white, though she had looked steady on more than one battlefield; she took a pace backward, and he could tell she was fighting not to draw her own blade. She did cross herself.

Ignatius stepped forward and spoke in Rudi's ear, quickly and quietly. "I think the Corwinite cult take their trainees very young, Your Majesty," he said. "And I think this man has just lost all the years since they did. Pardon me."

Then louder, with a kindly tone: "Your mother is not here, my son. What is your name?"

The Seeker stood erect; you could see the effort it took him.

"I'm Bobby," he said, with a quaver in his voice. "Bobby Dalan, sir. Bobby Dalan from Scrabbledown

Ranch. You get me back home and Mom and Dad will be real happy, sir."

He wiped at his eyes with the back of one hand. It was a grown man's hand, and a warrior's, scarred and sinewy. That made the gesture shocking, and . . . Rudi found himself blinking too.

"I will look after you until you can go home," Ignatius said. His voice became a soothing murmur. "Here, my son, come and sit by the fire and be warm. Would you like to sleep? There's a blanket you can use. You are sleepy, aren't you . . ."

A silence deep enough to ring had fallen when the priest rose a few moments later; wonder on most faces, and horror among the troops of the Sword of the Prophet who'd followed the adept so long. Ignatius wore a quiet smile when he came back to them, and he crossed himself.

"God's mercy is very great," he said. "Great beyond our comprehension."

Rudi's mouth quirked. Ignatius wasn't the sort of Christian cleric who was always shoving his piety in your face, but it was bone-deep.

"It's the Sword of the *Lady*, Father," he said.

The smile grew broader. "And the Lady of Sorrows is most merciful too," he said, and chuckled at Rudi's snort. "That is a thing to which I can personally bear witness."

Then he grew entirely grave. "And so are *you*, Your Majesty . . . which, since you *are* to be High King, is re-assuring to know."

"We've been in each other's sporrans for years now," Rudi said. "I'm not a man who enjoys killing and never was."

Fighting, sometimes, yes, he admitted to himself. *Be-*

Barnes & Noble Bookseller #2718
Sheridan Blvd
Westminster, CO 80030
303-425-1748

STR:2718 REG:003 TRN:2953 CSHR:Hailey M

High King of Montival (Emberverse Series) 9780451464019   T1
    (1 @ 9.99)   9.99

Subtotal   9.99
Sales Tax T1 (8.600%)   0.86
TOTAL   10.85
VISA   10.85
  Card#: XXXXXXXXXXXX8535
  Expdate: XX/XX
  Auth: 020357
  Entry Method: Swiped

A MEMBER WOULD HAVE SAVED   1.00

101.31A   08/07/2013 08:40PM

Return Policy

With a sales receipt or Barnes & Noble.com packing slip, a full refund in the original form of payment will be issued from any Barnes & Noble Booksellers store for returns of undamaged NOOKs, new and unread books, and unopened and undamaged music CDs, DVDs, and audio books made within 14 days of purchase from a Barnes & Noble Booksellers store or Barnes & Noble.com with the below exceptions:

A store credit for the purchase price will be issued (i) for purchases made by check less than 7 days prior to the date of return, (ii) when a gift receipt is presented within 60 days of purchase, (iii) for textbooks, or (iv) for products purchased at Barnes & Noble College bookstores that are listed for sale in the Barnes & Noble Booksellers inventory management system.

Opened music CDs/DVDs/audio books may not be returned, and can be exchanged only for the same title and only if defective. NOOKs purchased from other retailers or sellers are returnable only to the retailer or seller from which they are purchased, pursuant to such retailer's or seller's return policy. Magazines, newspapers, eBooks, digital downloads, and used books are not returnable or exchangeable. Defective NOOKs may be exchanged at the store in accordance with the applicable warranty.

Returns or exchanges will not be permitted (i) after 14 days or without receipt or (ii) for product not carried by Barnes & Noble or Barnes & Noble.com.

Policy on receipt may appear in two sections.

Return Policy

With a sales receipt or Barnes & Noble.com packing slip, a full refund in the original form of payment will be issued from any Barnes & Noble Booksellers store for returns of undamaged NOOKs, new and unread books, and unopened and undamaged music CDs, DVDs, and audio books made

*cause I do it well, and it's necessary work, and it calls forth
all you have in you of strength and heart and wit. But killing in itself, no. Though it's part of living and also sometimes necessary, even killing in cold blood.*

The warrior-priest shook his head. "I knew that you
were not a man of blood, my King," he said. "But you
had very good personal reasons to hate the Corwinite
magus, and excellent reasons of policy to kill him as well,
and it lay within your rights in law. That you chose not
to . . . speaks well of how you will rule."

Rudi looked around. Several of his companions were
looking disappointed . . . but they all nodded as he
sheathed the Sword once more, and there was awe in
their eyes.

"Major Graber," Rudi said.

"Yes?" the officer replied, crossing his arms on his
chest.

He had an outward calm; his men were younger, and
looked rocked to their foundations. That was the disadvantage of a creed that preached inevitable victory: its
doctrines tended to be silent on what to do if you lost.
Particularly if the loss was not merely a matter of swords.

"There's a village on this island," Rudi went on, nodding to Ingolf to show where he'd gotten the tale of it.
*Some of them were refugees from the mainland from just
after the Change who came with stock and seed and tools,
and the rest were Indians from this place—from the same
time as the forest, brought forward with it—who had their
own knowledge to add to the mix.*

"They're fishers and gardeners and hunters of the
whale; good-hearted folk, from what I hear. They have
more women than men, and it could be they'd take in any
of you who wished to stay here. The rest may return to

the mainland with us, but closely watched and unarmed, and the journey westward will be perilous at best."

The man nodded, a swift hard gesture. "I was tasked with assisting the High Seeker," he said, in a voice that might have been forged from iron.

"The High Seeker no longer lives," Rudi pointed out. "Now there's only the boy who was murdered to make him."

After a slight hesitation, Graber went on: "My family is in Corwin. My wives, my children."

Rudi shrugged. "You tried to fulfill your mission; it's for you to decide if you and your kin can await anything good from your rulers because of it. But you've time to think, all of you."

When he turned back to his friends, Mathilda linked her fingers together and tapped her paired thumbs on her chin, a habit she'd picked up from him.

"Do you think you can trust this Graber?" she said softly.

Rudi shrugged. "Within reason. My judgment is that he's a hard man, with little mercy and no yielding in him, but not without honor of a sort when left to make his own choices. There was a poet of the ancient Greeks . . . he said something about a perfect man being hard to find . . ."

Father Ignatius nodded. "I think I know the one you mean," he said. "Simonides of Keos."

Then, quoting: "*So I will never waste my lifespan in the vain unprofitable search for a blameless man. If you find him, send me word. But that one I will love and honor who does nothing base from free will. Against necessity, even gods do not fight.* Undoubtedly he was among the virtuous pagans."

Rudi nodded. "Like myself?" he said ironically.

Ignatius smiled slightly and tapped one booted foot on the ground; *if the shoe fits . . .*

Rudi and Mathilda chuckled; the younger man went on: "Graber . . . is as good a man as can be expected from his upbringing, and the time and place of it. Raised elsewhere, he'd have been a good man by our way of thinking as well. I'll kill him if I must, but I'd rather not."

He turned his head. The corsairs had moved a little farther away, as if to disassociate themselves still more from the surviving Cutters and whatever their fate would be. As he watched they spread their prayer mats and knelt on them, bowing eastward, where *their* Holy City lay.

Now, what shall I do with the lot of you? he thought. *That's less of a problem, for I did promise quarter to those of you captured in Kalksthorpe in return for sailing me here. As for the others . . . well, in honor I can do nothing but extend the same terms to them. Yet you* are *pirates, and honor doesn't require me to be an overtrusting fool. Mercy to the guilty can be cruelty to the innocent, as the saying goes.*

Abdou al-Naari rose. The crews finished their prayers and stood as well, rolling up their mats. Rudi Mackenzie had been waiting quietly until they were done with the ritual; Abdou had to admit he was polite in such matters. The five daily prayers were God's will unless something very urgent intervened, and besides that it was good to reestablish routine; it helped the men's spirits.

And it helps mine, Abdou thought. *Sorcery is more often heard of than seen, even since the Change, but I have seen it now.*

Witch doctors and shamans were as common as pea-
nuts in the Emirate of Dakar, for all that strict law forbade
them, but he had never put much credence in them. Yes,
there was more than natural law to the universe—even if
he had been inclined to believe anything so impious, the
Change was a stern warning to the contrary. God could
do as He willed, and He had created many beings other
than men, some with strange powers. But this . . . was
enough to put all of them in fear.

*All men fear. Only cowards allow the fear to govern
them. Call on the One and meet your fate, Abdou.*

Then he took a deep breath and went on to the infidel
leader:

"My friend Jawara, of *Gisandu* captain, say . . .
says . . . that there were snakes in his head, while sorcerers hold him by spells. Now they gone. He thank you."

Djinn fly away with English! Abdou thought. *Why
can't the misbelievers speak some civilized language?*

He was captain of a Saloum rover, which meant he had
enough mathematics for navigation, and he could design
a ship besides—or a bridge, or an aqueduct. He was flu-
ent in the Hassani dialect of Arabic, which was his father's
tongue, and in the Wolof and Serer languages common
throughout the Emirate of Dakar; he knew enough
Mandinka to get by; he could read the classical tongue of
the Holy Book, and some of the dead French speech—
enough to appreciate poetry as well as to read books on
practical subjects like engineering.

But his English had been learned strictly by rule of
thumb for trade and war, and in present company he was
humiliatingly conscious that when he spoke it he sounded
like some peasant from the back of beyond.

Or like a baboon sitting in a baobab tree and scratching

its fleas. Or like a tongue-tied foreigner, which is another way of saying the same thing.

Pride kept his back stiff as he bowed and touched brow, lips and heart with the fingers of his right hand in a graceful gesture. His wounds no longer pained him when he performed the courtesy; somehow they'd had time for more healing, when he felt nothing but the space between one breath and another. Another strangeness.

"Thank you for rescuing of him and men. Thank you for exposing false marabout who led us here. Peace be upon you, and God's blessing for you, your sons, and the sons of your sons."

The so-called holy man whose "visions" had brought Abdou's little two-ship fleet to these bleak northern waters lay on the snow-speckled sand not far away. The corsairs had taken care of him themselves, as soon as they'd woken, and they hadn't needed any weapons to do so despite the man's unnatural strength; his head now looked out over his shoulder blades, and his arms and legs were visibly broken in several places as well. The green turban had rolled away, and the edges of it fluttered in the cold breeze.

"Blasphemer," Jawara said in Wolof, and spat on the corpse, his full-featured black face contorted with hate. "Apostate. Sorcerer."

Abdou translated; he shared the sentiment wholeheartedly, even if he was less given to showing his feelings. The infidel chief nodded, his straight and implausibly sunset-colored hair swaying about his jaw. The Moor had never seen anything quite like it, though many English had hair the hue of sun-faded thatch or reddish wood. His face bore the starved, angular look whites had and which Abdou had never liked; in Rudi's case you had to admit that he was handsome enough in an alien fashion. One disastrous encounter in the fight where he'd been captured had shown Abdou that the infidel's long-limbed body could move with a leopard's speed and strength.

That had been honest combat, though; he averted his eyes from the pommel of the sword the man carried now. Such things were not lawful for Believers. Best to think of it as little as possible.

"When we home, there is . . ." He made washing gestures with his hands.

"Making clean," Rudi said. "Cleansing."

Abdou nodded, his face grim. "Cleansing of marabouts of the Mouride Brotherhood, if any more like this. I go Dakar, Emir's court, speak there. For this too, we thank. The Faith is pure. For any to . . . make it not pure, not clean . . . that is a great evil."

"You are welcome," Rudi said. "And that cleansing will be a thing to benefit the whole world, not just your own land. Now, how is the ship? We've that little journey to Kalksthorpe to make."

Jawara spoke far less English than Abdou, but he understood a little. They both looked at the *Gisandu* and sighed; now she and her cargo were lost too. The *Bou el-Mogdad* was simply *gone*, and the Kalksthorpe folk had her load of treasures already. And the corsairs' families and clans would have to pay ransom for their return as well. It had been a disastrous voyage in more ways than one. His kin had put many years of labor and hard-won wealth into those ships.

"Ribs good, none stove in," Abdou said after they'd conferred for a little; his vocabulary was better for nautical matters than general conversation. "Need spare boards to patch hull leaks, once we caulk sprung seams.

We refloat her with anchor out to sea, capstan, when patches all done. For long voyage, need to pull out of water, refit with . . . special tools, supplies."

"You've only to get us back to Kalksthorpe," Rudi pointed out. "Less than a week's sail to the northward."

"Now you know we deceived by false marabout, should give ship back to we," Abdou said. "As you say, home need cleansing. Faster if we have ship. We take you back, go home, never sail these waters again. By God and His Prophet, I swear."

If you do not try, you will never succeed. And I mean that oath. If I never even hear *of these waters again it will be too soon!*

Rudi grinned, teeth flashing white. "You were pirates before you met this marabout," he said. "He used no magic to make you willing to fall on the Kalksthorpe folk, kill them and plunder their goods. Count yourself lucky your lives are spared, but your wealth is forfeit."

Abdou shrugged. The accusation was not *completely* without truth. Mostly his business was salvaging in the dead cities along the old American coast; there were far fewer such remains of the ancient world in his native land, and his people needed the metals and goods. But that often meant fighting, with the bands of mad cannibal savages who haunted the ruins, or with others on the same venture. The Kalksthorpe folk often clashed with his, being great salvagers themselves. For that matter, as pagans they were legitimate prey by law, but he didn't expect Rudi Mackenzie to grasp that point, being only a *kufr*, an unbeliever, himself.

God's will, he thought. *The Merciful, the Lovingkind, does as He wishes, not as we wish. It is not for mortal men to question Him. I live, my son Ahmed lives, my blood brother*

Jawara lives. We will purge our homeland of a great wickedness. Praise be to the One!

He sighed again and went on aloud: "Ready to sail, *Inshallah*, with the morning tide in week, ten days, if all work hard and we no need cut timber. Not much food though, for all people these, even for short voyage. We all go hungry before end."

Rudi Mackenzie showed his teeth in an expression that did not even pretend to be a smile. "Needs must. I grudge every day. My people need me at home, and they need me *now*."

Then a voice cried out: "Sail! *Sail ho!*"

CHAPTER TWO

BEND
CAPITAL, CENTRAL OREGON RANCHERS ASSOCIATION
MARCH 20, CHANGE YEAR 25/2023 AD

"This city is going to fall," Signe Havel said bluntly.

The Rancher-delegates who made up the CORA assembly roared—some in agreement, some in protest, some to hear themselves make noise, as far as she could tell. It echoed off the walls of the old pre-Change theater; shouting faces shone desperate in the light of the gas lamps, a thick smell of sweat and burnt methane and hot lime, wool and leather and linen. The representatives of the city itself and the smallholders who farmed the irrigated land upstream and down mostly just stared at her wide-eyed.

"Why can't you stop them?" someone shouted.

Signe leaned forward and braced her hands on the sides of the podium, and the lames of her articulated suit of plate clattered slightly against each other, despite the backing of soft leather. Moving quietly in armor was like trying to tiptoe in a suit sewn with cowbells. She wanted them to notice it; notice the nicks and the indented lines that looked like someone had taken something sharp and pushed it against the steel *very hard*. Which was exactly what had happened, and she still had the bruises underneath.

"You may notice we've all been *trying* to do exactly that, your people and mine."

She paused to let the way she looked—and for some of the closer delegates, smelled—reinforce the words.

Rationally it's silly to wear sixty pounds of metal to talk to people, she thought. *But then again, who ever said war is a rational activity? And the whole* world *went crazy when I was eighteen. It's been getting worse ever since. My armor is a symbol, and Mike taught me about the value of symbols. He used them and knew he was using them, even when he believed in them himself. Because symbols hit down below the part where* knowing *makes any difference.*

She was very tired, tired enough that her eyeballs felt as if they'd been rolled in a mixture of fine grit and cat hair before they were stuffed back in their sockets. There was probably enough red around the pupils to drown out the blue.

I'm forty-three now. I can't go for days without sleep anymore. Willpower makes up for the tired and the hurt and the hungry, but every time it takes a bit more water from the well and someday soon I'm going to run dry.

"It hasn't been working, no matter how hard we try, because they outnumber us three to one," she said, when the noise had died down a little.

If anyone but Mike Havel had been flying that light plane over the Bitterroots on Change Night, she and her family would have died like hundreds of thousands of others. Signe thought of them sometimes, whenever the present seemed too grim to bear: astronauts in orbit when all the city lights below went out and the ventilators died, passengers in 747s at thirty thousand feet glancing up in a flickering moment of pain and silence, people in submarines or down at the bottom of gold mines when the pumps stopped.

Mostly they'd been the lucky ones, at that. For them it had been fairly quick. Five billion and more had died in what followed, died slowly of thirst and hunger, of plague, or killed for what little they had or the meat on their bones.

And thanks to Mike we survived. Survived the plane crash, survived that year after the Change, survived . . . life. For a while. Life's so dangerous nobody gets out of it alive, he used to say, and he's been dead fourteen years now. I've got this bad feeling about what's coming down the tracks.

She poured strength into her voice, *willing* desperate men to see sense:

"The Prophet's maniacs *alone* outnumber all the troops the countries of the Meeting . . . the High Kingdom of Montival—"

Freya, we're calling the whole country something because someone barely old enough to shave suggested it in a letter. What next? How desperate for hope are we?

"—can muster. The United States of Boise outnumbers us by about the same margin. If we try to meet them here in open country, they'll crush us. They didn't beat us at Pendleton last year because they were better, they beat us because they were good *enough* and there were Loki's own lot of them. They *want* big decisive battles. We can't afford to fight on their terms; we have to make them come to us. Bleed them until they're down to a level we can tackle."

A man got up; elderly, leathery: Rancher Brown of Seffridge. A good man, steady. He'd been an ally of the

Outfit in the wars against the Association in the decade after the Change.

"What's wrong with Bend?" he asked; they'd agreed on the question beforehand. "They have to come at us here, and we've got the city wall and plenty of food."

Signe made herself grin. "You have to ask? The wall's good enough against a bunch of bandits or Rovers. It's too long and too low for an army with a good battering and assault train—wheeled belfries, siege towers, trebuchets, which Boise has and will lend to the Corwinites. And the water supply can be cut off. You people should really have thought of that."

She saw embarrassed winces. The CORA had trouble agreeing on the time of day, normally. War wasn't normal times, but it was a bit late now for major engineering.

"I thought that . . . that thing that happened was supposed to stop places falling to the Cutters," Brown said.

People made the signs of their various religions, or muttered prayers . . . or curses, or both. Signe kept calmness, but only just. That flash of pain and the ringing voice in the middle of Juniper Mackenzie's ceremony:

Artos holds the Sword of the Lady, she remembered that tolling voice speaking from within her. *The Sun Lord comes, the son of Bear and Raven! The High King comes, as foretold! Guardian of My Sacred Wood, and Law! His people's strength, and the Lady's Sword!*

She cleared her throat, swallowed and went on: "That means their spooks can't hoodoo men into opening gates anymore," she said.

She added to herself: *We think.*

Aloud: "It does absolutely nothing to keep them from coming over the walls on ladders. When—" She nearly said *if* and then went on: "When Artos gets back, things will be different. Until then we're on our own."

Another roar, and a general shout of *What good are you, then?*

She slammed a gauntleted fist down on the podium. "We Bearkillers stand by our promises, and by our friends!" she shouted.

That had the double advantage of being true, and being known to be true. Over the years the Outfit had shed a lot of blood, their own and other people's, making sure everyone knew it. Everyone, including the people expended, had thought it was worth it. Quiet fell, slowly and incompletely.

"Bend will fall, and with it everything this side of the Cascades, before we can hope to get help. Before Rudi . . . Artos gets here. Your homeplaces aren't fortified, not really, not the way the PPA's castles are up north. But if we hold Bend long enough, you can get your families and your livestock through the passes, which have forts we *are* strong enough to hold. Hold for a long time, long enough for the snow to close them, while you hit and run and pull back into the space you've got so much of out here. We—and the Clan Mackenzie and the Corvallans and everyone else in the west—guarantee you lodging for your people and grazing for your stock during the rest of the war, and all the help we can give after it, to rebuild. We'll take your families in. Nobody starves as long as anyone has food."

That set off another explosion; she waited it out, while the sensible ones argued the hotheads into line. It took less time than she might have expected; but then, they *were* ranchers, not farmers. Losing buildings and the crops some grew would be painful, but their real wealth was their flocks and herds.

With those and their people safe, they'd be willing to scorch their land as well as fight across it. Turn it into a wasteland where the enemy would starve while they battered at the Cascade passes, and mounted guerrillas harassed enemy outposts and supply columns.

I hope. I never liked you, Rudi. I see Mike with Juniper when I see you. When I think about you. But we need you, and badly.

When the meeting ended and Signe was back in her rooms, she sank into a chair and stared at the ceiling, watching the lamplight flicker on the stained plaster and smelling hastily cleaned-up mustiness, as if this suite had been boarded up right after the Change and opened only when Bend started getting crowded with people pushed ahead of the Prophet's armies.

She was too limply exhausted to even think about removing her armor, much less hunting up food and drink. She felt too tired even to *sleep*; the sort of bun-fight she'd just been through took more out of you than work or even fighting, and her mind stayed hopping-active even when her eyes closed. She started slightly at the feel of someone working on the buckles and catches.

Her son shook a finger at her when she looked, Mike Havel Jr. in all the tireless glory of seventeen years. *He* looked like Mike too, more and more every year. Taller already, just a sliver under six feet, though his hair was yellow-blond to his father's raven-black.

Which makes him look more like Rudi too, even if there's no red in it.

Otherwise the same hard-cut masculine good looks emerging from under the last of childhood's padding, high cheekbones, straight nose, square cleft chin, long-lashed light eyes that had already cut a swath through the more susceptible females of his generation.

"Mom, you need to get some sleep. You need to eat first. And no disrespect . . . but you need a bath, real bad, too."

All Gods witness, I still miss you, Mike, she thought, then smiled at him.

"Glad to see someone's attending to business, Brother Havel," she said.

He'd earned that title, and the small white scar of the Bearkiller A-list between his brows, young as he was. Earned it on a battlefield, while still a military apprentice.

He knew it too, from the moment's flash of reckless fighting-man's grin; it sat a little oddly on a face that was still nearly a boy's. That she still *saw* as a boy's, unless she made herself look at him as a stranger might.

"Someone has to do it, Sister Havel . . . Mom."

She groaned a little with relief as the last of the war-harness was removed, and a junior took it away clanking in a canvas sack to be cleaned and have the dents hammered out. Mike Jr. went to the door and returned with a tray.

"Eat, ma'am," he said again.

He placed it in front of her; a slab of rare prime rib, some fried potatoes, pickled vegetables and a half loaf of bread and butter on the side, with a wedge of dried-apple pie and cheese to follow. Winter food, but good.

Mike stood at parade rest with his hands behind his back and his eyes fixed on the far wall.

"You're in the field," he said. "You don't know when you'll get another chance at a hot meal. Never pass that up."

"At ease," she replied.

The smells tickled at her nostrils, and she took up a fork and dipped a chunk of potato in the spicy Bend-style ketchup and pointed with it before she put it in her mouth.

"Sit."

He relaxed then—Bearkiller discipline bit deep—and sat in the chair across from her. The suite was comfortable by modern standards, which meant there was a blaze going in the fireplace and you only needed a sweater despite the chill early-spring night of the high desert.

"So . . ." he said. The order had put him back in pupil mode, which meant he could ask questions. "What the hell are we going to do now?"

"Fight," Signe said succinctly.

The first bite had made her ravenous; there had been nothing but field rations for the past week, and not always that. She ate with slow care anyway. He was right; this might be the last chance for a good long while. It was something Mike Sr. had always said too. He'd probably gotten it from her, though. He hadn't been old enough to remember his father, not really. For him the first Bear Lord was something put together out of stories, and out of the shape his life had left in the world he helped to make.

"Mom, you were right out there. If we go at them straight-up, well, they'll know they've been in a fight, but then it's pork chops at Odin's All Night Diner for us until Ragnarok."

"We *have* to fight. A delaying action at least. Evacuating this bunch of range-country anarchists is going to be a nightmare, especially considering how late they've left it. We have to cover them . . . us and the rest. I hope the

PPA can send some help but that's iffy. Boise is pressing them hard, even with the castles."

"Time," Mike Jr. said soberly. "We have to play for time. Until Rudi gets here."

Her mouth twisted slightly. If he hadn't been so self-controlled, Mike Jr. would have sighed in exasperation. She caught it anyway, of course.

I am his mother, after all!

And she had that odd floating feeling you had when you were very tired, or sometimes very drunk; as if you were perfectly lucid but some part of your brain was missing. The part that decided what to say and what to leave out.

"Don't worry," she said dryly, tearing a chunk off the bread and buttering it. "I'm not going to let it get in the way of business."

"I didn't think you would, ma'am."

Signe swallowed and chuckled. "The hell you didn't. You're growing up now—you're old enough to be told things—but you're not forty yet. I don't know if emotions get weaker as you get older, or you just get better at controlling them. That's supposed to be part of growing up."

His expression was perfectly calm, but it radiated: I *am* grown up!

No, you're not, she thought. *You're getting there, you've fought and seen bloodshed and you're not a virgin anymore either, but there's a lot more to it. I want you to live long enough to be an adult. I want to see your children. And there's not a damned thing I can do about it except to try to win this war, or at least not lose it.*

Aloud: "But one way or another I've got it covered. Hey, Brother Havel—what matters most, what you're *feeling*, or getting the job done?"

He snorted; there was only one answer to *that*, for a Bearkiller of the A-list. For a Havel. A hesitation, then:

"You know, Mom, *I* like Rudi . . . Artos, I suppose, now . . . fine. Always did."

Signe nodded, mopped the plate and began on the pie. "You're his brother . . . half brother. He's blood kin to you."

"And a hell of a man." Another hesitation. "I, well, I always thought he had something of Dad in him."

"Yes, he is, and yes, he does. Even as a kid, you could see what he was going to grow into; Mike was proud of him, though he didn't say much about it. But to *me* he was also always a reminder of your father straying. And *don't* let either 'get over it' or 'that was before you two were married' go through your mind. You're going to find that you don't get over things that easily; feelings become a habit, after a while, and they're hard to kick. Even when you're *tired* of them. And the other part . . . all that shows is that you're a man. Or male, at least. Which I suppose is for the best."

He managed to suppress the infuriatingly smug smile until she gave a weary grin.

"Artos is . . . well, if we have to rely on somebody, he's the one I'd pick, ma'am. Plus that Sword thing. Whatever."

Signe nodded. That *was* business, and the appraisal was accurate, of the man and of the situation. She'd manage to smile and cheer at the coronation of Artos the First, if they won. Life hurt, and then it hurt some more, and then you died. What mattered was that you did what you had to do without sniveling about it.

And if we don't win, we'll be too dead to care.

"Bath," she said. "Sleep. Work tomorrow."

CHAPTER THREE

Rudi grinned to himself, catching Mary Vogeler's glare at her husband from the corner of his eye. All his party were assembled to greet the little armada that had brought the Sea-Land tribe from their village a bit west of here. Their boats were drawn up on the shore, eight craft shaped like long whaleboats, each with a single gaff-rigged mast a third of the way back from the prow. They'd carried a score of men and rather more women from the village farther west along the narrow island's coast.

One of the women had headed straight for Ingolf, beaming and waving. More than the damp chill salt wind flushed Mary's pale cheeks red, and her single blue eye snapped. Ingolf spread his hands.

"Honey, that was more than a year before we even *met*," he said desperately. "He's nearly *three*, for . . . ah, Manwë's sake."

The young woman of the Sea-Land folk held her child—and Ingolf's—by the hand and beamed at them both; the toddler beamed too, showing gaps in his grin, and waved his free arm. The resemblance was unmistakable, down to the dark blue eyes, though the plumply pretty mother was half-Indian, her cheekbones high and hair raven-black. Her little tribe was mostly similar mixtures in varying degrees, offspring of the time-displaced inhabitants of this ancient Nantucket mixed with a party of refugees from Innsmouth just after the Change.

"Well, *introduce us*," Mary said, crossing her arms.

"Ummm . . . this is, ah, I think it means *Dove*," Ingolf said tightly. "She's, ah, the daughter of the chief here. The guy Rudi's talking to. That's her mother interpreting."

The woman touched a gray feather woven into one braid; it had a tinge of pink along its edge.

"Doh-uv," she said carefully, and then repeated it in her own tongue.

The language was like nothing any of the questers save Ingolf had ever heard, but you could pick out English words in it, like plums in a Yule cake. Nor did the situation need much in the way of detail to be obvious.

Mary snorted, dug a stiffened finger into her man's ribs, then relented and went down on one knee. The boy came forward fearlessly and returned her hug. Ingolf put a hand on his head, smiling a little, a wondering expression on his face as he saw himself there.

"You don't think . . ." he said slowly. "Or at least I didn't . . ."

". . . when you're passing through and having fun along the way that there might be *consequences*?" Mary said, and snorted again. "Men!"

And to be sure, my brother-in-law has been a wanderer for many a year. Best not to mention that right now! Rudi thought. *They'll be easier when we're gone and have left this little reminder behind.*

The warriors stood gravely impassive, lean strong-armed muscular men; the hair was shaved off the sides of their heads, stiffened into a roach above and braided into a queue behind. They wore leggings and breechclouts, mostly covered by well-sewn jackets of sealskin or rabbit pelts or woven mohair adorned with shell beads—a few pair of Angora goats had come with the mainland refugees—and soft boots of folded and sewn leather turned fur side in laced up their calves with thongs. Their weapons were harpoons, spear-throwers for the darts held across their backs in hide quivers and knives and hatchets at their belts, but they'd obviously come in peace.

For that matter, those are tools of the hunt rather than made just for man-killing, Rudi thought. *Though doubtless they'd be stout fighters at need. Ingolf said they'd beaten off raids by Eaters from the mainland. Nor do timid men hunt whale in boats like those!*

The women wore leggings too, but under knee-length tunic-dresses, and their hair was mostly in long braids. They smiled and spoke and signed as they unloaded bundles from the craft; smoked and salted fish, jerked goat meat, sacks of cornmeal and beans and potatoes, dried vegetables and edible seaweed, and the carcasses of deer and rabbits along with baskets of scallops. Rudi gave a mental sigh of relief; that would ease his band's logistical problems considerably. His mouth watered a little at the thought, the more so as the women briskly stoked up the fires and went to work.

He nodded gravely to the chief of the Sea-Landers, in a gesture that was almost a bow.

"My thanks to you, Kills Orca," he said sincerely to the stocky, deep-chested older man.

These people weren't poor, as his generation judged such things; their goods were well made if simple, and they didn't look as if they went hungry often. He didn't suppose they would starve because they were feeding his folk from their winter stores, though they numbered half as many as the whole tribe; but this food was something they would not have as a reserve against ill fortune, and it had been won with sweat and effort and sometimes danger.

The first scents of roasting venison made his stomach rumble; it had been a while since he'd had fresh meat, and the mainlanders who brought the Sea-Land tribe seed corn and spuds had apparently also had garlic and herbs along.

Kills Orca was what the man's wife translated the name as; she was about his age, in her forties, and her gray-streaked braids had been yellow once. Her English came fluently, though a bit halting and mushy with lost teeth; she'd been nearly a woman grown at the Change, and now showed every one of the hard years and many children.

"Strong Man"—she indicated Ingolf and went on as her husband spoke in his own sonorous tongue—"saved our son Frank . . . High Wave . . . when this was a place of bad magic. Now you've made that go away, so our homes are safe. You are friends. Friends help each other."

"Indeed they do," Rudi said gravely.

"Threefold return," Mary said unexpectedly.

"For good or ill," Ritva added. "Ingolf's getting it, and we as well."

Rudi nodded; that *was* the way the world worked . . . though it could be a very long time indeed before the Powers reckoned up the balance.

"As ye sow, so shall ye reap," Ignatius said; which was another way of putting the same thing.

"Tell Kills Orca that I hope he will accept these gifts from us," Rudi said, making a gesture with his open hand.

They were lavish, thanks to the *Gisandu*'s helpful cargo of salvage from the dead cities. Stainless-steel blades for knives and spearheads, hatchets and axes, fishhooks and imperishable nylon cords and nets, woodworking tools, hoes and pitchforks and trowels, pots and pans and mirrors, cloth found sound in sealed locations.

He was fairly sure the locals would have extended the same hospitality even if he'd had nothing to offer, though the men looked pleased and the women enthusiastic. And . . . Graber's men were helping the Sea-Land women unload the boats, and exchanging smiles. Kills Orca didn't seem to mind. Ingolf had mentioned that the tribe had tried to get *him* to stay, the first time he'd come here. These Sea-Land folk were perilously few, in a world where they had no kin for neighbors; in need of men to work and fight, and of fresh blood to father children not dangerously closely related to their future mates. They didn't seem to have any prejudices about those who looked different from themselves either, which put them a step up on some folk he'd met.

The major started towards his men, or former men; Rudi caught his eye and shook his head slightly.

"You've made your choice, and they shall make theirs," he murmured to himself.

The words wouldn't carry, but they didn't need to. The officer of the Sword of the Prophet was nobody's fool. He nodded in return, turned and stalked off along the beach, with his left hand making occasional movements as if to rest on the pommel of a shete that wasn't there and his little tuft of chin-beard bristling.

"That may solve one problem," Mathilda said.

She looked over to where the ex–High Seeker was doggedly dragging a long piece of driftwood towards the fires. Her eyes narrowed; he knew she found the five-year-old in the man's body disturbing in a way that went below words. The more so because the child in the man wasn't merely lost. You could see hints of a sunny-natured boy named Dalan, brave and willing. And you knew what had happened to him.

"Perhaps him too?" she said hopefully. "There would be worse ways for him to make amends. Father Ignatius thinks he'll . . . mentally age . . . enough to do a man's work. Eventually."

Rudi thought, then shook his head, though he'd have been just as glad to see the last of the man as she.

"No. I have the feeling he may be . . . useful."

Ignatius nodded. "Nor would it be safe to leave him alone, I think. He is vulnerable. The malice of the Adversary has been defeated here, but not destroyed."

"No indeed," Rudi said softly, his hand caressing the hilt of the Sword. "Not yet."

"Bows out, y'lazy beggars!" Edain Aylward said.

"Shouldn't we be getting aboard?" Hrolf Homersson asked, nodding towards the refitted *Gisandu* where she rested at her anchors with furled sails.

He was one of the Norrheimers they'd picked up at Eriksgarth to replace casualties; a very big man with a braid in his brown beard, whose favorite weapon was a four-foot ax with a war-hammer's serrated shape on the side opposite the broad blade. He handled it like a willow switch.

"We've a few hours yet till sundown," Edain said, and grinned. "And what better way to spend them than practice with the bow? We're off on the morning tide tomorrow."

He heard muffled groans, and a voice that muttered: *Sleep? Food? Beer?* from the background, and he didn't try to see who. It was the sort of cold, dank day in the Black Months when your thoughts turned naturally to a chair and a crackling fire; and hot cider, and apples and nuts roasting on the hob while you worked on a bit of harness and yarned with your friends and smelled supper cooking.

"So back to work!" he said, putting a sergeant-major's snap into it that he'd learned from his father.

It worked, too. He paced up and down the line, his own longbow in the crook of his arm, watching critically.

Asgerd Karlsdottir was off a farm near Eriksgarth too, tall and lithe, with the ends of hacked-off hair the color of fresh honey sticking out from under her knit cap; she'd been trying stubbornly to use the longbow he'd tossed her, but her string-arm gave a betraying quiver at full extension.

"This stave's too heavy for me," she said bluntly, glaring at him. "I'm over-bowed."

"No, you're not," he said. "I made that one with Ritva in mind, and you're as tall, and near as strong. You're drawing from outside the bow, sure and y'are. *That's* the problem."

Another glare, raw and belligerent. He'd noticed that Norrheimers were touchy, and she had extra reason—her affianced man had been killed by tribes allied to the Cutters. She was here because she'd taken a vow before the Gods of Norrheim, what her folk called a *bragarfull*, to take ten lives for his one, or die in the attempt, and sworn service to Rudi for the accomplishing of it. Edain intended to see that she did so and lived.

It would be an offense against the Lady of the Blossomtime to let a lass that fair die unwed.

"What does *that* mean?" she said. "Outside the bow?"

"Gather 'round, ye infants!" he said.

They did; the Norrheimers and the men of the Southside Freedom Fighters—who'd been savages in the Wild Lands of Illinois, until the chief and he had picked them up last year. The Southsiders nudged one another. They found the *asatruar* folk of what had been northern Maine a bit heedless and arrogant. Also they'd had him drilling and bully-damning them into shape considerably longer.

"The folk who taught you archery were hunters before the Change," he said. "Or they learned from such."

"So?" Ulfhild said.

She was the sole other woman in the war band the original questers were building, dark and built like a barrel, and she'd been having the same problem. The Norrheimers were good shots; their people depended on wild meat for a good bit of their diet. But they weren't battle-archers as the Clan thought of it, and they tended to think of fighting as mainly an affair of cold steel at arm's length.

He'd seen fights won where the enemy never got to within twenty yards of a longbow harrow-formation, and that was the way he liked it best. Against horsemen particularly, which the Cutters mostly were in their home ranges.

"Hunters can make do with light staves," Edain said. "And take their time about a shot. Me dad practiced all his life with the war-bow, yes and made 'em too, for all they had those gun weapons back then. As pastime, and because it's old in my family, the Aylwards. He taught me—all us Mackenzies—how you draw from *inside* the bow."

They looked blank. He took his own weapon and tossed it to Hrolf. "Draw that, big man, and yourself so strong and hearty."

The big man did; his eyes widened as he pulled it to full draw, grunting a little.

"Heavier than mine! A good deal heavier!"

Edain nodded; he was thick in the shoulders and arms himself, and deep-chested, but of no more than average inches. Asgerd was tall for a woman, and within a finger-width of his height; their eyes were level with Hrolf's chin. He took the bow back and held it before him, elbows out, one hand on the grip and one on the string.

"This is outside the bow," he said, pulling.

Then he shifted to a real stance. "This is *inside*. Push at it. Like you were in a doorway and pushing on the jambs from the inside. Bend your whole body into it. Feel the curve from left hand through your body to your feet and out your right. The bow stave is a spring; make your body a set of levers and springs to push it. Inside the bow, and sit into the draw."

He did, twisting and sinking down a little.

"You look like you're drawing with the weight of your arse," Ulfhild said, and laughter barked.

Edain grinned himself. "But it works."

"Maybe with an arse like yours."

"Ah, well, y'need a heavy hammer to drive a long nail," Edain said cheerfully, and there was another laugh.

The Mackenzie bow-captain put the snap back into his voice: "Try it! Right hand past your ear, past the hinge of your jaw. Open your chest right out, that uses your back muscles—they're stronger than your arms."

They did, and Asgerd's eyes went wide. "I can hold it! Long enough to shoot . . . but it makes aiming harder."

"Don't aim! Aiming's for beginners. Don't look at the arrow at all. Look at where you want to hit. *Think* the shaft home—and once it's clear of the bow, don't think of it at all. Shift to your next at once. You only get one try at a deer, and then it runs away. Men are different. They come at *you*."

He turned . . . and suddenly a shaft was in the air. Two more followed before the first hit in the driftwood log a hundred and fifty paces down the beach: *tock-tock-tock* in the hard sea-bleached wood.

His great half-mastiff bitch Garbh looked up at him to see if he wanted her to fetch the arrows. He dropped a hand to her head and she leaned into him, showing her long yellow man-killing fangs as she grinned and lolled her tongue.

"No, girl, not yet. That log will be an unhealthy place for a few hours more."

Under his determined cheerfulness ants seemed to be crawling under his skin. They were needed at home, and home was a continent away.

KALKSTHORPE, NORRHEIM
(FORMERLY ROBBINSTON, WASHINGTON COUNTY, MAINE)
MARCH 12, CHANGE YEAR 25/2023 AD

"Kalk, how long have we been arguing?" Heidhveig said sharply.

"Off and on, since we met!" the old man said, his seamed face pushing towards her like a snapping turtle's.

Somehow the resemblance was greater for the fringe

of white hair around his bald skull; he'd been bare on top when they'd met, twenty-five years ago.

Aesir witness, he's older than me.

They were sitting in her loom room—mostly used by her daughters and granddaughters and their apprentices these days, and for *seidh*. The pale winter sunlight washed over the vertical frame from tall windows on two sides. Also over a scattering of hanks of spun wool, and a stuffed tiger (made of real tiger skin) with one ear chewed off by a great-great-grandchild, a horse on wheels . . . The room smelled of wool, faintly of ash from the fires that had run wild during the corsair attack on the town a few months ago, and strongly of cod-and-onion stew and baking rye bread from the kitchens. Always a little of the sea, out where the Grey-flood met the Atlantic. Noises too; someone singing, children's voices, a dog barking. Her household here had started out large, and grown more by births and weddings and simple accretion than it had lost by youngsters moving away.

"No, when we *met*, you persuaded me that the Change was about to happen, which is why I moved my family here from California," she said.

He nodded. "It was good advice."

"And I took it. I've given *you* good advice since, haven't I? As a friend and a seidhkona."

His nod was a little more grudging; her fame as a seer-ess was nearly as important to Kalksthorpe as its trade and crafts were.

"So believe me when I say Rudi and the others *will* be back soon. I've seen it." She sighed. "Care to *bet*? Say, that long table with the carved edge against . . . oh, four bolts of woolen?"

"Done," Kalk said.

And a child of seven ran into the room, her unbound

maiden's hair swirling like black mist beneath a fur cap
with earflaps and the rosy flush of the day's chill still on
her cheeks. A tiny gold horse hung on a linen cord
around her neck, the sign of Gná, Frigg's messenger.

"Sails, Amma!" she said, her voice crackling with excitement. "A ship! A big, big *ship!*"

"Njord sink me, I should know better by now," Kalk
muttered. "Take the table, take it!"

"Feet!" Heidhveig said sternly to the girl, hiding her
smile and pointing.

"Yes, Amma. Sorry, Amma."

Gundridh Thorvinsdottir was actually a *great*-
granddaughter, but that was what all the youngsters
called her; the half of Kalksthorpe under sixteen mostly
did, for that matter. The child hopped from one foot to
another, taking off the muddy overboots she had forgotten and holding them in one hand; there was mud on the
hem of her thick burgundy sumac-dyed wool skirt too.
Her eyes still glittered; Kalksthorpe was a fishing town
and a port in a not-too-small way by today's standards,
but a strange vessel this early was still a rare break in routine.

"I wonder what ship that could be?" Heidhveig said
dryly to her old friend. Then: "Well, fetch me my staff,
girl!"

Gundridh did, grinning again. She carried the staff
carefully, though: it had a brass knob on the end, with
carvings of a raven, cat and bear below, set with amber
and garnet and a small compass. Her boots were tucked
under one arm—which wouldn't do her dress any good
either. A brindled tabby jumped out of a basket of wool
and onto the warm spot on her chair as Heidhveig walked
down the hall to the stairwell and descended with a

thump and grunt for each tread. She was well for someone with her years; you were well or dead, at her age and in this time and place. But her joints hurt in cold weather nowadays.

Before the Change someone had told her that you started groaning like that when you were past prime breeding age—it let the predators know you were old enough to be safely culled from the herd. She grinned a little at the thought as she came to the big hall that ran the length of the house on the ground floor and gave on the front-door vestibule. There were two hearths blazing, and it had a multitude of uses, from ritual to storytelling. But the family's arms were also racked on the walls, and now people were bustling about quietly; the menfolk of the house and more than a few of the women were donning nose-guarded helmets and war sarks of metal-studded leather or mail shirts, and handing out spear, shield, sword, bow and ax. Even the dogs caught the mood and waited quietly. Everyone was still of a mind to be cautious after the corsair raid last year—though it was very unlikely they'd be so unlucky again anytime soon.

"Don't count any man lucky until he's dead," she said to her son Thorleif, when he said that. "But this time you're right."

He grinned back at her, showing blocky irregular teeth, and lifted his seven-foot spear to demonstrate that he wasn't taking any chances; he was well into middle age himself now, silver in his receding dark hair but still strong, a bold-featured man with a square jaw and beak nose. Then he thumped the ashwood shaft of the weapon against the boss of a round shield painted with a black raven on a red field. The loud, dull *boom* caught everyone's attention.

"Carefully!" he said. "I don't want anyone stabbing someone in the ass because you're hurrying needlessly. Chances are it's nobody hostile. Keep good order and keep the points *up*. Karl, you're still not fifteen—door-guard for you."

Heidhveig thumped her staff on the floorboards in turn. "It's Artos Mikesson and his folk, returned with the Sword of the Lady, as the High One foretold. I felt it when he drew the blade. Everyone on this continent with the Sight did! And a good many others."

"I didn't," Kalk observed sourly.

"You saw the Change coming," she said. "How often since?"

Kalk grunted wordlessly.

"Right, Mother," her son said. "We'll still turn out. Practice never hurts."

He turned to his wife. "Though if we're to have guests . . ."

"We slaughtered that pig just the day before yester-day," she murmured, her eyes going distant. "We haven't started on that. Plenty of potatoes . . . I'll start some tor-tiere and sausage thawing, get out some apple pies we froze last fall, and put more dough to rise . . . you get going!"

Heidhveig donned her padded coat and a long, dark blue cloak fastened with a valknut, pulling a knitted cap over her braided white hair. Her household's fighters crowded out the door, joining the others of the town; everyone had his assigned place. For the Heidhveigssons that meant down by the docks and boatyards. The alarm bell tolled from the *stave-hof*, the temple, but paced slow and steady. That meant the others could suit their pace to hers and Kalk's determined stump rather than dashing;

the old asphalt and new cobbles were slippery under a
layer of wet slush, and she picked her way cautiously. Falling and breaking a hip was not a good idea these days.
Breath misted white in the damp air, and edged metal
gave a watery gleam. They passed half a dozen construction sites littered with tools and sawdust and chips, where
houses wrecked in the raid were being replaced, solid
fieldstone-and-log structures replacing old pre-Change
frame for the most part.

The towering roof-upon-roof of the hof was in the
center of the town's only open square, with its gilded
carvings and dragonheads snarling from the carved rafters. Folk mostly followed their trades in their own homesteads these days, but past the temple lay the part of town
down by the Greyflood and the piers which held busi-
nesses smelly, smoky or requiring more space; fish-salting
works, renderies that turned whale oil into soap or candles, foundries, worksheds, tanyards, timber-yards. The
half-built ribs of a ship rested on a slipway.

A low palisade with gates marked off the town from the
docks proper, much lower than the double log wall that
ringed the town elsewhere. Most of the seaward defenses
were out in the water, a sunken pattern of great logs set in
the harbor bed tipped with steel blades waiting to rip out
the belly of any ship that didn't know their pattern. Block-
houses at either seaward end of the wall held catapults that
could smash boats trying to row foemen ashore. The fishing boats were mostly hauled up in long sheds, but the
larger salvage craft rested at their moorings, the long slender bowsprits reaching over the cobbled roadway. The savage figureheads below were dismounted and stowed; no
sense in risking the landwights' anger.

Nearly anyone who could walk at all was behind the

fighting levy, peering past shoulders and shields and spears. Thick patches of mist lay on the estuary's ruffled gray water this morning; warmer water was coming in from the south, meeting the still-strong hand of winter. Then the tips of two masts appeared, ghosting slowly forward under the slight onshore breeze.

"Schooner," Kalk muttered, peering; his sight was still keen for distant things. "Big one . . . Moorish-built . . . no, it's not that one we captured and Artos took south! Close, but not that one . . . looks like she took some damage somewhere . . ."

The crowd tensed, then broke into a hum as a flag appeared at the mainmast; blue, with a green white-topped mountain, overlaid with a longsword whose guard was the crescent moon. Anchors rattled and splashed, and the ship swung steady, pitching slightly with the waves. A tall man sprang to stand on the frame of the bow-catapult, standing easy as a cat on the slippery moving metal. Redgold hair hung to his armored shoulders, a bright dash in a world of gray and brown and dark green.

Then he drew his sword. A low murmur of awe went through the watchers at the silvery flash of blade and pommel.

"Hail!" someone shouted, and in a moment the crowd had taken it up:

"Hail! Hail!"

Heidhveig shivered a little and drew the cloak closer with her gloved hands. There was a glitter to the steel that was like music—like trumpets and drums, like the silver chime of bells on the bridles of destriers, a song that could seize the hearts of men and transfigure them.

"More potent than Tyrfing, forged for the hand of a King," she quoted softly: those had been the High One's

words, spoken through her while she was in trance on the *seidhjallr*, the Chair of Magic.

"What do You plan now, old man? Your daughters will bring you many a hero before this is finished."

The rhythmic shouting broke apart in cheers, and boats set out to shuttle the crew ashore. Heidhveig waited, leaning on her raven-headed staff until Artos came through. Gundridh was riding on his shoulders, yelling shrilly and waving his flat raven-plumed Scots bonnet in the air, and the same frank grin she remembered was on his face. It died as he swung the child down and faced her, bowing his bright head for an instant.

"Merry met again, Lady Heidhveig," he said gravely, and put the back of his right fist to his forehead for a moment.

She met his blue-green gaze and then bowed herself, more deeply.

"*Come heil*, Artos King," she said, using the formal greeting from the old tongue.

Some buried fragment of her wondered what the young woman she'd been a lifetime and an age ago in Berkeley would have thought if she could have seen this moment. The rest of her was entirely grave.

His mouth quirked a little. "Not King in *this* land," he said.

"But King indeed," she said. "You've changed."

A matter-of-fact nod, and the soft burring lilt went on:

"That I have, Lady. For a man must suit himself to the work fate and the Powers give him. I led a band of friends to find the Sword. Find it I did; and now I must raise a host, win a war, and found a kingdom!"

"Hopefully you won't need to fight a dragon as well," she said dryly.

"That too, Lady. That too—though not one with scales or wings, perhaps."

They bustled him and his folk back to her house; the talk went on through the afternoon and into the early dark. By then the dinner trestles had been set up, and besides her own family others were drifting in to hear the tale, and of course you couldn't refuse hospitality. She winced slightly at the expense as plate after plate of basted ribs and sizzling pork chops came out, piles of sausage and platters of French fries and round rye loaves and butter.

This wasn't the mead-hall of a *godhi*, a ring-giving drighten chief; it was just a big house. A *godhi* was expected to be openhanded to all comers, but he had his own lands and the scot from his yeoman followers to supply the means. And this had been a hard winter in Kalksthorpe, with their losses from the attack; late winter and spring were the hungry times in Norrheim anyway. Her family's share of the corsair ship's cargo would help, but in a country as thinly peopled as theirs it would take time to translate it into things they could eat and use.

Her mouth quirked a little. She'd loved the old stories even before she came to the old Gods, but the people in them had seemed a little crazed for booty at times. It wasn't until you'd lived in something like their world that you understood how thin the margin could be between comfort and desperation, and how important it was to build up a reserve. Nor would anyone who'd survived the first Change Year ever take food for granted again.

Though most of her neighbors were at least bringing along a dish, fish casseroles, a ham, loaves, butter, cheese. Another thing you learned in these times was how much you depended on other folk, for all that Norrheimers boasted of their independence. Artos-Rudi and his companions tore into the dinner with the thoughtless voracity of the young and active who'd also been on short commons for some time.

"The winds were against us much of the time," Artos finished. "With the ship so crowded we were weary and no mistake, by the time we made the Greyflood! *And* hungry!"

A hammering came at the front of the house. The buzz of conversation died down. The lanterns and candles guttered in the sudden draught; someone had pushed through the inner vestibule before the outer door closed, spilling heat. Her heart hammered, almost painfully.

She didn't recognize the man; from the cut of his clothes he came from far inland, in the farmlands where most of the Norrheimers dwelt. He was young, just old enough for a downy show of brown whiskers on his cheeks and chin, the hood of his parka thrown back to show longish hair held by a leather headband. Youngster he might be, but a sword and seax-knife hung at his belt, and a round shield over the pack on his back. His boots had the raised toe of the type you wore on skis.

It was the arrow in his hand that drew everyone's eyes, and brought shocked silence. It was painted bloodred from tip to fletching. That was shown for one thing only; to call out the full levy of Norrheim against a foe who threatened them all.

"War!" he shouted, shaking it in the air; his voice cracked across, and that made him pause, swallow and continue with a little more calm:

"The Bekwa have come through the north woods and crossed the border, thousands, killing, burning. A *trollkjerring* leads them, a sorcerer in a red robe, and the

terror of him makes brave men run; the troll-men swear
they will eat our hearts and lay all Norrheim waste. *Godhi*
Bjarni Eriksson calls the fighting-men of all the tribes to
rally to him—in Staghorn Dale, at the Rock of the Twin
Horsemen—or we will be overrun piecemeal. Every true
man. And he asks you, holy seidhkona, to come as well to
battle the red-robe."

The young man stopped, gulping, swaying on his feet;
someone gave him a cup of hot cider, and he drained it
eagerly, a little running down his chin as he gulped and
half choked. When he looked up his blue eyes went wide.

Artos stood, and the mild good cheer had left his face
altogether, making it a thing of angles and planes. He had
hung his sword belt over the back of his chair. Now he
took the scabbard in his right hand and set his left—his
sword-hand—on the long hilt. The crystal of the pommel
caught the light of fire and lamp, breaking it back in shiv-
ers of red and orange.

"Bjarni Eriksson and I swore blood brotherhood on
the golden oath-ring of his folk, in the name of his Gods
and mine," he said. "And the Threefold Herself gave me
this Her Sword for just such tasks as this. Your chief shall
have the help he sought, and more besides."

The great blade flashed high suddenly. "*War!*" Artos
shouted, his voice a huge silver peal in the long room.
"*War!*"

Men stood, and women; fists and drinking-horns and
knives flashed in the air as they took up the chant.

Heidhveig shivered a little in her chair, suddenly alone
and a little lost in this her home.

War, she thought. *War indeed*.

CHAPTER FOUR

"They attacked us!" Kalk said furiously.

His voice rose under the high roof of the three-quarters-empty warehouse the town was using to muster its fighters.

"They're *pirates*," he half shouted.

"They are pirates, and they did attack, and most of them are dead. The survivors are forty-four first-class fighting-men, and neither you nor I can spare them. Nor are folk who make *viking* a term of honor in a position to be . . . what was the word they used . . . picky," Artos said.

It was becoming more natural to think of himself by that name.

Artos is *my name,* he thought. *It always was, in the Craft. Rudi . . . Rudi I can be in private, I suppose.*

Most of the Kalksthorpe fighters were mustering here, ready to leave at dawn; it was hard cold outside the town wall, and the granular snow was still thick enough for skis. Their families were there to see them off, and a low murmur of voices sounded. Most of the good-byes were quiet and solemn, with fewer embraces or tears than there would have been among Mackenzies, even when a mother tucked the last bundle of fruitcake or rolled socks into a young man's haversack. Everywhere about love met necessity with a fierce dignity.

Rudi turned to the Moors, who stood in a clump amid a circle of empty space. Abdou al-Naari was there, and his son beside him, a slim young man just old enough to journey with a war band; his arm had healed while his father was in Nantucket. Abdou's blood brother Jawara stood by his other hand, smiling grimly as he fingered the edge of a broad-bladed spear. He looked to have shed years or gained inches with a weapon in his hand again, a leopard's hunting eagerness on his broad features.

"Is it agreed?" Rudi said. "You join us for this one fight. If we win, you get your ship and enough food to sail her to your home, and pledge your word of honor by your own God that you will trouble these lands no more. The cargo is still forfeit."

"Agreed," Abdou said. "May God destroy me if I break the oath. *Inshallah*, God willing, we will begin our revenge on those who tricked us and blasphemed the Faith."

He turned slightly and repeated the words in his own language. An eager baying snarl ran through the corsairs.

"And an equal share of any loot," Abdou added, in a more matter-of-fact tone.

"Agreed, though the savages aren't likely to have more than hard blows to give us. Stay close to my band, Abdou al-Naari. These folk may accept the bargain but they don't love you for it."

Abdou shrugged and smiled. "I not love ugly pagans either, we same-same so there," he said.

Artos turned to Kalk. "The cargo is worth more than the ship; consider that wergild."

"I'd rather have blood for blood," the Norrheimer said.

The Mackenzie smiled at him, and the grim old man blinked a little at the savagery of the expression.

"And so you shall," he said quietly. "Do you think they'll all come through such a campaign as this unhurt? They *could* have stayed safely here waiting for an English ship to pick them up. Instead they're offering their lives. For their own reasons, but that won't make their blood flow any the less red, eh? When a man takes up the spear of his own will in a country not his own, he consents to his death and makes himself a sacrifice whose blood blesses the land."

Heidhveig chuckled mirthlessly. "I *told* you he used his head for something besides a helmet-rack," she said. "Now do you see why the High One said he would found a line of Kings that lasted forever in the tales of men, if he lived and won his victory?"

Kalk nodded wordlessly and turned away to his sons. Artos looked at her:

"If you can keep up, you're welcome," he said bluntly. "But if you can't, Lady, then you must ask the Gods for protection, for I cannot stay to offer it."

The seeress inclined her head. "My sleigh should be enough."

"Pray for cold, then. If we get a thaw and then mud . . ."

"I will. We've held our *blót* and spoken with the wights and cast the runes. Now it's in Victory-Father's hands."

Rudi turned his head. "Matti?"

"Arms and armor in good condition, enough arrows, and the food supplies look adequate assuming we can restock at Eriksgarth," she said.

"Ignatius?"

"Our medical kit is full—the healers here are excellent. Enough are coming along that I can be spared for combat duty."

"Ingolf?"

"They've got no cavalry at all," the Richlander said in frustration, and Virginia Thurston scowled agreement. "Mounted infantry at best."

Rudi sighed. "You fight with the army you've got, not the one you might wish. The ideal one that has a core of well-drilled pikemen and longbowmen, with field artillery to suit, three thousand good light cavalry, and a thousand knights on destriers . . . It would be a nightmare getting enough fodder anyway. Wait until we get farther west! Fred?"

Frederick Thurston turned his hands upward, the pink palms contrasting with the chocolate-brown of his skin.

"There's not much unit articulation in this lot," he said, frowning slightly. "They fight by households. Given a week or two—and if they listen to me—I could at least get them to sort by the way they're armed."

Artos hid a smile. Fred was young—still short of twenty—but he was very intelligent and very well trained in his father's army. The problem was that the army of the United States of Boise was a superbly disciplined precision instrument, and he judged everything by that standard. As village militias went, the Kalksthorpe *fyrd* weren't bad at all. He'd have to learn to be a bit more flexible.

"We'll do that along the way; but Fred, remember it's the art of the possible. Ritva, Mary . . . I need to know more than *there are thousands of them* and *gather at Staghorn Dale*, and I need to know it quickly. Can you do it?"

The two Dúnedain gave identical nods. "We can travel three times faster than this bunch," Mary said.

"There and back again," Ritva added, despite her sister's glare.

Rudi signed agreement; a war band traveled at the speed of the slowest. And the Rangers trained hard in just that sort of scouting and endurance trek. He himself could keep up with his half sisters cross-country, but he didn't know many others who could.

"Go, find out who's where with what, and get back to me. Hopefully by the time I reach Eriksgarth." Then he added: "*Hortho le huil vaer, muinthel nín.*"

That meant *fair winds speed you on, sister*. He'd never had the time to spare to learn the Rangers' special tongue, but he had a fair assortment of stock phrases. Ritva and Mary both put their right hands to their hearts.

"*Harthon cened le ennas, muindor nín,*" Ritva said solemnly: "I'll see you there, my brother."

Mary spoke to Ingolf: "*Unad nuithatha i nîr e-guren nalú aderthad vín.*" When his lips began to move in silent translation, she leaned close and whispered:

"Nothing will stop the weeping of my heart until we are once more together."

Ritva added a wink—he thought at Hrolf Homersson—and they picked up the skis that leaned against a pillar, put them over their shoulders and left at a tireless springy trot.

Artos took a deep breath and jumped to the top of a great hogshead full of something heavy.

"Folk of Kalksthorpe," he called.

His voice wasn't pitched very loud, but absolute silence fell; he could hear the cold wind hooting around the logs of the walls.

"You've agreed to follow me to this war-muster," he said; his glance went to Thorleif Heidhveigsson.

The man nodded soberly. "I did," he said.

Kalksthorpe didn't exactly have a chief, besides Kalk himself; they settled matters by a folkmoot where every adult had a voice, much like a Mackenzie dun. The settlement was small enough for that to work, just, if most were sensible. But the seeress' son was a leading trader and craftsman, a respected man whose word carried weight. Hers carried even more, and the word of the Gods through her.

"*I'm* not going to quarrel with the High One's opinions about war," the householder said, confirming Artos' thought. "Who here is fool enough to do that? He's the Father of Victories."

Nobody volunteered to put on the offered shoe; Artos held his grin within himself. He didn't doubt for a moment the truth of Heidhveig's vision, but it *was* politically convenient as well, and no mistake.

"Do you all swear to it?" he said.

A moment's silence, then a crashing shout of agreement from the two-hundred-odd fighters; most of them hammered weapons on shields, a hollow booming thunder that turned into a roar as it echoed back from the rafters.

"We swear!"

"Then hear my word! You will obey my orders; a war band without a leader is like a ship at sea without a captain, food for the carrion eaters. And you will take those orders through those I appoint as if from my own mouth. Doubtless there are many men of mark among you, but we've no time for me to make their acquaintance. Frederick Thurston here is my chief of staff—"

The dark young man nodded. He had the specialist training for it . . . and Fred had come to follow the same Gods as the Norrheimers, over the past year or so; the Lord of the Ravens had personally claimed him as a follower through Heidhveig. That would give him added authority.

"—and Ingolf the Wanderer is my second-in-command."

Ingolf crossed his muscled arms on his chest over his mail hauberk. Even to someone who didn't know him, he looked to be exactly what he was; a fighting-man vastly experienced, shrewd, and dangerous as an angry bear when the steel came out. And unlike Fred Thurston he was accustomed to making do with scratch bands of amateur warriors.

"Princess Mathilda is in charge of our logistics . . . our supplies; she will set rations and give all orders concerning forage and shares. Virginia Thurston is horse-mistress."

The rancher's daughter nodded. She also snorted a little; to her way of thinking nobody here knew *anything* about the beasts.

"Father Ignatius is master of the making of camps, the setting of watches, and all matters concerning health and order. Edain Aylward is master-bowman and chief of archers. *Don't* waste my time quarreling with any one of them. Understood?"

Sober nods. These Norrheimers were more stiff-necked than his clansmen at home, and almost as fond of argument and dispute, but also a bit more practical. Vastly more so than, say, nobles of the Association.

"Then let's be off. *March!*"

*　　*　　*

He paused a half hour later, to look back over the cleared snow-covered fields to Kalksthorpe, squinting against the sun before they entered the shade of the low pines.

"What's wrong, Rudi?" Mathilda said, snowplowing her skis to a stop beside him and thrusting down her poles.

He frowned and rubbed his left hand across his face. The right stroked the pommel of the Sword; he did that often now, a habit that felt ancient already.

"I . . . I don't know," he said. "It's . . . as if I'm *concentrating* all the time."

"You're a King and running a war, Rudi!"

He shook his head. "It's not just that. It's like I'm concentrating *all the time*, sure. As if it stops only when I make it, instead of the other way around. Just now I found myself looking through the list of candidates for Chancellor of the Realm in Montival! Which is not only odd, but premature in the extreme!"

She smiled at him. "Oh, that's easy. Father Ignatius."

She's right, he thought; something *clicked* in his mind in acknowledgment as she went on:

"Though you may have to hit him alongside the ear and throw the chain of office over his head while he's dazed."

Artos chuckled. *He does take that* humility *business rather seriously*, he thought.

Aloud: "And I feel like a *pipe* a lot of the time. Like a pipe with something rushing through it, and being worn away by it."

Her thick brows frowned in concern. "What does that really mean?" she said.

"I don't know!"

He made a gesture of apology as she flinched a little;

he seldom raised his voice. Then he looked down at his clenched fist and forced the long sinewy fingers to unfold.

"You know that engine they have down in Corvallis, at the university? The one that can be set to do all sorts of calculations?"

She nodded, and he knew they were thinking of the same thing. The great room, and the cogs and gearwheels and cams, moving smoothly as the hydraulic turbine whined, and the white-coated attendants like priests of a mystery, or a glimpse of the ancient world.

"The Analytical Engine."

His mouth quirked a little bitterly. "Thinking about what the Sword does . . . I feel like a *dog* in that room with the Engine, looking at it and trying to understand it, with my nose going around in circles and my ears drooping!"

Forlornly, she tried a joke: "I didn't understand it anyway, Rudi!"

He sighed and rubbed his forehead again. "And sometimes I can feel things *happening* through the Sword. As if it was carving a path from . . . somewhere . . . to somewhere . . . to do . . . something. But I haven't the least idea what."

COUNTY OF THE EASTERMARK
BARONY OF DAYTON
PORTLAND PROTECTIVE ASSOCIATION
HIGH KINGDOM OF MONTIVAL
(FORMERLY SOUTHEASTERN WASHINGTON STATE)
MARCH 16, CHANGE YEAR 25/2023 AD

Eilir ghosted through the chill darkness to where her mother waited beneath a big lodgepole pine. She slid the knife back into the sheath along her boot after she'd wiped it, and sank down beside the older woman. This was as far as they could get towards the encamped enemy convoy, even with Dúnedain doing the Sentry Removal. The United States of Boise's army was extremely disciplined and tended to operate by the book; the problem was that they used a *good* book, one that had definite things to say about putting out a wide net and checking on it often. The raiding party had a hundred Mackenzie archers along too, and *they* wouldn't have gotten this far without open fighting, although they hid and skulked quite adequately once the way had been opened for them. There were five times that number of enemy troops camped down on the roadway.

Ready? she said in Sign.

Juniper Mackenzie's face was in shadow, hidden by the fold of her plaid that she'd pulled over it like a hood. She was on one knee, with her rowan staff leaned across her kilted thigh. The head was the Triple Moon in silver, waxing and full and waning, two outward-pointing crescents flanking a circle.

Readier than I wish, Juniper signed.

The moon was down, and starlight hid her face. Eilir Mackenzie hadn't seen her mother in some time and had been a little shocked at how much she'd aged; the once molten-copper hair was faded and heavily streaked with gray now. Whatever it was that had happened in that ceremony back at Imbolc—that voice tolling in her head and the flash of light like nothing since the Change—it hadn't made her any happier.

Be careful! Eilir signed, laying a hand on her shoulder. *If they see you too soon—*

Juniper's hand covered Eilir's for an instant. *I'm the one who taught you how to move through the woods, my girl!*

Eilir's eyes prickled. For a moment she was struck by an almost unbearable memory, of herself as a little girl with her mother in the woods on the mountainside above Dun Juniper . . . or what had just been their house in the hills then. Her mother's hands parting the grass ahead of them, and the fox cubs tumbling over each other in the little clearing ahead, drunk with play and prancing in the moonlight. The way she'd taught her daughter to move quietly, even when Eilir couldn't hear noise herself.

Now Juniper took a deep breath and stood. Then she walked towards the enemy camp in the valley below with her rowan staff moving in precise scribing motions in her right hand, glittering and swooping. The silver head glinted in the faint starlight, but no more brightly than the hoarfrost that covered rock and brush and pine tree. The snow-clad tips of the Blue Mountains were the merest hint behind; not far away a waterfall brawled down a rocky slope, heavy with spring melt. Most of the men ahead were in their little tents, or shapeless mounds of sleeping bags under the wagons. Breath puffed white where the draught horses dozed, their bridles tied to picket ropes, each strung between two trees.

Eilir Mackenzie's breath caught as she saw a sentry rise and heft his long iron-shod javelin, the big oval shield marked with Boise's eagle and crossed thunderbolts up under his eyes. Things were moving in the air about her mother, things the eyes couldn't see but the mind sensed as a tangle of something like lines of bright and dark.

Uh-oh. Mom's in Spooky Mode. Heavier than I've ever seen.

Eilir made the Horns with her left hand. She couldn't hear what her mother said—sang, rather, soft and eerie and gentle. She'd been deaf since birth, but she knew the words. The little hairs along her spine tried to rise, and her belly wanted to cringe beneath the armor and padding where it rested on the dirt. The soil beneath her seemed to *hum*, somehow.

"Sleep of the Earth of the land of Faerie
Deep is the lore of Cnuic na Sidhe—"

The sentry's challenge came slow, and then slower, softer, his lips barely moving. He swayed as she let the staff stop and blew across her bunched fingertips into his face. The Boisean soldier's face went from hard suspicion into a tremble; then he wept, sitting down and burying his face in his hands as sobs shook his armored shoulders.

"Hail be to they of the Forest Gentry
All dark spirits, help us free—"

Another sentry came running; he seemed to stumble, to draw into himself. Then he halted for a moment, set the butt of his spear against the earth and the point to his throat. Juniper moved, her staff knocking the javelin aside so that it merely gave him a nasty cut on the face; the rank salt-and-iron scent of blood filled the air, and it seemed to smoke with Power. He lay facedown, hands and feet making vague gestures. Juniper paced between the banked fires with her left hand going to her belt and then out in a sowing motion as the rowan wood of her staff passed over the sleepers:

"White is the power of the state of dreaming
Light is the song to make one still

Dark is the power of Death's redeeming
Mark but that one word can kill—"

The longbowmen around Eilir were all wearing war-
cloaks. They shed them as they rose, a wave of motion
and a quiver through earth and air and forest, a gleam on
the bodkin points of the arrows and the savage swirls of
war paint on their faces. She came to one knee herself,
hand going to the wire-and-leather-wrapped hilt of her
sword. Then she began to move forward, flitting from
tree to tree to rock and on, until she was close enough to
see faces. The chant continued:

"Sleep!
Poison in your dreams
Some will not awake
Nothing's as it seems
Iron bonds will break
Hearts will be set free
Wrongs will be made right
Sleep and death will be
Justice in the night
Sleep will be
Justice in the night
Death will be
Justice in the night!"

Sleeping men twitched and whined and thrashed and
called for their mothers. Then one rose, and *he* was in
command of himself. The robe he wore was the color of
clotted blood, almost black in the night. Jeweled color
showed on his wrists as he lifted his hands and the loose
sleeves fell back.

"I . . . see . . . you . . . little witch. You . . . are . . . too . . . late. The end . . . of . . . everything shall . . . swallow the light in . . . perfection."

Even lip-reading, the words *thudded* into the world, as if language itself strained and buckled under their burden. She remembered the reception room at Pendleton last year, and looking into the Prophet Sethaz' eyes, like a window into nothing, a caterpillar eaten out from the inside by larvae. The missing part of her left ear seemed to throb.

"And we see you," Juniper replied. "Dark sun-light and shining Moon; the balance of the light and dark; perfection is un-life. We are living Mind and living World and we will *never* be perfect. *Go!*"

The two figures locked into stillness, but she could have sworn that they were fighting . . . or were they dancing?

Not my business. I'm a war-chief of the Dúnedain Rangers. Get working, woman!

She drew her sword and slid the shield onto her left arm. The soldiers were getting up and that *was* her concern. But mostly they were staggering, mouths open in shouts or cries or howls, their eyes seeing things that weren't there . . . or at least things that *she* couldn't see, and was very glad that she couldn't see. None of them were putting on their armor; one was thrusting his hands into a banked fire, into the bed of hot embers beneath the ash. Another blundered towards her, his shortsword jabbing the air in front of him. She twisted aside—he wasn't really trying to strike her—and knocked it out of his hand with the metal-shod edge of her shield. For good measure she slammed it into his head behind the ear with precisely calculated force and dropped him cold as a banker's charity.

A wave of the blade, and the hillside erupted. The Rangers came first, to secure the enemy commanders and the fieldpieces that squatted on their wheeled mounts. The Mackenzie archers were just behind them; they moved among the Boisean soldiers, binding hands behind backs with spare bowstrings and making sure they didn't harm themselves further. All of them gave her mother and the Corwinite magus a wide berth. She was Chief of the Clan; she was also Witch-Queen and Goddess-on-Earth, and right now that was more obvious than anyone liked, especially after what had happened at Imbolc.

Which left her daughter free. The problem was that while the CUT's adepts were not invulnerable, she knew by experience that they were *very hard* to kill.

Back of the neck . . . she began; then the thought was interrupted.

A huge figure trotted down the broken asphalt of the road from the northward, six-seven and three-hundred-odd pounds of John Hordle, her handfasted man . . . or as he usually put it, she was *the missus*. She pointed with the blade of her sword, and he nodded grimly. He'd been in Pendleton too. His own weapon was slung over his back, and it had a four-foot blade. His great auburn-furred paw went up to the long hilt and the bastard sword came out as he spun, astonishingly light and quick for a man his size.

The red-robe tried to turn. Even before the heavy steel struck he crumpled, his attention divided. Hordle gave a grunt as the edge struck.

"They're tough, but that'll put the bugger down, roit enough," he said with satisfaction as the body pitched to one side—the head went considerably farther.

Juniper Mackenzie collapsed as well; Eilir had her arms about her mother's torso before she was halfway to the ground. The green eyes blinked at her, and then rolled up in her head. Her mouth opened; Eilir could feel the vibration of the shriek through the throat. She pinched one earlobe sharply; the rigid shaking stopped, and Juniper looked at her with her waking gaze.

"I'm—" she began, then turned aside and was copiously sick.

Eilir held her until it was finished, produced a handkerchief and wiped her face, snagged a nearby bedroll to place beneath her head. One of Hordle's ham-sized hands came in sight with a canteen, and she helped her mother rinse and spit.

A tap on her shoulder, and she looked up. John spoke, waiting until she had her eyes on his lips:

"Is she roit, then?"

No, Eilir signed bluntly. *This sort of thing backlashes at you. That's the price. The more oomph you have, the worse it is. And someone . . . Someone or Something . . . was giving Mom lots of oomph.*

". . . like wrestling with a rotting corpse," Juniper whispered.

Eilir gave her more water. *Rest!* she signed.

"I'm not a baby!"

The protest was feeble; her daughter smiled. *You took care of me long enough. Let me return the favor.*

John squatted as Juniper's eyes fluttered closed; they looked sunken.

"We've got to clear out as soon as we've looted the wagons and put thermite on them fieldpieces. Thurston's men respond bloody quick, and Corwin's lent them more cavalry. Let me take her."

He did, lifting the slight body as if she were a child's straw dolly.

"Lighter than she was," he said soberly. "She's wearing herself down to a nub."

We all are, Eilir signed.

She looked eastward for a moment, where the first hint of dawn was paling the stars over the mountains.

I just hope they're coming.

That's them, Ritva signed.

All Rangers learned Sign; the younger generation from their cradles. Partly that was because of Eilir Mackenzie, their cofounder with her *anamchara* Astrid, the Lady of the Rangers. And because it was simply so useful, almost as much as Sindarin . . . which few outside the Fellowship ever had the patience to learn either.

She peered carefully around the pine trunk, body and head shrouded in the hooded war-cloak with its mottled green-brown-white surface and loops for bits of pine twig.

I make it about two thousand in this bunch, she estimated. *The tail of them is over about a mile thataway.*

Damn, I'm still not as good with estimating distances as I was before I lost the eye, Mary replied fretfully. *Oh, well, one more bit of payback, coming up.*

Then she silenced herself by raising her monocular, tilting it cautiously to keep the bright pale morning sunlight from making a revealing glint on the lens. Or her *palantír en-crûm*, as it was called in Edhellen. Down on the coast where the Greyflood, the St. Croix that had been, merged with the Atlantic in a tangle of little islands, you could tell that spring was coming, even if it wasn't quite there yet. Even the snow had a grainy, tired look.

Up here near the edge of the North Woods it might as well have been February, except that the days were a bit longer. Their breath smoked, and even the scent of the big tree's sap was faded to a ghost of itself, the rough bark hard as cast iron beneath her gloved hands. The fresh snow glittered. More of it made a fog about the feet of the Bekwa column, kicked up by their snowshoes.

If you can call it a column, she thought snidely. *I'm not expecting Bearkiller standards, but really!*

The wild-men the Norrheimers called Bekwa—apparently only some of those gangs called *themselves* that, but it served—came on in no particular order, in clots and clumps and straggling files, a dozen here, a score there. Some of them grouped around standards on long poles—the antlers of a moose, the skulls of tigers and wolves and men, bits of leather or cloth scribed with crude symbols. A few carried the rayed sun of the CUT, gold on scarlet. Others just trudged; a few drew sleds, or walked behind others drawn by dogs or ponies. One of those keeled over as she watched, going to its knees and then struggling to rise as its owner beat it with a stick. Then it fell; the man drew a long knife, cut its throat and whipped off his crude steel cap to catch the blood. Hoots and yells rose as others crowded close to butcher the animal, many of them haggling off bits of raw meat to eat before it cooled. Inside five minutes nothing was left but the raw bloody skeleton and some of the guts. Others scrambled to add the sled's cargo to their backpacks or toboggans.

They're not organized, exactly, but they seem to get things done, Mary signed thoughtfully. *They're a lot better equipped than the Southside Freedom Fighters were when we first met them, too.*

Ritva nodded. *I don't think they crashed quite as hard after the Change as happened in Illinois,* she replied. *Bit more space between the cities, maybe. Not good, but less absolutely bad.*

All the Bekwa seemed to have a spear at least, solid weapons with heads ground down from pre-Change steel and well hafted. Belts bore knives of various sizes, and hatchets. Quite a few had shields, usually the archetypical barbarian's *Stop* sign nailed on a plank backing, although many read *Arête* instead. There was the odd ax, filed and cut down from woodchopping models; the originals were far too heavy to fight with, of course. Plenty of metal-headed clubs, too, or war-picks. Distance weapons were equally divided between buckets of javelins and real bows; it was impossible to tell how well those were made at this distance, but the sentry-scouts they'd met on their way in had had a straightforward wooden-stave self-bow, competently made but light in the draw.

Hard to tell if there's much body armor, Mary signed. *But I'd bet on a fair bit.*

Could be underneath their coats and furs, Ritva replied.

She didn't expect mail coats or brigandines, much less articulated plate. But the Bekwa could make leather; a jacket of boiled moose hide was pretty good protection, enough to turn a glancing cut or a thrust that didn't hit straight on and hard. Even better if you fastened bits and pieces of metal to it, and washers and lengths of chain and the like could be found in any of the dead cities. Certainly a number of them had bowl helmets—literally made from old stainless-steel kitchenware. Not nearly as good as what a workshop in Montival or Iowa made, or for that matter the spangenhelms the Norrheimers used, but better than nothing.

It could be taken for granted that all the wild-men were skilled fighters, and tough as old shoes; if they weren't, they'd have gone into someone's stew pot over the past generation, or ended up with their heads on a stick if the local tribe had put its Change-era culinary indiscretions behind it. The two Rangers waited patiently, pitting muscle against muscle in motionless exercise to avoid stiffness. When the last of the Bekwa had passed they slipped their hands into their climbing-claws and went down the big white pine cat-fashion. It was as natural as walking, when you'd spent a lot of your life in and out of *flets* in forests that made these look like brush-wood.

The twins landed softly, not far from the body of the Bekwa sentry; Sentry Removal was a Dúnedain specialty.

Then six men rose from behind a curtain of blueberry canes, the points of the bolts in the firing grooves of their crossbows glittering and the thick steel prods bent.

"*Calisse de Tabernac!*" one of them swore, the tassel on the end of his knit cap dangling over a villainous squint. "What we got here, eh? Biggest dam' raccoons I ever see!"

"Uh-oh," Mary said, keeping her hands carefully motionless and in view.

"*Dulu!*" Ritva said. *Help!*

CHAPTER FIVE

One of the six Bjornings who stood by the upright rune-stone was a young man in a mail byrnie, but he moved with a bad limp. The others were women, equipped with spear or bow, swords at their waists. They all exclaimed at the sight of the war-party from Kalksthorpe—about two hundred, plus Abdou el-Naari's forty-four, and fifty more picked up from lonely steadings along the way. Artos suppressed a smile at the obvious relief the man was trying so hard to hide, and thumped a fist on his own brigandine-armored chest in greeting as one of the women slipped away.

"Ladies . . . and . . . Erland Johnsson, isn't it?" he said.

The young man nodded, flushing with pleasure at being remembered from a brief meeting during Rudi's passage through Eriksgarth.

"Yes, lord; *hirdmann* to the chief. I was here when you came at Yule, and the seidhkona made prophecy, and you and the chief swore blood-brotherhood."

"You weren't limping then," Artos said.

"That thumb-fingered idiot Halfdan Finnursson

dropped a crate of hardtack on my foot while we were loading the supply sleds!" Erland burst out, flushing; the flush grew deeper when one of the young women snickered. "That's why I was left behind when the *fyrd* marched."

"But you can stand and hit. Your chief must value you highly, to have you defend his home and kin while he's away."

Out of the corner of his eye Artos noticed two of the Norrheimers he'd sworn to his service, Hrolf Blood-Ax and Ulfhild Swift-Sword, glance at each other and roll their eyes a bit. The young man—he was about seventeen, Artos judged—nodded without noticing; his face was self-consciously warrior-stern, but there was a pleased note in his voice as he said:

"Pardon, but I must signal."

Then he pulled an ox-horn from its sling at his tooled leather belt and blew: *huuu-huuu-hu-hu-hu*. The snarling blat of the horn trumpet sounded across the bright snowfield. You could just see the high roof of Bjarni's meadhall there over a clump of trees and his father's grave-mound to the westward. And the glint of his tribe's *stave-hof*—it was farther away, but taller and sending bright eyeblinks from its gilding and painting. Post-and-board fences sliced the snowfields into square shapes, curving around an occasional rocky hillock or clump of dark green spruces or leafless birch and maple.

"Lady Harberga will be happy to see you; come with us! It's her might that holds the garth while the *godhi* is away."

Edain led a spray of bowmen out first. Before the main column had joined him, Artos heard a high, ringing neigh. A black mare had been standing hipshot in the turn-out field; you could scarcely call it a pasture, with new snow half a foot deep. Night-colored beauty seventeen hands high tossed her head and trotted in a circle, with the other horses in the crowded paddock giving her room.

He laughed, for a moment as carefree and joyous as a boy, and called out ancient poetry in a bard's voice he had learned at his mother's knee:

"*One horse is black, broad-thighed, fierce, swift, ferocious, war-leaping, long-tailed, thundering, silk-maned, high-headed, broad-chested; there shine huge clods of earth that she cuts up with her steel-hard hooves, and her victorious stride overtakes the flocks of birds!*"

Then he whistled loud and shrill; she took ten quick strides and leapt the six-foot rail fence with contemptuous ease, pacing over to him with her tail lifted like a flag and her mane flying in the breeze of her speed. Matti was on his right; the horse casually shouldered her aside and stood by him, turning her head to butt him in the chest and nip slobberingly at the ends of his hair. He blew into her nostrils, a greeting kiss in the horse-tongue, and gave her a piece of dried apple which she deigned to accept, with an implication of forgiveness for his long absence.

"I could get jealous of Epona," Mathilda said. "Is she your horse, or your leman?"

"Nonsense. We're just very good friends." Artos grinned. "You were at Sutterdown Horse Fair, you should know the true story of Artos and Epona."

No, he thought. *I was just Rudi then. Ten years old, and Matti a kid as well, sure, when I found Epona. Or she found me.*

"I wasn't watching when you jumped in that paddock. My hair went *white* when I heard. She'd just tried to *kill* a man. Several men!"

"I'm sure she's not jealous of *you*," he said.

"I know that," Matti said dryly. "She hasn't tried to kill *me*. Yet."

Artos winced slightly as he ran a hand over Epona's withers. She was well into middle age for a horse . . . or would have been, if she was like most horses. Even her vitality had been worn down by the terrible midwinter trek eastward, the grinding effort and bad food. Now she was glossy-sleek, her neck a smooth arch of power and the long mane shining, her coat as smooth as the winter growth would let it be; he thought he saw a wicked glint in the eye she rolled towards him.

"They've been stuffing you," he said mock accusingly, breathing in her grassy scent. "Maple sugar with the oats, and warm mashes each night, blankets, fresh straw every morning. Some adoring girl currycombing every chance she gets, and teasing out your mane and polishing your hooves as if you were a holy image in a shrine."

"Which means she'll savage someone soon," Matti said. "Poor baby," she added.

He nodded. Women were relatively—not absolutely—safe around Epona. The horse trader who'd mistreated her as a filly had been a man, and so had his assistants, and had bred a long-lasting feud with humankind in her breast, starting with the male half. All except for him. She followed at heel as he stepped out of his skis, put them over one shoulder and moved on. Every now and then she'd nuzzle him in the back.

Eriksgarth's heart was an L-shaped combination of a big pre-Change white frame farmhouse sheathed in clapboard and the two-story mead-hall, squared logs on a hip-high foundation wall of mortared fieldstone. The regular whitewashed plank of the one and the flamboyant carved dragonheads and steep roof of the other ought to have clashed, but over a generation they seemed to have grown into each other. The snow-patched shingles on each roof even shared the same spotting of green moss.

Smaller homes for the chief's carls and *their* families made another arm to turn the L into a U; a little farther back were big hip-roofed barns, the low sunken rectangular structures they called potato-houses here, and granaries and stables and workshops, all the necessities of a busy community's farming and crafts. Right now it was more busy than ever, but not with its normal round of churn and loom, saw and smith's hammer. Wagons and sleds were parked densely in the gaps between the buildings, lashed together with ropes and chains to make fighting-platforms. The windows of the houses had been closed with loopholed steel shutters, and a buzz of voices showed that the population had swollen manyfold.

"Some of those are folk who fled the Bekwa," young Erland said, ignoring the pain of his foot and using his spear as a walking stick. "Their families, at least. And more the families of the *bondar*"—which meant *yeoman*, near enough—"hereabouts sent in as part of the Defense Plan. Erik made the Plan, Erik the Strong, the chief's father. Families to rally at the strongest places while the *fyrd* is out."

Rudi nodded. Bjarni's father had been head of an Asatru kindred much farther south; he'd also been a soldier in the old American army for most of his life before the Change. This part of the world hadn't been cursed with the great cities whose witless hordes killed all around them when the Change came, and it had enough goodish farmland to feed the dwellers despite the stark climate, like an island in a sea of forest. But it had been in chaos when Erik arrived with his followers and those picked up along the way. Chaos could kill as certainly as numbers, if more slowly. You couldn't plow and plant if the forest-edge was likely to vomit armed men at you on any given day. The more so when old ways of doing had to be re-learned in desperate haste by stumbling through books or from a few who'd known them as hobbies.

Erik and his men hadn't conquered the land once called Aroostook, not exactly. From what he'd heard it was more that they'd organized it, with a fair bit of fighting now and then, against bandits and reivers and refugee gangs from the north and south and locals too stubborn to admit what needed to be done.

And I grew up on stories of that sort, he thought. *Erik sounds a good deal like my blood-father Mike Havel.*

Folk came boiling out to meet them. They seemed a little surprised when the newcomers didn't do likewise. Instead Fred Thurston made a signal, and troop-leaders barked *Halt*. That came a little raggedly, but in silent unison.

"Attention to orders!" the son of Boise's first General-President snapped.

"We'll break long enough to load food and get the news," Artos called. "And then we're off. No more than two hours—don't get settled. Dismissed!"

Then more quietly: "Good work, Fred."

Fred grinned, snapped a salute and then dashed off. The crowd of Norrheimers parted and Harberga Janets-dottir came through. She'd been well along in pregnancy when he met her, and wasn't now.

"The babe is well?" he asked, with a little anxiety. "And yourself?"

"A boy this time, strong and healthy," she said, smiling forgiveness of his breach of formal manners. "I find the second time goes easier."

Gudrun Eriksdottir followed—her husband's younger sister and about seventeen herself. Gudrun walked in breeks and jacket and boots this time, helm on her auburn-tressed head and spear in hand. Harberga was in Norrheimer women's garb, a long hanging skirt of fine green wool embroidered at the hem with golden triskels, and a linen apron held at the shoulders with silver brooches, with a shaggy bearskin cloak over all. She was tall and a year or two older than he, her fair hair braided under a married woman's kerchief according to local custom, and a look of tight-held worry on her face.

Her blue eyes went to the sword at his waist—to the Sword—and then flicked up to his face, going a little wider. He nodded very slightly, and saw her sternness melt a bit. Then he bowed a little with the back of his right hand pressed to his forehead. That was the greeting a Mackenzie man gave to any hearth-mistress, whether in a lordly hall or a crofter's cot. Harberga handed him a drinking-horn that one of her women had brought.

"Drink I offer, tall helm-tree," she said, abbreviating the local formula of welcome a little.

"Hail to the giver, to the Powers and the folk," he said, doing likewise.

It was hot cider, and grateful in his throat, tasting of summer afternoons. They made good cider in this land, and fine whiskey, and excellent mead. The beer . . . well, they flavored it with spruce buds and had no hops.

He touched a finger to the drink, flicked a drop aside in offering to the spirits of place, then raised it and drank again with his own folk's toast:

"To the Lord, to the Lady, to the Luck of the Clan! Now, Lady Harberga, it's tidings I need; after that, trail food for those with me, if you can spare it."

"We can. We're well supplied and we were expecting . . . well, not you, but the folk from Kalksthorpe at least; they're the last of the *fyrd* to come in. We were hoping for our allies from Madawaska, but there's been no word; we don't know if the messengers got through or if they're under attack too and can't spare help . . . Gudrun, see to the supplies!"

The *godhi's* younger sister pulled Mathilda away, and they started to compare tallies and lists. Barrels and crates and sacks began coming out to fill near-empty sleighs— crackerlike rye hardtack, oatmeal cakes, cheese and dried smoked sausages, with some maple sugar. Concentrated foods, ready for use in the field; several hundred human beings ate a quarter of a ton a day when they were working hard. Meanwhile servers brought the newcomers cooked food from the kitchens, and the improvised camp-style cauldrons that drifted a mist of woodsmoke through the crowded settlement. Artos accepted a chipped plastic bowl of hot bean soup with chunks of meat in it, and a slab of rye-and-barley bread with cheese melted into its surface. The smell of the good plain food made spit run into his mouth; traveling hard on skis in cold weather burned the body's fuel faster than anything else in his experience.

Harberga spread a map the size of a large towel on a trestle resting on barrelheads, and Artos' chief followers crowded around, looking with busy spoons but careful not to mar the precious thing; Heidhveig came over as well, using her staff and assisted by her apprentice Thorlind, herself middle-aged. The Lady of Eriksgarth looked a little askance at Abdou al-Naari, who politely ignored her, eyes kept down on the map itself. It was a new one, copied from a topographical survey of the ancient world onto a carefully tanned white sheepskin with a hot needle, the names and places modernized and twining bands of serpentine gripping beasts added for a border about the edges.

"The muster of the *fyrd* was here, at Staghorn Dale. A short day's march northwest," Harberga said, tapping the surface.

"How many?" Rudi asked.

"Eight thousand and a little more when Bjarni moved against the foe. More were coming in each day, but he didn't want to delay; if there hasn't been a battle yet, then . . . perhaps nine thousand?"

Artos cleaned the inside of his bowl with the heel of the bread, crunched the hard crust down and handed the empty container aside, tapping a thumb on his chin. Nine thousand was more than a tenth and less than a fifth of Norrheim's whole population. Subtracting the many children too young to fight and the sprinkling of elders too old for it along with the sick, halt and lame the total came to about half the folk of warrior age. It meant Bjarni had called up every man between fifteen and fifty who was fit for war, and a fair proportion of the stronger women. He was throwing the dice with everything he had for table-stakes. Artos nodded slowly in respect. Many would have tried to hedge their bets, and traded a possibility of swift victory for the certainty of slow piecemeal defeat.

"The enemy?"

"Less certain, but more than the *fyrd* by a quarter to a third. All the wild-man tribes of the north along the Great River from Royal Mountain to the Stone-Halls. We have a treaty with the Madawaska Republic—"

She pointed to a narrow strip shaded along the upper St. John to the north and east of the Norrheimer settlements, with a symbol that looked like a porcupine in a circle of stars beside it.

"—and we were expecting a thousand men, but we've heard nothing."

Artos' breath hissed between his teeth. "And your last word from Bjarni?"

"Two days ago. They were here," she said, moving her finger westward. "Skirmishing with the troll-men's out-runners, and the foe seems to be gathering all their gangs into one horde."

"They're going to accept battle, then," Artos said thoughtfully.

Sure, and it can be surprisingly hard to make men stand and fight if they don't want to come to the dancing-ground, he mused. *Especially if neither side is cramped for room.*

She nodded. "Bjarni said he'd try to have them come to him on his chosen ground, he knew the place he'd prefer to fight. Six-Hill Field, it's called, used for summer pasture by the northernmost of our folk. The old roads run through there; it's the only way to get large numbers into our farmlands quickly."

Then Artos blinked. The map seemed to be . . . over-lain somehow. As if he were hovering above the land like a raven, and the war bands were like little writhing lines of men coming together; and yet he could hear them, the murmur of voices, the shuffle of boots and skis and snow-shoes. But at the same time they were like living numbers, swinging balances of supply and distance and time in his head, a consciousness of every factor in a dynamic balance. It was the way a God might see them . . .

And not the way I would choose to do so, at all. Useful, though!

The others were looking at him oddly, as if he'd gone away for a moment. He shook his head.

"Yes, that's where the fight will be. Almost certainly.

No word of Mary or Ritva?" he asked. "I sent them on a scout, and they were to rejoin here if they could."

"Your half sisters?" Harberga said, frowning. "No, nothing."

Ingolf moistened his lips, then visibly took command of himself. Rudi-Artos felt his mind stutter. One part was worried; the other was . . .

Not indifferent, he thought, turning the eye of attention inward. *Not that. But as if I had ten thousand thousand sisters, and all were somehow equally dear to me. And that too is how a God might look on things, and no comfort to a man. But it's perhaps a lesson to a King.*

Then he regained his self's balance, feeling as if he should be panting. But that was no calm center. It was more as if he rode a rushing wave, as a longboat does from a ship off the surf-beaten Pacific shore to land softly on the gravel beach that might have ground its bones to splinters if it wavered.

"We'll take this path, cutting the cord of the circle," he said. "That will give the best chance of catching up in time. The river ice is still hard?"

"For now," Harberga said. "But the weather could turn warm anytime. The weather-wights are flighty in this season."

Artos looked up, at a sky white with high thin cloud, felt the air through his skin and breathed the stinging cold. He folded the gift-map.

"Not for a week," he said absently, watching the others get the war band ready to move; it went quickly. "Probably ten days. Time enough to find Bjarni, and fight a battle."

Matti returned, giving him a quick report—full provision—and then checking her horse's tack. The gray titanium-alloy mail of her hauberk and vambraces seemed to suck the pale light out of the day. Gudrun was with her, but carrying a young babe swaddled in one arm and leading Swanhild, Bjarni and Harberga's three-year-old daughter. The little girl was much graver than Artos remembered her, great turquoise eyes sad and worried. Children that age could smell trouble like a puppy, though the words might be beyond them. Her gaze lit when she saw him, though.

"Little Swan-battle!" he said, and got a smile in response to his; then she went to cling to her mother's skirt. "And this likely lad is—"

"Erik. Erik Bjarnisson," Harberga said, taking the infant. Then, suddenly: "I wish I could be out there, fighting for them, beside my man. For our homes! Instead I have to . . . to sit here and fill stew pots and make bandages and *wait*."

Artos shrugged to settle the long kite-shaped shield across his back, hung the sallet helm on the saddle bow and handed Epona's reins to Matti.

"Lady Harberga," he said gently. "May I hold him for a moment?"

She looked puzzled, then handed over the bundled child. He cradled the small body expertly, looking down into the softly unformed face, just past the red and crumpled appearance of a newborn.

"Such a little thing," he said softly. "Such a little thing, with such a greatness of might-be within!"

A tiny, perfect hand clutched at one long, calloused finger as he touched the baby's chin, and it grinned toothlessly at him.

Now, there is perfect joy, he thought happily. *With the glow of the Summerlands and the Cauldron still upon him.*

Then he went down on one knee and held the child out in both hands.

"Lady," he said as Harberga took him back, meeting her blue eyes steadily. "Haven't you fought for your son already? Haven't you gone under the shadow of the Dark Mother's wings for him and his sister, walking the blade-thin bridge in blood and pain? If your man fights with weapons, and the rest of us beside him, it is for this . . . this wonder. Only for this."

Slowly she nodded. He drew the Sword and held it up reversed, pommel uppermost; the pale winter sunlight caught in the crystal and broke back in flickers of colored fire. The baby's chubby fist clutched it with a crow of delight, and the mother's hand closed around both. A singing note rose within him; he didn't think the Lady's gift glowed, not to the eyes of the body at least, but there were gasps around him.

"Give us your blessing, Lady."

She did, standing tall.

NORRHEIM, LAND OF THE WULFINGS
SIX-HILL FIELD (FORMERLY AROOSTOOK COUNTY, MAINE)
MARCH 25, CHANGE YEAR 25/2023 AD

Crack!

Bjarni Eriksson wheezed and took the ax-blow on his shield. Impact shocked through the battered, tattered round of plywood and sheet steel, through his aching hand on the central grip and into his shoulder.

"*Yuk-hai-sa-sa!*" he screamed, and cut with a swooping arc.

The sword bit, though the edge was duller now; through the Bekwa's leggings and thigh and into the bone. The foeman wailed and toppled backward down the hill, thrashing and spurting red against the gray trampled snow. Despite its chill the air stank of it: blood like rust and seawater, and the hard fetor of cut-open bodies and sweat. For a moment he blinked at the sight, then realized that the dying man *could* fall, without being held up by the press of living warriors behind him; the enemy were giving ground, fast until they were out of bow-range, then more slowly, then stopping in a way that spoke of sullen readiness to come again. The long slope was littered in clots and clumps and single shapes, mostly still, some yet moving and moaning. More Bekwa than Norrheimers, but too many of his people as well.

The mind-blanking surf-roar of battle died, thousand-fold screams and shouts and the endless waterfall rattle and crash and drumming of steel on steel or wood or leather. Only the lighter threnody of pain from the mangled and dying remained, a shocking quasi silence under the cold wind. He put the point of his sword against a dead man's moose-hide jacket and leaned forward with both hands on the hilt, heaving air in through an open mouth for a moment before he could stand on legs suddenly a little wobbly.

His face was nearly as red as the brick color of his short-cropped beard, and sweat dripped off his nose and soaked the padding under his knee-length mail byrnie. His body was strong—not overly tall, yet broad in the shoulders, thick in chest and arms—but he ached in every inch, though the morning sun was still low in the eastern sky and the battle was as young. The sweat stung in minor cuts he hadn't noticed until that instant, and places where the mail coat had been hit hard enough to rasp skin raw even through the stiff quilted padding of the gambeson.

Healers and helpers dragged the wounded back towards the tents and surgeons' tables at the center of the shield-wall circle. He saw one wisewoman in green with the *laguz*-rune on her chest, her own hand bandaged, helping along a warrior whose leg was drenched with blood and who cursed every time that foot touched the ground. Around him hale men were stepping back to the rear rank, letting the fresh second file move forward.

"Where's Ingmar?" he said, asking after the guardsman who was assigned to ward his right side.

"Dead," his uncle Ranulf said succinctly, and jerked his helmeted head back; there was a gilded boar on the crest. "I'm going to see to the rear of the shield-wall."

He took off at a springy trot, despite his forty years and the weight of his gear. The whole array shook itself in the moment's rest, passing canteens from hand to hand or taking spare weapons from the stacks behind the rear ranks. A few had the strength to hoot insults or jibes at the enemy, where they'd drawn off. His standard-bearer stood behind him to the left, a younger cousin holding the tall lance with the Bjorning war-flag—made by his long-dead mother of heavy black-edged white silk, straight along the upper rod-stiffened edge and the pole, but joined by a loose curve. Gold streamers edged it, and on the cloth was a black raven shaped of jet beads, with wings outspread and seeming to beat in the wind. Over its chest was the blazon of the pre-Change war band his father had served in, two letters—AA, but with the outer arm of each curved and the inner vertical so that they made a near-circle together.

The cousin set the point of the shaft in the ground and took Bjarni's sword, wiping it down and giving it a quick touch-up with his hone. Someone else handed the

chieftain a fresh shield; a sword would last a lifetime
with luck, but a shield was lucky to endure an hour of
sharp steel and strong men and heavy blows. Bjarni
worked the strained fingers of his sword-hand inside the
steerhide glove and shook out his wrist. On that side
was Syfrid Jerrysson, the chief of the Hrossings, leading
his fighting tail of *hirdmenn* and levied farmers, a tall
lank man with a dark brown beard showing the first gray
threads. His long-scale byrnie was made of polished
washers riveted to a leather backing. The overlapping
disks of stainless steel were spattered with the filth of
battle, but enough metal still showed to give a cold glitter in the pale sunlight of earliest spring. Fresh scratches
showed as well.

The fifteen-year-old who held the Hrossing banner of
a stylized white horse on green looked pale and gulped
down nausea; from disgust at the sights and stinks, Bjarni
thought, not fear. The sword in his free hand wavered a
little.

"Never seen death before, Halldor?" Syfrid gibed at
his son; the boy flushed, took stance and braced his back
and the pole that bore his tribe's standard. "It's time,
then!"

"I haven't seen this *much* death before either," Bjarni
said; he'd been in fights since he came to a man's age, but
not pitched battles. "Not all in one place."

"I have," Syfrid replied. For a moment his voice was
remote. "In the year of the Change, yes . . ."

Then he went on briskly, but with a grudging note in
it: "You chose the battlefield well."

The Hrossing chief checked the broad blade of his ax
for nicks as he spoke—the helve was four feet of reddish-
brown hickory, and thick with blood and bits of hair and

matter for most of its length. He scrubbed at it with a cloth to clear the grip and continued:

"And the array, that was clever too. You've that much of your father in you, at least, as well as his looks."

Bjarni nodded. Syfrid and he had never been friends—the older chief had been a right-hand man to Bjarni's father, and had wanted to be first man in Norrheim himself when Erik the Strong died. Most folk felt that Erik's son, the chief of the Bjornings, should have that place. Young as he'd been then, only a little older than Halldor was now, he'd managed to keep it. That rivalry was a great part of the reason the talk of selecting a King for Norrheim had stayed just talk; that and the fact that Bjarni was of two minds about the matter himself.

Or I was, he thought. Then: *Let that keep to sunset, if we're still alive.*

Syfrid grinned at him now, showing strong yellow teeth, as if he'd been reading his thoughts.

"So, we end up fighting side by side like brothers, youngster," he said. "If we win, we can take up our disputes. If we don't . . ."

". . . we can fight each other to our hearts' content every day in Valhöll, and then feast and drink together all night," Bjarni completed dryly.

A canteen came his way and he took a long swig. It was one part apple brandy to four of water, just enough to make it safe to drink from unknown streams when you didn't have time to boil. Then another draught, and the sweet liquid poured down his throat like new strength; he thought he could feel it running out through his body, making the parched tissues full again.

"Ahhh, that was made from the Apples of Life," he said, passing it to Syfrid.

Horn-signals went through the Norrheimer host. They were deployed in six groups of a thousand or more, each atop a hill not too far from the rest, in a loose shallow V running from north to south. The strongest clump was here in the center, with the Bjornings and Hrossings together. The formation had been enough to tempt the wild-men to try ramming through the low ground between each position to surround them. Bodies showed where those attacks had broken under a hail of missiles, and then the swords and axes of men charging downhill.

He eyed the enemy, pushing back his helmet by the nasal bar until it rested on his forehead and then using his father's binoculars. Distance leapt closer, and men turned from ants to doll-figures. They'd suffered heavily, but . . .

"They're still ready to fight. Though we killed them two, three, maybe even four for one," he said meditatively. "We've better gear, we're in better order, our men are more skillful and the foe have to come at us uphill. I think they're hungry, too."

"And they still outnumber us three to two or better," Syfrid said. "They can afford losses."

"If they're willing to take them. I didn't expect them to be so many, or so fierce. They fight like men who want to die."

"If I was a Bekwa savage *I'd* want to die, too," Syfrid said, and they grinned for a moment.

"Or like men who have to win or starve to death," the older chief went on. "Men who burned their boats behind them."

"Or they fight like men who feel the hand of their God, or both."

He raised his eyes; ravens rode the wind, and crows. Even a few hawks.

"*They* will feed well today."

It was chaos over there among the enemy host, but patterns were appearing in it, like ripples in water. More and more warriors gathered around a central banner, the rayed golden sun on scarlet. Their chanting rose, breaking louder and louder across the half-mile distance:

"Cut! Cut! *Cut! CUT! CUT!*"

"They're going to try and smash us here in the center," Bjarni said. "That bunch is massing to come straight down our throats. Well, let's bite hard."

"Do they have enough spearmen for that and to guard their flanks at the same time?" Syfrid wondered.

"We're going to find out," Bjarni said. Then louder: "Our hospitality is so warm on a cold day they can't get enough of it. Honor requires we give every one of them enough feasting that he'll have to be *carried* away to sleep it off."

"And we'll furnish a deep bed to do it in," Syfrid said, flourishing his ax.

Grim laughter rippled through the ranks, and then farther away as the joke went from mouth to mouth; you had to show you were confident. A chieftain's main, his soul-strength, ran all through a war band. While it did, Bjarni gripped the silver Hammer that hung around his neck on a chain and spoke within his mind:

Thor, old friend, You are also the Friend of Men and guardian of Earth who is Your mother and mine. I have made offering to You many times. Now lend me Your might as I fight against etin-craft for my folk, my home, my woman and our children!

Through the binoculars he could see a figure standing before the wild-man host, a man in a dull red robe with a shaven head. He drew a blade and flourished it, then pointed at the Norrheimers—and it felt as if he pointed at Bjarni himself. He grunted slightly, like a man punched in the gut.

"The *trollkjerring*," someone whispered fearfully, and it rippled through the Norrheimers. "The sorcerer. He comes with them this time. We fight trollcraft!"

"Give me one," Bjarni said, pointing to a stack of javelins upright in the ground behind them.

Syfrid raised his brows but did so. Bjarni cased his binoculars, pulled down his helm, hefted the spear thoughtfully—it was well balanced—and stepped out of the ranks. At his gesture the signalers blared out a sustained hoarse call on their long bullhorns. Eyes swung towards him along all the Norrheimer line. He filled his lungs. Casting your voice was a skill a chief had to have, whether speaking on a battlefield or from the Thingstone when the folkmoot met.

"*To you, Victory-Father, the blót!*" he shouted.

So that those beyond hearing but in sight should know what he did, he tossed the javelin up into the air, a high whirling circle, and caught it as it fell again to smack against the hard calloused palm of his hand before he signed it with the *Ansuz*, the rune of the High One.

Then he took three steps forward and threw it towards the enemy. The point gleamed a little as it reached the height of its arc over a heap of the foemen's dead and wounded, then slanted down and stood in the hard snow-covered earth. A roar ran through his men, long and deep and fierce. They knew what he meant by that, boast and threat and prayer together: he had dedicated every soul in the enemy host to the One-Eyed, the rider of the Death Horse, the Lord of the Slain to whom the warlords in the sagas gave men. That meant a fight to the knife, without quarter or mercy. Invoking Odin was never done lightly.

Bjarni stepped back and took his fresh-honed sword from his bannerman; the edge of the hard steel gleamed as the familiar weight filled his fist. The enemy were moving, first the rayed sun flag and the sorcerer, then thousands . . . and all of them seeming to aim at *him*. All around Bjarni and on the other hills men were coughing to clear their lungs and then breathing deep over and over to give a little more strength, hefting weapons, stamping their feet to make sure of their footing. Chiefs and their *hirdmenn*, their sworn guards; strong stolid yeomen of the levy, their sons and carls and hinds; youngsters wild to prove themselves heroes out of the sagas and bearded fathers of families anxious about the spring plowing, and a scattering of strong fierce women; all fighting by the neighbors and kin and blood brothers who would see their honor or their shame. Spears snapped down like a bristling porcupine, and shields overlapped in a wall.

The second rank came closer, to support the first with shield against back and stab over their shoulders. Syfrid crouched a little, his teeth bared in a taut grin, the great war-ax held slantwise across his body in armored gauntlets, one hand just below the broad blade and the other near the end of the haft. Just now Bjarni was very glad indeed to have him close. He might not be quite as strong or quite as quick as he'd been in his fights beside Erik the Strong, but he had a generation's unmerciful experience to compensate.

"*Cut! Cut!*" rang out.

"*Ho La, Odhinn!*" bellowed back.

The enemy grew closer; first at a steady jog-trot that rumbled through the ground until he could feel it in the soles of his boots, then faster as archers shot from the inner part of the Norrheimer position over the heads of the front ranks, then at a pounding run as they came in range of volleys of throwing-spears and stones from whirring slings. Men fell as the bale-wind blew arrows and edged metal and lead slingshot at them, silent or screaming. The rest shrieked bloodlust, teeth snarling in bearded faces often streaked with blood already, or patterned with ritual scars.

Bjarni raised his shield up under his eyes as missiles came back at the Norrheimers. But fewer; it was harder to shoot and attack at the same time. Two arrows struck in the shield with angry *thwack* sounds and an impact he could feel like hammer blows in the metal-sheathed birch plywood, and three or four more banged off his mail or his helmet, bruising-hard. Scores of shafts arched towards the *trollkjerring*, but none struck. He loped forward as easy as a wolf, turning and jinking but as if he was anticipating the arrows rather than dodging them, not bothering to use his shield. Closer, and Bjarni could see him smile, look into his eyes . . .

And the sword drooped in his hand. The eyes *pulled*. He blinked, and saw himself dead, standing rotting amid corpses yet still seeing and feeling, and Harberga crouched with shreds of his son's flesh dangling from her grinning jaws. His hall was ash in a world of ash, where dead moon and gutted sun collapsed into themselves. Still his living corpse stood and watched, and love, honor, hope were dead, had never lived, as the stuff of the world itself decayed, and the blackness was forever. But that was good, for at last there was purity—

"Thor with me!" he groaned, and raised his shield.

Slivers of wood and metal spun away as the red-robed

man's blade hammered. Bjarni staggered backward, his left arm numb. Blow after blow rained on the shield, and then it fell in shattered pieces from the handgrip. A cut landed on the mail covering his left leg, and it buckled beneath him. He fell on his back, and the blade went up to kill.

CHAPTER SIX

G arbh lifted her nose and growled very softly; there wasn't much wind, but what there was came from ahead. Then she pointed, silent now, the thick shaggy barrel of her head trained to the northeast. Artos flung up his right hand, clenched into a fist, and eased back in the saddle. Rhiannon wasn't quite what her dam was, but she was an intelligent horse and very well trained; she stopped instantly, with only a white puff from her nostrils as she snorted.

His own war band stopped too, then spread out to either side with minimum fuss as he waved the hand from left to right—there was a clop of hooves muffled in snow-covered pine-duff, a rattle of bits and bridles, but much of that was because many of their horses were local mounts picked up catch-as-catch-can. The Kalksthorpe levy and the rest of the Norrheimer *fyrd* were slower, but they managed it, and few spoke questions; those mostly got a hard hand across the mouth from their neighbors. Scouts fanned to the sides and forward.

It was dim here, and quiet, though from ahead he thought he could *almost* hear a dim confused burring sound like heavy storm surf beating on cliffs a long way away.

Sound's deceptive in forest, he thought. *The more so when there's snow on the branches.*

They'd come along an overgrown road most of the day through oddly uniform stands of pine that all looked about fifty years old, but now they were in mature forest or old second growth tall enough to shade out most underbrush; white pines, hemlock and leafless sugar maples. Dry powder-snow lay thick on the boughs, fetlock-deep on the horses.

Edain looked a question at Artos, who held up three spread fingers, turned them towards his eyes and then tapped them forward towards the brightness ahead. There the sun of midmorning broke through a generation's scrub growth of birch and alder that was spreading out into the open ground.

Edain nodded, caught two others with his glance and slid to the ground himself, moving forward through the brush as easily as his totem Wolf might have done, bow in hand. Asgerd followed him; she was good at skulking in these woods. Ulfhild went too, and she was very good indeed; a little surprising, since you didn't expect that degree of slinking marten grace from someone built like a white-oak barrel. Garbh ghosted along at her master's heels, head low and thin black lips drawn up silently over long yellow fangs that knit together like edges of jagged broken glass. The mottled gray-white-brown wool of the scouts' coats and hoods disappeared almost instantly.

The rest waited, apart from dismounting to spare the horses; there wasn't much point in doing anything else until they knew the facts. After a half hour a raven went *gruck*, or something that was very close to the real thing, and from what sounded like the forest edge ahead. Eyes came up, and spearpoints and drawn bows; Artos let one corner of his mouth quirk up, and then answered with the same call. Garbh trotted into sight, and the three scouts after her. Asgerd looked grimly tense; Ulfhild was grinning, blood on the Norrheimer broadsword naked in her hand; Edain jogged with the same tireless hunter's pace he always used unless he was sprinting.

"Action?" Rudi asked.

"*Acht*, nothing but a scuffle, Chief. The Norrheimers are there, all right, and they're between us and the enemy. We met a few of the Bekwa, stragglers, is all, the which was unluckier for them than us."

Fred Thurston had the map out before he arrived, and the young Mackenzie sketched on it with one finger.

"On all the six hills. They're close enough to support each other—half-bowshot. Well, half for Mackenzies; three-quarters, here. We got close enough to shout, and the Bekwa are led by a red-robe right enough . . . but only the one *bachlach*, the exceeding luck and good fortune of it. The fighting-men are all Bekwa, none of our old friends from Corwin."

Artos nodded. "They could send a few missionaries to convert men," he said. "Easier than armies."

"That's a good formation, if they keep coming straight at him," Fred said, his black eyes narrow on the map and then glancing up abstracted as he built a model in his mind. "Good when neither side has field artillery, that is."

"They will keep coming," Ignatius said. "From all our experience with the CUT, most of their . . . priests . . . can think of nothing but hammer blows."

"Numbers?" Mathilda asked. "Hammers work, if you have a big enough one."

"Eight thousand Norrheimers, eight thousand and a bit," Edain said. "Half again as many of the enemy, maybe, but it's harder to tell because they've about as much order as so many rats in a grain-bin. The Norrheim men are holding their own. High ground, and I don't think near as many of the savages have armor, or real swords. It's a *big* battle, though. Big as that one in Idaho."

Fred swallowed slightly; that had been where his father died. At the hands of his own brother, at that. His voice was steady as he spoke:

"Father Ignatius is right; Corwin's *soldiers* know their jobs, but their . . . spook-pushers . . . aren't soldiers."

"No," Artos said softly. "But they are accomplished at what they do, and that is why we must bring the Sword into play, and quickly. This isn't just a battle of men."

"And the Bekwa aren't soldiers either," Ingolf said. "I know their kind."

He'd been a leader of salvagers in the dead lands by trade; that had taken him to Nantucket, and from that . . .

"They're not quite the animals, the Eaters, you'll find in places like the east coast, but they're still wild-men, savages. Hunters and raiders, not soldiers," he went on. "They can *fight*, but stand-up, toe-to-toe . . . it isn't their style, sure as shoot it isn't."

"Right you are, brother," Artos said.

He looked into the white-hazed blue of the morning sky; it was odd to see it serene and beautiful while men tormented the earth. Two more ravens launched themselves from an ash tree, circling overhead and heading out over the battlefield before them. Possibly chance, but he felt things moving within himself as he rested the palm of a gauntlet on the hilt of the Sword. Like planes of greased crystal, turning, moving, coming to a *now*.

Artos began to strip off his parka and the brigandine beneath, unsnapping the latches under on his left flank.

"Destriers forward and barded," he said quietly. "Everyone gear up; full panoply. We're close."

I would have suspected that, before I found the Sword. Now I know it, he thought.

The war-mounts were led forward, and the packhorses with the armor. Many hands made quick work of the task. The men of the Southside Freedom Fighters had practiced since he took them into his service last year, and even the Norrheimers he'd sworn at Yule had had enough time to be useful at it.

Epona came of her own accord, and stood still save for a stamping of a forefoot; she knew what all this meant, and tolerated others touching her as they worked the straps and buckles of the barding, the horse-armor. It was of fine-wrought steel plates jointed with strips of mail and riveted to leather that was padded on the inner side. Chamfron for the head, articulated crinet on her neck, peytral on her breast and flanchards for the shoulders. Epona tossed her head, and the gear clattered on its backing. Her breath puffed white in the cold midmorning air, and the pale sun seemed to shatter on the coal-black of her hide and the gray metal of the horse-armor, and the silvered spike between her eyes.

Heavy cavalry—knights and men-at-arms—were unknown outside Montival, and common only in the Association territories there. Raising and training them took endless trouble and expense, and there were other drawbacks besides. A horse so burdened could run fast but not for very long, not even the tall muscular warmbloods, and it couldn't *travel* far with the barding on and an armored man in the saddle, so that every knight needed a train of attendants and palfreys and pack beasts. Light horse with room to run could melt away before a charge and then swarm back to sting like wasps around a tiger. The problems went on from there.

But when they were used just right, they hit like a mailed fist punching down on a ripe tomato.

So Matti's father wasn't simply obsessed with the ancient days of knights when he put so much effort into bringing them alive once more, Artos thought.

He stood as hands lifted a long tunic-coat of quilted linen over his head; it had mail sleeves, extended to cover the vulnerable spot beneath the armpit. Mail-covered chaps laced onto its skirts, covering the outside of his legs; plate greaves went on his shins, with linked steel splints to protect his feet. He slapped the vambraces onto his forearms; after the brigandine was buckled back over the padding on his torso he ducked his head for the coif, more leather covered in mail, making a tight-fitting hood and covering his neck and a semicircle of chest and back.

Then, wryly: *Or he wasn't* just *obsessed with the days of the knights, sure. And if he hadn't been obsessed, he wouldn't have learned those skills in a world where they were no more use than tits on a boar. I don't blame him for loving the ancient stories, either. For being a red-capped brute of a powrie in the flesh, yes, now there I do blame him. Yet Matti his daughter and I Mike Havel's son will wed, if we live, and our children will unite the blood of the Bear Lord and House Arminger and Clan Mackenzie. Let the dead past bury its feuds. We Changelings have our own wars to win.*

Mathilda looked at him as she adjusted her own coif,

smiling a little as the lustrous titanium-alloy mail framed her slightly, pleasantly irregular strong-boned face.

"Are you sure you're not going to set *me* to waiting and cooking stew instead of fighting?"

He grinned at her, lifted a little out of his thoughts. "When you're pregnant or nursing, that I will, by the Blessing! If I have to chain you to a rock to do it, too. Or lock you in a castle solar to look out the tower window and comb your hair and pine, like a princess in a story."

"You could try!"

"Ah, but acushla, beat of my heart . . . then we'll be married, and by your Christian rites that means you'll have to promise your God to obey me, won't you? The which our Mackenzie witch-girls do not, by the way. *And* I'll be able to command you as High King to vassal lord."

She stuck out her tongue at him; he winked back and settled his sallet on his head, tightening the chin-cup. Twin tufts of raven feathers stood upright from each temple of the helm, and the surface was scored in patterns set with niello that made more feathers. Close-tailored pads of old sponge rubber and new felt gripped brow and head within; he flicked the visor down and up. Then he twisted and bent, squatted and sprang upright, to make sure everything was settled and nothing was going to shift at a—critically—wrong moment. Uncoiling, his long legs drove him to a chest-height leap before he landed again; not exactly lightly, but with a tensile grace on the balls of his feet and flexed knees.

One of the Norrheimers behind him swore softly in amazement. Artos—Rudi for that moment—caught Mathilda's eyes as she lifted one eyebrow; yes, it was a bit of a boast, but why not?

The gear weighed about seventy pounds, not counting

his slung shield, and hung mostly from his shoulders; a suit of the latest modern plate would have been no heavier, better distributed, better protection and just as flexible, but it would also have been impossible to repair in the field away from the Association's experts. Any good smith could fix what he was wearing; he could do most of it himself, given the tools.

"Ready," Ignatius said.

"Ready," Mathilda said.

"Ready," Artos replied.

"Ready," Ingolf said in turn.

They checked each other's gear, squire's duty back in Montival. The four of them were the ones with the mounts and training to fight knight-fashion.

"And we lugged this stuff all the way from home," Mathilda said. "How many times have we used the full set in all that time?"

"Three or four, that I recall, my child," Ignatius said calmly. "But when we've needed it, we've needed it *very badly*, Your Highness."

Virginia snorted. She and Fred were in western light-horseman's gear of the sort used all through the ranch-lands of the Plains and the mountain-and-basin country, waist-length mail shirts with short sleeves and bowl helmets, armed with recurve bow and curved sword.

"That stuff slows you down," she said. " 'Specially the tinware on the horses, and in *snow* at that. If God"—she glanced at her husband—"the Gods had meant horses to be arrer-proof, they'd have given 'em scales like an armadillo."

"No, it's worth it, when the target doesn't have room to run," Fred said, ignoring her frown. "Paper beats rock, and scissors cut paper, but rock smashes scissors."

He has a strong personality, sure and he does, Artos thought.

He was half amused, half making notes for the future. The High King would have to deal with his vassal lord of Boise . . . and his lady, and his heirs . . . all the rest of his life. Assuming they all survived, of course.

Hers is the stronger will, though; she hides it most of the time, but usually he ends up taking her position when they argue. Yet his father trained him so well that when it's a matter of war-craft, nothing else matters to him but the rightness of it.

Abdou al-Naari and his son and several of their men were in gear halfway between that of the plainsmen and the knights, armed with bow and broad-bladed spear and scimitar, exotic in spired helmets and armor with Koranic verses worked into the mail with brass links; evidently nobles such as he fought on horseback in his homeland as well, and he rode as easily as he conned a ship. Most of the others looked . . .

Like sailors on horseback, Artos thought whimsically. *Or like a sack of oats would, if it could fear falling off. Fishermen at home, I'd judge, when they're not pirating, or farmers too poor to own a horse.*

Hrolf Homersson handed Artos back his sword belt; the big Norrheimer was a very brave man . . .

Not least because he dared take up with Ritva!

. . . but he was notably cautious about the weapon, avoiding touching anywhere near the hilt. Artos himself felt a slight easing as he swung the heavy studded belt around his hips again and drew it tight; being out of reach of the Sword made him uneasy now, as if he'd lost a sense like hearing or sight. Which made him uneasy itself in turn. Was he to be forever incomplete without it, a cripple without that fifth limb of not-really-steel?

"Ready!" he said crisply. "Make your peace with your Gods, comrades, for now we do battle."

Mathilda crossed herself, kissed her crucifix and tucked it back beneath her hauberk. Ignatius did likewise, and murmured under his breath:

"Holy Mary, Mother of God, Queen of Angels, I am your servant and your chosen knight. Strengthen me in soul and body, that I may be worthy of your trust and vanquish the enemies of God and our people. Intercede for us all, comrades and foemen, now and at the hour of our deaths. Kyrie eleison. Christe eleison. Amen."

Then a little louder: "*Deus lo vult!*"

"*Allahu Akbar!*" the Moors chorused, which meant approximately the same thing.

The rest of his own war band all had horses to carry them to the fight, if not to fight from. He looked at Thorleif, the leader of the Kalksthorpe folk; they were on foot or ski.

"Follow as quickly as you can and keep good order," he said.

Thorleif nodded. "*Swine-array!*" he said aloud.

The Kalksthorpe men shook themselves out into a blunt wedge; Thorlief and the man bearing the banner of an orca black-and-white on silver were three men back from the point. Lighter-armed fighters with bows and slings spread out from the base of the triangle.

"I wish Odard were here," Mathilda said quietly.

Artos nodded, a little surprised at his own sincerity. "*Ach do làmhansa bhi, Odard, mo chara.* I wish his hands were with us now."

He was a trained knight, and a good one. And by the time he died, he was a true friend—a prickly and difficult friend, and one given to saying things that disquieted a man, to be sure. A King could have worse companions.

Artos paused a fraction of an instant for his own prayer: "Morrigú of the Crows, Red Hag of Battles, to You I dedicate the harvest of the unplowed field of war. Be with Your children now; and when my hour comes, I will welcome You."

When he did that, *Someone* always answered. Often with fire-shot darkness, so that he woke later scarcely knowing what he'd done, save for the blood. Now it came on him in cold certainty; the world seemed to recede until everything was small and bright and perfect, seen through panes of crystal. He took up a clod of snowy earth where Epona's hooves had torn through winter's coat to bare the soil's flesh, and touched it to his lips:

"Earth must be fed."

Behind him Edain did the same, and the Southsiders who'd come to follow the Old Religion. It was acknowledgment that you only borrowed your body from Earth the Mother for a little while. And that to slay in battle was to consent to your own mortality and make your killer free of your blood.

Then they swung into the saddle, with no more than low grunts of effort. One of the tests of knighthood in the Association was to vault into the saddle full-armed, but nobody felt like showing off right now. Artos held out his hand and Edain tossed him the lance. He caught the twelve-foot length of it in his left hand below the bowl-shaped guard, resting the butt on his thigh. They'd had them made up in Richland, Ingolf's homeland in Wisconsin, to a west-coast pattern, and stowed at Eriksgarth with their horses when they came through at Yule.

Lances didn't last long in use, either.

A little wind dropped powdered snow on their heads from the pine branches overhead. The long man-at-arm's shield slid onto his forearm. Its surface was painted with the new arms of Montival, blue field with a green mountain topped by a crown of white snow, and the silver Sword across it. He left the reins of the bitless hackamore bridle knotted on the high arched steel-sheathed pommel. Even an ordinary destrier didn't need much rein control in battle, and Epona and he talked at a level far beyond that.

"Forward, my friends," he said, and dipped his lance.

CHAPTER SEVEN

Approaching Castle Todenangst, Crown demesne
Portland Protective Association
Willamette Valley near Newburg
High Kingdom of Montival
(formerly Western Oregon)
March 24, Change Year 25/2023 AD

"So, is this Toddyangst place really a castle?"
John Red Leaf said to Juniper Mackenzie,
standing in the stirrups and looking eastward. "Some sort of fort, I suppose it means?"

They'd gotten horses at noon in the Crown stables by
the railway station in Newburg a little west of here, along
with a Portlander escort to join her six archers; the sun
was behind them now, throwing their shadows onto the
damp off-white crushed rock of the roadway. Luckily the
spring rains had relented today and the sky was blue,
studded with drifting high-piled shapes of white cloud.

The two Sioux had changed into carefully packed formal costumes back there; moccasinlike boots, doeskin
trousers with fringes of hair down the outer seams, and
leather shirt-tunics worked with shells and beads and porcupine quills. Red Leaf was the elder, a thickset proud-
nosed man in his forties with a hard square face the
ruddy-brown color of old mahogany, lined and grooved

by harsh summers and worse winters; he added a headdress of buffalo horns and mane on his steel cap and a
breastplate of horizontal bone tubes. His son Rick Three
Bears was in his twenties, either a Changeling or on the
cusp of it; he had a look of his father but lighter of skin
and narrower of face, with a broad-brimmed Stetson on
his head and a few eagle feathers in his dark brown braids.
Both of them had the shoulders of bowmen and the instinctive seat of those who spent most of their lives in the
saddle.

"No, Dun Juniper is a fort, and a village, and other
things, my home being one," Juniper said. "Todenangst
is . . . hard to miss, you might be sayin'. And the huge
and imposing castle it is, without doubt or question
whatsoever."

She'd had Rudi's letters to describe his meeting with
the Sioux leaders last year in what had once been South
Dakota, and evidently they'd been impressed enough
with her son to treat *her* as friend and ally from the beginning. Those letters and a day or so in Red Leaf's company gave her the impression that the Sioux tribes who
now dominated the northern High Plains bore a closer
resemblance to their ancestors of the time of Crazy Horse
and Sitting Bull than her Clan Mackenzie did to the actual pagan Gael of the *Táin Bó Cúailnge* . . . but not all
that much more.

Which was no surprise; she'd seen since the Change
that you couldn't re-create the past no matter how you
tried, though *myths* and *stories* about the past could be a
most powerful force in how folk built new ways to live in
this new-old world.

"Way! Make way! In the Crown's name, make way!"

The harsh cry of the golden-spurred knight who com-

manded the escort moved aside passersby on foot or bicycle or pedicab or mounted horseback themselves, and
once a group of villagers doing their corvée duty by filling
in potholes looked glad enough to take a rest and lean on
their shovels. They threaded around and through and by
wagon trains and stagecoaches and oxcarts, flocks of
Romney sheep with their fleeces silver or gray or white, a
little girl who stopped to curtsy, with an udder-heavy Jersey behind her on a leading rope, a gray-robed Franciscan
friar telling his beads . . .

The plate-armored Portlander men-at-arms jogged
along swapping jokes and stories with the half-dozen
Mackenzie archers who accompanied Juniper.

*Amazing and delightful it is, how a common enemy
wears away old hatreds!*

"Holy shit!" Red Leaf blurted a few moments later. "I
thought Disneyland was in California!"

Juniper Mackenzie chuckled. "And we surpass it, these
days. That's not lath and plaster, by all the Gods and the
fae as well!"

The laugh had a tired sound to it—she was always exhausted now, down to her very bones, and they'd come
just as fast as they could up the valley. But her amusement
was genuine.

"Are these people for real?"

"Oh, yes," she said. "Most exceedingly so."

The representatives of the Seven Council Fires of the
Lakota *tunwan* had come much farther and faster than
she, and mostly by some very rough mountain back roads
still dangerously close to winter.

*They are without doubt hardy men. But then, they live in
tents through winters in Dakota!*

Single-minded speed meant this was their first real

glimpse of the PPA's style when at home. She'd been here often enough in the years of peace since the War of the Eye that Norman and Sandra Arminger's exercise in pseudo-medievalist megalomania seemed just another very large building most of the time. Now she tried to see it through a stranger's eye . . .

"As I recall, they used the Château de Pierrefonds as a model. Scaled up considerably, to be sure. With elements of Carcassone, if that means anything to you, and a dash of Mad Ludwig of Bavaria's Neuschwanstein, the which Walt Disney also admired, and hence the family resemblance. With a little *Gormenghast* for flavor."

The great fortress-palace on the butte ahead had a curious skyward thrust and delicacy to it, despite the brutal massiveness of the structure; it was built of ferroconcrete, since not even the first Lord Protector's demonic will had been able to summon whole legions of skilled stonemasons from nothing. Mixing cement and aggregate and pouring it into molds had been much simpler, and the fact that it was coated in glittering white stucco helped with the effect, she supposed. A forty-foot curtain-wall formed the outer perimeter, studded with scores of thick round machicolated towers more than twice that height, and the butte below had been cut back to form a smooth glacis down to the moat. Gates punctuated the circuit in four places, with towers and defenses that turned them into smaller fortresses in their own right.

"And just a touch of Hearst's San Simeon on the inside, which you will see," she added judiciously.

The inner donjon reared where the summit had been; two towers at north and south were taller than all the others, the first sheathed in palest silver-gray stone, the second covered in some glossy black rock whose crystal inclusions glittered in the bright spring light. Conical roofs of green copper topped all the towers, save for the gilding that turned the tip of the dark spire into a sun-bright blaze, and colorful banners flew from the spiked peaks.

Light blinked from the spearheads and polished armor of soldiers on the crenellated parapets. Then a heliograph began to snap from the highest point, sending a message flashing towards the perfect white cone of Mt. Hood on the eastern horizon, beyond the low green forested slopes of the Parrett Mountains. In the middle distance north- ward another tower, toy-tiny with distance, began to re- peat the coded lights to somewhere else.

"Christ, this was built *after* the Change?" John Red Leaf said. "That black tower must be a hundred and fifty, two hundred feet high! How did you manage it without machinery?"

"*We* didn't," Juniper said dryly. "We Mackenzies, or Bearkillers or Corvallans or the Yakima League or the Kyklos or . . . well, all the others. We had other priorities, sure and we did."

He's what . . . perhaps halfway between forty and fifty? A man grown in 1998, but younger than me. Still, not a Changeling like his son there. He has more sense of what must have been involved.

Aloud: "The Portland Protective Association built it . . . which is to say Norman Arminger did. Quickly, too. Though furnishing the interior's still going on."

"Norman Arminger . . . he was Mathilda's dad, right?" John said.

"That was him. Sandra . . . the Regent . . . uses the Silver Tower there as her headquarters; the black one was Norman's lair while he was Lord Protector, but it's full of bureaucrats now."

And the whole of it bears the mark of him, she thought; it was like an arrogant mailed fist smashed into the face of heaven.

"There's many a castle in the Association territories; they built scores to hold down the land, but only one like this. It goes with the flag, you see," Juniper added.

John turned in the saddle to look at the pennants snapping from the lances of the men-at-arms in their suits of gleaming plate. They were troopers of the Protector's Guard, and the narrow fork-tailed flags bore the undifferenced arms of House Arminger; a lidless slit-pupiled eye, argent on sable, wreathed in scarlet flame.

"It's an eye; Matti had something like that on her shirt. So?"

"That's the Eye of *Sauron*, my dear. Or it was in origin, at least. And a good thing that copyright died with the Change, eh? Though it would be a bold lawyer who sued the Armingers in the seat of their power."

His eyes flicked from the banner to the fortress. "Black tower . . . eye . . . Sauron . . . you've *got* to be shitting me, right?"

"No, that was Norman's little joke. His sense of humor was just a wee bit eccentric, so to say. Though his main obsession was with the Normans . . . William the Conqueror, Strongbow—bad cess to him—and Roger Guiscard and Tancred and that lot."

"The dude thought he was bad, right?"

"Oh, you have no idea. This is Castle *Todenangst*, for example."

"Which means?"

"Castle of the Anguish of Death, roughly. Or Death-Anguish, to arrange the words Germanically. I'm afraid he was every bit as bad as he thought he was, too, the creature. They say there's a man's bones in the ground for every ten tons of concrete and steel in that thing there; when they didn't just throw the bodies in the mix. Fortunately he wasn't quite as *smart* as he thought he was, the joy and everlasting good fortune of it."

Rick Three Bears whistled quietly to himself and said:

"Rudi's father killed him, right? Not your husband, that Mike guy, I suppose he was your boyfriend then?"

"Very briefly," Juniper said dryly. "That was just before he married Signe . . . who's the mother of Mary and Ritva, whom you met. Yes, Mike killed Norman, and vice versa, *ochone* . . . ah, he was a lovely man, Mike Havel was, and he's badly missed now."

"Rudi and his bunch didn't want to talk about the details much, seemed to me," Rick's father noted.

"Understandable, and it wouldn't be altogether tactful for either of you to mention all this in Sandra's hearing. Remarkable it is to contemplate, but she really did love Norman. There's no accounting for taste."

"So, you're friends with these folks now?" Red Leaf said.

"Oh, I wouldn't go quite so far as to say *that. Ní dhíolann dearmad fiacha*; a debt is still unpaid, even if put out of mind. Mathilda's a wonderful girl—"

"I was impressed with her."

"Rightly so. But then, she spent half of each year with us Mackenzies after the War of the Eye, in my household; that was part of the peace settlement. She's like a daughter to me. Her mother, Sandra, the Regent, is much, much more clever than ever Norman was, and Norman was no fool except where his hatreds and lusts blinded him."

"What's she *like*? Sandra."

"Well, some say she's a sociopath. Some say psychopath. Sandra says her chosen phrase would be: *Very focused.*"

The commander of the escort was riding ahead of them but well within earshot; she could see his helm jerk a little in horror, and then he slid his visor down as if to cut himself off from such sedition. Of course, you *were* a bit cut off from the outside world in a visored sallet, one smooth curve of steel from bevoir to crest interrupted only by the vision slit.

"What's your opinion?" Red Leaf asked.

"A little of all three. We spent ten years fighting each other, and fourteen since then as . . . allies of a sort. Not that she's not good company, when she chooses, and she's devoted to Mathilda, and looks after her supporters very carefully. I don't think you could call her *cruel*, exactly, either. They don't hang folk in spiked iron cages here. Not anymore. But there's more mercy to be found on the edge of a razor than in her mind or soul."

His eyes went back to Castle Todenangst; they were closer now, and the sheer scale of it was daunting.

"I still can't quite believe it. It makes you feel like a bug."

"That was precisely the intention, I believe, and just exactly how Norman regarded everyone but himself, and perhaps his wife and daughter. The materials he scavenged . . . I think the ornamental stone came mostly from banks and office buildings as far away as Seattle, the concrete and steel from construction sites and factories."

"But how did he *get* it all here?"

"Hauled on the railways, mostly. Horses were scarce then, so he used men for that and the rest. Used them up. They were going to starve anyway, he'd say, and might as well work first. The Pyramids were built by hand too, without even steel tools or wheelbarrows to help."

He whistled silently and rode wordlessly for a few moments, craning his neck up.

"I see where your boy got his accent," he said, changing the subject.

For which I do not blame him. He's here to negotiate with all the countries of the Meeting at Corvallis . . . of the High Kingdom of Montival . . . and not to hear our old feuds. Though the man does need to know what he's dealing with; I owe him that and more, for the rescuing of my son and Mathilda.

His own speech was a slightly twanging rural mid-American, with just a hint of something else and an educated man's vocabulary. She shrugged ruefully.

"At least with him it's genuine. My mother was Irish, from Achill in the west—she spoke the Gaelic to me in my cradle—and I can put on County Mayo at will. Over the years I've let it have free rein, so that at least the real thing is available as a model, so to speak. Most of my people—"

She glanced back at her own guard with fond exasperation as they rode along in kilt and plaid and green brigandine marked with the Moon and Antlers. The six-foot yellow staves of their bows slanted over their backs, and arrows fletched with gray goose feathers rattled in their quivers.

"—imitated what they *thought* was the accent, for all that I'd tell them they sounded like Hollywood leprechauns from *Finian's Rainbow*. And their children grew up hearing that, with a result that is now wholly indescribable without using bad language, so it is, the more so as they don't realize it. I try to think of it as just the way Mackenzies talk."

Red Leaf grinned. "Yeah, I thought some of the others sounded like . . . I had a friend, this Mongol guy named

Chinua, studying range management at South Dakota State University while I was there, who was crazy about John Wayne. One night he ran a movie on his VCR where the Duke played this boxer who went to hide out in Ireland because he'd hit someone too hard . . ."

"*The Quiet Man*," Juniper said with a wince. "A fine movie if you don't mind assuming my mother's entire people were a race of happily drunken potato-faced wife-beating peasant yokels with room-temperature IQs who thought with their fists when they weren't clog-dancing or killing each other in fits of mindless religious fanaticism. It's annoying that sort of thing can be."

"Tell me," the Indian said dryly. Then, softly: "I miss VCRs sometimes, though . . ."

They paused for a moment, both lost in memories of a world that had perished in an instant of pain and white light. Then they looked aside in mutual forbearance; there were some things that were too hurtful to be called back from their graves, best left in a time that was now remembered mostly as myth. If only because thinking of that made you think of what had followed, in the years of the great dying.

No wonder so many who survived sought escape in dreams of ancient times! As if that age just before the Change had never really happened, something to be passed over with a shrug.

Red Leaf cleared his throat, as his son rolled his eyes, very slightly and probably without conscious intent.

Arra, Changelings are often like that, when they hear their elders babbling of meaningless things like television and movies. Sadly: *And soon there will be nobody who understands us, really, as we die off one by one, we survivors who remember the ancient world.*

"Pretty country," John said, looking towards the fields north and south of the road.

It was, gently rolling hills vivid green with the spring rains and burgeoning warmth of this mild and fertile land. The orchards of peach and plum, apple and apricot were in bloom, a froth that sent fragrance drifting on the mildly warm air to compete with the smells of dung and horse and sweat and metal, turned earth and woodsmoke. Willows dropped their drooping branches in the little river to the south, amid oak-dotted pastures studded with pink and blue hepatica.

"Makes me feel closed in, though," Three Bears said unexpectedly. "Sort of . . . cramped."

"All what you're used to," Red Leaf said. "It sure ain't the *makol*."

When Juniper looked a question at him he translated that: "*Makol*, the short-grass prairie, the High Plains. Our country."

Peasants in hooded tunics rode sulky plows on the northern side, turning under green sod in their field-strips as the patient oxen leaned into the traces and soil curved rich and brown and moist away from the plowshares, the smell as intoxicating as fresh barley bread. Others farther away on a south-facing slope worked with hoes flashing in a vineyard whose stocks were still black gnarled stumps after winter's pruning. Then the almost metallic bright green of winter wheat, with its slight undertint of blue. It grew ankle high and rippled away towards a line of poplars; a prosperous-looking village clustered there, brick cottages with tile roofs peeping through the trees around the gray square bell tower of a church and a manor hall's roof.

The castle was south of that and across the highway

and railroad right-of-way. A squad of crossbowmen in
half armor doubled out of the gate to stand with their
weapons presented at the salute; the great steel leaves
were already open. It wasn't a full-dress ceremonial reception, though trumpets screamed beneath proud banners. The Lakota mission wasn't exactly confidential but
they weren't trying to draw attention to it yet either; a
mass of alarming unconfirmed rumors was the objective.

Red Leaf and his son stayed quiet through the massive
gate-halls, shrewd eyes taking in the details of catapult
and ballistae and firing-slits for flamethrowers, and through
the courtyards and gardens, fountains and roads and
sweeping stairways and galleries where pillars supported
pointed arches beyond, and into the donjon; the interior
of Todenangst was like a small city in itself, a city and a
building at the same time. It included a cathedral of some
size, rows of houses against the curtain wall's inner side
as well as barracks, stables, armories, workshops, reser-
voirs, grocers and bakers and cobblers' shops, cold-stores,
granaries, taverns, schools, libraries and printshops, joust-
ing grounds and even a theater. The escort vanished off
to their quarters, save for the knight, taking her archers
and the horses with them.

"My lady, my lords," the man said. "This way."

He accompanied it with a stiff bow—it was difficult to
make any other sort in a suit of plate complete, even one
with an articulated breastplate. He also had a limp, and a
pointed brown chin-beard and green eyes that showed
when he pushed his visor up. His shield's main blazon
was the Eye, but an inescutcheon in the upper left showed
a series of wedges of gold and black meeting in the center, with a flaming motorcycle painted over it.

Gyronny sable and or, a Harley purpure . . . the Were-

tons of Laurelwood; they were Hells Angels before the Change, when they decided to back Norman. They hold Laurelwood by knight-service; an armigerous family but not titled, enfeofed vassals of the Barons of Forestgrove in County Chehalis. And that's a baton of cadency across the arms, and he's very young, so he's the tail end of the second generation—his elder brother was about ten at the time of the Change and had that lance-running with Mike Havel in the War of the Eye. And I heard that—

"Ah, Sir Joscelin," Juniper said, searching her memory. "Congratulations on receiving the accolade, and I hope your wound is healing well."

"Thank you, Lady Juniper," the young knight blurted, fighting down a smile.

He showed them through the entrance of the Silver Tower into the vast hall at its base, with an arched groin-vaulted ceiling and great spiral staircases on either side, lit by the incandescent mantles of gas-burning chandeliers. It was fairly crowded; secretaries and clerks in plain tunics; visiting delegations; soldiers of all descriptions, from hairy leather-clad foresters to military bureaucrats; a nobleman in a surcoat of blue silk lined with yellow whose extravagantly dagged sleeves dangled to his knees, attended by pages and squires, and a lady in sweeping dress and pointed headdress who was as gaudy and haughty as he; clerics, from a bishop in crosier and miter to tonsured monks and robed nuns . . . And one section blocked off by planters full of roses and lavender and set with tables and chairs.

"One double-cheese pizza, one chicken stew, two bacon cheeseburgers with fries, right, gentles?" a server in a commoner's tunic-and-shift said with the singsong intonation of phrases infinitely repeated. "And two glasses of Pinot Noir and one mug of small beer. Bread, butter and cheese are complimentary, but manchet bread is extra. That'll be one silver piece and three pennies."

John Red Leaf blinked. "A food court? The Black Tower of the Dark Lord has a *food court?*"

"Well, even minions have to have lunch, and not all of them can go to their own hearths," Juniper said. "And technically, this is the *Silver* Tower. The pizza is fine, but I have my suspicions about the hamburgers, that I do; they taste far too breadcrumbish for honesty sometimes."

"OK, OK," he said. "What *floor* is she on?"

"The seventh, usually, a bit more than halfway up, which is quite a climb, but—ah, here we are. The VIP treatment."

At the rear wall, the one facing the interior of the donjon, was what looked like a small room lined with an openwork trellis of bronze wrought into vine leaves; Sir Joscelin bowed them into it, stepped back, closed a door of the same construction and pulled on a tasseled rope.

"Godspeed and good fortune, my lords, Lady Juniper."

Somewhere far below a bell chimed faintly. Young Three Bears did start in alarm when the elevator lurched into motion beneath them, and a slow chiming music sounded from above. His father grinned—he undoubtedly hadn't ridden in an elevator since March 17, 1998—and swore admiringly.

"All the comforts. How does *this* work?"

"Convicts on treadmills down in the dungeons turning the drums with the cables," Juniper said, holding out one hand with the index finger pointing downward.

Then she rotated it towards the roof, where the icy music sounded over and over, like the chiming of Elven bridles on a midnight heath:

"Rigged to a carillon as well."

"Well, fuck me, elevator music isn't dead after all."

The elevator didn't travel very quickly, but it was much faster than trotting up ten flights of stairs. They went from one story to the next and the light outside brightened as narrow arrow-slits turned to real arched windows with glass panes in their stone traceries, albeit with steel shutters that could be barred and bolted.

A young woman was waiting to greet them at the seventh stop, dressed in a long embroidered cotehardie and a wimple of yellow silk bound with jeweled wire. The bright cloth complemented skin the color of chocolate truffles; she had an Associate's jewel-hilted dagger at her woven gold belt as well as the usual rosary and embroidered pouch. Her narrow black eyes were somewhere between elaborately guileless and extremely shrewd, her delicately full features expressionless save for a bland smile of welcome.

"God give you good day, my lords from the east, my Lady Juniper," she said, holding her skirts and sinking in a curtsy that let her trailing oversleeves touch the birch-and-maple parquet. "I shall bring you to the Lady Regent."

"Wait, demoiselle," Juniper said. "You're . . . Lady Jehane Jones, aren't you? Lord Jabar's youngest."

"Yes, I have the honor to be the Count of Molalla's daughter, my lady," she said. "You and I have met only once, though. And also I have the honor to be amanuensis to the Lady Regent."

Which meant she was something between *confidential secretary* and *general gofer*, a post of considerable importance if your principal was high on the totem pole. Juniper stopped herself from raising an eyebrow; it was the first time Sandra had allowed that job to go to one of the greater nobility. There must be a story there. The Regent liked using people she had some strong hold on, ones whose fortunes were linked to hers, not those with independent power bases and blood links to the ruling houses of the Association.

The young noblewoman went on: "If you'll follow me, my lords, my lady?"

She led them down a long corridor walled in pale marble streaked with darker gray. Arched windows to their left overlooked a rooftop garden surrounded by high walls grown with blossoming roses, and the interior wall held paintings—mostly Impressionists and Post-Impressionists along with some of the obligatory Pre-Raphaelites—or objets d'art in niches; a thirteenth-century Persian bowl showing warriors battling around a tower, an ancient savage-looking Shang Chinese mask in jade and gold, and more.

Sandra still has her salvage teams at work, I see, Juniper thought; they'd gotten as far as museums and galleries in San Diego.

"Bet the economic pyramid comes to a mighty sharp point here," Red Leaf murmured in her ear; she nodded silently.

Knights of the Protector's Guard crashed gauntleted fist to breastplate outside the last door, burnished cocobolo, teak and maple carved with scenes from Tennyson's *Idylls of the King.* A tinkle and buzz of music from lute and rebec and hautboy from within died away as it swung noiselessly open.

"My dear Juniper," Sandra Arminger said, rising to greet them.

She was small and neat and elegant and smooth in her

white-and-gray cotehardie, and a pearl-and-platinum
headdress that wasn't quite a crown over an elaborately
folded white silk wimple. It framed a round slightly
plump middle-aged face, entirely ordinary . . . until you
looked into the brown eyes.

"And John Red Leaf and Rick Mat'o Yamni," she said.
"*Hau Kola!*"

The Presence Room in the Silver Tower emptied at the
Regent's gesture, with even her Persian cats being carried
out protesting in baskets. Of the entourage there remained only Jehane and a tall blond woman in black surcoat, jerkin, hose and turned-down thigh-boots. The
surcoat bore Sandra's arms quartered with her own,
sable, a delta or over a V argent. She stood behind Sandra's chair with her left hand on the plain hilt of her longsword and her right turning a rose beneath her chin,
watching with eyes the color of moonlit glaciers.

The room was uncluttered and elegantly spare, pale
stone and tile, with the color mainly in the glowing rugs
where tigers wound through thickets beside the Columbia
Gorge and lords and ladies rode out with hawks on their
wrists through fields of asphodel. Before she left one last
lady-in-waiting set out a coffee service on the blond wood
of the table, along with petits fours and nuts and dried
fruits; the rich dark scent of the Kona Gold mixed with
the lavender sachets and the floral scents from arched
Venetian-gothic windows open on a little patio garden.
They all sat silent for a moment, considering one another.

One thing clashed violently with the room's decor. A
long carved ceremonial pipe with a spray of eagle feathers
along its underside rested in a wooden holder, along with
bowls of sage, sweetgrass and tobacco and a brass censer
of glowing coals.

Red Leaf's brows went up as he saw it. "Why do I get the feeling that's a sure-enough *chanunpa*, ah, Lady Sandra?"

"Why, it's best to be prepared," Sandra said with a slight smile. "In case we come to . . . serious matters."

Red Leaf returned the smile. "You know, Rudi struck me as a really smart guy. And he's sure-enough death on two legs in a fight. But I got the impression your girl Mathilda was more subtle. Twisty."

Sandra's smile grew to reveal a dimple and she spread her hands palms up.

"Why, my lord Red Leaf, you say the nicest things!"

"And that's real coffee, isn't it? God, it's been over twenty years!"

"By all means," Sandra said.

Jehane put her shorthand pad aside for an instant and poured for all of them; Rick Three Bears gave her a shy smile and then struggled manfully to hide it; Juniper judged he was fascinated by her alien looks, as well as the fact that she was simply a very comely woman of a bit less than his own age. Black people apparently weren't common on the High Plains. They weren't all *that* common here in Montival either, but the twists and turns of post-Change politics had made them very well represented among the PPA's nobility.

Red Leaf sipped the coffee and sighed; his son followed suit, winced, and poured in more cream and sugar. The elder Sioux rubbed his palms together.

"Let's get to business, then."

Sandra held up a hand. "Before we do, let's make our own positions plain. I am the Lady Regent of the Portland Protective Association; I make the Association's foreign policy in peace and war. Jehane is my personal amanuensis and has my full confidence; you may speak as if we were alone. This"—she indicated the tall woman behind her—"is my Grand Constable . . . supreme commander . . . Baroness Tiphaine d'Ath; she also enjoys my full confidence, and is here to give me any military advice I need. Lady Juniper you know. I represent the Association, which is about half of Montival. Lady Juniper is *the* Mackenzie, the Chief of the Clan and Name, and sufficiently influential that she can more or less commit the remaining powers as long as we don't do anything too outrageous. Signe . . . the Lady of the Bearkillers . . . couldn't be here, and Corvallis can't get anything done without six days of debate. There are over a dozen minor states . . . cities . . . leagues . . . tribes . . . autonomous villages . . . kibbutzim . . . but as a matter of practical politics they'll fall in with whatever the big four decide. Correct?"

She glanced over. Juniper shrugged:

"It would be more accurate to say that everyone else trusts you to do the negotiations . . . and trusts me to keep watch on *you*, Sandra. And that Corvallis can't do anything without six days of debate, including deciding on what's for dinner, much less who short of a committee of dozens should have plenipotentiary powers. Which is why the people there, if not the Faculty Senate, are keen for the High Kingship."

John Red Leaf looked around, apparently noticing that he and his son were the only males in the room. "Ah . . . you folks got some sort of matriarchy thing going here?"

"Not exactly," Sandra said dryly. "Though it can seem that way at times."

Tiphaine spoke for the first time; she had a strong soprano, with a tone like cool water sliding over gravel in a mountain stream:

"You might say that a lot of our first-generation leadership came down with mutually terminal cases of testosterone poisoning."

Three Bears looked puzzled, but his father barked amusement. "Yeah! Seen a fair bit of that in our neck of the woods too. A bunch of guys who thought they were a lot more like Conan than they really were. Watching the wrong movies'll do that to you."

Then both he and his son took a sudden second look at the Grand Constable. Juniper had fought occasionally with her own hands in the early Change Years, but she didn't claim to be any sort of warrior; at only a little over five feet she just didn't have the heft, for starters. But she had a very good fighting-man for her handfasted husband, and had been around many others for decades now. She knew exactly what they were looking at—details of stance and subtle movement, the wrists and hands, the thin scars that showed under the sleeves of the surcoat and shirt and on her tanned face. Other things that showed only in the chilly gray eyes, and the worn sweat-stained look of the leather and wire wrapping on the longsword's hilt, shaped by constant use to fit the wielder's palm. A sudden slight wariness showed on both their faces, and a small, brief, bleak smile on Tiphaine's; she gave them a very slight nod.

The Sioux leader turned back to Sandra and hesitated. "Ah . . . you understand, this place has been a bit of a shock. I mean, your daughter Mathilda . . . the *Princess* Mathilda . . . and the others described things for us but I thought she was, ah, maybe being a bit colorful."

Juniper intervened. "They're finding the Association a little . . . picturesque, Sandra."

"Perfectly understandable," the PPA regent said.

One slim, tastefully plucked brown eyebrow went up at the headdress the Sioux leader had put aside on the table, and the rest of the tribal finery. Red Leaf's heavy-featured face split in a smile.

"OK, I admit, you've got a point . . . Lady Sandra. This stuff's *your* warbonnet."

"And then there's Dun Juniper," Sandra said.

"It's as big as this?" Red Leaf said, surprised.

"No, not nearly as large, but it's every bit as *picturesque*. I've heard it described as looking like . . . ah . . . the biggest, gaudiest Celto-Chinese restaurant in the universe."

Juniper stifled a laugh, and Sandra went on: "But enough pleasantries."

Her slight smile died: "Can you commit the Seven Council Fires, then, Chief Red Leaf?" she asked, with gentle implacability. "Can you say yes or no to this alliance?"

"In theory, no," Red Leaf said. "Yeah, we've got a lot more organization than we did the last time we were independent, but we don't have a King or Bossman or Dictator or anything like that. We didn't *want* anything like that. Mostly the *tunwan*, the nation, handles foreign affairs and leaves us alone except for keeping us from fighting each other."

"Except for horse theft, from the intelligence reports," Tiphaine commented, in her cool-water-over-rock voice.

"Yeah, that's the national sport. That and football. But I helped put the whole thing together at the beginning, I talked things over with the other VIPs before I left, I'm pretty damned influential, and this *is* about foreign policy. So I can make promises for all the Seven Tribes, provided I don't go completely . . . off the reservation . . ."

Sandra and Juniper both winced very slightly. Red Leaf grinned and continued:

"Everyone will be together for me to talk to when I get back. We've got a mutual problem, and his name's Sethaz, aka *the Prophet,* and his merry band of fanatics and magicians and general all-around cutthroat scumbags out of Corwin. *And* his buddy in Boise, General-President Thurston."

"Or his name is legion," Juniper said.

Sandra nodded. "They are . . . alarming in some respects."

"Yeah, our Sacred Men say the same thing, and I've met some of the Cutter . . . High Seekers they call them. Once was more than enough; those bastards seriously creep me out. They're not natural; there's something else living in there, like . . . what was that Howard guy, not the one who wrote *Conan,* the one who wrote the horror stories . . ."

"Lovecraft," Juniper and Sandra said together.

"Yeah, like that. And just before we left to make this trip, all our Sacred Men and Wise Women and whatnot went bananas about something. Especially my uncle, who did the *hunkalowanpi,* the making-relatives ceremony for your kids when we adopted 'em last year. Started talking about the *akacita wakan.* That's some . . ."

His mouth twitched ironically. ". . . heap big medicine."

"*Akacita wakan*: Sacred Messengers, specifically," Juniper said clinically.

She'd studied more Ways than her own from her girlhood, and had looked up more when her son's letters spurred her interest; that had led to her arranging this meeting.

Red Leaf spread his hands in a balancing gesture. "You know, I was always all for the old ceremonies. It reminds us of how we're a people . . . which with all the, um, volunteers we got right after the Change was a pretty good thing. But I never took it all that seriously before, myself."

Three Bears looked uncomfortable; his father nodded at him. "Right, I know it makes you antsy to hear it, Rick, but this is time for putting cards on the table."

Sandra nodded. "I had very much the same attitude," she said. "Allowing for local circumstances. Until recently, as you said."

"Until recently, and that's a mouthful. I was wrong. My uncle said the *wakan* people, the spirits, were finally getting real tired of the Cutters. About fff . . . time, if you ask me, the way *their* spirits seem to have been beating on everyone in the vicinity."

"That would have been at Imbolc," Juniper said crisply. "I doubt that anyone who has the Sight . . . anyone on this continent at least . . . *didn't* sense that something had happened."

"I've had a dozen new crazed preachers proclaiming that a Crusade against Corwin is God's Will since then," Sandra said. "One of them's traveling around with a tame wolf, talking to the birds, too. Not to mention bishops. Even bishops I didn't put up to it myself. Marvelous are the works of God."

Jehane crossed herself, despite her liege-lady's obvious irony; Tiphaine touched an owl-shaped amulet around her neck.

"What *did* happen back then?" Red Leaf asked.

"Rudi told you of the Sword?" Juniper replied.

"Ummm . . . yeah. That was the part I found hardest to believe."

"*Et moi aussi*," Sandra murmured. "But it appears I was wrong too. We have that in common."

Juniper took a deep breath. "When Rudi was very young, at his Wiccaning . . . it's a rite of our Old Religion equivalent to baptism . . . I had a vision."

Sandra raised a finger. "I was a skeptic myself. But please take this seriously."

"I named him *Artos* then, in the Craft. And I spoke words." Her voice deepened a little:

"Sad winter's child, in this leafless shaw—
Yet be Son, and Lover, and Hornéd Lord!
Guardian of My Sacred Wood, and Law—
His people's strength—and the Lady's Sword!

"And then Ingolf Vogeler showed up at Sutterdown a little over two years ago now, telling us what he found on Nantucket . . . and you know the story of *that*. What happened on Imbolc was that Rudi—think of him as Artos now—reached Nantucket, *found* the Sword of the Lady in the World beyond the world, returned and drew it in the light of common day. And at that moment Earth's foundations shook, as they had not since the Change itself."

"So, he's got the Sword and he's coming home, and he's pissed?"

Juniper nodded; her leaf-green eyes looked beyond the wall for a moment. "*The Sun Lord comes, the son of Bear and Raven*," she said softly. "*Lugh of the Long Hand comes again, in His splendor and His wrath.*"

Silence closed down for a moment. Nobody who heard her could doubt her perfect sincerity . . . and she judged that *nobody* here was altogether ruling out the literal truth of what she said, either. She went on more matter-of-factly:

"And in the meantime, the Cutters have been some-what weakened. And all we who stand against them strengthened. At least as far as their ill-wishing and ma-lignant abuse of the Powers are concerned."

Sandra sighed and rested her chin on one small fist. "I must admit that . . . that was a real problem."

Tiphaine nodded from behind her. "We lost castles in ways that just couldn't be accounted for," she said. "Lost more than we could afford; we'd been relying on our strongholds to delay them. But now apparently we can play that game too."

She inclined her head towards the Mackenzie chief: "Lady Juniper here bagged us an entire battalion of Boi-se's troops just last week."

"That was you?" Red Leaf looked at her, surprised. "I heard they surrendered, which is news 'cause they're tough bastards generally, but . . . you *hexed* them or something?"

Juniper winced and rubbed the fingertips of her right hand over her forehead. "I cast troubles into their dreams, and they'll be none the worse for it. Eventually. Most of them. I wouldn't have done it if there hadn't been a High Seeker out of Corwin with them, because there's a price to be paid for that. And I do *not* wish to discuss it, so."

"But we must," Sandra said. "If these things are pos-sible now—"

"They were *always* possible!" Juniper snapped. "Magic is . . . not a matter of clicking your heels and having boul-ders fall upward. It's a thing of mind and soul and will. I will admit—" she said reluctantly. "I will admit that things have become . . . easier since the Change. And much easier since Imbolc. The Veil is thinner. Something . . . or someone . . . moved through me; it's not the first time, but it was the most disturbing. The which is linked to Rudi bringing the Sword. A new thing has come into the world."

"Indisputably so," Sandra said. "It's disturbing, as you say, but I'm not going to deny the evidence of my senses. *That* would be irrational. Though I've tried prayer and it doesn't seem to do any more for me than it ever did."

"Of course it doesn't!" Juniper said sharply. "You don't believe in anything; you pray to nothing for something and you get . . . nothing!"

"Is *nothing* sacred?" Sandra murmured.

Juniper made an impatient gesture; then she spoke very softly. "This frightens me, Sandra. More than it does you. I really know the implications, and you don't. We're not talking about a better breed of catapults or . . . or D&D hit levels. We've always walked with our legends. But what happens if our legends start to walk with *us*? What will the world be then? Will the Powers burst the everyday asunder in their contentions?"

"At least we're not at a disadvantage in . . . non-material terms anymore," Tiphaine said. "Which just leaves the fact that we're badly outnumbered."

"Yeah," Red Leaf said, visibly putting other things aside. "OK, I've seen enough here to know you guys can put up a stiff fight. But as matters stand, Corwin and Boise between them have you beat in the next couple of years, right?"

"It's not inevitable," Tiphaine said. "But when you're fighting someone who can replace losses and you can't—" A shrug. "It's the way to bet. Particularly if they don't make any big mistakes or take big risks, and so far they haven't. Grinding forward costs, but they can do it if they're prepared to pay the butcher's bill. They've already overrun most of our part of the Palouse, and even more south of the Columbia."

"And having disposed of us, the Cutters will turn on you," Sandra pointed out.

"Possibly," Red Leaf said. "Or maybe Corwin and Boise will have it out and whoever's left standing won't have any attention left to pay to us. They're partners now; that won't last forever."

"If this were merely a war of men, that might be so," Juniper said. "But Corwin has no partners. It has only prey. The CUT is an infection that spreads like mold through bread."

Silence stretched. "OK, you got something there, too," Red Leaf said. "But we fought them once before and we got beat. Not whipped, but beat."

"With us on your side, the odds would be much better," Tiphaine said. "You could bring, what, fifteen thousand men into the field?"

"Ten to fifteen if they're going to be away from home for a while," Red Leaf said. "But—"

"But they're all light cavalry, horse-archers," Tiphaine said. "No siege train, no infantry and no logistics beyond foraging and what they can carry in their saddlebags or drive along on the hoof. Plus they all need grazing for three horses each."

"Yeah," the Indian said. "Most of the Cutters fight that way too, Ranchers and their cowboys, but they've got drilled infantry, and they've got the Sword of the Prophet—regular troops. Not tin-plated like you guys in the Association here, but more punch than our riders in a stand-up fight. And they've got forts. With Boise on their side they've got another big tough army, *lots* of forts, and field artillery, too—how they square that with the crazy religious thing about no gears or machinery, God only knows. We don't have a ban on machinery, but we just don't run to that war-engine stuff. It doesn't go with moving around the way we do. And we've had some painful experience with it."

"We *do* have field artillery and a siege train," Tiphaine pointed out. "Taking all of . . . Montival . . . as a whole, we've got a *great deal* of field artillery; we and the Bear-killers and the Corvallans make some of the best. And we have relatively recent experience at using it. Mostly on each other, back a decade and change."

"Yeah, but you're on the other side of them from us. It's our guys who'd have to ride into the teeth of bolts and round shot and balls of napalm at three times bow-range without being able to hit back, or try climbing stone walls on ladders while the people inside pumped flaming canola oil on them. Not good."

Sandra almost purred as she held a hand out to Lady Jehane. The amanuensis slid a folder from an accordion file and pushed it under her liege-lady's fingers. It was correspondence, on heavy parchment-like paper, thick with official letterheads and seals.

"As it turns out, something can be done about that. You're aware of what happened in Iowa while Mathilda and Rudi . . . Artos . . . were passing through?"

Three Bears spoke: "The Cutters who were chasing Rudi, and some of their local butt-monkeys, managed to kill the Bossman of Iowa while they were trying to get at Rudi and his friends. While they were his guests. The Iowans are totally ripshit and aren't going to calm down anytime soon. But how did *you* guys find out?"

His father glanced at him; Sandra chuckled a little, a warm comfortable sound.

"No, it's a good question. We have a route of communications *around* the Cutters now."

"Through the Dominions?" Red Leaf asked sharply.

"Exactly."

The Dominions of Drumheller, Moose Jaw and Minnedosa spanned what had once been the prairie provinces of central Canada from west to east. They had settled governments, and a scattered semblance of civilized life in farm and ranch and small town, as far north as the Peace River country. Drumheller abutted on the lands ruled by the Prophet, and also had a border with Montival, through the Association's holdings in what had been British Columbia.

"How come?" Red Leaf asked. "They've always been pretty isolationist. I thought the Cutters had 'em spooked, Drumheller in particular."

"They've reconsidered," Sandra said. "Or possibly simply considered where they'll be when Corwin and Boise have destroyed us."

"Or where they'll be if *we* win and they're surrounded by hostile neighbors they refused to help," Juniper pointed out. "I think Iowa helped persuade them."

Sandra gave her a considering glance and murmured: "Dear Juniper, occasionally you remind me that honesty isn't *necessarily* linked to stupidity."

Louder, to the two Sioux: "And these letters are from the new Regency Council of the Provisional Republic of Iowa. In the names of the Regent, Lady Catherine Heasleroad, speaking for her son Thomas who is the heir to the Bossmanship, and the Chancellor, Abel Heuisink, for the rest of Iowa's government. Both speaking for *the*

Sheriffs, Farmers and People of Iowa, as they rather quaintly put it; or *Barons, Knights and Commons,* in our terminology. Offering a very substantial military force, from Iowa and the neighboring states. Fargo, Marshall, Richland, Nebraska, Concordia, Kirksville. They'll be abundantly well equipped and as numerous as the supply situation permits; that's the most densely populated part of the whole continent from Guatemala to Alaska now."

"The logistics are pretty good, too," Tiphaine put in. "If the railroads were put back into commission—and they also have plenty of labor and good engineers, and even rolling mills for light rail—"

The two Sioux sat bolt upright; Red Leaf choked slightly on a mouthful of coffee and clashed the priceless Sèvres cup down in its saucer.

"Now, wait a minute! We fought the Square Staters too, over the Red River Valley, for years. No *way* are we letting them get that sort of foothold on Lakota land. Railways and forts . . . where the hell have I heard *that* song before? Iowa alone outnumbers us something like ten to one. We held them off because they *didn't* have any way of supporting armies on foot out in the short-grass country. Nobody was all that organized back then, anyway, but that's changed too. People know what they can do now, and how to do it."

Juniper nodded sympathetically. "Well, now, my dear, we have thought of that. Your fear is that having come to help you, the Iowans may decide to outstay their welcome and help themselves, to whatever they please?"

"Damn right!"

"Well, then, think on this; if *we* go down, then not only will Corwin eventually turn on you, but you'll be caught between two millstones: the Cutters' empire, and

Iowa and its allies. Alternatively, the Iowans could decide to fight their way through you to get at Corwin. Which would leave you after the war with no friends and no bargaining power at all."

It wasn't a pleasant thought and she could see both of the Lakota mulling it over. The High Plains were a sparse hard land where the Mother's gifts were given grudgingly; they could yield a decent living if the folk there had many acres per head and used the scanty grass and water skillfully, but they couldn't support the great farms and towns possible to the east or west. Not in the world after the Change.

Ogma of the Honey Tongue, lend us your eloquence! For we are speaking for our lands and homes and folk.

She felt an impulse to reach out and shake sense into Red Leaf and his son . . . which would do no good whatsoever, of course.

"But," Sandra said, raising one finger, "there is an alternative. One which will assure that the Iowans go home after the war."

"Provided we win, of course," Tiphaine qualified.

Sandra nodded. "Operating on that assumption, yes, Baroness d'Ath, since we'll be too dead to care if we lose. Your Lakota country is drier than the Midwesterners like, anyway; they have land enough to feed twenty or thirty times their number lying idle inside their own boundaries, and more vacant to the east and south down the Mississippi Valley when they've brought all that under the plow. It's one acre after another around there, fat black soil and well watered, the best farmland in the world."

"Yeah," Red Leaf said. "They don't *need* our territory. That doesn't mean they wouldn't *want* it if they were *standing* on it."

He frowned, looking as stubborn as a bull bison, and as dangerous, almost ready to bellow out a challenge to the world and charge heedlessly. Then he took a deep breath:

"So, what's your plan?"

Sandra made a graceful gesture. "You know Rudi's to be High King in Montival?"

"Yeah. Whatever the hell a High King is, as opposed to just plain King or President or Bossman or whatever."

Juniper took up the story: "An *Ard Rí* . . . a High King . . . isn't an Emperor or Bossman or anything like it. We haven't settled all the details of the thing, but you may notice there are many peoples out here, with many ways of doing and living that have grown up since the Change, their own laws and ways and Gods."

Red Leaf's dark eyes narrowed above his high cheek-bones.

"So?"

"A High King will . . . so to speak . . . reign over the whole of Montival lightly, more than *rule* it. All the peoples . . . city-states, clans, the Association, the monks at Mt. Angel, the Faculty Senate in Corvallis, and others besides . . . will keep their own laws and govern themselves. Each will guarantee the borders of the others and aid them if they're attacked, under the High King's direction."

"Nobody gets to settle on our land without our permission," Red Leaf said bluntly. "That's non-negotiable. We learned *that* lesson real good."

"Precisely. Nobody to touch so much as a blade of grass without your leave," Sandra said soothingly.

"Free trade, of course," Juniper put in; she wasn't going to sweeten the pot with bad treacle. "The *Ard Rí* won't have a big standing army, only a guard, but everyone is to send contingents when needed, and there'll be a tax—not much of a one, but to be paid—and the High King's court will hear disputes between communities, or their members. You can consult the Three Tribes Confederation of Warm Springs if you like, and see that we around here keep our word. And while nobody is compelled to take anyone *in*, everyone is to be free to leave where he is, and most places welcome any pair of hands that go with a willingness to work, since land is so much more abundant than people to till it. Which means no slavery or serfdom anywhere, unless it's truly voluntary—which would take away the whole point of such."

"And in return you get *our* backing if anyone tries to attack you," Tiphaine pointed out. "The Association's knights, the Mackenzie archers, engineers and pikemen from Corvallis or the Yakima League. We are most assuredly not interested in anything to the east of you but we're willing to push the border that far, and help hold it. As part of Montival you'd have enough weight behind you that even Iowa would have to think three times before tangling with you."

"And we could have our reservation as long as the grass grew and the sun shines," Red Leaf said dryly; his voice was skeptical but not utterly hostile.

Juniper shrugged. "If you call everything you've got now a *reservation*," she said. "And that's what . . . half the Dakotas and chunks of Wyoming and Montana and Colorado and a bit of Nebraska? Which is more land and more people than ever you had in the old days."

"Including . . . ah . . . volunteers," Sandra observed. "There are more of you than there are Mackenzies."

"Which means you'd also be a fairly big element in the

High Kingdom as a whole," Tiphaine said. "Not least in the number of troops you could field. Nobody would be in a position to bully you, even if they were so inclined."

"What about Boise? And New Deseret?" Red Leaf asked. "They're between us and you as well as the Cutters."

Sandra steepled her fingers and raised her eyes slightly. "You may have noticed that the late General-President of the United States of Boise had more than one son. The elder killed his father and usurped his position. The younger . . . you met. Traveling with Mathilda and, um, Artos."

"Oh, *ho*," Red Leaf said, and gave her an admiring look. "Well, yeah, that's a definite possibility. You think Boise may come apart over that?"

"That and their alliance with Corwin, which we understand is *not* popular. Martin Thurston is trying his best to pin the blame on his brother, but the true story has been circulating . . . aided by us. And New Deseret is desperate, what's left of it. We've been helping their guerrillas in the occupied territories as we can. They're very . . . upright people. Usually gratitude is worth its weight in gold, but they actually seem to practice it. Marvelous are the works of God."

Red Leaf nodded and rubbed his hands together; the heavy stockman's calluses bred of rope and rein, lance and shete, went *scritch* against each other.

"OK, whoa, this is going to take a bit more thinking. I *can't* commit all of us to *this*. Some of it sounds good, but I'm not going to say yes or no yet, and it's above my pay grade anyway."

"Oh, certainly," Sandra said. "We'll have to have extensive talks even for a temporary alliance, and you'll have to consult your Council about anything more. But . . . we *do* need the Iowans. And we need them to march in, fight, and then turn around and go back with hearty thanks ringing in their ears. And we need them *now*."

"What do they get out of it? Besides hearty thanks and gratitude . . . which, you're right, are usually worth their weight in gold. Or diamonds."

"A long-term menace disposed of," Sandra said. "And in terms of their internal politics, in which my daughter had a hand, they get unity behind House Heasleroad— there's nothing like a successful foreign war to rally support. Now let's start with a few details—"

She settled into her chair, as content as one of her Persian cats confronted with a bowl of fresh cream and salmon on the side. Juniper sighed silently and settled herself as to a task that had to be done.

Rudi, my son! Where are you now?

CHAPTER EIGHT

Bjarni Eriksson saw his death rising with the heavy curved sword. Thunder pounded in his ears; it echoed in the ground beneath his back like hooves. He struggled to raise his sword and meet the blow still fighting. A man lived until he died, and not an hour more.

"Fare You well, Thor, until the weird of the world!" he choked out. "Harberga—I come, father—"

The thunder *was* hooves. A great black horse whose head and neck and shoulders gleamed silvery breasted the slope, and Bekwa scattered aside like sandy soil before the coulter of a plow, like birch leaves in an autumn wind. In the saddle was a man with the head of a raven, and in his hand was a lance. The *trollkjerring* turned, raising his shield. The lance struck it and shattered, with a sharp stuttering crackling impact that seemed to strike his own head between the eyes. The red-robe staggered back, but the great warhorse staggered as well, almost falling.

Bjarni blinked, even then. It was like seeing a hammer hit an egg and watching the *hammer* bounce. The man in the high war-saddle kicked his feet out of the stirrups and threw himself to the ground, landing even as he drew his sword.

Shock ran through the world.

The flash that came with the long blade shone through his flesh to his bones, making him transparent as fine glass of the ancient world, without being anything his eyes could see at all. It lit the *mind*, as if his inner being had stared into the sun. Bjarni saw the way the smooth curve of the man's visor drew down into a point that almost hid his bared teeth. Eyes of cold blue-gray glinted through the narrow space of the vision slit.

The sorcerer crouched, snarling. **"You . . . can . . . slay . . . the vessel . . . but . . . not . . . us,"** he said, in a voice like the world ripping. **"For . . . we . . . are . . . legion."**

"I don't have to," the man said, his voice like a trumpet. "I have only to put you back where you belong, in my time and in my land; for even you are a part of things. The which I will do, now, so."

The red-robe screamed and struck.

Shock.

The world shook again, as if it were a painted drawing whose fabric trembled in a high wind. Steel met the Sword and shattered, and the blade looped back. A hand spun away in a rising arc, and blood trailed behind it and spouted from the wrist and in a circle from the follow-through of the Sword. Bjarni stumbled upright again, as if released from bonds; his leg hurt badly, but he could make himself move. Everyone about him was moving too. The red-robe clutched at his severed wrist; the cold malevolence was gone from his face, leaving nothing but a vast bewilderment as he sat down to die.

*   *   *

Artos let the momentum of the strike carry him around. The Seeker of the Church Universal and Triumphant was no threat anymore—just a man, and a dying man with no heart to fight, at that. A spear thrust at him, a length of rusty steel pipe with the end hammered and filed down to a point. The thing was too massive to be agile, but the thick-shouldered savage had already begun a two-handed smash that would have driven the mass of metal through anything a man could wear. It scored across Artos' shield and left a peeling thread of the facing sheet behind it; the Sword struck upward and the front three feet of the crude weapon went pinwheeling away. There was a tug on his sword-wrist as the Sword of the Lady cut through the tough alloy, like the hesitation he'd feel if he lopped off a dried reed. The thrust that followed snapped out faster than a frog's tongue, crunching through the thin bones of the man's face between the eyes and back before he even began to crumple.

Wheel, slash a man's legs out from under him, turn another spear-thrust with the shield and smash its facing into the wielder hard enough to crack bone, kick backward against a knee, thrust and ribs parted and the man jerked forward into another Bekwa's path as Artos wrenched the Sword free—

Most of his consciousness was in a peculiar and very specialized place, one that saw only threats—spearpoints, blades, the glimmering edge of an ax—and targets, joints, throats, unarmored bellies. Everything else blurred into a mist of irrelevancy. That part of him danced light-footed across the field of war, shield and blade moving in a continuous blurring whirl from which blood *splashed* in arcs and circles, leaving horror in his wake. Very far away some other part winced when the Sword hammered through metal, a reflex of training that told him he was destroying it.

It was the first time he'd *fought* with the weapon the Ladies had given him, and the supernal rightness of it filled a warrior's soul with wondering joy. As if all other blades were mere children's copies of lath and rattan, and this was the original pattern as it had been in the mind of the Maker. The Sword was many things, but it was a *sword* beyond all swords at the very least.

Yet he could see the whole battle now, as well as his part in it, without breaking the diamond point of concentration that a man required when he fought hand to hand for his life. As if he were more men than one.

He could see the others following in his wake, the three lances dipping in a synchronized wave, light breaking from the honed steel of the heads, the heads of the horses pumping like pistons in a watermill as their hooves threw divots shoulder-high. See/feel/hear them strike, massive thudding blows, turning in the riders' hands to pivot free, coming down again. Mathilda releasing her lance when it jammed in a pelvis and sweeping out her sword, her destrier soaring in a capriole that ended with lashing hooves knocking back a whole clot of the enemy as she seemed to hang suspended for a moment. Epona rearing, smashing her shod feet down on faces and shoulders. Abdou al-Naari throwing his spear into the breast of a Bekwa chief with an antlered headdress and drawing and slashing with his scimitar in almost the same motion . . .

Arrows feathering past as Edain and the others slid free of their saddles and shot in a deadly ripple as fast as they could draw and loose, a bodkin point cracking out through the breastbone of a man about to hit Artos on the back with a sledgehammer filed down to a blunt cone. The Kalksthorpe men scrambling up the hill and slotting themselves breathless into the crumpled face of the Norrheimer shield-wall, pushing it out to stop the breakthrough.

Suddenly he was in the waking world again, panting beside Bjarni and a brown-bearded man with a dripping ax.

"And the top of a fine morning to you, blood brother," he said to Bjarni.

The Norrheimer grinned at him, through a face spattered with blood that thinned and ran with the sweat.

"Where's my signaler!" he cried. "Now, now, without the *trollkjerring* they're ours—"

"Not yet," Artos said. "Wait, wait. I can feel it, I can feel the balance shifting."

Bjarni halted with his hand half raised. The youth with the banner a few steps behind him suddenly shouted:

"There, *godhi*. Behind them! Is it more of them?"

He sounded frightened and trying not to show it. Bjarni's face was grim as he stuck his sword point down in the frozen ground and opened the steel-lined case at his belt that held his binoculars. Then the grin came back.

"The flag of the porcupine! Madawaska!" A slight frown. "And there's another with it . . . a tree, and seven stars, and a crown."

Ingolf let loose with a whoop: "*That's my Mary!* Egleria gwenn *and all the Elvish bullshit you want for the rest of your life!* She found your Madawaska and brought them here *right* on time."

"By Thor's almighty prick, they're charging!" Bjarni

said. "Right into the rear of the foe . . . stopping for a volley with those crossbows of theirs . . ."

Artos blew out a breath he hadn't known he was holding. "Then, yes, Bjarni Eriksson, this is the time. And it's your battle to win, you and your folk's, and we but helpers."

"The spirit's gone out of them, the *main*," Bjarni said thoughtfully, scanning the battlefield. "Signalers! Call number five, the Boar's Tusk call!"

He's right, Artos knew, following his gaze.

The fight still went on; right here the enemy were giving ground, but he could see the blurred heaving violence of shield against shield to either side, double long bowshot east and west; see it well, since this was the highest spot and at the base of the V of the Norrheimer formation. The noise was stunning, like an avalanche of scrap metal on a concrete floor even through the padded coif and the helm—there was a reason warriors shouted most of the time—but you could sense the realization that . . .

That they are well and truly fucked, as my blood father would have said, Artos thought.

. . . as it soaked through the enemy ranks. Then a brabble, and Bekwa even in the front ranks were skipping back a little and looking over their shoulders.

Several men raised the long horn trumpets to their lips. The call was a blatting bellow that thundered deep, carrying well through the rattle-stamp-crash-shriek sound of war. Other horns took it up, from one end of the line to the other, on all the six hills, until the triumphant braying *haaaaah-haaaaah-huuuu-huuuu-huuuu* rhythm sounded over and over again. No silence fell when they stopped, but there was a trembling pause where Bjarni's shout could be heard:

"Form the boar's head and forward, Norrheimer men! Kill! Spare none; make safe our land, our homes! Thor with me! *Ho La, Odhinn!*"

Epona butted Artos between the shoulder blades. He swung into the saddle; it was harder this time. Mathilda fell in at his left, and Ignatius beyond her, with Ingolf on his right. From the tall horse's back he could see how each hill's shield-wall shook and reshaped itself as this one did, the standards of the chiefs coming forward with their armored guardsmen behind them to make the tip of a blunt wedge with the farmers of the levy as the shoulders and base. The light-armed bowmen and slingers fanned out, and now the Norrheimer line had turned from a chain of shield-wall forts into the blade of an inward-curving saw. The men of this land evidently didn't know many tricks of war, but this was a good one. The Madawaska newcomers were running forward, blocking the only exit from the sickle shape.

"*Forward, Norrheim!*"

A roar: "*HO LA, ODHINN!*"

And the saw began to cut.

Six hours later, Artos reined in below the slope where Bjarni Eriksson stood silhouetted against the quick sunset of early spring; the others were with him, save for where Abdou al-Naari grieved over the body of his blood brother Jawara. Mary and Ritva had the stars-and-tree flag, and a wizened-looking little man came with Madawaska's porcupine.

The *godhi* still had his sword in his right hand, but he'd dropped his tattered shield and found a spear to grip in his left as a walking stick; evidently the bone-bruise was starting to really hurt. His face was drawn, but that was probably just the aftermath of battle, and realizing what it had cost.

Less than it might, Artos thought, looking around.

This fight had been typical in one way; the real killing had started after one side broke and ran. You could chase and strike, but running left your back bare to every point and edge. It was worse this time than most, because the Bekwa had been trapped until they were a mass too crowded to use their weapons; an acre or more was bodies piled two deep. If Bjarni's people wanted more land, there wasn't going to be anyone to stop them to the northward for a generation at least. The stink was overpowering, even to someone used to the aftermath of human bodies cut open by desperate strength and edged metal, but at least it was cold—getting very chilly indeed, in fact. Men and the wisewomen were attending to the most urgent chores, getting the wounded gathered in and kept warm by small efficient fires while they bandaged and stitched and splinted; everyone else could roll themselves in their sleeping bags and eat trail food tonight.

Mathilda muttered: "What *are* you up to, Rudi?"

"What needs doing," he said quietly.

What Artos *knows is necessary. For once, that's something Rudi agrees with all his heart* does *need to be done.*

The majority stood or sat or wandered aimless, eyes empty for the moment, or tracking back and forth as if in disbelief over the field of war they'd survived. Some searched for kin or friends; he saw an older man sitting with a youth's head in his lap, thick blunt fingers inexpertly brushing a lock of hair back from the dead face. More and more gathered as Artos and his party came cantering by. Almost all looked up when he reined in and Epona caracoled; he stood in the stirrups and thrust the Sword skyward.

Nobody ignored that. It didn't seem possible. Even the grave chiefs of the tribes—Hrossings, Wulfings, Kalkings, Verdfolings, Hundings—fell silent.

Artos met Bjarni's eyes, saw a question there, and smiled, then filled his lungs:

"Hail, victory!" he shouted.

Silence echoed. He could feel the pressure of eyes on him, thousands of them; somehow the Sword seemed to reflect them all, glittering itself—with the evening light, and with the fires of their hearts.

"Hail to the victor! Hail, Bjarni—hail Bjarni, *King in Norrheim! Hail Bjarni King!*"

Silence *crashed*, until another voice took it up. Then another, and another, hoarse from throats raw with the day's shouting. A spear boomed against a shield, and the flat of a sword, then more and more. The leaden exhaustion left Bjarni's face, first giving way to alarm, then stiffening as the wave of sound roared across the battlefield:

"Hail Bjarni King! Hail Bjarni King!"

After a moment the chiefs took it up as well; last the one under the white horse of the Hrossings, his mouth quirking.

"Hail Bjarni King!"

NORRHEIM, LAND OF THE BJORNINGS
ERIKSGARTH (FORMERLY AROOSTOOK COUNTY, MAINE)
MARCH 27, CHANGE YEAR 25/2023 AD

Artos looked at Fred Thurston. "You think it'll work?" he said.

"Sir, I *know* so. Dad . . . the President . . . came up with the tactic and we did test runs. One of them was my Junior ROTC class, and we were just *kids*, not one of us over fifteen, and we managed it fine in the field. Yeah, the rail lines will be more screwed here than even in the Idaho backcountry, but not *that* much more screwed. It really is a way to move a medium-sized—up to battalion-sized—unit cross-country fast without being able to forage locally. I can't guarantee that it'll work, but it's a very high probability."

"And we've scarcely a battalion's worth of warriors to move," Artos said thoughtfully. "Less than twoscore."

"Well, that may be a problem. You need a certain number to do the work."

Artos stripped the flesh off the roast duck drumstick with his teeth and chewed the rich dark meat with relish. The long cavern of Bjarni's mead-hall was bright tonight, with the circles of lanterns drawn up on the tall white-pine pillars carved with gods and heroes that ran in a double row down the center. Light glinted off curled gripping beasts wrought into the wainscoting, off the painted shields and honed weapons racked against the walls, on tapestries that hung from the railings of the second-story gallery and stirred in the draughts. Blazing logs boomed on the firedogs of the great twin hearths, casting warmth and a scent of pine beneath the smells of roast pork, steaks, blood sausage, mounded heaps of loaves, French-fried potatoes, ripe cheese, dried-fruit pies and ice cream. Barrels stood on X-frames, ready to refill mugs and horns as the appointed *valkyries* went about.

Part of it was the ongoing victory feast, part grave-ale for the fallen . . . and to be sure, part was the politicking that Artos himself had started, though he'd kept strictly in the background since. These Norrheimers had a straightforward approach to such things; the battlefield had been a lawful moot like their annual *Althing* because it held a quorum of their adults . . . and because it would be silly to pretend that a King's throne didn't rest on the spearpoints of his people. He'd come to know these folk a little, and they prided themselves on common sense as much as they did on courage or stubbornness.

So Bjarni Eriksson would be King in Norrheim; Bjarni Ironrede, they were calling him now, Bjarni of the Iron Counsel. Then they'd started the real haggling. He recalled what one of the chiefs had said to Bjarni. It had been Inglief of the Hundings, he thought:

You're a man of honor and you'll be a good King. We have to settle what the King can and cannot do now because someday there may be a King who doesn't *respect our rights of his own will. Then we'll need a chain of laws to hold* him *back, as Fenris was chained.*

Right now small groups were huddled together on the benches, chiefs and prominent men and women talking quietly as they ate, a serious thread beneath the boisterous celebration around them. Bjarni had made it plain that after the third day the cost of the roast meat and bread and pastries would come out of *their* storehouses, not his, which gave an added incentive for haste.

Whoever had built this hall had understood acoustics; the folk on the dais could hear each other. Bjarni turned towards Artos after Fred spoke, his gold-bound horn in his hand. The fair skin of his face was flushed, but the hard cider had only put a bit of a glitter in his eye.

They may be solemn in their every-day, these Norr-

*heimers, but by Brigid who makes the grain to grow and by
Gobniu who first brewed it into beer, they can* drink, *and no
mistake!*

"Not a battalion? I have something to say to that," the
new-made King said. "Yes, and a few other things."

He rose from the High Seat with its curly maple pillars
carved in the images of hammer-wielding Thor and Sif of
the golden locks, and silence gradually fell through the
hall; in one or two cases when heads were rapped sharply
against the tables by neighbors more sober. Harberga sat
at his side, her long headdress bound with gold as yellow
as her hair, love and pride and fear in her gaze on him
behind an impassive public face.

"Abdou al-Naari!" Bjarni called. "Come before me,
you and your son."

The wiry corsair captain came and bowed slightly before the high seat, his hawk-featured brown face impassive, slimly elegant in the best outfit he'd had aboard his
ship, sweeping over-robes of pale blue trimmed with
pearls, cut at the neck and chest to show a snowy white
beneath, and a turban colored indigo wound around a
spiked steel helm. There was no sword at his waist, but a
curved dagger in a sheath of chased silver was thrust
through the silken sash. He shook back the broad sleeves
of his garment and bowed again, touching brow and lips
and heart with the fingers of his right hand. It was extravagantly polite and proud as an osprey's flight, as if he
were the one who sat in power dispensing favor, rather
than a prisoner on probation.

"*Za'ima-t,*" he said in his own tongue, and translated:
"Lord."

"Abdou al-Naari, you made war on my people. But
after war a peace may be made. You and yours have paid

wergild duly accepted by the families of the slain. By our law, blood-price freely taken ends a feud, and you have shed your own blood by our side against a common foe."

He laid a hand on Rudi's shoulder for a moment. "My blood brother made oath that you should go free with your ship if you fought with us. His honor is mine, and his pledged oath; free you shall be, and with provisions for your voyage."

A slight pawkiness crept in, and his blue eyes held a hint of cool menace: "Your voyage *home*."

Abdou smiled slightly, the inclination of his head acknowledgment of things that need not be spoken.

"My great lord is gracious beyond my due."

"I will be the judge of what is due; so take this gift of me," Bjarni said.

He reached up his thick arm and took a gold arm-ring, graven in sinuous abstract patterns, leaning forward and holding it out.

"As a mark that you may come in peace to Norrheim to trade, if you will. Let no more blood come between us, but guest-friendship instead."

The Moor came forward and took the heavy ring with a graceful gesture; Artos reflected that he knew how to accept like a gentleman. He'd also obviously practiced a store of more formal English for this.

"My lord is generous as well as gracious!" he said. "May Allah, the Merciful, the Lovingkind, reward him according to his deeds."

"And this for your son, who fought bravely in his first pitched battle, so far from his home and kin; he has shed his blood on the soil of Norrheim, and that of my enemies."

He held out another, and the young man stepped forward, repeating his father's gesture with a dignity more self-conscious.

Still, he carries it off well for a youngster, Artos thought. *He'll be formidable when he has his father's years.*

The elder Moor spoke: "If I come to these waters again, only in peace I shall be. And my son Ahmed ibn Abdou after me. Also I shall speak of peace between his land and mine with the Emir, though I am not ruler in Dakar. This I swear by God and His Prophet, on my hope of Paradise and on my honor before my shipmates and my kin."

His son bowed beside him, his face still a little stiff with the stitched scar that ran from ear to chin, a mark he bore with more pride than pain. Artos hid his smile; you could see the lad taking in the alien wonders of the hall and the bare-faced beauties, storing up tales he'd be telling *his* grandchildren about hairy barbarians he'd fought in a far land, and shameless golden-haired viragos of the frozen northlands. The Moors backed, bowed again, and then trooped out as courteous and graceful as cats. He nodded; they couldn't really join the feast, being theoretically forbidden strong drink, and unwilling to eat many of the local foods in theory and practice both. There would be more goodwill this way. Perhaps there would be peace between their breed and the Norrheimers, perhaps not, but in either case it would be the normal friendship or enmity of men and men's concerns, the things of common day.

And not that thing which speaks through the CUT and its like. I did a better deed than I knew when I rescued Kalksthorpe from the corsairs, and them from the man who misled them.

A buzz went down the long benches; comment, and

approval in the main. Bjarni waited until it ran down; he'd been handing out golden rings for the past three days, reward and gifts of honor both.

What the ancient world called medals, eh?

Artos leaned over to speak softly to Harberga. "He's a stout warrior, your man, and a cunning war-chief, and careful of his honor. But he's careful of the honor of others as well, no hothead who reaches for his sword as his first resort, no lover of blood. And he knows the strength of his folk is best built by their labors in peace, not by glory or plunder, so a wise King serves them by standing as the shield that lets each reap what he sows. What a praise-song my mother could have made for him!"

Harberga turned her head slightly to answer him. "From what I hear, you could have had the throne as easily as him, if you'd stretched out your hand for it."

Artos shrugged. "This is your land, and I have my own," he said.

Which is the truth, and more polite than saying I wouldn't have Norrheim on a bet!

There was a stark beauty here, but he wanted to be *home*. For a moment he was standing looking through mountain mists at the glowing checkerboard of the Willamette country gold to the harvest, and the pain of it was like cold steel in his chest. He wanted to be *home*, to hear the speech and see the ways of his own folk in his own land.

I wouldn't have great Iowa itself in exchange, much less this frigid remoteness.

Then he forced lightness into his voice:

"In Montival I must be High King, for the land's sake and to do the will of the Powers. Given my own way I'd stay at home and farm and hunt with no thought for anything but the harvest and the Wheel of the Year."

She snorted slightly. "Wyrd may weave many things for you, aetheling, but to sit peacefully in your hall is not the Orløg which will rule your days, I think. And I think you praise my Bjarni—praise him truthfully, mind you—by giving him the virtues you hope for in yourself."

Mathilda hugged his other arm with hers for a moment; he turned his fingers to interleave with hers as she spoke:

"And he has what he hopes for. He will be a great King, and make Montival great in turn!"

Harberga looked across him at her and smiled at the passionate belief in the younger woman's voice, but with a little sadness in the expression.

"He will," she said. "And you will have to share your man with a throne all the days of your lives together, sister. As will I, now. Power will be a cold and thankless third head on your pillow."

Mathilda smiled a little and shook her head. "He was born to be a King; it will complete him. And my father and mother were rulers before me, and his before him as well. It's . . . it's the family trade on both sides."

By then the hall was quiet again, and Bjarni's voice rang through it:

"The true folk have hailed me. *I am King!* Does any man here dispute it?"

His eyes scanned the benches, cold and considering, lingering on each *godhi* who headed one of the Norrheimer tribes. Silence enough this time that the crackle of burning wood was the loudest sound.

"We have yet to hammer out all the metes and bounds of what it means to be King in Norrheim. But one thing is not in dispute; it is for the King to call the folk to war, and to lead them against foreign enemies."

Farther down the hall someone cried him hail as victor. He flung up a hand.

"No! What's the saying of the High One: *Call no man lucky till he's dead?* So we shouldn't call any King victorious until the war is over. And this war is not. We have won a victory, in a battle greater than any my father fought in the land-taking. But the Bekwa were only the point of a spear in another's hands."

"The *trollkjerring*," someone said.

"Yes. And he was one of many, in the service of their ruler far to the west, in what the old world called Montana."

"The wolf gapes ever at the gates of the Gods . . ." murmured Heidhveig.

Bjarni nodded respectfully. "True, holy seidhkona. So we have won a victory, but not a war. If we sit here eating roast pork and guzzling beer and telling each other how brave we were, other armies will come against us in the end, ones we will have no hope of defeating. Led by sorcerers. I will not leave to my children work I feared to do myself! My blood brother Artos Mikesson, High King in Montival, goes west to fight that war. Are we of Norrheim such cowards, such nithings, that we will let him go fight it alone and without any help of ours, after he and his sworn band aided us? I tell you now, that if the kingdom will not help him, then I will—my word binds me, sworn in this hall on the Oath-Swine of the Bjornings. And a King's public oath is laid in the Well of Wyrd and binds the fate of all his people."

A murmur, and then Ingleif of the Hundings rose. "Lord, you are King. Your honor no man doubts and your words do you credit. Much of what you say is true, though these are strange matters; but I will not dispute what the holy seidhkona says of the Gods' wishes for true folk. Yet we cannot march the levy of Norrheim across the whole wide world! It's not to be thought of. There are our homes to guard, and we can't take that many men out of the fields for long or everyone will go hungry. We haven't settled the term of a war-levy, but it won't be years at one time."

What exactly does Bjarni have in mind? Artos thought, slightly alarmed. *Fred's thought gives us a way . . . but I can't haul an* army *all the way through the dead lands to the Mississippi! Getting a substantial force from Iowa to the theater of war will be hard enough.*

Bjarni stood with the thumb of his right hand hooked through the broad belt that cinched his waist; the buckle was a gold-and-jet dragonhead, and the sinuous designs tooled into the black leather made it a serpent like *Jörmungandr*, the World Snake that Thor lifted. Harberga's hands had woven the crimson wool of his coat, and embroidered it with curving gripping beasts in gold and silver thread along collar and cuffs and hems. His shoulder-length hair was held back by a golden band. He looked every inch the King now.

Syfrid of the Hrossings rose as Ingleif sat. "As *godhi* Ingleif says, our King is a man of honor. And as our King says, his oath to the . . . valiant stranger . . . Artos Mikesson . . . binds the fate of the kingdom and the folk. Even in a matter so distant as wars a world away."

"It does," Bjarni said, his voice hard. "For the lord and the land and the folk are *one*."

"But Ingleif is also right. We cannot march a war-levy that far. What is needed is a picked band of strong fighters. And who better to lead it than our victorious young King? The more so as we already have an heir."

Harberga's face might have been carved from fine-grained birchwood, but her breath hissed out. Bjarni smiled slightly as he nodded.

"You were always a right-hand man to my father, *godhi* of the Hrossings, and for your wisdom as well as the blows of your ax. What better way for Norrheim to show its united strength than to send its best to fight the common foe of men and Gods?"

Carrying off the King you hailed against your will, and his strongest supporters, Artos thought, glancing at Syfrid casually. *And leaving you as much time as you need to do whatever you wish here at home; or if Bjarni were not to return . . . well, much may happen before a babe grows to a man's strength.*

Bjarni's grin made Syfrid blink. "And that band must include men of every tribe. And their chiefs, when those are noted men of war . . . such as yourself, Syfrid Jerrysson."

There was another pause. This time the buzz held an ever-so-slight undertone of amusement, though nobody dared smile to Syfrid's thunderous face. He couldn't possibly refuse, not without branding himself a coward among this warrior folk, or treacherous and so hated of their Gods—Gods who valued a man's sworn oath above all else.

Is the Hrossing so simple? Rudi thought. *I'd thought him a cunning man, and a bad foe.*

Evidently he thought loudly. Mathilda still had his hand; she leaned close to whisper in his ear.

"No, Rudi, he's not stupid. But he's no genius either, and he was a man in his prime when Bjarni was still a little boy of six, in the year of the Change."

"Ah," Artos said.

That explains it. Bjarni is a lad to him still, not a man of thirty with children of his own. Not in his inner heart. And so he underestimated him, expecting rashness and vainglory. There is a lesson I will remember well. And another that I learned long ago; my Matti has wits enough for both of us.

CHAPTER NINE

The crowd stirred. It was a raw day, gray-overcast but much warmer even at dawn than it had been on the day of the battle. A few lanterns shed yellow light, and torches smoked and guttered and paled as the glow behind the clouds strengthend. The tall carved rune-stone that fronted the grave-mound glinted, where flecks of mica ran through the granite; for the negotiations had been finished, and the King's powers drawn, and he had dared the night-long vigil atop his father's howe.

Then Bjarni strode down the slope of dead winter-grass, with the bloody hide of the horse he'd sacrificed at sundown wrapped around him like a cloak and its face-mask above his own head. Beneath he was naked save for a loincloth, but he didn't seem mortally chilled. Heidh-veig paced beside him, her long staff thumping the turf. When he came to the level ground Artos could see his eyes. Normally they were shrewd and forthright, the gaze of a strong-willed man who was a good friend and a dangerous foe. Now they were . . .

"Something else," he whispered, inclining his head in acknowledgment and awe and a little . . .

Fear, he thought. *Fear of what I see in my own future. For though I'm called High King now, the thing itself can only be done in my own land. And there too it will be a first time, and we must feel our way towards the rightness of it. I'm glad to have witnessed this, though it's only a hint of how Montival must be courted.*

His hand gripped tighter on the Sword.

"This is a true King-making," he said. "The land has welcomed him as the Lady does the young God at Beltane."

Matti and Ignatius crossed themselves. Mary and Ritva laid right hand to heart and bowed; after a moment Ingolf followed suit. A low murmur ran through the rest of his band, and through the great watching crowd; then silence so complete that the sough of wind through the ash grove was the loudest sound.

Syfrid was spokesman for the *godhar* of the tribes— each of them was also a man who made sacrifice, of course, though there was probably a little irony in their choice of him. He was a bold man too, but he moistened his lips and looked a little aside from that blue stare before he spoke:

"What have you seen, Bjarni Eriksson?" he asked. "What word do you bring to us from the world beyond Midgard?"

"I spoke with my father," Bjarni said, his voice calm and distant as if he still dreamed, but carrying easily across the assembly. It grew stronger:

"And with the Norrheimer folk who have shed their blood on this soil that fed them, and the old Americans who tilled these fields and so made them their homeland, and with the ancient tribes, the First People who came here when the Ice withdrew and worshipped the Gods who were before the Gods. Theirs is the land's unrest and its deepest peace. . . . Many and strange were the things told me, many and strange were the sights shown me."

Heidhveig spoke, firmly but weary; the ordeal had worn harder on her:

"The dead have accepted the King's oaths, and the land acknowledges him."

A mass intake of breath, and a sigh.

"What is your oath to us and Norrheim, Bjarni King?" Syfrid asked formally.

"To be father to the land, and the folk; to rule honorably the living, respecting olden law and right, and to give their rightful due to the ancestors, the wights and the High Gods in the name of all our people. To die into the land at last, and watch over it with my might and my main as my father does."

As he spoke the humanness came back into his gaze bit by bit. There was a brief crashing cheer, and then he stepped forward. The chiefs joined him, and they walked forward together under an arch of rowan and ash-withies, covered with sod cut from the earth around the mound. When they had all bowed beneath it he hung the horsehide on it as well.

Heidhveig raised her staff and called: "The earth of Norrheim is your mother! From this day, you and your tribes and your kindred are reborn as brothers, and the common blood of Norrheim runs in your veins!"

Another cheer, and Harberga came forward with a thick cloak. *Now* Bjarni shivered a little, and clutched it around his shoulders, taking the horn of hot mead she handed him. She chanted as he raised it to the four corners of the world and flicked a drop aside for Earth:

"Mead I bring thee, thou oak-of-battle,
with strength i-blent and brightest honor;

'tis mixed with magic and mighty songs,
with goodly spells, wish-speeding runes."

"I thank you, Harberga, my wife who is now Queen in Norrheim and Lady of this land," he said hoarsely, before draining it in one long draught.

"Now," he said, his eyes meeting Artos'. "Now I want a steam bath, and some clothes, and food . . . and then, my new brothers, and you my tall blood brother, we have *work* to do!"

Mathilda groaned a little and stretched. Working with her hands was something she was fairly used to; her months every year with the Clan Mackenzie had meant living as the clansfolk did, and even the Chief of the Clan and Name did a lot of her own chores and helped with the harvest.

But I don't get the same sort of enjoyment out of it some do, she thought, watching Father Ignatius.

He was wiping thick black grease off his hands as he bent over the plans tacked to a board easel, careful not to smudge them. The barn was close and damp, with cold draughts through gaps in the boards alternating with blasts of heat from a pair of improvised charcoal hearths. At least the rain was no longer beating down on the strakes of the roof; the interior was littered with parts and machinery and workbenches, amid a clanging and grinding of metal on metal, a rasp of saws and files and drills on wood as smiths and carpenters labored. The acrid sulfurous smell of hot metal mixed with sawdust and glue, and feet scuffed on the planks of the floor.

Near a hearth of salvaged brick a squat muscular man

was working something on an anvil, a *tinka-tinka*-clang! and showers of sparks on his leather apron and everything else around him, with a boy waiting with a bucket of water in case they caught. Ignatius looked that way, nodded approval, and went on to his audience, composed of Fred Thurston, Ingolf and the twins:

"—the two rolls at right angles can groove and shape the strip at the same time, if we feed it in at red heat," the warrior-monk said. "Then we can hammer-forge each wheel, heat-shrink it on and hand-file to fit, tedious but possible with the gauges to measure—"

Mt. Angel trained its members in many skills; their missions took them to strange places, and they had to teach and practice the trades of living as well as preach the Church's message and fight evildoers.

On the one hand, he's my confessor and a very good one who's helped my soul and understands me, and he's a very holy man and a good friend and I love him like an elder brother as well as a man of God, Mathilda thought. *On the other hand, sometimes when he finds a new toy, he's like a little boy with a wind-up horsie on the First Day of Christmas. There was that balloon thing in Boise . . .*

She slipped outside, past a bevy of Norrheimers carrying in bundles of ashwood poles; the tough springy wood was honey-pale, well seasoned and probably originally meant for spearshafts, or pruning hooks or ladders or sleigh-frames or something of that order. Outside it was raw, but she had a good wool jacket with fleece lining. Behind the barn was an open fenced field with a roofed open-sided shed along one side; from the straw, it was usually used to hold steers for fattening. The mud-and-manure surface wasn't too bad, but she wouldn't have chosen the footing for anything difficult. The smell was familiar to anyone who'd spent their life around livestock, hardly noticeable except in concentrated doses.

Rudi was there, next to a row of oak posts seven feet tall and as thick as her thigh, hammered solidly into the earth.

Pells, she thought.

The things you endlessly whacked at when you practiced with the sword, until your shoulder ached and your tight-wrapped wrist shot stripes of pain up your forearm and your hand felt like a wagon had run over it. They were battered and surrounded by chips hammered off them by dulled practice weapons; Bjarni had been using this ground to test the *picked men* flocking in to make up his war band. Artos stood before one of them with the Sword at his right side, held horizontally with that hand on the sheath and the left resting lightly on the hilt, fingers and palm just touching it. He took a deep breath . . .

And drew. There was a shock, a faint glitter of light that really wasn't there, a feeling as if her currently rather grimy skin had been soaked in a sauna and scrubbed with soap made with meadowsweet and the sensation had gone inward to her bones and her very self. It wasn't as strong as it had been when the blade was drawn on a battlefield, and it didn't have the same fierce clean *anger* she'd felt then. This was cooler, more subtle, just as disturbing.

He gripped the long hilt with both hands, the right towards the crystal pommel and the other just below the guard. The blade rose until the point was at throat height; then he spun it and thrust backward without turning, up again and a slice and a slice, his feet moving as if on the sanded planks of a *salle d'armes*. Dancing with the blade in the two-handed *nihon* style, the most graceful of the sword-arts, if not the most practical in a world of strong shields and steel armor. The moves were fast, but so smoothly coordinated with the motion of his whole long body that there was no sense of hurry. Simply a flowing, flickering grace that held a smashing power as well.

It's different, she thought. *He was always like some pagan God of war when he used the blade . . . but he's . . . calmer, somehow? Cooler. Look at his face; the only reason his lips are open is to breathe. It's like a statue. Where are you, Rudi? Where's the boy I knew, the man I love?*

Then he turned and cut again, his whole body and the momentum of his motion behind the blow. A lifetime of her own training rose in an instant's instinctive protest—a battle sword was a precision instrument delicate as a scalpel. You didn't cut at baulks of oak as if it were an ax. A blunted practice weapon was good enough for smacking into a pell; this was almost cruelty—

Thack.

The Sword struck, the follow-through perfect as Rudi's hips twisted, left hand leading on the hilt to press and right pulling it through the cut, knee bending and other leg outstretched. The top three feet of the post's seasoned hardwood toppled away, the slanting surface that remained as smooth as if burnished and waxed. Cut like the rolled reed mats used as ordinary targets to test a blade. Now there was a slight *huff* of breath, and he pivoted and thrust in the same two-handed style, one hand guiding and the other with heel to pommel ramming the longsword's blade forward with all his strength. The point glittered through the wood, then the post's upper half fell away as he withdrew and swept the successor cut in a horizontal slash, turned and struck and struck and struck—

"Rudi!" she said sharply.

He turned to her, and his green-blue eyes were . . . not empty, but full of something. Something great. Not evil; instead her soul recognized it as *terrifyingly* good, but a goodness beyond men's hopes and fears. Beyond comprehension, save as her mother's cats understood Sandra Arminger's love.

"It doesn't chip, the edge doesn't turn or blunt, it doesn't break," he said, eerily calm. "I don't think I *could* break it."

"*Rudi!*" she said again, her voice rising a little.

"Watch," Artos said.

He pulled a long red-gold hair from his head and tossed it into the air. It fell slowly, curling and drifting, bright in the gray gloaming; his wrist presented the Sword so that the edge intercepted it square-on. Despite her concern, she blinked as the hair struck and fell into two pieces that floated apart.

"Like a razor, like *light*, but nothing dulls it."

"Rudi, *come back.*"

He blinked, and a little of himself did come back into his gaze.

"It's so easy," he said, his voice calm but no longer empty. "It's as if I can see what I'm doing from outside myself, and all I have to do is tell my body to do it and step aside."

He looked down the row of hacked, cloven posts and blinked. "And it will do things *as* a sword no sword can do . . . but that is . . . a flattery, an indulgence, I think. So that I can bear it at my side and say to myself, *I carry the Sword forged in the Otherworld*, and the bewilderment and glory of it is as a tale told to a child to reassure him—"

"*Rudi, wake up!*"

He shook his head, the coppery gold of his hair an explosion of color against the dun browns and grays and off-whites of the early-spring landscape behind him.

"I . . . I . . ."

Then he smiled. "Matti!"

She hurdled the fence, the splintery pine of the upper rail gritting beneath her palm, and ran to hug him. He sheathed the weapon before she could, and caught her up. His arms were living steel around her, his body warm and living and *him* again, and he breathed into the hollow of her neck and shoulder.

"Matti, I keep *seeing* things."

"All those things that might be?"

"And . . . and as if I'm seeing beneath that, too. To the essence of the world, all the worlds, and it's . . . it's like *numbers* somehow, mathematics, and I feel, not know but sense, that if only I could make sense of the numbers *I* would be like a God making and shaping worlds by wishing it so, but the thoughts go by in my mind like great creatures rushing through the night and myself beneath their notice . . ."

He shuddered against her, the grip growing almost painful. Then he pushed back a little, looking down into her face, and it struck her that he was a man in his prime now. There was only a shadow left of the boy who'd started out from home, the one with a sparkle in him like a lad going to steal apples from a grumpy neighbor's orchard.

"Oh, Matti, acushla, it is so good to have you here. I could not bear it else," he whispered into her ear.

"I *am* here, Rudi. I always will be."

They stood together for a long moment, and then he straightened and looked at the mutilated posts and a boy gaping openmouthed as he stood with the basket of potatoes he'd been fetching forgotten.

"Well, I could always find work as a woodcutter, I suppose, if this High King job doesn't work out well."

Mathilda snorted laughter. "Let's see what's for dinner. It's growing dark and getting cold."

"Let me guess," he said. "Roast pork. Blood sausage. And red cabbage and potatoes, and rye-and-barley bread and butter. The savor and the delight of it! To tell you the truth, I'm getting a little tired of that menu."

She looked at him and made her eyes go wide, putting on the Norrheimer accent that swallowed the "r" and elongated the "a."

"Ti-aahed of *food*?"

Ten days later Artos stood in a muddy field and spoke his farewells.

Not least to you, my lady, he thought as he bowed his head to the Norrheimer seeress.

"A very wise man told me, Lady Heidhveig, that if I sought to do the will of the Gods and help men upward through the cycles—by which I think he meant what your folk would call achieving the strength that lay within them—it would arouse a legion of enemies against me. But that I would also find friends and wisdom in unexpected places," Artos said.

Heidhveig smiled. "You are not the first wanderer to find it so."

He laid his hand upon the Sword. "This and much else you helped me to, Lady. My thanks, and the thanks of my House and blood for as long as either shall endure."

"My child, you have returned the blessing," the wisewoman replied. "Your deeds here are part of our saga now; our people won a great victory through your warning and your help. And now there is a true King in Norrheim."

Her eyes went blank for an instant with an inwardness he recognized.

The Sight, he thought. *Mother has that look sometimes.* When she spoke there was a distant note to her voice for a moment.

"And that has laid a fate in the Well of Wyrd that will govern the story of the true folk for many lives of men, and in lands that now seem very distant. Yes, one that will touch the very Gods . . . and I think that a certain One had his hand in that. I will pray to my God to keep an Eye on you, though He scarcely needs encouragement from me!"

Her lips quirked in a rueful grin. "And give my greetings to your mother—from one survivor to another—when you reach home at last."

"That I will!" he said, smiling in turn, thinking of how her eyes would light. "Forebye the thought of her happiness when she hears that you still live, and of what you've built here, is another reason to hurry home."

He bowed his head as she reached up to him, and twitched as he felt runes being drawn on his brow.

"*Raidho* . . . and *Elhaz* . . . to ward your journeying. *Sowilo*, that you may follow the sun-road to victory . . . *Ansuz* for Odin's blessing, and at the end of it, *Wunjo* for joy . . ."

The syllables vibrated through him, expanding in layers of meaning as they were amplified by the Sword. Then her dry lips brushed his forehead in the kiss he had been half expecting, and the power she had invoked settled into a hum of protection.

She stepped away, and he saw on her furrowed cheeks the shine of tears.

"Farewell. We shall not meet again in this life."

Well, and weren't his own eyes smarting too? Then he heard Edain calling him. He turned, and when he looked back, Heidhveig had gone.

Spring had arrived in the way it apparently always did here—grudgingly, with little of the lush sweet sense of dreamy unfolding he'd grown up with. The temperature was above freezing while the sun was up; there had been rain only a little mixed with sleet several times. Ahead of them the fields stretched in a mottled pattern of old off-white snow and emerging brown mud showing the fall plowing's clods, a chill silty smell giving notice that Ostara was past and Beltane only a month or so away. Most of the Norrheimers here were the band accompanying their King; they'd made their good-byes earlier. Harberga had done so with a smiling calm, the farewell horn of mead she handed her man steady, but her eyes had been red. A few were here now for a last word, including a girl with hero worship in her doelike eyes who gave Ulfhild a rather clumsily knitted sweater, to the latter's visible embarrassment.

"Enough waiting, the which I hate," he grumbled. "I've a war to fight and a throne to win. Let's *go*."

"We're not really *waiting*. We're getting ready to move fast," Ingolf pointed out. "We'll save the time ten times over."

"I know that," Artos said. "I said I hated it, not that I wouldn't do it, sure."

"The cherries will be blossoming at home," Mathilda said wistfully. "And the apricots, and then the apples. Buds breaking in the vineyards, meadowsweet in the pastures . . ."

That they will, Artos thought. *And the grass bright tender green by now, and the spring lambs butting at the udder, and folk making ready the Beltane bonfires. Ostara the promise, Beltane the fulfillment, the Black Months well past and life running strong like sap in flowers. A time for weddings and beginnings and begettings.*

Grimly: *And the time of war. Another two months, and the Cascade passes will be open enough for armies.*

"*I'm* sorry to miss the rest of the sugaring time," Bjarni said. "It's the best part of the mud season."

Artos nodded, and belched slightly. Breakfast had been endless stacks of pancakes made from buckwheat flour, studded with dried blueberries and slathered with the maple syrup, besides bacon and fried potatoes. Forest loomed in the middle distance, and he could see sledges moving amid the maples. The work of the land didn't wait, and it was doubly urgent here in a land where the world lay so long locked in the Holly King's grip before He yielded to the Oak Lord.

"We couldn't have done the job any faster anyway," Fred said. "They've got good woodworkers here and some fine smiths, but it was complicated and there's very little in the way of machine tools."

Ignatius looked up from checking a frame. "All that we needed were a few rollers to groove wheel attachments."

Fred nodded: "I'm a bit surprised there were even enough stored bicycles; I thought that would be the bottleneck."

Ingolf sucked at a skinned knuckle and grinned. "It was fun to do some hands-on work with machinery again."

"My father and his chiefs salvaged a lot of the cycles,"

Bjarni said. "They're handy enough in summertime, and the parts can be made into a dozen sorts of useful machines for winnowing and grinding and pumping and chopping."

Artos slapped his hands on the shoulders of Fred and Ingolf where they stood beside him. It was an accomplishment, and it was also always a pleasure to see those who really knew what they were doing at a task.

"Good work!" he said. "Very good work, my friends!"

"We had plenty of good *help*," Fred said. "We couldn't really have done it without Father Ignatius, either."

The cleric made a final check of wheel bearing-boxes, waved and went back to his infinitely patient examination and reexamination.

"He's a *real* engineer," Fred said.

"You had the concept, my son," he said without looking up. "And a good deal of the details. After that, it was merely a matter of execution. And I have worked on railroad equipment occasionally since I was a novice. Only permanent types, granted, but this is a logical extrapolation."

The first cart lifted easily in the hands of those who would pedal it. Four bicycles were at the front, locked into a frame of seasoned springy ashwood held together by bolts; a V of saw-blade was held out on two arms in front, to cut light growth. A like set of bicycles made up the rear, divided from the first by the flat load-bearing section. The flanged wheels on the cycles went onto the rusted steel of the rails with a hard *clunk* sound. Then they loaded it; the bed between was a mat of strong resilient wickerwork, and on it they lashed the small tent the men would share, food enough for two weeks, and their camp gear, spare weapons and the rest of their needs. It was far more than they could have carried on their backs, or on a bicycle even on smooth well-tended highways.

The which are rare in this part of the world. The Norrheimers are too few, too scattered and each little garth of them too self-sufficient to spend much time keeping roads repaired; it would be too much labor for too little return.

Fred went forward, and took out his stopwatch. Mary Vogeler bent one ironic eye on his seriousness, but she and her sister responded with disciplined speed when he barked:

"Team One!" he called. "Remember to keep your interval . . . ready . . . go . . . *now*.

"There's a work party at the first break south of here," he called proudly over his shoulder as they pushed the car to trotting speed and he leapt into the saddle, wiping his hands on a cloth. "They'll walk back. After that it's up to us."

Virginia winced. "Going to be *lots* of breaks," she said.

The thought of being held to a single line of rail didn't appeal to her. Fred gave her a pawky look; probably also because she had a true range-country down-the-nose attitude towards work that couldn't be done on horseback, or at least didn't concern livestock or their products. In the Powder River country where her family's ranch had sprawled over scores of thousands of acres, that sort of labor had been done by Change-driven refugees from the towns and their descendants, the people on the bottom of a social order ruled from the saddle.

"Team Two!" he called. "Remember to keep your interval . . . ready . . . go . . . *now*."

Then he nodded. "Yeah, honey, there will. From what the documents Bjarni got us say, this line was about to be abandoned just before the Change anyway! I've been down it and we'll have brush that'll have to be cleared, washouts, blocked culverts . . . Bridges down will be the worst. The thing is that the people in front can go ahead *fast* and start working on them, thirty miles an hour or better. Either to repair it—it's all right to take up rail behind us, after all—or to build a portage track around it, or at worst backtrack a ways and find an alternate route. Then by the time the horse-drawn sections have come up—"

He nodded towards the rail-wagons they'd made, each drawn by three horses hitched in line ahead. *Those* carried the heavy loads, food and cracked oats and barley for fodder and tools, tons of it. Some of them could be rigged to carry wounded or sick men; several were set up as rolling kitchens. On steel rails a horse could pull fifteen tons or better, far more than it could manage even with a sleigh on river-ice.

"—everything will be ready . . . Team Three!" he called, in a louder voice. "Remember to keep your interval . . . ready . . . go . . . *now*."

Then conversationally: "It'll be slow getting around the gaps, but there's a lot more intact rail than gaps; say a hundred to one, from what that preliminary survey indicates. Our *average* speed will be about what we could make on good roads with no breaks and supplies available en route. Call it twenty miles a day, day in and day out. Not too hard on the horses, either, since we'll have good high-energy feed for them, and a portable forge and all. We should hit the Mississippi in say a month, if, ah, Wyrd will have it so."

I trust Fred's judgment, and Ingolf's and Ignatius' even more, Artos thought. *But if they're wrong, we're all likely to starve to death somewhere between here and Lake Michi-*

gan. Or be so long on the road that the war is over and done with before we reach Iowa. There's a lot more to this Kinging it than swinging your own sword, or even the Sword, and I've seen that a good deal of it involves depending on others.

"Why didn't we think of it?" Bjarni Eriksson said; he sounded a little disgusted with himself.

"Sure, and that's obvious: you didn't have any *need* for it," Artos pointed out. "Norrheim's not so large, and you had no neighbors on land to trade with—trade anything but blows and knocks, so to say. What outland trade you have goes by sea or river."

Bjarni nodded. "Still, now that I've seen it, I can see uses for it. Do you use the old rails so often in Montival?"

"Well . . . yes and no. We've kept up long sections of them, and joined more together after the War of the Eye; you can go from south of Ashland to the Okanagan in the north, or from Astoria on the Pacific to Spokane; where freight can't go by water, it uses rail when it can, and pedal-carts are far and away the fastest way to move people or light goods. But we generally switch to foot or bicycle or hoof or wagon wheel when we're in the lands where they *haven't* been kept up. It takes a good deal of work to maintain railroads, so, but far less than *making* those cuttings and tunnels and the like."

"This is a military application, really," Fred said, a little shyly; it was getting easier to forget how young he was, but every now and then you could still tell. "Dad thought it would give us surprise, if we had an offensive campaign . . . you know, for Reunification. We'd be able to move strike forces really fast."

Artos gave him a considering look. "I'm thinking, Fred, that it's odd your father didn't do more of that.

Offensive campaigns, that is. He was strong for reuniting all the old America, and he was an able man and a forceful one, and he certainly put enough effort into *preparing* for such. That army he built is a wonder and no mistake."

"Team Four!" Fred called. "Remember to keep your interval . . . ready . . . go . . . *now*."

Then he looked down at the greasy rag in his hands. "I . . . don't know. I *think* . . . I think the reason was that he didn't want to fight other Americans. Not really, not all-out. Yeah, bandits, Rovers, scum like that, sure. But not whole . . . whole countries like your people, or New Deseret, or, ummm . . ."

He stopped and looked at Mathilda for an instant before glancing away.

"The PPA."

Now, he was going to say even the PPA, sure and he was, Artos thought, nodding helpfully. *Matti's wincing a bit. For the Association was everyone's boogeyman, until we had Corwin and the CUT to concern us. And at that, the Association today is not what it was in Norman's time.*

"I think he really expected to have the others join in freely as soon as he got Idaho really organized. But that took so long, and by then . . . well, by then things had sort of *set* in other places, like concrete going hard. It ate at him, I know, and really disappointed him. And—" He stumbled and went on. "I think that's one reason why so many younger officers were ready to back my broth . . . to back Martin. They'd spent all their lives training for Reunification, and then it looked as if it wasn't going to happen."

Grimly: "Martin doesn't mind fighting anyone. Everyone knew that, too."

Artos nodded sympathetically. Though it wasn't just

that Martin Thurston was coldly ambitious, and ruthless in a way that made him equal even of Mathilda's father. To a man like the elder Thurston it still *was* America. To those born after the Change, or too young to remember much of the old world, it was *natural* to think of those over the next river or mountain range as strangers, the more so if they followed different Gods or customs. And the Gods knew enough strange little enclaves and cults and tribelets had spawned in the last generation, crystallizing around someone with a strong will or vision . . . or just luck, or all three.

Like my own mother, to be sure. Or my blood father. Or Matti's parents.

The young man drew a deep breath. "Well, we're ready for you, sir . . . Your Majesty. Your Majesties, I should say."

Artos looked over his shoulder. Epona was hitched behind one of the horse-drawn wagons on a leading rein, and not looking happy about it, but it would be work enough for the destriers to keep up with nothing on their backs. He strode forward and grabbed the lifting handle on the front right side of the next pedal-cart. Mathilda took the front left; that had the added advantage that each of them had the shield arm facing out. Edain was behind him, and Asgerd beside the bowman. Ignatius, and three of the Southsiders—Tuk and Samul and Rattlebones—were on the rear pair of cycles.

The assemblage thumped down on the rails; the deep rust of a generation already showed a glinting strip where it had been worn away to show the untouched metal. Left to itself a few more generations and this would just be a long mound with a ruddy streak in the soil; already it was far too weak to have borne the huge engines and loads of the ancient world. But it would serve this time; it would serve . . .

Their gear was prepacked, and it was the work of a moment to lash it down. Garbh leapt up and curled to rest on Edain's sleeping bag. The huge half mastiff was a little plumper; even a dog could be a hero of the Battle of the Six Hills, and trade on it for many a rib or titbit.

"I swear that beast looks *smug*," Mathilda said, smiling. "*She's* going to ride at her leisure, most of the way!"

"Team Five!" Fred called. "Remember to keep your interval . . . ready . . . go . . . *now*."

Artos swung into the saddle of the bicycle. "Hup!" he called, letting his left foot bear his weight down on the pedal. Everyone else in the team did likewise. "Hup! Hup!"

Steel grated on steel; one wheel skidded amid Southsider curses not intelligible to anyone who hadn't grown up with their little tribe in the Wild Lands of Illinois. Then the weight of the cart moved forward, slowly at first and then faster and faster. His long legs pushed at the soft steady resisting force. He'd pedaled carts before back home, but this wasn't quite like the streamlined aluminum pods used in most of Montival for fast transport. The wind in his face was colder with the speed of their passage, but not too uncomfortable for any of them, accustomed as they were to hard labor of one type or another outdoors in all weathers.

Behind Mathilda, Asgerd blurted in a tone halfway between shock and exhilaration:

"This is as fast as skiing downhill! Faster than a galloping horse!"

"Not quite." Edain grinned. "Still, it's better than walking, eh? And no more effort."

Better if you're in a hurry, Artos thought. *And to be sure, better than mud!*

There was plenty of that to either side as they covered the stretch of open fields southward; doubtless in a month or so they'd be planted to grain or buckwheat or potatoes or timothy and clover, but right now they looked the sort of glutinous quasi bog that would suck the boots right off your feet or break a horse's heart. Then they flashed into the woods, with dapples of shade running across their faces and blinking brightness in the intervals; it was colder where there was shade, and most of the ground was still snow-covered. Occasionally the framework would shake and sway as they hit a patch where some gravel had washed out below the ties or rails had bent a little in a storm, but mostly their passage was smooth.

The sugaring party they'd seen looked up from emptying buckets of wood or old-time galvanized metal into the tank on a sled, moving their spears or bows to stay in arm's reach as they went from tree to sled and back. A black-and-white dog with them dashed in a circle and barked at Gharbh, who turned her head away in ladylike indifference, and a boy or girl of around seven called from the box of the sled, waving with the hand that didn't hold the reins.

Artos waved back, and Asgerd called a greeting lost in the speed of their passage.

"My family has a fine stretch of sugar-woods," she said. "They're a little east and north of here. Nearer to New Sweden. It's a good farm; my mother's family held it before the land-taking. Good woods for timber and firewood and sugar, good pasture, good land for grain and spuds and flax, and fishing rights on a lake."

"Your mother's?" Edain asked.

"All her kin were killed by outlaw reivers before Erik the Strong came in the first Change Year. My father, Karl, was one of his followers . . . joined him after the Change but far south of here, in a place called New Hampshire where he was a warrior who kept the peace . . . a policeman, that was the word . . . and he helped rescue her. There are six of us children—my brothers, Grettir, he's twenty-four summers and just wed, Hauk and Erik, and me and then Brynhildr, she's fifteen, and little Tóra's ten. Tóra loves sugaring time. When we make candy by dropping the hot syrup from the boiler in the snow."

The words were plain enough, but there was an undertone of longing. Glancing over his shoulder, Artos saw her head turned as well, with wisps of honey-colored hair escaping from her knit cap. Doubtless she was thinking that she might well never see it again, or the land where she'd been raised and had thought to live all her life and her children after her.

"Why didn't you stay?" Edain asked, a little more bluntly than Artos would have phrased it.

"My oath," she said flatly. "You were there when I swore it at the *sumbel*, master-bowman."

Artos faced forward again; Mathilda glanced at him and winked.

Edain shook his head. "You swore to kill ten of the enemy to pay for your man," he said. "Ten followers of the red-robes."

Asgerd Karlsdottir's intended husband had been killed by the Bekwa before the open war started, while he was on a trip to find salvage goods in the dead cities to the northwest; what her people called *going in Viking*.

"And I think you've killed the half score you promised

your God," Edain went on; Asgerd had the three inter-linked upright triangles that were Odin's mark on a pendant around her neck. "Met it or bettered it at the Six-Hill Fight."

"That's not certain," she said bleakly.

It wasn't *absolutely* certain. Often in a pitched battle there was no way of knowing if your blow went home, the more so with arrows; everything was a whirling shifting chaos. But he'd be surprised if it wasn't a moral certainty, given the way the pursuit and merciless slaughter had gone after the Bekwa broke.

"And . . ."

She was silent for a long moment; when she spoke again it was hard to hear beneath the creak and rattle and hum of the pedal-cart. Then softly:

"That's near where Sigurd and I were to make our homestead. I don't care to live where we spent so much time planning our life together."

Louder: "Besides, I made oath to Artos Mikesson too. He's my lord until he releases me, and he hasn't."

"That I have not," Artos said, hiding kindliness under the stern tone.

The rails stretched on ahead, rising and falling, winding through rolling hills and patches of forest that gradually grew larger; now along a small river still mostly frozen, then by a lake with black water showing between chunks of rotting ice. On a straight stretch he could see two teams before them toiling away in front, and a quick look over his shoulder showed five more behind. The woods grew thicker still, until they were traveling through a tunnel, green with pine and spruce or showing the writhing bare branches of hardwoods whose buds were putting out their first faint swelling. The air had an intense cleanliness that you got only at some distance from men's dwellings—no dung or woodsmoke.

"Your folk don't use this part of the country much?" he said.

"No, lord," Asgerd answered. "The farmland's better north and eastward, that's the heart of Norrheim. All the folk in these parts who didn't die in the Change Year moved up to join us. Ayuh, where there were enough people to help defend each other and do the work. And over there"—she pointed westward—"is land that was dedicated to the forest wights by a *godhi* of the old Maine-folk whose blood I share. He was a chieftain hight Baxter. There, nobody lived even before the Change. But the hunting's very good—deer and boar and bear and moose. Wolf and catamount for their skins, and tiger too, but they've only become common these last few years."

"Isn't it a little far to pack out meat?" Edain asked with interest. "Or do you stop to smoke and salt it?"

"We wait for the frost so it'll keep," Asgerd said. "Or even later until first snowfall, when the beasts are still fat but we can sled it back home. Don't you Mackenzies?"

The master-bowman shook his head. "Not near where we live. You can't count on it staying cold there—chilly and wet, to be sure, but not freezing-cold; it'll keep the flesh from spoiling a while, maybe, but not long. Up in the mountains, yes, but it's too dangerous to go there much into snow season; you can get buried fifteen or twenty feet deep in a few hours with no more warning than the first flakes."

He grinned. "The chief and I and Ingolf the Far-Traveler *did* get buried just like that, two years ago less about a fortnight, when we crossed the High Cascades going east."

The smile faded a little. "Just away from home we were, and spring blooming hard around Dun Fairfax down in the valley."

"How did you survive?" she asked.

"Built a quick hut of saplings and pine boughs against an overhang in the cliff face and waited out the storm, telling tales and sleeping," Edain said. "'Twasn't even very cold, once the snow blanket piled up, and we had plenty of food and firewood. And Garbh was warm!"

The dog lifted her broad head at the sound of her name, then laid it back on her paws.

"We had a chimney of bark to keep the air fresh, pushed up through to the surface, d'you see."

She nodded; snow made good insulation, if you had something to keep it away from your skin, and plenty to eat to stoke the inner furnaces. But it could still be deadly in a dozen ways if it trapped you far from home or help.

"And how did you get out afterwards?"

"Tunneled out, then walked over the pass on snow-shoes we'd made while we waited. The snow wasn't near as deep once we were over the crestline; the peaks block the wet winds from the sea however much she blows. Not a comfortable pair of days, but no great danger."

His tone was offhand, which was the most effective type of boasting.

"Well . . . I'm glad to see that your rich warm land hasn't made your folk soft," Asgerd said.

Artos grinned to himself. Every word of what Edain had said was the truth. What his fellow clansman *hadn't* mentioned was that it was Ingolf Vogeler who'd shown them what to do when the storm struck, with a trick from his Wisconsin home; they'd probably have died without him. The Kickapoo country around Readstown in the

Free Republic of Richland was nearly as bleak in winter as Norrheim.

The Clan Mackenzie's territories were not, not down in the valleys where their farms and duns lay and where they spent the Black Months in rain and fog with only occasional brief snow cover. You could pasture stock outside right through most winters, with only about thirty hard night frosts in all. His people dealt with the huge mountain snowfalls of the High Cascade range by simply not going there from Samhain to Beltane, for the most part. His own experience of mountain snows had been limited to downhill skiing at Timberline Lodge, a possession of Mathilda's family on Mt. Hood, with great hearths and well-stocked pantries for stormy days.

I somehow doubt the kilt would have caught on in Norrheim the way it did among us, regardless of fashion!

Despite the mid-forties chill they were all sweating a little after an hour or two. Water bottles made the rounds occasionally, and cold pancakes rolled around jam fillings.

"This is a rest," Artos murmured to Mathilda as Edain and the Norrheimer girl chatted behind him.

"Rest?" she said, wiping a dab of blueberry jam off her chin with her thumb and licking it. "Well, it's not as hard as pushing sleds through snowdrifts on the shores of Superior and wondering if we'd have to eat the horses."

"Rest it is, like a downy bed."

And you beside me in it, he *didn't* add aloud.

That would have been a natural joke among Mackenzies, but not among Associates in mixed company. Instead he went on:

"All we have to do is *pedal*. The future runs ahead on rails, and I don't have to *decide* a single bit of it! The knottiest problem we're to be confronted with the now is whether to heave a log off the track bodily or cut it up first."

She laughed a little, but nodded. "And we're headed *home*," she said with longing.

He nodded. "And . . . the Sword seems quieter. It's whispering to me, rather than talking with an annoying insistence in a language I can't really understand."

Mathilda reached over and touched his shoulder. "Perhaps it does what's, um, necessary. And not more. And it will leave you alone when, when all this is over."

"It's hope you give me, Matti," Artos said. Then he smiled. "But you always did."

CHAPTER TEN

Three days later they camped not far from the abandoned town of Brownville Junction. Bjarni was frankly incredulous:

"Ninety miles in three days! Five hundred men and seventy horses and all their supplies!" he said, shaking his head and looking out over the disorderly array of tents.

They had been hastily erected amid scattered snags of brick and cinder-block ruin overgrown with saplings and brush, equally hastily cleared. The corroded lumps of cars and trucks stood among them, or tangles of wire where telephone and power lines had fallen in some storm or fire. Woodsmoke and cooking smells predominated, with badly washed warrior and horses and their by-products a close second, but water was heating for hasty baths. You didn't want to expose more of yourself wet to the air than you had to, even if it was merely chilly muddy spring and not winter now.

Artos was checking Epona's feet; there was some wear on the Norrheimer horseshoes from the gravel and the railroad ties—they shod with rather soft metal here, hand-hammered from rebar, rather than the harder machine-made types common in Montival. They'd do for a few more days, though, and the hooves and legs were fine, which gave him a gut-deep feeling of relief. He didn't quite know what he'd do if she started to break down when they were so committed to an unrelenting schedule.

Actually, you do know what you'd do, boyo. That's why you're relieved. And she's toughening up again nicely after the winter's rest, but this isn't stressing her so badly as the trip east. So far.

He put her left forehoof down, slapped her neck and watched her mooch off towards the rest of the herd.

"Fred's idea seems to be working"—*so far*—"and that's the truth," Artos agreed.

"You're fortunate and well served in your companions," Bjarni said.

"And *that's* the truth, Bjarni King," he replied, feeling an inner glow. "No man better."

The Norrheimer was thinking hard. "When I come back, I'm going to see what more we can do with railroads. Though I don't see how we could ever make rail once it rusted or wore away, and I don't like to think what it would cost to buy from the English."

"You wouldn't have to," Fred Thurston said. "The old Americans used steel rail because it was easy for them, and because they ran giant engines and cars moving fast as arrows *on* the rails. To support a horse-drawn wagon or a pedal-cart all you need is wood with a metal strip spiked on top. My father had some of that worked up by our engineers in Boise for test purposes. It does just as well and it's a *lot* simpler to make."

Bjarni grunted thoughtfully. "Perhaps I can find

some—what's the word—engineers in Montival. My folk are breeding many strong sons and daughters, and we don't like being crowded. If we did more with rail, we could settle the empty lands around us without losing touch with each other, be close enough to help each other. Going overland is hard—there isn't much good farmland to be had for many miles outside our present boundaries; it's like an island amid the forest. Long distances on foot to more good land, but short *this* way."

Artos grinned and slapped him on the shoulder. "Spoken like a King! Perhaps your saga will say that thought was the beginning of great things, eh?"

Bjarni snorted. "My saga? Is this my tale then, or yours?"

"Now that, my friend, will I think depend entirely on who is doing the singing of it. In Montival, it'll be my epic, and you a friend and ally met on the way and your battles and strivings and loves and hates mere incidents if they're mentioned at all. Material to burnish me, as it were. In Norrheim, the reverse."

"Ah," the Norrheimer said, rubbing at his short red beard; Artos could see him turning the thought over. "And which will be the true tale?"

"The both of them will be entirely true! Or untrue, for if the King *is* the land and the folk, yet his story is really theirs, and bigger than any single man."

"Bigger than a King?" Bjarni asked, grinning at his earnestness, and looking up to exaggerate the difference in their heights.

"Even one with a fancy gewgaw on his head and a fancy chair beneath his arse. The which he must wipe with a wisp of straw just like his subjects if he's not to stink like a midden."

Bjarni laughed. "Too deep for me! See you tomorrow."

"And I'm a minor character in either story," Fred said ruefully.

"Not necessarily, boyo. When you're home in Boise with your family—"

"It's been a long time since I saw Mom and my sisters," the young man said wistfully.

Artos nodded. "Well, *you* will be there, and a man of mark."

Ruler, in fact, if I have anything to do with it. And, I strongly suspect, if Virginia has anything to do with it either, and she will, she will.

Aloud: "I'll be . . . the High King will be . . . far away, for the most part. That's one of the virtues of an *Ard Rí*. Do you see? He leaves most of the songs to be sung about people's own hearths and their own close doings, not seeking to be always before their eyes."

"You've got a point. Sort of like federalism," Fred said.

Or feudalism, Artos thought but did not say. *Still, the two have more than a little in common. And another virtue of an Ard Rí is that he's there at need, should some local lord become too much of a bully.*

They walked on to his own campfires—three, including one for the original companions of his quest and two for the Southsider and Norrheimer retainers he'd sworn—greeting his followers by name. The heads of two deer were set on the ground nearby with the hooves and tails; he made a reverence as he passed.

Thank you for your gift of life, sisters, as he brought his palms together twice before his face and bowed slightly over paired hands. *Go in peace to the Summerlands, and be reborn in joy.*

No more was necessary, since he wasn't the one who'd hunted the animals and didn't need to ask leave of Cernunnos, the Horned Lord of the Beasts; that had been the twins, as they returned from their latest scout ahead.

Fred joined Virginia and they shared a long kiss. Artos sank on his blanket beside the fire and sighed. Mathilda had no objection to kissing . . .

But it's just a trifle *frustrating with nothing to follow but anticipation; that it is. Particularly if I'm to be walking upright the now without frightening the countryside. I think the Lady made women so that it's easier for them to wait, especially those who don't know what they're missing.*

Hastily he pushed the thought away and cocked an eye skyward; there was plenty of gray cloud, but with patches of afternoon sky blue between and not looking like rain just now. An aluminum pot of something thick and brown was bubbling over the low embers of the fire, smelling much better than it would probably taste. Even though hunger made a good relish.

He nodded thanks as Ignatius ladled him out a bowlful and added a couple of bannocks and a lump of hard white cheese. The coarse twists of barley bread were made from flour mixed with baking powder and a little salt, and were palatable enough when fresh—particularly if you had butter, of which they still did a little. The stew-soup-whatever was buckwheat groats with dried onion, dehydrated vegetables and bits and pieces of venison mixed in—lean, stringy venison at this time of year, but meat was meat, and you got the most out of it by cooking it this way.

Artos shoveled down the thick *kasha*-style porridge-soup and enjoyed the feeling of relaxation and the warmth in his middle. Thirty miles wasn't all that far to cover, not when you were cycling on smooth steel. This stretch was the last that had been reconditioned by the Norrheimers while the expedition put together their pedal-carts and rail-wagons. Each day so far had been brief, lest they outrun the capacity of the horses to catch up before nightfall. Even on ordinary roads bicyclists could run horses to death; on rails there was no comparison at all. In the west there were ways around that, but they required skills and machines the Norrheimers couldn't possibly acquire in time.

He settled in and looked around. Mathilda was over at one of the other fires, teaching a couple of the Southsiders their letters. He waved and she returned it, then went back to using a stick of charcoal and pieces of old board from a wrecked building not too far away; more of that had gone under their tents and blankets to keep out the damp. Fred took out a hand abacus and soon was in some deep calculation; he played a game of chess with Virginia at the same time. Edain was methodically checking the fletching on his arrows, fingers delicate on the thread as he bound on another goose feather to replace one that had been disturbed by use; as he worked he sang a song old in his father's family:

"Here's to the bowmen—the yeomen
To the lads of dale and fell;
So we'll drink all together
Drink to the gray-goose feather
To you, and to you, to all hearts that are true
And to our land where the gray goose flew!"

His voice sounded well, though old Sam Aylward's was fit to frighten a rook; singing skillfully was as much a part of being a member of the Clan as shooting with the bow, since Juniper Mackenzie had been a bard by trade before the Change. Asgerd was not far away, knotting her brows over a book that had a man in a mail shirt and conical helmet on the cover, drawing a longbow to the ear—*The Free Companions*, by Donan Coyle, one of Artos-Rudi's childhood favorites and one of three he and the younger Mackenzie had brought with them all across the continent. She absently scratched Garbh's ears as she turned the pages; the wolf-mastiff was lying with her head in the girl's lap, eyes closed and chin thrust forward in bliss. At the last lines of the song she looked up:

"What do you mean by *hearts that are true*, master-bowman? We here call ourselves the true folk."

"True to what?" he asked in turn, holding the arrow point-first to the fire and looking down its length as he gently turned the shaft to check the twist of the feathers that would twirl it in flight.

"True to the Gods—Asatru. True to their kin and their friends, true to their oaths."

"Ah, well, then. The song means much the same thing, perhaps with a little less talking about it. Mind you, it's an English song—me da was born there and his family forever before him, farmers and fighters in a land called Hampshire. But it's widely sung among Mackenzies; we say that a man can lie with his lips, but not with a bow, and if you watch him shoot you'll know his soul more than you would from an hour's talk."

She snorted slightly, looked at the book again, and said quietly: "*More than you would from an hour's talk.* I like that. I like the tale in this book too; the folk are brave and true, and they know how to take joy in life even in hard times. Even if they follow the White Christ and not Thor Redbeard."

"Some of my best friends are Christians," Edain said, and tipped one of them a wink to the side.

"Finish this," Ignatius said gravely, and handed the young man and woman the last of the *kasha*. "Waste is an affront to God. And here is the last of the apple turnovers, only slightly stale."

He turned to Artos. "Perhaps we'd better see to the scout report, Your Majesty."

Artos scoured his bowl, rinsed it out and rose; they strolled over towards the spot where the twins were huddled over their latest map, with Ingolf looking on, but they went roundabout. And stopped by a pile of gear wrapped in burlap; bundles of arrows and little kegs of apple brandy and rounds of hard cheese and boxes of rye flatbread harder still. The warrior-monk chuckled under his breath.

"I'm not even the oldest of our company . . . or Fellowship, as your half sisters would put it. But sometimes those two there make me feel an ancient of days."

"I know what you mean," Artos said, brushing his bright red-blond hair back out of his eyes. "Dancing around each other like grouse in the spring."

He cocked an eye at the cleric. "You approve?"

"They are two fine young people, and I think there is more in their attraction than the body's needs . . . not that there is anything wrong with those, when properly governed. There are many ways of serving God; and most often, we do it by turning to the service of others. Duty to a wife, a husband, a beloved child; the fulfillment of such are reflections of the one great duty our souls owe to Him. If they wed and work together to raise a strong family, then God is glorified indeed."

"Even a pagan family?" Artos teased. "Two varieties of

pagan, at that! Sure, and if you think so well of them, shouldn't you be converting them?"

"I pray for it," Ignatius said, perfectly serious, but also with an ironic note in his narrow black eye. "As I pray for you, Your Majesty. We are all called to tell the glad tidings, but again, not all in the same way. Some are so blessed that they speak with the tongues of men and angels and set a fire in the souls of those that hear them. That is not my gift. I . . . try my poor best . . . to make my life an imitation of Him, and hope that does His work."

"You're not without eloquence yourself, Father. You've strengthened Matti in her faith, that I know, by example and by word both."

The priest smiled, and for a single instant his face seemed as if lit from within. "Thank you, my son. By serving her who will be our Queen in Montival I serve the Queen of Heaven whose knight I am. How could I do otherwise, when she laid that charge on me herself?"

"That One could have bound you to duties far worse than being Matti's guard and guide," Artos observed.

And I pray to the Lord and Lady and to my Luck that your duty as you see it never clashes with mine. For you make an excellent friend and a rare comrade, knight-brother of the Shield of St. Benedict; but you would be a very dangerous foe indeed. And I would very much regret the day I had to kill you.

Ignatius laughed softly. "No, that One could *not* have bound me to a duty that was other than good. But I know what you mean. She has the seeds of greatness in her, our Mathilda; her mother's cleverness, her father's strength of will and ability to dream grandly, but also a sound heart which—frankly—neither of her parents did or do, and a nature that seeks truth and justice strongly, not counting the cost to herself and not forgetting that to others. Nurturing those seeds and seeing them come to their fullness is a task worthy of everything a man can give; or a priest. So does God turn even great evil to lasting good."

He inclined his tonsured head towards a little fire off to one side, where the man who'd been a Major of the Sword of the Prophet sat brooding and staring into the flames, and Dalan the ex–High Seeker whittled industriously at a stick and whistled.

"Even in *those* men there is good; buried, crippled, twisted by the perversions of the Adversary, but there. The Church teaches us that no living man is ever beyond redemption."

"And you've made me think better of your Church, for producing such a man as yourself. My lord Chancellor."

Ignatius shrugged off the compliment, then did an almost comical half step as the rest of it sank in, like a stutter made with the feet.

"That . . . I'm far too young! Other men, wiser and more experienced—"

Artos laughed and shook a finger at him. "Take up your cross, knight-brother of the Order! Yes, I'll have wise older advisors; my mother, and my foster father Sir Nigel, and Matti's mother, and your Abbot-Bishop, and many another. But if I'm to be a young High King in a kingdom younger still, I'll want a young man to help me lay the foundations and shape the timbers. A Changeling, like myself."

"Technically I'm not—"

"Do you remember the old world? Do you, Father?"

A sigh. "Not really. Perhaps a few glimpses, and I am

not sure if they're memories or things I was told often when I was very young." He paused. "Do you really think me capable of filling such a post, Your Majesty?"

"Yes," Artos said crisply. "What you don't yet know, you can learn. We've been in each other's sporrans for two years now, man! I think I know your quality, if I'm any judge of men. And if I'm not, I'm not fit for a throne myself."

The cleric sighed. "When we called you King, you told us, you *warned* us, that you would spare neither yourself nor us. I see you meant it. Not that I had any doubts. I would rather be a simple monk following the Rule of Saint Benedict . . ."

"I know you would," Artos said. "And *I'd* rather stay home and let the world rave as it will. Neither of us will or can do that."

The dark eyes turned shrewd. "And the fact that I am Catholic . . . and a religious . . . and that it is, by now, generally known that I was granted the high honor of a vision of the Blessed Virgin . . ."

"None of those hurt at all, at all," Artos conceded. "Better than half the folk in Montival are Christians, the most of them Catholic ones these days, while only a quarter follow the Old Religion and they're nowhere a majority outside the Clan Mackenzie's lands. Mathilda helps there, of course. But with a witch-boy for a High King, it takes a Queen *and* a Chancellor to balance it, wouldn't you say? And while you're a Catholic, you're *not* from the PPA."

"Quite the contrary," the man from Mt. Angel said.

They both smiled; the fortress-monastery's rulers had been stout opponents of Norman Arminger's ambitions and even more of his schismatic Antipope Leo all through the wars with the Association.

Ignatius put his hands in the wide sleeves of his habit and stared down at the earth for most of a minute; then he straightened, left hand on the hilt of his sword, and met Artos' eyes squarely.

"Your Majesty," he said evenly. "If you insist on laying such a task on me, I will fulfill it to the best of my ability and I will pray that our Lord Jesus Christ and Holy Mary who is my patroness and all the bright company of Saints give me the strength and wit to do so. But . . . Artos King . . . I am already a man under obedience. To my superiors in the Order, to the princes of the Church and His Holiness, and to the Most High. If ever those vows conflict with my duty to follow your wishes, though I love you as a brother and though I honor you as my captain and my High King, I will obey my vows, and God, not you. Let the consequences be what they may."

Took the thought right out of my head, so you did, my friend, Artos thought. Aloud he said:

"The which is just exactly what I expected you to say, Father, and wouldn't it be proof positive of your unfitness if you said anything else? I'm mindful of the example of Henry and Thomas à Beckett, and have no desire to repeat it!"

"So be it." A grin. "And while I am *willing* to wear the martyr's crown, I have no *desire* to do so!"

They shook hands once, firmly, then walked on to the twins. Mary and Ritva looked up at him, made a final notation on the map, and presented it. He looked with interest as they spread the results of their labors before him on crackling paper protected with a thin coat of wax; their labors were done in grease pencil on that. The candlelike smell added to the camp odors.

"Fifteen miles to the first blockage," Mary said, tracing the line that ran west from Brownville Junction towards the old Canadian border. "Not too bad, just a tangle of fallen timber; we should be able to clear it in, oh, two hours. Eight miles after that there's a bad one, a long train left on the rails after the Change; it looks as if it was carrying logs and at some point they burned, which buckled things. Parts of the roadbed there were undercut by water after *that*, and the weight of the whole thing turned over a long section of the track and sort of sank into a mixture of mud and rock. We'll have to set up the winches and drag a lot of wreckage out of the way before we can get the roadbed patched enough. Substitute poles for the wrecked bits of rail, or take up some from behind us."

"We'll do the bit with the fallen logs easy enough, and then all the men can get up to the place with the abandoned train before midafternoon that day," Artos said. "Get a start setting up the winches and pitching camp, clear it the next day, rest the night, start fresh the morning after."

"Beyond that, thirty miles clear to a forest fire and a mudslide; that'll mean clearing burnt logs and digging out mud and rock. I'd say less than a day but more than a couple of hours."

"If it's not too bad the men can have a fair start on it by the time the horses arrive. Might even get it finished soon enough to start the morning after."

"Beyond that, twenty miles to a washed-out bridge. That will mean a portage, and it'll take a full day. At least. We'll have to knock everything down, pack it upstream to a crossing, then back down and onto the rails."

"Doable. The average is working out acceptable, sure and it is. Next?"

"We only went twenty miles beyond the bridge, but no obstacles on that beyond a little brush trimming."

"Man-sign?"

"None that we could be sure of. But if we go much beyond there, we'll be into Bekwa territory."

Ingolf grunted. "After what happened at the Six-Hill Fight, I doubt if any of those tribes are going to get in the way of five hundred Norrheimers. *Or* listen to the Cutters much."

"Unless the survivors are mad for revenge," Artos pointed out. "And they might harass us—arrows in the night, that sort of thing. But I know what you mean. If they didn't lose three of every four men able to carry a spear, it's surprised and astonished I would be. Once we're past the Montreal area . . . Royal Mountain, our hosts call it . . . we'll be into fresh territory. There some of the wild-men may try to bar our way. Still, at need we can cut our way through most savages by sheer weight of men and metal, where we couldn't on our way east. Five hundred spears are a good many, and they're thinly scattered there at best."

"We've been lucky so far, too," Ingolf observed.

He poked at the fire with a stick and stared at the embers, then coughed a little as the wind shifted a gust of smoke his way. His eyes were looking beyond the present.

"Lucky?" Artos said.

"The way this area here is completely clear of people. It's just wilderness, not . . . haunted. I went through to Boston south of here back when I was on my way to Nantucket that first time, and it was a nightmare every step, even with my Villains and all our gear. Not fighting every day, no, but you never knew when the Eaters would try something, try to snatch someone. And you knew they were always watching, waiting, looking for a moment when you let your guard down."

"Does it really matter if you know they're going to eat you after they kill you?" Mary asked curiously.

Ingolf nodded. "Yeah, darling, it does. Feels different, anyway. Every one of my Villains was pretty much a hardcase even before they went into salvage work—"

"Went *in viking*," Artos said.

Ingolf nodded, but his mood didn't lighten: "And I didn't know one of them who wasn't creeped out by it. Even Kaur and Singh, and half the time they didn't care whether they lived or died."

Artos nodded. Much farther south and there would be at least scattered bands of Eaters—the savage descendants of those who'd lived through the Change Year even in the heart of the death-zones of megalopolis. Never very many in any one spot, but there were a great many spots.

Such wild-men were not always irredeemable. The Southsiders had been a band who'd started as near-children in the outskirts of Chicago before drifting to the banks of the Illinois River, and though pathetically ignorant of even the simplest arts they'd been good-hearted. But most Eaters were considerably more vicious than any animal, if only because they were more cunning; their parents had generally made it through the first year by hunting and eating men, that being the easiest source of food and the only one they had skill to catch at first. Being raised by insane cannibal murderers didn't make their children more agreeable and often they were just as crazed themselves.

The Powers have a good deal to answer for, Artos thought.

His hand caressed the pommel of the Sword, and images flitted through his mind. The alternatives to the Change were something They could show him. He shook his head violently, *pushing* the thoughts/visions/knowledge away; there were worse things than the Change, evidently, but he didn't want them paraded always before his innermost eye.

I'm a Changeling. I wasn't hag-ridden by seeing the old world die; hearing about it and coming across the leavings is bad enough. Leave me that, will you!

Ignatius seemed to sense his mood, and returned to practical things, tracing his finger westward: "Then south of Montreal . . . Royal Mountain . . . southwest through the old province of Ontario to the ruins of Windsor-Detroit, then across the base of this peninsula . . ."

"Michigan, they called it," Ingolf said. "That whole part that looks like a thumb. There's some farms and little towns up north. Nothing near those cities but wild-men."

"Then a swing south of Chicago and back north, and we will be in striking distance of your home, Ingolf. By Readstown we'll be out of the Wild Lands, and back to the settled realms."

"Readstown's my *former* home," Ingolf said, and looked over at Mary. They reached out and wove their fingers together for an instant. "I guess home's in Mithrilwood, now, even if I've never been there."

Mary smiled, a remarkably piratical expression with her eye patch.

"For a while!" she said. "I don't want to drive you away! I'm not inclined to hang around Aunt Astrid all my life. That can get a bit tiring. I don't think you'll want to either. I've been thinking—"

Which means we've been thinking, Artos thought. *Ingolf may have wed only the one of them, but he's gotten a conspiracy as well as a bride.*

"—and when the war's over, we could lead some of the

Dúnedain southward, south of Ashland, the way Legolas did from Mirkwood to Ithilien after the War of the Ring. The Westria project will be getting under way, and settling new land they'll need Rangers. More even than in the older parts of Montival. It's beautiful country, from the stories and the pictures, and the first comers will have their pick."

"Redwoods! They say they make Douglas fir seem like *saplings*," Ritva said. "What a place to build a *flet*."

"Sounds like fun," Ingolf said, stretching with a far-away look in his eyes. "I would like to have a homeplace for ourselves, and that's a fact."

"Let's win the war first," Artos said dryly. Then: "But kinship apart, Ingolf, you've been a true right-hand man to me and will be even more in the days to come; and so have you been a strong support, my sisters."

He made a gesture, the Horns with his left hand: "Fate and Fortuna willing, vacant lands will be in my gift, and you won't find me niggard. They say there were fine vineyards in old California. I'll expect many a glass of the best when I come visiting, to play bear with my nieces and nephews before the hearth!"

Ritva cleared her throat. "Ah, Rudi . . . Artos . . . Mary and I were thinking."

Something warned him as he looked up into her turquoise-blue eyes, as innocent as the gaze of heaven. Behind the two women Ingolf held both hands up palms out, waved them a little as if to say *Don't blame me!* and walked away towards the horse herd. There was always something a man could find to do there convincingly. Ignatius seemed to evaporate; he was an exceedingly quiet man, both in his body and in the calmness of his mind, and could do that without fuss or bother.

"Thinking of what?" Artos asked. "Because the last

time I saw you *thinking* with just that expression was when you two put garden slugs in my bed when I visited Stardell Hall in Mithrilwood."

"Oh, Rudi!" Ritva said. "That was years and years ago! And it was just a joke."

"Not to the one whose toes were covered in cold dead slug."

"We'd only just decided to become Rangers. We were just kids then!"

"Says the crone of twenty-one summers," Artos said dryly. "Get to it, please!"

"No, no, this is *serious*."

"Very," Mary added.

"It's about the Sword."

"Ah, is it so?" Artos asked.

He sank back against the stump, hitching up the blanket a bit and laying the scabbard across his knees.

"Well, you see, it's a sword of the far *West*," Mary said, a slight frown knotting her yellow brows. "Isn't it?"

He nodded at the rhetorical question; the compass directions had special significance for the Rangers, since the Histories made goodness proceed into or from the West, rather like an ethical version of water running downhill.

"True," he said cautiously.

"And it's supposed to *defend* the Uttermost West. Which Montival is, because if you go farther west it turns into East, since the Straight Path to Aman the Blessed was closed back in the Second Age at the Fall of Numenor, you see."

"True," he said, his voice even slower. "According to the *Histories* at least."

And everyone's entitled to their own beliefs. Though sometimes not to their own facts.

The other twin took it up—it was easy to see that it was Ritva because she had two eyes, unlike the old days when they'd often tag-teamed him and others. It was still a little disturbing, like listening to someone with a stutter.

"And have you noticed that when you draw it there's this sort of *flame*? At least it *seems* like a flame. And it's going to be the sword of the Kings of the Men of the West, too!"

"So it's the Sword of the Lady, but it's also the Flame of the West, and it would make Aunt Astrid so *happy* if—"

"*NO!*" Artos roared, leaping to his feet, almost entirely Rudi again.

Mary and Ritva bounced erect too, moving back with graceful speed, hands held up in a soothing, placating gesture.

"Now, Rudi, don't be silly. You have to see that it's sort of *fated* that—"

"*I risked my life for this! Men died for this! You are not renaming the Sword of the Lady Andúril Flame of the West and the suggestion itself is enough to warrant a hiding—*"

Artos was very fast. Mary and Ritva were very nearly as fast and fifty pounds lighter per head; they accelerated more quickly, and they were even able to fit their climbing claws from their belts to their hands as they ran, inches ahead of his swatting scabbard. Each picked a tree and leapt, scampering upward like cats a stride ahead of an angry dog.

"Rudi! You're being *unreasonable* again!" Ritva called.

"Ingolf! *Do* something!" Mary shouted.

"What, help him?" Ingolf called over his shoulder. "It's a fucking silly idea, sweetie, and I told you so. Told you he'd be pissed off, too."

Artos stopped, suddenly conscious of how many people were looking at him. Then he began to laugh, tossed the sheathed Sword into the air and caught it by the hilt and pointed the chape on its end at his half sisters.

"It's a bargain I'll be making with you," he said.

"What?" Ritva said suspiciously.

"You agree to never mention this nonsense again."

"We still think . . . well, and what do *you* do?"

"I agree not to whale the stuffing out of you both and throw you in a mudhole."

He was still chuckling when he settled back on his bedroll and watched Mathilda combing her hair; the rhythmic movement was both pleasing and soothing somehow. Garbh lifted her head and growled slightly, but he'd been aware of ex–Major Graber's approach. The man had stayed in the background, helping to look after the little boy living in the shell of the High Seeker and doing his share of camp chores uncomplainingly and skillfully despite being alone and unarmed among those whose feelings towards him ranged from indifference to bone-deep hate. Nobody had dared attack him against Artos' order reinforced by Bjarni's, but it could not have been an easy passage. Now his face had more of its customary granite rigidity than ever.

"My lord," the man from Corwin said. "I am obliged to speak to you."

"You're welcome to, Major Graber," Artos said courteously, laying aside his sword belt wrapped around the scabbard.

Silence still stretched; a muscle twitched on one cheek, and there was sweat across the older man's forehead. "I . . ." he began.

Artos glanced aside to give him space to speak. He cleared his throat and began again.

"I have been reconsidering many things. I must tell you of the conclusion I have reached."

"Yes?" Artos said, meeting his eyes steadily now; he stayed seated to remove any possibility of looming over the man.

"I . . . have been misled. Those in authority over me have distorted the meaning of the Church Universal and Triumphant's teachings. I do not think that they are truly in the service of the Ascended Masters at all."

Rudi sat up cross-legged, conscious that Mathilda's hands had halted their steady movement; Edain was gaping at the man's back, Asgerd was glaring, and Father Ignatius looked back down at the pages of a small breviary with the merest fugitive hint of a smile.

"Yes, I would agree with that, Major Graber," he replied, his voice pleasantly neutral.

This is not a man you can push; he will neither bend nor break, only die. But a rock may move of itself, at times.

"Accordingly, I withdraw my allegiance from them. They have misled me and caused me to mislead others. Many of my men . . . my entire *regiment* . . . died in pursuit of a mission I led them on. I must accept responsibility for this."

"You did as you thought best, given what you believed and as you were raised, in a cause that your men also followed," Rudi said, choosing each word with exquisite care. "A sorrow it is that they died; but that they were brave and steadfast is a good and lovely thing in itself and by itself. And they were both, as I can testify from my own knowledge."

Graber swallowed and looked down. "The responsibility is still mine. And my . . . my country and my family are still mine, and the men of my service, even if they would kill me for an apostate. And there *must* be truth in the teachings of the Church Universal and Triumphant, even if it has been perverted. Therefore I must think more on the best course for me to atone for the sins of which I have been guilty. Thank you."

He turned on his heel and walked towards the small tent he shared with Dalan, the ex-priest of the Corwinite cult.

"Well, well, and three times, *well*," Artos said into the silence that followed. "Sure, and no man is all one thing or all of a piece."

Ignatius nodded. "While we live, there is always the possibility of redemption and atonement."

"I wouldn't trust him as far as I could throw him," Virginia Thurston said with conviction.

"Trust him not to decide he must fight us?" Artos said. "No, that's possible. But I think I'd trust him to do what he thinks right. And after this, I think I could trust him to inform me if that meant to take up arms against me again. That at least."

CHAPTER ELEVEN

COUNTY OF THE EASTERMARK
BARONY OF WALLA-WALLA, NEAR CASTLE WAITSBURG
PORTLAND PROTECTIVE ASSOCIATION
HIGH KINGDOM OF MONTIVAL
(FORMERLY SOUTHEASTERN WASHINGTON STATE)
MARCH 31, CHANGE YEAR 25/2023 AD

"**W**ere they really evil? What lies or threats brought them here to die . . ." she began, looking down at the dead men sprawled beside their dead horses.

You're quoting *again, Astrid!* Eilir signed. *I've been listening to you do that since we were both* fourteen!

"That doesn't make it any less true, soul-sister," Astrid Loring said calmly. "They're not necessarily bad men, even if they are Cutters and from Montana. Good and ill are not one thing in the Third Age and another now."

The identity of the men they'd ambushed was fairly clear from their mixed gear, which was the sort of thing a Rancher's retainers put together from what came to hand, and from the common element: the rayed golden sun of the Church Universal and Triumphant. The younger Dúnedain behind her nodded solemnly; those words *were* from the Histories after all, and apt.

It was the quiet time when sick men died, not-quite-dawn, and the blood of men and horses looked more black than red; chilly enough to make it smoke a little too, though the days were already mild even this far inland. It made an iron undertone to the sweet cool smell of spring and green growth; a few trees beside the roadway had already burst their swelling buds to show a mist of green. A quivering birdcall sounded, and the Rangers on the slope looked sharply southwestward. Another call followed and they relaxed; just afterwards the first clatter of hooves sounded on the old asphalt of the roadway, patched with pounded gravel. A spray of light cavalry went through first, several score local levies riding with arrows nocked on the strings of their recurved saddle bows.

I'll go with them, Eilir signed. *We'll have to coordinate.*

She swung into her saddle and trotted over to the local nobleman leading the horse-archers, who was in three-quarter armor himself; this far east the Association produced its own ranch-style fighters. John Hordle followed—he rode a destrier-bred warmblood even when in light gear, as at present—and a file of a dozen Dúnedain *ohtar*.

Then a heavier drumbeat on the broken, patched asphalt, and a long column of heavy cavalry came up the roadway, the butts of their twelve-foot lances resting on their right stirrup-irons and their kite-shaped blazoned shields across their backs. The riders were knights and men-at-arms in plate cap-a-pie from the sabatons on their feet to the bevoirs that guarded their chins, the metal of their harness bright with the polish and chamois leather and elbow grease of squires and varlets.

They're going to fight, she decided. *The destriers are barded. She* might *have told me in advance, rather than just saying "if circumstances allow."*

The figure at their head reined aside, warhorse looking almost insectile behind the laminated armor; the raised curved visor of the sallet showed a face that was . . .

Not all that different from me, Astrid admitted grudgingly.

They were both around five foot ten, both blond, both in their late thirties, and both moved with a leopard's assurance. The Grand Constable had gray eyes rather than blue, and her face was a little harsher-boned, but otherwise they might have been sisters.

And we've hated each other for what . . . nearly fifteen years now. Since the War of the Eye. Since I killed Katrina Georges, and even worse, since I spared Tiphaine's life, which she'll never really forgive. Even after she saved mine at Pendleton last year . . . which I find rather hard to forgive, may the Valar forgive me.

"My lady Astrid," Tiphaine said; or at least her lips did, in a coolly polite tone that probably disguised something like *you gibbering lunatic*.

She bowed in the saddle with impeccable precision— acknowledgment of Astrid's status as sovereign of an independent realm, albeit not *her* sovereign, as opposed to her own high military rank and middling social status within the Association's nobility.

"My lord Alleyne."

That to Astrid's handfasted husband, with a bow fractionally deeper than that to an equal, since he was a ruler's consort. He replied in kind, with a minuscule lift of one pale eyebrow.

"*Hirilen o Ath,*" Astrid replied, then at the blank look remembered to shift to the Common Tongue and repeat it in English: "My lady d'Ath."

You orc, she added to herself. *No, not an orc. A Black Númenórean? Yes, that would fit. But a* very dangerous *one*.

"Thank you for the report, my lady, my lord," the Grand Constable went on. "Very complete, and very convenient since we're out of heliograph communication with Castle Waitsburg for the moment. I'm glad to hear they haven't deployed caltrops. And you took out their scout network very neatly indeed."

"Thank *you* for being so timely," Alleyne said. "They're going to notice within ten minutes when they don't get a man going back to check in; they're not stupid. I trust all goes well with Lady Delia?"

"My Châtelaine is in excellent health, but pregnant. Again," Tiphaine said, with the slightest hint of a grave wink. "Now let's get to work."

"You're going to try and break the siege?" Alleyne asked. "And not just raid them?"

His smooth voice still held a trace of the officer-class Englishman he'd been before he arrived during the War of the Eye to court and win her; Astrid thought it added a touch of distinction to his Sindarin too. The way some of her folk treated the "r" sounds or butchered the vocalic umlauts . . . but at least the Noble Tongue was being spoken again, here in the Fifth Age of the World. That love of the Histories was what had first brought them together.

Well, that and he looked *so dreamy*, she admitted. *And the charm, and his laugh, and that he's so smart.*

"We're going to try," Tiphaine said. "Break through, destroy the siege works, reinforce and resupply the castle and evacuate the noncombatants at least. Make them commit their field force to reestablish a siege, and tie down more men here. For once I think we've gotten in-side their decision curve; it'll make the—"

"Special mission, yes," Alleyne said crisply. "We've been briefed."

"—disguise for the special mission more convincing if we do them some real damage. A raid with this strong a force would look too much like a demonstration to cover something else unless it had an objective of commensu-rate importance."

They all swung into the saddle and moved forward, like the ghosts of horsemen in the dawn gloaming. The Dúnedain peeled off to the right as the bulk of the men-at-arms deployed; Astrid thought there were probably twenty lances of them—two hundred riders, more or less.

The sun was just beginning to peek over the rolling hills eastward, and it caught at a lancehead here and there, or the colored pennants with the arms of count and baron and knight. As they came over the rise they saw the long gentle slope below running down to the river. The besiegers' camp was there at the bridge, then the occupied ruins of the village, and the castle on the first ridge beyond. It was a rectangle with a tallish square tower in one corner and smaller round ones at the others; a standard design of a type the Protector's labor gangs had built by the dozens in the Association's years of ex-pansion after the Change. This had been the northeastern boundary, until the PPA divided the Palouse with Boise well before the current war started.

Woodsmoke drifted down from it, and the besiegers' camp, a familiar musty-sharp scent on the cool morning air; she even thought she could detect a faint hint of scorched bacon. The castle was probably densely crowded with the villagers who'd fled within the gates when the enemy came. Certainly there were plenty of tiny heads between the distant crenellations.

This is a better use for the place than its original intent.

Which had been to intimidate anyone who objected to having their land handed out willy-nilly by the Lord Protector as fiefs for his newborn lords.

The alarm had just been given down there. The Boisean infantry had been digging like moles; they already had one of their square marching camps within twelve-pounder range of the castle, the Stars and Stripes flying defiantly from a pole topped with a gilded eagle. They'd been digging a trench and barrier all around the castle too, a brown scar against the green of the winter wheat and pasture, but it was incomplete. Now they were swarming out of their orderly rows of tents and from their working parties, falling in with smooth precision outside the southward facing camp gate with its stubby wooden tower above. She took her heavy binoculars out of their lamb's-wool-padded steel case at her saddle bow; they were a treasure and heirloom of her House, a mechanically stabilized Zeiss 20x60 S-type bought by her father a few years before the Change.

And prying them out of Signe was a complete pain. Honestly, she got Larsdalen and all the rest of Dad's stuff, but she's such a clutchfist! Bad as a dwarf. Of course, I got the original editions of the Histories signed by the Great Translator, but still.

The field glasses were cumbrous, requiring both hands and full attention, but worth the trouble: the enemy sprang to within arm's reach instantly and the image stayed centered. The United States—"of Boise" to outsiders, simply "of America" to themselves—equipped its heavy infantry with big curved oval shields, marked by crossed thunderbolts and a spread-winged eagle. Each man wore identical armor of bands and hoops of steel for his torso and shoulders, with mail sleeves and a plate vambrace for the right arm, a complex helmet with hinged cheek-guards and a flare to protect the neck, and a sporran-like spray of metal-shod leather straps covering the groin. Their weapons were a dagger, a short broad-bladed stabbing sword worn high on the right side, and three long javelins, two with cast-iron balls beneath the yard of metal point to add armor-piercing weight to impact.

Each eighty-man platoon was commanded by an officer they called a centurion, with a transverse crest on his helmet, a vine-stock swagger stick and a scarlet cloak. There were four of them; that meant a half battalion, a little over three hundred men if they were at full strength, which they probably weren't. One of the centurions looked back at her through his own binoculars, then over at the Portlanders. He nodded to a signaler beside him, a man with a trumpet and a wolf's head and hide over his helmet and shoulders. A standard-bearer had the old American flag on a pole topped by a gilded hand.

The curled *tubae* brayed, and the first row of Boisean soldiers went down on one knee, their shields overlapping and a spear in each right hand snapping out in a quick uniform bristle. Another call, repeated by the officers' silver whistles, and the ranks behind brought up their shields and cocked a shaft ready to throw. It was hardly like watching individual men move at all; more as if the signals were playing directly on their nerves, like some automatic machine of the ancient world. The formation gave fairly complete protection from arrows, and even heavy horse would often flinch from a line of unbroken points.

The men shouted as they lifted their shields, a unified *hooo—rahhh* sound, deep and guttural. Then a crashing bark of: "USA! USA!"

"They *are* stretched thin," Astrid said with satisfaction, counting them. "I wouldn't start a siege this close to an enemy force without at least twice as many men."

"Nice to know we're not alone in that overextended feeling," Alleyne added dryly. "I've been feeling like too little butter—"

"—scraped thin on too much bread," she completed for him.

"For over a year now," he finished.

He took the heavy binoculars from her for a moment, returned them, and began checking his gear. They were in Dúnedain light armor, open-faced sallet helms, no limb protection except their buff leather boots, and torso protection of fine chain mail made from stainless-steel wire riveted inside a soft green leather tunic.

Behind the Boiseans a scorpion spat from the north wall of their marching fort, throwing a bolt on a long blurred arch towards the castle and warning its garrison not to interfere. Stone and cement spalled away where the pyramid-shaped steel head punched into the wall above the gate. A harsh unmusical *taaank!* sounded at the impact as hard alloy steel deformed where it met the dense mixture of concrete and crushed granite.

"They think they can see the knights off," Alleyne said. "And thanks to our bit of Sentry Removal, they don't know about anything else coming their way."

"If those pikemen ever show up," Astrid said. "But I agree, it was a mistake."

"Reasonable, if aggressive, but perhaps a bit arrogant. I'd be more cautious in his place."

Astrid nodded in quiet satisfaction. She'd dreamed of being a warrior like those of the War of the Ring from her early youth—someone like Éowyn, but less Anglo-Saxony—but before she actually took it up as a trade after the Change she hadn't realized how much craftsmanship there was to it, as opposed to simple derring-do.

And archery and horsemanship and swordplay, but I started those when I was a little girl, when I first read the Histories. The rest of it . . . is more like a combination of chess and tennis, more or less. You are playing against your foeman's mind, when you are in command.

Her brother-in-law Mike Havel had started her education in that, and she'd learned diligently from many instructors over the past generation. Including the people she'd fought.

The Montival light horse spurred down the long slope towards the Boisean troops. Their equivalents came to meet them, and arrows twinkled as they arched in long flat trajectories between the two formations of horse-archers. The Association men-at-arms walked their horses forward at a steady pace, halting just out of practical catapult range of the fort, about three times the distance of a long bowshot. The enemy mounted archers withdrew, with Eilir and John Hordle and their troop chivvying them north and west; they were outnumbered, and anyway had no place on a confined field where armored lancers and heavy infantry might clash, any more than a wasp did between hammer and anvil.

Over the crest of the hill behind Astrid poured a stream of soldiers on bicycles, puffing as they pumped at the pedals in low climbing gear. Their leader was on horseback; he spurred over to the Grand Constable, then stood in his stirrups and waved to his command, about six hundred men. They skidded to a halt, laid their cycles on the kickstands and ran to deploy between the Portlanders and the smaller group of Dúnedain. One carried a red-white-and-blue flag on a tall pole; it streamed out in the cool breeze, showing . . . she blinked.

"Ah, they *did* make it," Astrid said. "And in time, too, for a wonder. Thanks be to the Lord and Lady."

"Hazards of coalition warfare . . . Is that a bloody *teapot* on their flag?" Alleyne asked. "Surrounded by seven stars? I call that cheek!"

Their eyes went immediately to their own banner; the silver tree on black, surmounted by the winged crown of the Sea-Kings and surrounded by seven stars also.

She fought down a stab of irritation, and went on: "It's . . . yes, that's Zillah's banner. One of the Seven Free Cities of the Yakima League. Manwë and Varda alone know why they use a teapot. Wait, wait, there's a famous building there *shaped* like a teapot. Quite an old building, as Men of these later ages count years. Tourists used to come and see it."

"They're rather out of the way there. Doubtless some story behind it originally."

"Yes, they're a little like the Marish beyond the Eastfarthing," she said, running a soothing hand down the silky dapple neck of her horse, Arroach. "Full of odd notions and queer customs. I wouldn't mind paying them a visit after the war. I understand it's very pretty country, and the wine is certainly good."

Astrid watched with interest as the infantry deployed; the Yakima valley's prosperous but rather insular little cities—towns, by the old world's standards—hadn't come in her way much before. Their close-settled, intensively farmed irrigated countryside didn't need the Rangers to

put down bandits or beasts or guard caravans or convey
messages and parcels through dangerous territory, and
they were surrounded on all sides by Portlander fiefs anyway; they'd fought valiantly in the wars against the Association in Norman Arminger's time. The troops were
armored catch-as-catch-can, brigandines mostly, with
mail shirts and some leather jackets sewn with washers;
reasonable for infantry, though a bit old-fashioned except
for the modern turtlelike sallet helms, which were probably recent issue and looked as if they'd been bought *en
masse* from a Portlander arsenal, or someone else who
had pneumatic presses.

*About what you'd expect from a prosperous farmer's mi-
litia.*

The weapons were more standard, sixteen-foot break-
down pikes, glaives, and sword-and-buckler at their
waists. There was a long rattling clatter as the two sections of each long polearm were fitted together in their
metal collars, and then a shout as the pikemen raised
them in unison. Suddenly what had been a collection of
anxious tillers of the soil a long way from home was a
bristling hedge of foot-long steel points each on an ashwood shaft more than twice a tall man's height; the formation was six men deep and ninety wide. A bugle called,
one of the type that high school marching bands had
used before the Change.

"Pike points . . . *down*," Alleyne murmured to himself, reading the notes.

Another shout, and the front four rows of pikes swung
downward; the first two rows held underhand, the third
at chest height, and the fourth overarm at shoulder
height slanting down. That put four rows of overlapping
steel points in front of the formation; the last two rows of

pikemen held theirs upright, ready to step forward if a comrade before them in the file was struck down.

The rest of the Yakimans were armed with glaives or billhooks, six-foot shafts topped with heavy pointed single-edged blades, each with a vicious hook on the reverse side, capable of stabbing or yanking a horseman out of the saddle or a roundhouse chop. They formed up in columns to either side of the rectangle of pikes, making the formation like a thick I shape. The bugle beside the flag at the center blew again, and a quartet of snare drums beat: *rat-tat-tat-tat, rat-tat-tat-tat*. The soldiers began to mark time, marching in place; they counted cadence too, *heep-heep-heep*, but it took half a dozen paces before they were all keeping step.

"Not bad, for amateurs." Alleyne chuckled and stroked a knuckle across his mustache, which was corn-yellow with the first few gray hairs hidden in it.

The long Portlander trumpets—the oliphants, a name she'd always liked—gave a high silvery scream, and the formation of men-at-arms swung behind the Zillah infantry, split into two, and began to deploy on either flank. The pennants on their tall lances flickered and fluttered out as the destriers paced into the wind from the north.

His smile grew a little cruel: "That Boisean commander is going to be a very unhappy fellow; he thought we were digging in to defend Walla-Walla. *And* he'll be wishing he'd had his own men out on overwatch, not the Prophet's."

"We'd have killed them just the same, *bar melindo*," she pointed out. "He wouldn't have known a thing then, either."

"Yes," he drawled, sounding something a little more like *yaaaz*. "But *he* won't believe that. They're none of them very happy with each other in that alliance. Oft evil will—"

"—will evil mar," Astrid said happily, and they grinned at each other.

Eilir and John Hordle came up with their troop. Hordle had his greatsword out, looking like a yardstick in his massive paw; there was blood on it, and on the side of his face and neck.

"Nothing," he said to their questioning looks. "Just an arrowhead grazed me, loik. We got them going in the right direction, and I don't think they'll be back anytime soon."

Eilir leaned over in the saddle to deal with it; Hordle swore mildly as she wiped away the blood with a square of cloth soaked in alcohol, then ripped open a package of glazed paper with her teeth and slapped the adhesive edges of the sterile bandage to the shallow slice-wound on his neck behind the ear, under the tail of his sallet.

"Glad I'm not 'im," he grunted in Sindarin heavily accented with Hampshire yokel, nodding at the Boisean position. "Thanks, luv. You've got it corked."

A final rattle came from behind them as a six-machine battery of catapults came up, and then rocked up to a gallop. The field artillery were Corvallan demi-scorpions, six-pounders on spoked rubber-tired wheels pulled by four strong cobby horses each, the type used by farmers who preferred them to oxen. Each machine had the scowling beaver's-head blazon of that rich city-state painted on its shield in brown on an orange circle; those of the crew not riding on the teams were on mountain bikes. Astrid estimated heights, and her lips moved in a small smile.

"They can shoot over the pikemen with that slope to

help," she said. "And they can get into position to cover the whole ground between them and the earthwork of that marching fort. It's really not a very good position; he should have stayed inside, even before he saw the infantry."

"Boise's commanders still tend to underestimate how dangerous heavy horse are," Alleyne said. "Especially when you can't get out of their way."

Another bugle call and rattle of snare drums from the League's levy, and they began to advance at the quickstep, a hundred and twenty paces to the minute, thirty inches to the pace. The honed edges of the pike heads caught the early sun in a continuous blinking ripple as the shafts flexed to the pounding half trot, glittering as if on wind-ruffled water.

The Boisean commander evidently thought he'd made a mistake too; he looked over his shoulder as the fieldpieces slewed around. Their crews let the bicycles fall and sprang into action; one leading the horses back, two opening and spreading the legs of the trails behind the weapons, another attaching the armored hose to the outlet of the hydraulic jack built into the mount. The remaining four in each set up the pump, a rocker beam with handles on either side. Smoke rose as thick glass globes of napalm were set in the launching troughs and the gunners' mates set their lighters to the wicks of oiled rope wrapped around them. Pale flame ran over the hemp. Faint with distance she heard the shouted orders of the battery commander:

"Elevation thirty—" Hands spun the aiming wheels and the troughs rose. "Ready . . . battery . . . *shoot!*"

Tunnnggg- whack!

Repeated six times, as the throwing arms slammed for-

ward against the rubber-padded steel of the stops, driven
by massive coiled springs taken from the suspensions of
heavy trucks. The globes flew up the elevated launch
troughs and on long arching trajectories, farther than
granite or cast-iron round shot would have carried,
though not as far as finned bolts. The Zillah men stayed
steady, though some helmets turned as they followed the
flight of burning globes overhead, for which she didn't
blame them. Astrid winced at what came next. Two
landed short and cracked on the ground, sending sudden
gouting tendrils of flame towards the Boisean soldiers.

"Brave men," she admitted, as none of the Boiseans
flinched, only hunched a little behind their shields as liquid fire spattered the surfaces. "Very brave men."

*Fire may not kill you more dead than steel, or even be
more painful than a pike point through the kidney, but it's
harder to face somehow.*

"Magnificent discipline," Alleyne said.

"Got brass balls, that lot," Hordle added; all of which
meant much the same thing.

Ouch, Eilir said in Sign.

The next two came down in the middle of the enemy
formation, and shattered on upheld shields. There were
only a few pints of liquid in each missile, but that was
enough to spatter onto half a dozen men and run blazing
under their armor. The stuff clung like glue, too.

Not even the Republic's army had discipline enough
to keep still under *that*; men rolled shrieking on the
ground, until their comrades smothered the flames or
gave them the mercy-stroke. Orderlies ran out through
the gate to drag the wounded back, but the last two of
the balls had slammed into the side members of the gateway itself. It was heavily built, but of green pine timber

without the metal sheathing they would have added if they'd had a bit more time. The edges caught at once.

The battery's pump teams had started swinging their levers madly as soon as the first volley lifted, and in twenty seconds the water had forced the bottle-jack plungers forward against the resistance of the springs, until the trigger mechanisms caught at full cock. Gunners adjusted the aiming screws as hands passed more globes from the limbers and fuses were lit. Then:

Tunnnggg- whack!
Tunnnggg- whack!
Tunnnggg- whack!
Tunnnggg- whack!
Tunnnggg- whack!
Tunnnggg- whack!

Another flight of napalm globes soared over the advancing pikemen; this time all six burst in and around the gateway and threw a savage orange barrier across it. The whole framework of the gate began to burn as well, crackling and sending flame licking up towards the watchtower above.

"*Charge! Zillah forever!*" the commander of the pikemen roared, and pointed his sword forward.

The trumpets screamed, the snare drums sounded a long quick roll, and the pikemen broke into a pounding run behind their leveled weapons, shrieking wordlessly. Even with their tower burning beneath their feet the Boisean crews above the fort's gate fired their two scorpions. Their deeper note sounded beneath the growing white roar of the fire, and two twelve-pound cast-iron shot streaked out at point-blank range. The Zillah commander was running forward beside his city's banner when one of them smacked off his head in a spray of blood and fragments of hair and bone, and threw them and his helmet bounding behind the body that took two more steps and pitched forward. The other struck short, bounced and whipped forward at knee height, and an entire file of pikemen went down screaming as their legs snapped with a crackle like chicken bones in a dog's jaws.

"*Hooo-rah!* USA! USA! *Hooo-rah!*"

The guttural shout sounded again. Three ranks of the Boisean soldiers cocked their six-foot javelins back and then threw in perfect unison. Fifty yards away the charging block of League pikemen had just enough time to hesitate before the missiles slanted down out of the air at them. Pikemen didn't carry shields; they needed both hands for their unwieldy weapons. A hundred and twenty of the throwing-spears punched into their formation; about half of them hit rather than landing in earth or bouncing off pike shafts or glancing away from smooth pieces of metal, and men went down screaming as the hard narrow points punched through armor and flesh. Then another volley, and another.

It was a ragged line of pikes which rammed into the big shields of the Boisean troopers. But the Zillah men were still moving at a flat-out run, either brave enough to keep in mind that the way to get out from under a shower of spears was to close with the enemy as fast as they could, or simply too frenzied to think of anything but killing. The front ranks of the Boiseans snapped out their stabbing-swords and took the pikes on the faces of their shields or knocked them up, or hacked to cut the heads free from the shafts. Men ducked forward, shoving and pushing to get within reach of the Zillah pikemen. At arm's length they would be helpless against the stabbing-swords held underarm for the gutting stroke, but in the meantime men were going down with pike points in the face or throat or belly.

The whole Boisean force rocked backward; and then the Portlander cavalry hammered home on each flank, swinging in at a steady hand gallop like the jaws of a spring trap.

A bellow of *"Haro! Haro, Portland!"* and the lances struck.

Some horses went down at the impact, but far more men, run through shield and armor and body by points with a ton of horse and rider behind them, bowled over or smashed backward. Even then the Boiseans didn't break; men stepped up and flung javelins at close range, or stabbed and hacked at the vulnerable legs. Then the longswords were out, and serrated war-hammers, smashing down as the knights loomed like steel towers over the men on foot. The Boisean formation shrank as their commander ordered men from the interior of it to break back through the burning gate, throwing down their shields to make a temporary bridge through the flames; behind them their comrades stayed and died to buy them time. So did their commander, fallen beside his standard with its gilded hand on top, two lances through his body.

The watching Dúnedain bowed in their saddles, right hand to heart; part salute to the Grand Constable's handling of the little battle, part respect for the enemy's courage.

"Time for us to depart, if we're to meet those Indians," Astrid said.

Alleyne nodded and neck-reined his horse around to the east. "And I don't think anyone down there is going to be paying much attention. Really I don't."

CHAPTER TWELVE

"Now, that is amazing, so it is," Artos said quietly.

He stared up into a clear blue sky where a few small fleecy clouds drifted, and bisecting that view . . .

"The wonder of the world!"

He'd felt awe in his life; never more than on Nantucket, when he'd met something so—

So wholly grand and wholly beyond the grasp of humankind that my mind could not hold it, still cannot, so that I grasp and fumble after memories, memories not gone so much as too big, and I can contain only specks and splinters of them at any one time.

Or watching snow tearing from the peaks of the Three Sisters in a winter storm, or the Pacific thundering into a cliff beneath his feet and making the living rock quiver like some great beast in pain while the spray battered at him with chill salt hands. Or a tiger glimpsed moving like a yellow-and-black spirit of the Wild through the thickets along the Willamette. Awe at the Powers, or at the nature They embodied.

It was a little new to feel it at the works of mortal men like himself. Great buildings were common enough in the still-occupied ancient cities like Portland, so common that usually you didn't bother to notice them beside the modern life below. Or you looked at them as merely mines in the sky, sources of steel and brass and aluminum and glass and copper. There were plenty of that kind off northward to his right, some scorched and leaning drunkenly and others seemingly intact and everything in between, mostly of the usual upended-box profile. The ancients had had awesome powers, but very little in the way of taste, to judge from the things they'd built in the generations just before the Change.

The tower that reared over the travelers here near the edge of the lake wasn't a building, really. It was a narrow spire of concrete shaped like a Y in cross section, tapering inward like a lance or a finned crossbow bolt, but swelling out again to a pod near the top. Above that was a stepped metal spike. Only as they pedaled closer had he been able to get any feeling for the scale of the thing, and that mostly by how slowly it grew despite their speed on the rail. The Norrheimers were subdued by the dead city anyway; there was nothing even remotely as big where they lived, but if you'd seen enough ruins it was nothing extraordinary. The tower, though, was impossible to grasp until you realized that to see much of it from beneath you had to lie on your back.

"It fills the sky," he breathed.

"Nearly two thousand feet high," Ignatius said. "Possibly over two thousand, but I think a little under. One or two hundred feet under."

What I thought, but I thought I was getting it wrong, Artos mused.

He'd deployed the usual way of making a quick-and-dirty estimate of something's height, the one you used with a big tree or a castle tower. Do a rough cut of the distance from the base to where you stood, not difficult if you had something to give you the scale. Then stretch out your arm with the thumb extended and sight over it to the top of the object; with some practice that gave you the angle of elevation between the ground and the peak to within a degree or two. After that it was just a simple little bit of practical trigonometry, the sort anyone got with a warrior's or builder's education.

I just didn't believe it.

"*Surtr!*" Bjarni exclaimed. "Two thousand feet! That's . . . that's . . . three bowshots . . ."

"Two long ones," Edain said, craning his neck. "But *straight up*, d'you see! Can you imagine being up there in a thunderstorm? By the Dagda's dick, man!"

Bjarni signed the Hammer in aversion, and so did several of this folk.

"Can you imagine being up there *right now*?" Mathilda said eagerly. "Think how far you could see on a clear day like this! The Silver Tower at Todenangst would be *nothing* next to this; even a balloon or a glider wouldn't be the same. It would be like a mountain, but a mountain shaped like a needle, all by itself!"

Artos whistled softly as his half sisters cheered her. *That it would. Not like a mountain, not like a glider . . . not even like hang gliding in the Columbia Gorge. Like nothing else in the world.*

He looked around. They'd followed a set of multiple railroad tracks five or six pairs across into the ruins; usually even if one or two tracks were blocked by trains caught at the Change, or rubble slumped across in the twenty-five years since, it was simply a matter of switching the pedal-carts and rail-wagons over to another that was whole and clear. Most of the route inside the lost city was solidly bound in stone and concrete and metal, and still holding against the gnawing of nature. Nature was winning with its infinite patience—they'd just come through a section where water six inches deep ran over the rails—but that victory was delayed here where the hand of the ancients still lay so heavy. Hence there was less of the annoying minor scrub growth that was covering more and more rail as the season advanced.

Northward were broad streets still littered with a scattering of rusting, tattered vehicles, then the ruins proper. He wouldn't go anywhere near *that*; some of the streets had collapsed into the pits and tunnels beneath and were slow-moving swampy rivers now, and there might be dwellers, though they hadn't seen any, or heard drums in the dark either. Southward were elevated roads— freeways, they'd called them—and the tower, and another scattering of ruins in a narrow strip between the railways and the blue of the lake. Which was more like an ocean, since you couldn't see the other side.

Ritva and Mary reported the same all the way out of the vast necropolis to the west, so that the worst they'd have to do would be to set up the winches to topple rolling stock off the rails until it fell out of the way; they'd gotten that down to a science in their weeks on the trail.

"We'll do it," he said. "Those that wish to. The rest can stand guard. You Norrheimers may come back this way, but we of Montival will not, and it's an opportunity we'll never have again. Who's for it?"

Bjarni laughed and shook his head. "I'm a friend of Thor. His mother is Earth." He stamped his feet on the cracked concrete. "I'll bide here. That thing's like the Bifrost Bridge to Asgard, and I'll not walk that as a living man."

The party sorted itself; all his closest companions, and Asgerd, who wouldn't show doubt in front of Edain; he suspected that the bowman might have hesitated if she hadn't already loudly volunteered too. Garbh sat at the command of *stay* but growled dolefully as Rudi and the others walked off.

They took ropes and sledgehammers, pry-bars and bolt-cutters and hacksaws as well as their weapons with them, and a good assortment of torches—their tallow candles were long gone. They needed all of those in the tumbled entryway buildings; three false starts left them feeling discouraged before they found a way in.

Though those statues were worth the trouble, Artos thought; they'd been part of the big domed building next to the tower. *Bronze giants trying to squeeze themselves out of those narrow spaces, like ground meat from a sausage. I wouldn't call them beautiful, like the things Matti's mother collects, but striking? That they were!*

Ignatius stopped with broken glass gritting under his feet when they finally stood at the base of the huge stairway.

"Your Majesty, there is some danger in this," he said quietly. "Can a King take an unnecessary risk, when on his safety depends the welfare of the realm? We *must* get the Sword to Montival. And yourself to bear it."

"No, it's a necessary risk," Artos replied, giving him a quick grin. "Necessary because a King must be a man, and a man is more than a machine that does a task. Sometimes he must do a deed for the deed's own sweet sake.

If I become less than that, I'd be less than a man; and it's a poor King I would be."

Artos lifted his torch, watching the ruddy light of the flames sweep across stalactites of rust and plaster taller than him. Hibernating bats hung like thick fur from the ceiling, a few stirring at the light and noise; the smell of their droppings was thick in the damp musty air, and a littering of their dead sprawled mummified on the floor. Ingolf braced a foot against the wall and the door under his pry-bar squealed back. Artos ducked his head in and looked upward past the stairs; light vanished into a well of night, with wisps of smoke drifting across it.

"Dark and narrow, but it looks pretty dry," he said. "If there's not much water, the steel of the stairway should still bear our weight."

"Wish there were windows," Mathilda grumbled.

"If there were windows, there would have been more water!" Artos said. "Let's be at it. Everyone on the rope, now—through a good sound loop or ring on your harness, people. Be ready to grab hold if one of us falls through."

They joined themselves together, extinguished all but the lead climber's torch and began the ascent, not sprinting but keeping to a slow steady jog, careful to keep four or five feet of distance between each. Even for someone in hard warrior's condition he found his breath coming faster after a while and the thick air tired them all faster; there wasn't anything he did often that used *quite* the same combination of muscles, but he made his thighs into pistons to push against his weight and his gear. Rusty metal squealed and squeaked under their boots. He studied the wall for a while; sections were of heavy-gauge wire mesh, but mostly plastered concrete. Here and there a black trail showed where water *was* finding a way, to seep and freeze and expand and scale at the structure, or rot the steel wire within.

They paused after fifteen minutes. "Excitin' as a tunnel," Virginia said; she was mildly claustrophobic. "Only more work 'cause it's uphill."

"I just had a thought," Artos said. "Eventually this thing will weaken, and in ten years or twenty or fifty or a hundred will fall, so it will. Think of what a sight *that* would be to watch, the fall of a building two thousand feet high!"

"Jesus!" Ingolf swore. "Or Manwë."

Virginia whistled. "Goddamn," she said, pronouncing it *gaaawddaaa-ym*. "Now that would be sumthin' to see."

"Of course," Ritva said sweetly, "it *could* fall right now. Wouldn't that be something to *feel?*"

She snickered at Virginia's scowl; then the rancher's daughter joined in the twins' giggle, hitched at the baldric that supported her quiver, and followed as Artos started up once more. He estimated that it was about three-quarters of an hour from their start before they emerged into the first of the floors in the observation pod, and saw light streaming through windows shattered by storm or frost or the slow decay of their metal frames.

"Careful now!" he said sharply. "Everyone on a safety line, anchored solid to here! The support members and the floor could be much weaker than the tower itself."

To Ingolf: "No bones anywhere, that I've seen. Wouldn't anyone have made a fort of it? None easier to defend."

The former salvager shook his head; he had more experience of the dead cities than any of them.

"Too hard to get water up here," he said. "Nothing to

cook with. And it's conspicuous—show a light here and you'd be seen by anyone for a long way around. Plenty of *really hungry* anyones, for a while, until the city was eaten out and the last ones drifted out into the suburbs where there were rabbits and varmints."

They explored cautiously, until they were close enough to the windows to see out. They *did* come across some bones before then; a woman's, he thought, though it was hard to be sure when they were scattered a bit by birds. The human skeleton curled around a smaller one, certainly a cat's.

"Sedatives," Father Ignatius said, taking up a cylindrical plastic pill bottle from the finger bones.

The same type of container was still used and reused over all the world they knew, for everything from fire splints to spare needles; or even for pills.

"May God have mercy on her," he said soberly, signing the air over the remains. "I do not know if this could be *strictly* construed as suicide. Perhaps . . . but I hope not."

Ritva sniffled a little. "And she brought her cat. That's sad, that's really sad."

Artos shook his head silently. They were looking out over the graves of four or five million who'd died quickly if they were lucky, and more often in slow bewildered fear and agony and dread; the whole ruined city was a tomb, like a thousand others. Yet while the deaths of six billion were a story too hard for a mind to grasp, the death of one and her cat could move folk even a generation later.

We humans are made so, he thought. *We're creatures of the pack, and our packmates or those we can imagine as such are more* real *to our hearts than any number of nameless strangers.*

Then he came to the edge and leaned against the rope;

the windows had slanted outward here, so you could look directly down as well.

"Oh, my," he said after a while. "Oh, my. By flower-faced Blodeuwedd's all-seeing owl!"

It *was* different from a glider or balloon, yet oddly as if he were hovering suspended by a sheer act of will half a mile above the earth. The next surprise was how fair the view was. Water stretched south and east and west, white-ruffled blue beating in light surf on the curving shore, empty of sails but dense with birds nesting on green offshore islands. They rose in skeins like twisting trails of smoke as he watched, and other flights went honking through the air not far away—black-white-gray Canada geese for the most part. The ruins of the skyscrapers formed a huge cross, but soon they gave way to a mantle of green that must have started as tree-lined streets and gardens and now was a burgeoning forest with only occasional snags of brick peeking through; more birds flew raucous through the branches, and he could imagine deer and boar beneath, and rabbit and fox and badger and raccoon. From that wood of oak and maple, fir and spruce and locust, occasional apartment towers reared like monoliths, often more than half overgrown in a shaggy coat of climbing ivy.

Here there was none of the sense of brooding menace that filled the heart down among the buildings, the closed-in sense of hostile eyes always watching, and the awareness of the great dying beneath that. Here you could see how root and branch and leaf and burrowing beast were slowly reclaiming the land, and it gave you a detachment where the lifetimes of men waxed and vanished like morning light on the leaves. The air that blew in through the shattered glass smelled of the silty-wet lake and was otherwise clean.

"Does the Middle Earth of men look thus, from the

halls of the Gods in Asgard?" Asgerd said quietly. "Does the All-father's eye see so, the gaze that roams the Nine Worlds from his high seat?"

She turned to Edain: "I came up here because I was ashamed not to, Edain. Thank you for bringing my heart to it. I'd not want to have missed it."

His arm went around her waist. "It's a sight, and no mistake, eh? Something to tell the grandkids."

They stood looking outward. Ritva and Mary went the circuit of the round observation deck, pointing things out and exclaiming, the liquid trills of excited Sindarin marking their passage. Ingolf stood with his arms crossed.

"So damn *many*," he said in a brooding tone. "Madison, Chicago, Cincinnati, Albany, Boston . . . I've seen dozens of 'em and there's always more."

Father Ignatius meditated for a while, and then pulled a pad out of one of his robe's capacious pockets and began to sketch. Virginia merely blinked, then blinked again; Artos suspected she was trying to fit what she saw into a mind shaped by twenty years of Powder River ranch life, and succeeding only slowly.

"Well, I always thought the old folks mighty foolish when they talked about things before the Change," she said. "Maybe I was . . . sorta wrong about that. If they could do *this* . . ."

Fred nodded slowly. "I think I understand Dad a bit better now. They had this, and they *lost* it. It was all taken away. No wonder he was wild to get it back—get some of it back at least, the big *country* even if he couldn't get the stuff like this."

"But they *left* this!" Asgerd said. "For us to see, and sing of in our sagas."

Then, chanting:

"Yet all is not lost
For memory sinks not
Beneath the mold;
Till the Wyrd of the World
Stands unforgotten
High under Heaven
The hero's name!"

There was another moment of quietness. "And yet they died," Edain said. "And they're gone, almost as if they never were."

Artos shook his head. "They left *us*. We're not the ancients, but we're their children. Children of their seed, children of their dreams."

The dark young man from Idaho spoke:

"Rudi . . . Artos . . . do you think *we* can ever do something as, as magnificent as this? Or are we always going to be living in their shadows, tearing down their wonders and using them to build sheep-pens or hammer into spearheads?"

Artos put his hand to the hilt of the Sword, feeling the blur of possibility like currents beneath the surface of the world.

"No," he said. "We won't do anything like *this*. We'll do *different* things. Things just as grand! And maybe when we've proved we can, we'll get the power to do such as this back as well. Someday, when we're ready."

Mathilda took his free hand. He squeezed hers gratefully, and she said:

"I'm glad we saw this. But I'm glad it's only once. We can't let this sort of thing, umm, intimidate us. We Changelings have a world to make—our *own* world."

There was a murmur of assent, as they looked around at the bones of glory.

"And that's what's important," Artos said. "Important to *us* and our children and theirs after them. It's been an hour. Best we be going."

The nine of them collected their gear. Ignatius paused for a second, ripped out a page from his sketching pad, wrote his name on it and then folded the whole into a winged dart like a hang glider. Then he gave a dexterous flick of the wrist and sent it out the window; the wind took it and snapped it upward. The white fleck shrank into a dot that spun away.

The soldier-monk grinned; when he did you remembered he was still barely thirty, and saw the smallholder's boy who'd walked barefoot down the little dusty lanes below Mt. Angel.

"I used to do that when I was a scholarship student in the abbey's junior secondary school," he said, chuckling ruefully. "Before I decided I had a vocation. Mt. Angel's walls are high enough on its hilltop, though not as high as this. Sister Agatha would crack me over the knuckles with her rosary for wasting paper, and my confessor would set me penances for wasting the labor of those who made it—and made it for a tool of learning, not a boy's game. But I had trouble truly repenting."

His smile grew reminiscent. "One landed five miles away—and I got another switching from my father when he had to pay the man who brought it to us. It was worth it."

"And with that, let's take our leave of this wonder," Artos said.

When they were all in the stairwell he carefully shut

the steel door once more and wedged it against wind and storm with a bit of metal that he drove in with a blow of his heel. It made the door boom like a drum, echoing down the confines of the concrete passage.

"Why?" Ingolf said. "Won't keep the water out forever."

"Very little is forever," Artos replied. "It'll keep it out for a while, and that may mean the tower stands for another year. Which is not such a little thing, eh?"

CHAPTER THIRTEEN

Two more days took them well out of the last of the Toronto suburbs; those were now mostly forest anyway, with the roadways showing as patches of asphalt. Then they were in what had once been rolling farmland towards the center of the peninsula between Lake Erie and Lake Huron, with here and there a long ridge of glacial moraine covered in scattered oaks and beeches.

Twenty-five years after the end of the old world the farmland was forest too, of an odd transitional type that had never existed before in all life's history, for there had never been a time when tens of millions of prime acres were abandoned overnight. You could see where patches of woodlot had been, often on a bit of high ground. There the trees stood tall, massive hardwoods and scattered evergreens towering up a hundred feet or better, hinting at the majesty that would rear here one day if men left it be. Here and there was a smaller clump where a farmhouse had stood, or a line of them along what had been a road or a field boundary. From there waves of saplings had spread outward, fair-sized trees near to where their seeds had first fallen, rippling downward as the distance increased.

There were still open stretches, sometimes grassland where fire or grazing beasts had kept growth down; tangles of vine and ivy and bramble elsewhere; now and then the livid green and dried-reed brown of burgeoning marsh dotted with mallard ducks sticking their rumps in the air as they fed on the tender shoots pushing up from the mud, and grubs and bugs.

"Here," Artos said, signaling the halt.

That branch was broken; it's Ranger-sign. It points past the dead hedge.

It was about an hour past noon, the sky bright blue with some high thin clouds, and warm enough to make just a shirt comfortable when you were working. He swung the plaid back on and pinned it as they used the brakes and then he settled the flat Scots bonnet on his head; the two Mackenzies had switched back to their kilts, and so had the Southsiders, who took immense pride in the imitations of the Clan tartan they'd had made up in Iowa last year. Artos took a horn that hung from the handlebars of his bicycle and blew four long blasts, a blatting *huuuuuu-huuuuuuuu-huuuuuuuuuu-huuuuuuuuuu.*

Then they all jumped off to run a few last paces beside the pedal-cart before they grabbed the carrying handles and lifted it with a grunt and moved in lockstep through dead crackling canes of last year's scrub, hauling it a hundred paces, through a gap in the dead spiny growth of the onetime hedge and towards a section of brick wall that stood up from thick thorny scrub. That would make it the spot from which the practiced routine of pitching camp would start. Dense silence fell, broken mostly by the ticking of insects and birdcall—quarrelsome robins and fox sparrows, black watchful crows, fleeting wood ducks going *wak-wak-wak*. Small white flowers were blooming beneath their boots, trillium and snowdrops, and the new shoots of grass through the brown mat were dotted with yellow dutchman's breeches.

There was a small scrap of blue cloth snagged to the ruin at arm's length above head height, Ranger-sign for *here*. Roses had overgrown the brick, hiding almost all of it from sight in a thick tangle of bushy cane just showing their buds; the rest of the building had fallen into the cellar. The house had burned first, judging from the scorch marks he could see here and there, and from trees beside it that were dead stumps or dead on one side. In the years since, mud had flowed down into it until it was an overgrown depression in the dirt more than a hole, albeit one he wouldn't have chanced walking on if he could avoid it.

Bjarni hopped down from his cart as it pulled in next and walked over to him. "So soon?" he said.

"There's no break on the line for another day's travel beyond this, the twins say," Artos said. "We'll strain the horses if we go any farther today."

"A man can walk farther than he can run, I know, but—"

The Norrheimer lifted his floppy-brimmed leather hat and scratched his hair, which was just the color that showed where one of the bricks had cracked across. He'd taken a bit of the sun in the last few days of warm cloudless weather, and his face was tending that way too.

"It's odd, traveling like this. We're moving so fast, but often we halt so early. I feel guilty somehow!"

"Guilt I leave to Christians," he said, and Mathilda

stuck out her tongue at him. "We can always use more time for weapons training and drill! For now let's get our bows and look around. Take the lay of the land, and maybe get some fresh meat."

Rank had some privileges; that was necessary work, and who was to say they shouldn't be the ones to do it this time? There was an old well near the ruin, a circle of mortared stone with an iron top, and a piston-pump rising out of it. The rotted handle had been replaced with a new one roughly shaped from an ash branch; that would be Mary and Ritva's work as they came through scouting, and from the muddy section under the spout it had been successful. He took the handle and threw his strength against it. The first few up-and-down strokes were reluctant and ancient metal squealed amid falling flakes of rust, but soon water was gushing from the spout. He cupped his left hand under it and sipped. The water was icy-cold on his fingers and very clean, with only a slight iron tang added to the mineral tastes of the glacial sand and gravel far beneath their feet. He dumped another few handfuls over his face and neck, enjoying the feeling of the trickles cutting through sweat and dust.

"That's a stroke of luck," Edain said. "They stopped using these before the Change for some reason in most places, the eejits. Forebye they're the best way of getting good water I know. Or the surest. Even with a mountain brook, you can never tell if there's not a dead sheep rotting in it a few bends upstream waiting to give you the runs."

"My mother has one of these pumps in the kitchen of our house," Asgerd said, slightly boastful. "They had it there before the Change, she said, from her mother's mother's time. Water for the pumping, even in winter, and cold and good on the hottest day."

"Mine has one too," Edain said equably. "We make 'em, in Montival."

Strictly speaking they make them in foundries and machine shops in Corvallis and we Mackenzies buy them, Artos thought. *Though of course we* could *make them; it's just cheaper that way.*

They dumped their canteens and refilled them; the water they'd had was flat-tasting stuff, taken from a slow stream and boiled into harmlessness the day before. It was healthy and wet, and that was all you could say for it, but the well water made drinking a pleasure. From the flow, there would be plenty for their whole party. The next pedal-cart had pulled up; he turned and thrust one arm up with the fingers bunched into a spear, rotated it at the wrist, then made a fist and pulled it down.

Ingolf waved back to show his comprehension of the signals: *It's yours, take over* and *we stop here.* Bjarni beckoned to a Norrheimer and had him take the same message to *his* second in command, Syfrid of the Hrossings.

Then Artos stepped through his unstrung bow, braced the lower tip against his left boot, and flexed down with his thigh as he slid the string into the upper nock with his right hand. The rest did likewise. Edain reached into the plain brown leather sporran he wore—the fancy models with silverwork and fur trim were for special occasions—and rooted around for a lump of beeswax.

"In Norrheim, we teach men not to scratch there in public," Asgerd said. "Or are you bragging?"

"Mackenzie men have more to brag about, by the Dagda's favor which we enjoy," Edain said, and handed the wax to Mathilda.

They all gave their bowstrings a quick rub with it. As

he did, Artos quoted, thickening his accent and adding a Scots roll to the "r's":

"Och, laddie, I dinna ken where y've been . . . but waur 'ere it was, ye won first prize!"

The two Mackenzies laughed, and Mathilda groaned. When the Norrheimers looked puzzled, she gave them the ancient joke. Bjarni bellowed laughter, checking himself with an effort; they were hunting, after all. Asgerd groaned in turn and threw the lump at Edain's head; he caught it with a quick snap and dropped it back in the pouch.

They set out, Artos and Mathilda, Edain and Asgerd and Bjarni, with Garbh quartering ahead of them. All were hard to see in their roughly practical clothing; the green-brown of the Clan's tartan made good camouflage in this lush country too, and the little slivers of dull orange actually helped with that. Their swords hung at their waists, and their fighting-knives and belt-knives, but nobody bothered with armor or helm, or shields beyond the little soup-plate-sized steel bucklers clipped to the scabbards the three from Montival wore.

A space of bluegrass meadow only a little scraggly with brush sloped southward, past the remains of a swing and teeter-totter overgrown by a sprawling clump of lilac and a rotted rope hanging from the branch of an oak with the remains of a big tire lying on the ground beneath it. Then came an overgrown laneway, and after it a long-neglected orchard, grown into a tangle of dead trees, spindly saplings where fruit had fallen, and others run wild. A few of the apple buds were showing the first blossoms, and black-and-white-striped butterflies burst upward from around their feet as they walked. A jay with the long tail of the eastern tribe scolded and then flew away, sounding satisfied with work well done.

"I know the apples, but what are those?" Bjarni asked, pointing to another overgrown field that had been short trees in regular rows.

Edain glanced up from looking at the ground ahead for game-sign.

"Peaches over there. Cherries beyond that I think, and . . . by Brigid of the Sheaf, apricots! I haven't seen any of *those* for a while. Ah, my mother's apricot tarts! With good thick whipped cream."

"I'm beginning to think no woman could rival her, with you," Asgerd said dryly.

"None could, for cooking. But mind you, for dalliance—"

She snorted and made as if to clout him with her bow, then asked wistfully:

"What are apricots like?"

"Like peaches . . . no, you don't know those either, eh? Well, they're about *so* big, and yellow, and the flesh is sweet as honey when they're ripe, and the taste . . . well, how can I describe that?"

"I had some apricot brandy once, that vikings— salvagers—brought back from the dead cities," Bjarni said. He smacked his lips. "Not bad! But the fruit, no, I've never tasted it and can't imagine. That's like color to a blind man, I suppose."

They fell silent and walked quietly amid an intense fresh greenness for a half hour, enjoying stretching a different set of muscles and seeing the countryside without the constant onrush of wind in their faces. Each took in the lay of the land, and they instinctively avoided a marsh-fringed pond where a beaver dam had blocked a stream; they could hear a distant *smack* as one of the builders whacked his flat scaly tail into the water in alarm. Upstream of that to the west and north the creek flowed quietly between low banks over gravel, with yellow marsh marigold and dandelion-like coltsfoot and white-and-yellow bloodroot thick along it in the cool damp shade; a bit higher were shy little purple violets.

Long ago someone had set stepping-stones in the knee-deep water there, and they still ruffled the water aside in little standing waves. Willows dangled their long green tendrils in the flow, and a red-spotted brown trout darted away downstream into deeper water with a flick of fins as Artos looked.

Hmmmm. Would it be worth the time to tickle a few? No, the sorrow of it, however well panfried trout would taste. Not with a battalion to feed.

Edain hissed and pointed with the tip of his longbow as Garbh sniffed and bristled.

"Cat!" he said.

"Cougar?" Asgerd said doubtfully.

Mathilda crouched where the animal had come to the edge of the water to drink and held her open hands over the marks. She wasn't a small woman and her shapely hands were as big as many men's, but the pawprints were obviously wider than the span of her fingers.

"Tiger," she said succinctly. "Male. The pugmarks are square and the toes are thick, see? A big one, too; four hundred pounds or better, I'd say."

"They're more common here than in Norrheim," Bjarni said. "That's the third set of tiger tracks we've spotted and we've not been looking hard."

"And no wonder," Artos said. "Remember that sign we passed—*African Lion Safari Park?*"

"It said *lions.*"

"Yes, but it'd have many another sort as well. I'd say

it was likely the keepers there turned their beasts loose before they died themselves. That happened in many another such place, I know; and Father Ignatius has told me of others his order learned of. Some of the animals were eaten, no doubt, and some couldn't live with the weather here. Some survived to breed, which is why that one was drinking from this stream."

"But the tracks are old," Edain said. "I can't smell him even if Garbh can. Also I can't eat him, or won't unless I get very hungry indeed. I'm not livin' here, nor yet trying to raise stock in his bailiwick, nor yet in need of a tiger-skin coat. So if he'll leave me alone, I'll return the favor, and we can both bless the Lady each in his own way."

"Well said," Bjarni said with a grin.

He's missing home and wife and children, but this is a holiday for him as well, I think, Artos mused. *For a while he needn't be King.*

They scanned farther up the creek; there were signs of everything from raccoon to elk. Edain hopped across from rock to rock to the other bank and trotted up it for a minute before he gave a low call. Artos followed; the brush had been carelessly trampled down over a wide area, twenty or thirty yards, and the banks crumbled into the water.

"Cattle!" Asgerd said; the signs were unmistakable to the country-bred. "Are there herdsmen here? We've seen none."

"Man-sign?" Artos asked Edain.

"No. It's not a tame herd, Chief. The mix is wrong."

A domestic beef herd had far more young animals than one left to itself, and there were other differences.

"Feral cattle," Artos said to the others. "Messy eaters and messier drinkers. They're common in parts of Montival, common enough to be a nuisance."

The girl looked blank. Bjarni nodded. "We don't have them in Norrheim; the winters are too cold, I think. But I've heard that there are many farther south, from those who go there in viking. Swarms of wild cattle and wild pig, almost as many as the deer."

He frowned. "It's strange; the old-world folk died of hunger after the Change, mostly. Hunger and plague. I'd have thought they'd eat every beast before they started on each other."

Artos shrugged. "Every beast they could catch. For all the millions scouring for them, there were always *some* animals of each kind who survived until most of the humans were gone, if only by being out of the way. Cattle will double in numbers every two years, left to themselves."

"Pigs even faster," Bjarni acknowledged. "And the flesh-eaters were slower to build their numbers back, as well. Still it's hard to imagine people so ignorant they'd starve with game still in the woods."

"People before the Change didn't know *anything*, the most of them!" Edain said. "Me da still talks about how they had to be taught like babes when the Clan was starting, and how he and Lady Juniper and the others went scouring for people who knew things, real things, to teach."

"My parents too," Mathilda agreed.

"And mine," Bjarni said. "Erik collected them like treasures on his way north."

Edain went on: "If half what Da says is true, then it's a wonder any of those old folk lived long enough to be there when the Change came and killed them."

The Norrheimers laughed, but Mathilda spoke:

"That's not quite fair. Each of them knew one little

thing about their scientific arts, and they traded the results among themselves, and there were so many that that
was workable."

Artos nodded agreement: "But true it is that the most
of them didn't know the things we think are important . . .
how to farm, or fight with a sword, or hunt by bow and
spear, or butcher a cow, or how to milk one, or how to
make butter or tan leather or shoe a horse or . . . any of
that. The which is why so many people alive today are
those of the few who *did* know those things, or the children and friends and followers of such."

Bjarni had been kneeling by a cowpat to touch and
sniff. "Fresh," he said. "Not more than three hours.
Forty or fifty, I'd say. Quite a big herd, ayuh!"

"Wild cattle like to stay near water," Artos said. "And
they prefer brush and thicket and the edges of things to
either deep woods or open prairie, if they have a choice."

"Like deer or wild pig, then," the Norrheimer said,
storing the knowledge away.

"Very much."

He looked around; there were some big trees ahead of
them, mostly sugar maples, and smooth-barked beeches
with the odd oak and hickory, ash and yellow birch. Beyond that was thicket, and he thought meadowland beyond that; he could see farther through it than would
be possible in summer, when everything was in full leaf.
Above him a cerulean warbler gave the last sweet notes of
its song and fell silent as it took alarm.

Perfect, Artos thought. *They'll run for shelter if they're
spooked.*

"Pick a tree-stand," he said aloud. "You'll want to be
twelve feet up at least. They're dangerous."

"Cattle?" Bjarni snorted. "Swine, yes, but cows?"

"*Wild* cattle. The which I have hunted before, my friend, as you have not. I'd hate to know Harberga was a widow because you underestimated a bull."

"Hmm, right enough. It's surprising there are so many, too."

"You should see how the buffalo herds have grown, out west on the high plains, from the few hundred thousand kept on ranches. Millions is just a word, until you *see* it."

A light grew in the Norrheimer's china-blue eyes that was almost feral in itself. "Ah, buffalo! I've never seen one, of course, but I've seen pictures. That would be a hunt worth making."

"The Lakota take 'em on horseback, and it's just a wee bit exciting."

Mathilda snorted. "As in, they nearly pounded you into a thin red paste," she said. "It's a wonder my hair's not white already! *You jumped on the back of one!*"

"That wasn't the hunt—that was when the Cutters were after me," Artos said lightly.

In truth, he preferred not to remember it too vividly. There were things that made a good story over beer but could still have you wake up in the small hours shaking and sweating a year later.

Instead he went on: "Wind's towards us, that marsh is off to the left, and the woods get thicker off northwest there. This is a good spot."

Edain whistled sharply, then used the tip of his bow to mark a spot where the hooves had trampled leaves and grass into muck.

"Garbh! Take the scent!"

The big dog stuck her muzzle down, black nose quivering, body tense with happy excitement.

"Circle and drive, girl! Circle and drive! Fetch 'em, fetch 'em!"

She shot off through the brush like a bolt from a catapult, leaving only a few limbs and leaves quivering in her wake. Artos looked up; the big beech had a massive fork in its trunk the right distance above his head, and still quite a few of the brown serrated leaves from last year. He threaded through a thicket of root-saplings it was sending out, bent slightly and made a stirrup of his hands; Mathilda took four bouncing steps and leapt. Her right boot landed in his hands, her leg already bent; he straightened and thrust upward, throwing her hundred and fifty-five pounds of woman and gear upward with calculated force. She soared, gripped the sides of the V, and laughed softly.

"That was fun."

"Throwing you about is enjoyable, acushla," he said.

He grinned to see her blush, handed up his bow, and waited an instant until she had herself braced and a hand extended. Then he backed, ran at the tree, leapt, pushed off a knob on the trunk with one foot and landed with their hands clasped between.

"Well, fancy meeting a pretty girl in a beech tree," he murmured into her ear, suddenly acutely conscious of the scent of woman, clean but fairly strong. "Is it a dryad you are, sweet one?"

Mathilda flushed, gave him a quick kiss and sidled away. "We'd better get ready."

"I am ready . . . ouch!"

"Ready for hunting! *That* can wait for the wedding!"

"For the wedding? Even Mackenzies think it uncouth to set to *during* the handfasting—all right, all right!"

They each passed a loop of rope around the trunk behind them and then around their torsos, and hung their quivers on convenient stubs nearby. Artos patted the tree and gave it a silent word of thanks, then set an arrow to his string, a broadhead with four razor-sharp edges slanting back from the point, using his fingers to sort the others in his quiver so that the bodkins were at the rear. The Mackenzie mountain-yew stave he bore was an armor-smashing, man-killing brute that drew well over a hundred pounds, so he was grossly overbowed for the hunt, but that would simply slow him down a little—and he was a fast shooter even by the Clan's standards. Plus wild cattle were big beasts and had a hard grip on life; they could take a good deal of killing.

From here he could see out into the lower growth ahead; the afternoon sunlight was slanting through the trees, and the spring ephemerals were a pleasant scattering of blue and yellow and white and pink through last year's grass. Suddenly he heard a racking howl, mixed with snarls and barks. Garbh was at work, imitating a whole pack of wolves to the best of her ability. Then lowing and bellowing, including a bovine cry of pain that showed she'd gotten her teeth home; and an angry bull roared, a lower sound that carried well and seemed to shake in the bone. After a moment the tall grass and brush in the open space started to toss, and he saw the backs of the first of the herd; he could smell them too, a familiar barnyard scent carried on the wind.

White, he thought, or mostly; some had dark spots. *Big. Charolais by breed, I think, but they've gotten longer in the leg and leaner and they're all horned, many unreasonably lengthy and pointed in that respect. It's ten generations or more for them. Not winter-gaunt, but not fat either. Cows and young beasts mostly.*

No calves to speak of; the cows would drop them later in spring, and no grown bulls he could see, but plenty of younglings one to three years old, which were the ones he wanted. Like most Mackenzies he disliked killing any animal while it was pregnant if he could avoid it, as being possibly blasphemous and almost certainly bad luck, but you could cull males from a herd's numbers without damaging the stock. The first few were moving along at a lumbering trot-walk, looking over their shoulders now and then or facing back for a moment, but as more came into sight they picked up speed, feeding off each other's moods as cattle did. A herd could flee with its most timid member, or charge with the most aggressive.

Last the bull came into sight, all-white, rangy-massive, better than a thousand pounds of irritation with rage and steam pouring off his flanks and head, and a set of horns like forward-pointing scimitars. In front of him Garbh looked like a puppy, but she bounced around making a din with little threatening rushes, her tongue over her long fangs like a taunting scarlet banner. Then he lowered his head and his tail went up and he pawed divots of dark soil out of the ground; Artos grinned as Garbh replied with the play-gesture of her tribe, rump up and forequarters down.

The charge was like thunder and would have smashed any fence to flinders or any man, dog or wolf to bloody rags, but Garbh made a last-second leap, twisting in mid-air to avoid the rake of horns that spanned five feet from tip to tip. She landed nimbly and streaked after the rest of the herd. The bull twisted in his turn with an agility astonishing in an animal so large, and chased her . . . which meant he was running in the direction his charges had been going. *They* thought the bull was running away from the wolves too, and decided that discretion was the better part of valor for heifers and youngsters. In an instant heads were down, tails were up, and fifty-eight sets of hooves were churning. Which in turn meant the bull was disinclined to stop, lest his cows get out of sight. Garbh promptly dropped back around him.

I've met war-chiefs with less sense of tactics than that dog, Artos thought with a wide grin; he felt a familiar bubbling excitement. *This is one of the things the Gods made men for, as they did wolf and lion.*

The pounding of hooves grew into a rumble that shivered up the trunk of the beech and into his legs and backside, and bits of vegetation shot ten feet high as the herd smashed its way through all obstacles. It was a very good thing to be well *above* them. Closer, closer . . .

He threw the weight of arm and shoulder and gut against the stave, drew past the angle of his jaw and shot. The string twanged, and an instant later he could distinctly hear the wet meaty *thwack* as the point struck his target, slanting down from the base of the neck to sink feathers-deep in the body cavity. The big two-year male took three steps and crashed bodily into the trunk of the beech, making Artos lurch and also making him grateful for the safety rope. The animal recoiled backward and collapsed with blood pouring out of nose and mouth. Another shot, and a smaller yearling went down bawling with an arrow lodged in its shoulder-joint and the leg paralyzed. Then they were directly beneath him and he drove one more shaft into a spine at point-blank range, aiming between the shoulder blades to get the heart and lungs even if he didn't cut the nerve-cord.

Matti and the others were shooting as well, and whooping. After that, the survivors were past and spooked even more by the cries of pain and the smell of blood, showing no sign of stopping for miles as they thundered through the water of the creek in a wave of spray and splashing. He slung his quiver over his back again, dropped down lightly and bent his bow three more times, considered close-range mercy shots; you didn't leave an animal in hurt and fear longer than needful, but there was no need to risk taking the point of a horn in your belly or crotch in a last thrashing. The others were attending to the same task; when the beasts were still and throats had been cut, he and Edain each touched a finger to the blood, tapped it between their brows and passed a palm over the dead eyes and their own before they faced west with their hands raised.

Edain recited: "Thank you for your gift of life, brothers, sisters, and know it will not be wasted. Speak well of us to the Guardians of the Western Gate, and go in peace to the bright clover-meads of the Summerlands where no ill comes and all hurts are healed, to be reborn through the Cauldron of Her who is Mother-of-All."

Artos finished the rite:

"Lord Cernunnos, Horned Master of the Beasts, witness that we take of Your bounty from need, not wantonness, knowing that to us also the Hour of the Hunter comes at last. For Earth must be fed, and we but borrow our bodies from Her for a little while."

Mathilda crossed herself and murmured a prayer to St. Hubert, patron of hunters; the Norrheimers invoked Ullr, the *veithi-As*, the God of the hunt and the bow.

Then they set to work, retrieving their arrows and hauling up the twelve carcasses by cords threaded through the hocks between bone and tendon and thrown over convenient branches. It was brute-force work to get the heavy bodies in place, and nearly as much to hoist them up the necessary eight or ten feet, but they were all strong and five pairs of hands on one rope did the job quickly enough. There was no need to break and butcher; there would be help enough from camp for that with tools that included bone saws, but the meat would keep much better if it was thoroughly drained at once. They did do a rough gralloching of one young heifer, for the liver and kidneys and heart—incomparably best when grilled fresh right from the beast, with only a sprinkle of salt.

"That's the hunter's right," Artos said, laughing, stripped to his kilt and with blood to his elbows, tossing the organs onto a bed of broadleaf plantain.

"By olden custom," Bjarni agreed.

Asgerd kindled a small hot fire while they finished the work and washed in the creek, and whittled green sticks. That also gave them plenty of offal for Garbh. She waited anxiously with her nose following the business, but she was far too well-mannered a dog to feed on the kills until given leave.

Crouching with a string of smoking chunks of liver and kidney and heart on his stick, Artos bit into a flavorsome morsel and chewed blissfully, and started in on a second skewer. Then he caught Edain's eye and used his own gaze as a pointer. The younger Mackenzie nodded slightly, gulped, wiped his hands and rose, strolling away with Garbh at heel as if to obey a call of nature.

Artos swallowed a mouthful and called mildly: "Come and join the feast, friend, and introduce yourself. We're all the Mother's children and should share Her bounty."

A clump of blackberry canes not far away shook violently, and there was a choked-off cry and a low growling. Garbh came out, with her huge jaws clamped on the wrist

of a stranger, pulling him along by walking backward—
and perfectly capable of taking off the joint in one bite,
as the captive seemed to realize. Edain followed with an
arrow on his string.

"Nobbut the one, Chief," he said casually. "He hid
well, but not as well as Garbh and I looked."

"Thought so," Bjarni said, taking another pinch of
gray sea salt from his pouch and sprinkling it on his meat.
"Not much of a catch, hey? Not as much meat on his
bones as these cattle!"

Asgerd gave a violent start of surprise when the in-
truder was revealed, and made a nearly successful attempt
to disguise it by coughing as if she'd swallowed some
meat juice wrongly. Mathilda waved her skewer through
the air to cool it and looked the man up and down.

Artos considered their captive as well. He was young,
his beard just a patchy orange-yellow fuzz, straggled dirt-
and-sweat-crusted yellow hair falling to his shoulders,
blue eyes wide with fear. He was about five-eight and lean
but not too hungry-scrawny, his skin marked with a number of thick scars but no open sores or scrofula or scabies.
His pants were patches of hide on a foundation of pre-
Change denim, and his feet were bare and tough and
calloused, but he had a pair of the crudest moccasins
Artos had ever seen tucked into his belt, mere bags of
skin fastened with hide laces. His upper body bore a
sleeveless vest of small animal skins, rabbit and squirrel
predominating, badly cured with piss and brains, from
the smell.

The belt around his waist was braided from thongs of
raw cowhide, fitted to a salvaged buckle, and bore a knife
and a hatchet; a necklace of teeth adorned his chest,
human and wolf or dog and punctuated by two boar's-

tusks. Edain returned his arrow to his quiver, slung his strung bow and drew his dirk. Touching the point of the ten-inch blade to the skin behind the man's ear, he used his other hand to toss the weapons at his belt to the ground before Artos; they were pre-Change salvage too, but well cared for, sharp and shining with grease. The bowman ignored the crude buckler made from some sort of metal pot lid with a handle, which looked as if it had been hammered into a convex shape with a rock. Then he stepped back and picked up a bundle of spears, handing them to his chief.

Three were four-foot javelins balanced for throwing, with heads made from table knives ground down to points. The other was man-high and heavier, made for thrusting; the head looked like it had been fashioned from a strip of steel salvaged from a railing or something of that order, hammered and ground down by simple rubbing on rocks into a double-edged blade the length of Artos' hand from wrist to fingertips. All the heads were secured by butting the tangs into a slot at the top of the ashwood shafts, then binding tightly with a layer of wet rawhide thongs that shrank as it dried to an unbreakable grip. Hoof glue had been poured over the join to set in a resinlike mass and keep the leather bindings tight. The wood was straight, carefully shaped by a knife to give good balance, and rubbed with a little oil of some sort.

Not too bad, Artos thought. *Still, not what I'd use to hunt wild cattle by preference, much less a tiger. I'd say this lad's folk have fewer arts than the Bekwa, but more than my Southside Freedom Fighters did when I encountered them in the Wild Lands of Illinois last year. Whether they were Eaters or no in the dying time, I doubt they are now. Not as a*

matter of course; he looks too healthy, and you can catch
every disease there is by eating human meat.

"That's all his arms," Edain said. "Though if we could
train up his stink, it'd be a weapon of power to match
your Sword, right enough."

Artos nodded; the man had a hard dry smell about
him as if he'd never washed except by accident, and it had
been awakened by the fear-sweat pouring off his face and
flanks. He pointed to the other side of the little fire.

"Sit," he said.

The captive obeyed, or at least squatted on his hams.
Garbh released his wrist, backed three paces, and stood
staring at him, slightly crouched, her yellow-gold wolf
eyes fixed on his throat. Her lips were drawn back over
her long yellow teeth; she was at least the man's weight,
and the mouth in her massive head was broad as his palm.
He glanced at her out of the corners of his eyes and visibly decided to stay very still.

"Here," Artos said. "I'm Artos of the Mackenzies."

He pulled one of the sticks of organ meat from where
it rested over the fire on Y-shaped twigs, sprinkled it with
salt and handed it to the man. Their prisoner relaxed very
slightly as he took it. Then he gobbled with a roynish lack
of concern for manners, juices running down his chin and
dripping onto his chest. When he finished he wiped his
mouth with the back of his hand, licked his fingers to get
the last of the salty liquid, and then smeared his hands
across his vest and belched.

"Dik Tomskid," he said, and jerked a thumb towards
his breast. "Lunnunbunh."

Repetition made the syllables clear: *Dick Tom's kid, of*
the London Bunch.

"This dialect's even thicker than the Southsiders',"

Artos said aside to his companions. "Fortunately we don't have to learn it."

"It's amazing how fast the tongue can change its ways in these little wild-man tribes," Mathilda observed. "The smaller, the worse, it seems. It's only been one generation and I can hardly understand him at all—perhaps they were feral children, too."

"Easier for changes to spread when there are few speakers," Artos guessed.

The captive had been examining them more closely, now that he wasn't in a blind funk and expecting to be put over the fire himself.

"Yuh nuh Bekwa," he said. "Buh godda cuns widt."

"Yes, we have women with us, and indeed we're not Bekwa," Artos said. "We just killed a many of the Bekwa tribes and left them dead on the field."

That took more repetition to get across; Dik's smile showed an intact if discolored set of teeth.

"Yuh fukr dedum!" he said enthusiastically. Then, scowling slightly: "Nuh bunh ettin a-un Lunnunbuhn lan."

No other tribe eats . . . or does he mean hunt? *. . . on London Bunch land,* Artos translated; the Sword seemed to make that easier, though he'd always had a good ear. *Or it might just be* keep off my tribe's territory. *He's a brave man, to tell us so when he's in our power.*

"We go tomorrow," he said. "Go. Keep going. Go far away."

He pointed to himself and his companions, then traversed his arm from the east until it was aimed southwestward, which brought a nod of approval. Then he went on:

"You can have that one," he said, pointing to one of the yearlings hanging a good distance away. "We'll leave the hides of the others, and the horns and bones. Tell your folk that we come in peace, but it would be a very foolish thing to get in our way."

He stood and hefted one of the wild-man's javelins. Then he moved with a sudden skipping half step, and his long arm whipped forward. The captive fell backward to follow the flashing streak that ended with a *thunk* and a quivering hum as the point stood in a tree trunk fifty paces away.

Then Artos nodded to Edain. The Mackenzie wheeled, drew and shot three times in the space as many breaths would take, aiming for the most distant of the beef carcasses. There was a meaty *thwack-thwack-thwack* sound, and the big animal's body twisted and swung under the impact. All the shafts transfixed the beast's chest, all within a space the size of a man's palm. Dik's eyes went wider still, though presumably he'd seen at least part of their hunt. This close you could see how the arrows made nothing of thick flesh and cracked through the heavy bone of the beef ribs.

"Stay!" Edain said to Garbh, and dropped the wild-man's weapons near his feet. "And *you'd* best be going."

The savage snatched up his possessions, but he was careful to keep his movements unthreatening. He sidled over to retrieve his throwing-spear, grunted in surprise as he had to work it back and forth to free it, turned and raised it towards Artos. Then he ducked his head and trotted away to the northward. Edain retrieved his arrows before he and Garbh followed at a leisurely springy trot.

Bjarni finished his second skewer of meat. Then he took out the long single-edge seax-knife he wore horizontally across the small of his back and used it to cut a circle of turf. Artos drowned the coals in a hiss and sputter with the contents of his canteen, then pushed dirt over them with one boot and tamped it down and wet the results. Bjarni dropped the circle of turf in place and walked on it.

"You know," he said thoughtfully as he wiped the patterned steel of his seax on a twist of grass, polished it on his sleeve and sheathed it. "This is good land."

He dug up a handful from the space where he'd taken the grass, squeezed it to show the open, resilient crumb structure, tasted, spat and dusted off his hands.

"Very good land," he said, washing his mouth out with a swig from his water bottle and spitting again. "It tastes sweet. Not too heavy with clay, not too sandy, not sour either; there's plenty of wild clover—that means there's lime in the soil."

Artos signed agreement. "I've not seen much better. Iowa, yes, but this is more varied. I'd still prefer the Willamette country, but this is fine and no dispute. And there's a very great deal of it since we left your homeland."

Bjarni had a hungry look on his face as he considered the disheveled richness around:

"Good wheat and barley land, good for spuds and pasture and hay, and the weather's better than ours. You can see how much further along the spring is, and there are all those fruits we can't grow at all. Good hunting, enough timber, fishing in the big lakes, and we could ship cargo on those too. Plenty of fast-moving rivers for mills and forges. Good land all the way from Royal Mountain to here . . . and beyond, you say?"

"It's hundreds of miles from here to the Midwestern realms," Artos agreed. "The most of them are on the far side of the Mississippi. Nor are they crowded within themselves, and they have empty lands nearer them south of the lakes at need, or downriver. It will likely be a good-ish long time before they come here in strength."

The Norrheimer went on: "The English claim the coast south from the Aetheling's Isle—"

That took a moment to translate; it turned out he meant what the old maps called Prince Edward Island. Artos remembered hearing from his stepfather, Sir Nigel, that it had come through the Change very well, better than most of Montival, without famine or plague. And it had reforged its links with its ancient homeland. England was thinly peopled itself these days, with fewer inhabitants than Iowa; most of the survivors had ridden out the first Change Year on Wight and the other offshore isles. But Greater Britain was growing fast under William the Great, made broad claims, and had the ships to enforce many of them.

"—and the Empire men are rich and have much might. Let them have those lands along the coast I say, and fight the Moors for them; there are many old cities there, but not so much farmland like this, and there's enough salvage here too. That city with the great Bifrost tower alone would yield enough for a dozen generations."

Bjarni's smile grew worthy of Garbh. "And the wild-men here are so few, and so backward. Even more than the Bekwa tribes we beat! No armor, and none who know how to fight in a well-ordered array! Yes, it could be that in my son's great-grandson's time *this* will be the heart of Norrheim."

"The savages are thinly spread, but they're fairly numerous in total," Mathilda said shrewdly. "You're speaking of a *big* stretch of land, Bjarni King. Many times what your people hold now. There are what, seventy or eighty thousand of you? The Bekwa were as many, judging from the host they could raise."

"Not anymore," he said grimly. "And still less when their remnants have finished fighting among themselves; we saw that south of Royal Mountain."

Mathilda spread her hands: "But this land west of Montreal and north of the lake probably has as many again."

"You met some of the Bekwa north and west of here," Bjarni pointed out. "These wild-men are even more backward."

Artos shrugged. "They'll fight for their homes. The Bekwa we met in the North Woods on the Superior shores went around them, not through them, and they didn't try to settle here—though this is much better land for hunters as well as farmers."

The Norrheimer nodded. "A few families on their own wouldn't be safe. It would have to be carefully planned, with a chief and his followers as a core, as well as yeomen, all settled close enough to help each other and overmaster any little bands within reach of them. Starting near Royal Mountain directly west of Norrheim, and then west along the lines of rail and water as our numbers grew, and maybe east down the Great River too. The Bekwa and these other savages would have to flee, north into the pine forests, maybe."

"Lord," Asgerd said.

He looked up at her, startled out of his dream, and she went on, flushing a little but dogged and earnest:

"Don't the old tales say that sometimes the Gods walk among us in disguise, as homeless wanderers, beggars with nothing to bargain with, like that poor gangrel just now? Nerthus does, and Odin too. And they judge us by how we treat them. Also, didn't your father, Erik the Strong, make us one folk out of many, in the land-taking? Not only when he overfell foemen with his might, but by his wise words at the folkmoots as well, and by holding out a helping hand. That's how *my* father won bride and land, as Erik's follower; and my brothers and sisters are part of Norrheim's might now, ready to pay you scot and fight in your levy."

"In numbers is power," Mathilda observed. "Hands and backs to work and fight. Faster to school the ones that are already there rather than just wait for natural increase alone."

"A lot of these are unclean," Bjarni grumbled. "Eaters. Or their parents were . . ."

Then he nodded at Asgerd and quirked a smile.

"But you're no fool, girl; no shrinking flower, either. Yes, that's something to think on too. It would be a seemly deed if some of these could be lifted from being like beasts to a life as true folk, tilling the soil and following the Gods. Their children at least. I'll think on it."

A whistle brought Artos' head up. Edain eeled out of the brush, with Garbh following at heel.

"Our friend Dickie went straight home on his own back trail," the younger clansman said. "Didn't stop and didn't cast to either side. I saw some other man-tracks, but nothing very fresh."

"We'll warn the watch we set, but I don't think they'll be paying us a visit," Artos said.

They started back towards camp; walking directly it was only a half hour, and nothing would interfere too badly with the strung-up carcasses in the time it took for a working party to reach them. Eleven slaughter-cattle

would yield enough to give everyone several good meals
of fresh meat and they could finish it before it went bad.
Beef would be a welcome change, and it would help con-
serve their supplies. He noticed that some of the wild
plant foods were coming on now; nettles, Jerusalem arti-
chokes, wild leeks and some of the other spring greens he
recognized. Those would be welcome, and healthful—
and would help with constipation, which was always a
problem when you were living mostly off trail foods.

"The Histories of the Dúnedain talk a good deal about
food," he said aside to Mathilda. "Which is more than
many of the old tales do; the *Táin*, for example, save for
royal feasts. There are fights over the hero's portion, but
never any binding of the bowels."

She laughed, but briefly. He watched her brown brows
knot in thought.

"Yes?" he prompted gently.

"I was thinking of all the things we've done on this
trip," she said. "And . . . and the consequences, even the
ones we haven't thought of. The way our friend Bjarni
was talking, for example. Would he have had any of these
ideas if we hadn't met him and brought him on this trip
with us? And that may affect the lives of whole kingdoms,
for generations into the future."

"He might not have had the same thoughts; but then
again, he might. And—"

He set his hand on the Sword. "—I can see what
comes of them."

Vision flickered. For a moment he saw the wilderness,
but *overlaid*. This pathway was a rutted dirt road, flanked
by poplars and oaks. A girl in Norrheimer garb was walking along holding up the ends of her apron to make a
pouch full of berries, laughing with a youth who had a

bow across his shoulder, a brace of ducks dangling from his free hand and a dog grinning-panting at his heel. A brown plowed field stood behind them, and beyond it a building whose rafter ends were carved into the heads of dragons and gilded, and beyond that, tall forest. Another, and men in nose-guarded helms and mail byrnies tramped down the road; another—

She looked a little alarmed, and he shook his head to clear it.

"Nothing overpowering. I was granted the Sword for a purpose, and Bjarni's dreams bear on that only indirectly. A . . . blurred vision, as if I was seeing many might-be futures. In the most of them, steadings built of logs and broad tilled fields here, folk at work, and mead-halls and hof-temples such as we saw in Norrheim. Bjarni thinks to some purpose, it seems."

"He thinks like a King," Mathilda said. "Looking ahead, to find his people land and homes and food, and to make them strong against any enemy."

"True. But I don't think it's anything we need account to the Guardians for. It's like throwing a stone into a pond; the ripples spread as they may, and no one can tell beforehand just how they will. That there *will* be ripples, yes, but the only way to avoid that is not to act at all."

She tilted her head to one side. "I'm glad the locals haven't attacked us. The way it was going east, it seemed we couldn't step behind a tree for a call of nature without an ambush or an affray or a fight or something."

Artos nodded, and his hand closed on the pommel of the Sword. Crystal light seemed to seep through his flesh; was he imagining that, or the warmth?

"I think it's this, acushla. The Sword of the Lady. The enemy can't *see* us anymore, it comes to me. Not with eyes beyond the ones in their head, for Her hand is over us."

"They *could* see us? Before?"

That was almost a squeak.

"I suspected it, and now I'm certain. How else could they have dogged our steps so closely, again and again, through so many miles of wilderness? Even when we broke contact for weeks, there they'd turn up, like a debt collector from a Corvallis bank. But now . . . now we're on more equal ground."

"Good!"

They came back to the camp to the sound of raised voices. A crowd of onlookers was grinning and hooting; then the circle burst apart in two directions. In one a massively built Norrheimer stiff-armed his way through; that might have led to dangerous offense, except that the victims were laughing even after two of them fell on their backsides.

"Hrolf Homersson," Artos mused to himself. "Ritva's lover of the moment—"

On the other side there was a more flamboyant exit as someone vaulted onto a man's shoulders in a handstand and back-flipped back to the ground, twisting in the air as she did so. The indignant bob of the blond fighting braid was unmistakable as she stalked away. Edain and Asgerd chuckled with the innocent cruelty of happy youth.

"Hrolf on one side, Ritva on the other," Mathilda added. "Of the *previous* moment, I'd say!"

Bjarni strode forward, his broad-brimmed leather hat thrust back on his head; most of the crowd were men of his tribe, the Bjornings, but with a scatter from all the Norrheimer contingents.

"All right!" he shouted. "Is this a collection of picked fighting men, or a clutch of gossips at a quilting bee? Syfrid, can't you keep them working? In the days of the sagas, men so idle would be thought useless as anything but a sacrifice to the High One! I need a working party to collect our dinners, which will be roast beef and ribs and better than you wastrels deserve—you, you, you— each pick four more, and take as many horses. The rest of you, get your weapons and muster by your standards!"

Ingolf walked over to Artos and Mathilda and shrugged. "They had a fight. I thought it was better to let them have it out, since it was personal, but it sort of escalated. Short of throwing a bucket of water over them . . . well, she's my sister-in-law but your sister . . ."

"Ah, you've the right of it. Sooner shove your hand into a hornet's nest. What started it?"

"I'm not sure, but I think it was a rabbit."

"A rabbit?"

"Mary and Ritva got back from their scout, and they were pretty tired. Hrolf had just shot a rabbit, and he walked up and suggested that Ritva cook it for their dinner."

"Ouch," Mathilda said.

"Yeah. Then Ritva suggested he cook it himself since he'd been sitting on his ass all day pedaling while she did the real work. Apparently he'd heard that bit in those books where what's-his-name does up the rabbit with herbs."

"Sam," Edain said. "I always did like him best, of all the folk in those stories. Sensible lad. Me da thought so too."

Ingolf nodded, more as a placeholder than anything else, and went on:

"And Hrolf thought it was a big joke to quote that and say she ought to be able to do it just as well."

Artos winced. "And her response?"

"She suggested he cook it himself using his dick for a roasting-spit and then shove it up his ass with chili peppers on it—she said it in Sindarin first and then translated for him—and I'm afraid I laughed. Because in that language—"

"To say, *roast it on your man-spear with chilies and ram it up your back-hole* sounds . . . indescribable, so it does."

"Yah hey. Then *Hrolf* laughed, and things went downhill from there. They didn't actually draw on each other, but I don't think it was just a tiff."

Mathilda laughed herself. "And *you* can smooth down the ruffled feathers in your war band, my love. But I think you'd better be solemn, for she's not going to be seeing the humor of it all. That's how I'd guess, at least."

Artos sighed. "Ah, a joyful and heady thing it is, to be leader."

CHAPTER FOURTEEN

"**M**aybe it would have been better to go north and through the Dominions," Red Leaf whispered. "I need to get home soonest, but . . ."

"That would mean crossing the Canadian Rockies," Astrid pointed out, equally quietly. "At this time of year, very risky. They're much, much higher. Also colder, and not fond of men, like Caradhras."

He grunted, as if to say *And this* isn't *a risk?*

The eight Dúnedain and the two Sioux all sat quietly after that, gnawing on strips of jerky that tasted like salty wood. They didn't dare light a fire, and the steep lodge-pole pine forest was still and cold, quiet save for the scolding of a few jays; they were far inland now, over the old Idaho border north of the Salmon River and several thousand feet up. She shivered a little, as much with exhaustion as the chill; not far away their horses stood with their heads drooping. Still, it was a day when the sky was aching-blue above, and the thin air was full of the awakening scent of the pines. She pulled the air into her lungs and let it out slowly, over and over, until her spirit expanded to fill the high forest.

A warbling call from above and her head came up, swift but not jerky. Then another and she relaxed, coming to her feet and dusting pine-duff off the slightly damp seat of her soft leather trousers. The sentry slid down with no more than a few fragments of bark coming with him, his blurred outline shaggy in his war-cloak and gauze face-mask.

"*Man cennich?*" she said softly: "What did you see?"

"No sign," the young man said, nodding westward to where the slope fell away into a river valley. "They've lost us or they're better at hiding than we are at finding, Lady."

Astrid exhaled, hiding her relief. *I'm not even really sure they* were *following us,* she thought. *But that's two days.*

"Let's go, then," she said.

Then she turned eastward and moved her hands in the broad gestures of battle-sign: *Hold in place; await our return for the next three days maximum.* They'd need a clear path of retreat across the river, just in case, which was why Eilir and John Hordle were back there with the other half of the party.

It took a minute or two to collect everyone quietly; the Ranger band was spread over several acres of the hillside, for better concealment. While they did she consulted her map and compass, just to be sure. One of the things she'd learned long ago in the early years of the Rangers was how disconcertingly easy it was to simply get irretrievably *lost* in country you weren't thoroughly familiar with and end up going in circles. Particularly in un-roaded wilderness without man-made landmarks.

I'm happy Alleyne is ahead of us breaking trail.

Now they went in a widely spaced single file; her, then the Indians with her Rangers bringing up the rear and last a horse dragging a bundle of brush—which wouldn't hide their tracks completely but would make them much harder to read in detail. The two Sioux were nearly as quiet as her folk; forested mountains weren't their native range, but they weren't altogether unfamiliar with them either. The sun crept upward and the day warmed, enough to make her sweat a little under the leather-covered mail shirt she was wearing besides her travel gear. They rode and walked in about equal increments; that was good practice anyway, and the terrain made it impossible to do anything else.

The Ranger-sign Alleyne had left was faint, easy to miss if you didn't concentrate even when you'd helped invent it.

The Histories are frustratingly vague there. Runes, yes, like Weathertop, but that's not really very specific. Oh, well, it was long Ages ago. We're lucky so much was preserved.

A rough triangle of twigs, a scuff-mark, a broken weed, all things that could have happened naturally. At one point they guided her down to a rocky stream; they led their horses through it for half an hour. That wading was hard on the hooves and human feet inside the greased, waxed leather of boots, but the risk was worth it to break the trail so conveniently. When they were about to lead the animals back up the bank and check for loose horseshoes and change into dry socks themselves the horses grew restive and someone said quietly:

"Brôg!"

A bear it was, an adolescent male grizzly too young to be very massive yet but already near its full length, and thin with spring. For a moment it looked at the equally surprised humans, black nose wrinkling as it took in the scents of man and horse and metal, and then it reared up to its seven-foot height as if to say:

I'm dangerous, so take no liberties!

Grizzlies ate plant food as much as anything—this one had been nipping at green spring shoots—but they were more than ready to kill for meat when they could get it. She put her hand to Arroach's nose as the animal swung its head up in a startled gesture. Six of the Rangers brought their bows to half draw and two leveled spears in a moment of stillness that stretched. Then the bear decided to move aside, lumbering up with a crackle through the stiff vines and saplings at the edge of the creek. It wasn't afraid, nor moving fast, just reasonably cautious, which struck her as an eminently sensible attitude in a chance encounter. She'd hunted bear, but never without careful preparations.

"Go in peace today, Brother Bear," Astrid murmured.

"Yeah, heel and toe it, namesake," Rick Three Bears said in relief.

His hand was tight on the bridle of his nervous mount. If the big bruin had turned ugly they would certainly have lost horses before they could have taken it down, and probably warriors as well, since they were not in a position to dodge. Grizzlies took a good deal of killing.

Then the slopes gentled as they descended; they saw plenty of bird-life and game-sign, and now and then some mule deer, but they weren't pausing even to shoot for the pot. The sun was high enough that the grassy open expanse ahead seemed to shimmer with green and patches of bright blue as they caught glimpses between the trees. The other side was a line on the horizon, vaguely suggesting hills; it must be many miles away, to be so small from this height.

I hope we're just where I think we are. I don't want to blunder around wasting time looking for the rendezvous.

"Is that swamp, the blue?" Red Leaf asked. "Standing water with grass growing up through it?"

Astrid smiled and shook her head. "Camas flower," she said. "It's early this year, but later it looks even better. This is the *Nann i Camas*, the Camas Prairie I told you of."

She could feel the Lakota relax; she'd observed that they liked a big sky and a long view and felt cramped in close country. Dúnedain tried to be at home in all types of landscape, but there was no dispute that forest offered more scope for their particular talents.

"Yeah, we got camas in the *makol* too, but not nearly so many. Too dry, I suppose," Red Leaf said. "That's some good-looking pasture out there."

Astrid breathed a soundless sigh of relief as she saw Alleyne rise from a nest of branches and war-cloak that had made him the next thing to invisible. The rest of the column came up and spread out to either side of his waiting place at the edge of the woods, far enough back that no betraying glint would make them apparent to a patrol out on the prairie.

"Secure?" Alleyne asked.

"No sign of those cavalry. Eilir and John are holding the rear in case we have to move back quickly, but I don't think so."

He nodded and called: "Hírvegil, Imlos," while pointing upward.

The two young Rangers unwrapped their war-cloaks

from their packs, and donned them and their claws. Then each ran up a tree with a cat's hunching speed, picking ones with good fields of view on the back trail as well as ahead.

Astrid unshipped her Zeiss *palantír en-crûm* and leaned against a half-fallen pine to brace her elbows. Back and forth; no sign of man, save for a big herd of red-and-white Herefords already at the very edge of sight and slowly moving eastward with only two mounted cowboys in attendance; they'd vanished within an hour. This was rich farmland, well-watered dark basaltic soil planted to wheat and canola before the Change, but there was no need to till nearly as much now when crops weren't shipped to great cities far away. Most of it was sparsely grazed prairie where it wasn't outright abandoned these days, with planted fields only around the widely scattered ranch-houses and little hamlet-towns. The dirt roads that had marked it into square-mile sections had long since grown over in grass and brush, the telephone poles burned and fallen, plowland gone back to green wildness.

Like Eriador in the Third Age, and I saw the beginnings here back right after the Change, she thought, with a complex mix of emotions. *Remembering myself at fourteen is like remembering being someone else, almost. Then I was only beginning to know what my fate was, and what I must do in the Fifth Age.*

Man's hand lay lightly enough on the Camas Prairie now that she could see a lobo pack in the middle distance, trotting from north to south in single file. She smiled to herself as she watched them moving confidently with their heads high to keep them above the tips of the thigh-high grass, eight big shaggy gray adults a yard high at the shoulders and four youngsters, gawky adolescent one- and two-year-olds. Then they caught her party's scent; the wind was light, but from the west. She saw them halt and look her way, then give the canine equivalent of shrugs and head on their journey once more, wary of humans but not particularly frightened. A few bison cows and their calves an hour later were more cautious, veering away before they became more than dots to the naked eye.

Ohtar—warrior-squires—came by with water for humans and horses, and carrying the last of the cracked grain to feed the mounts. They were well-trained beasts, but it tugged at her heart to see them yearning towards that rich tender grazing when she had to deny them.

"You can graze tonight to your heart's content, my darlings," she murmured beneath her breath. "I know war is hard on horses."

The sun crept across the sky and moved behind her; she ate another stick of jerky and some raisins and ignored the way her stomach gurgled. She even tried to ignore the thought of how Diorn and Hinluin and Fimalen would be missing *her*, back at Stardell Hall. Children grew so fast . . . Diorn was past ten now and tried to hide his fears, but the twins cried whenever they saw her getting her war-gear together, though Míresgaliel was an excellent nanny.

Though I'd be even more upset if they didn't miss me. And I'd like to have at least one more. Another boy, say, though a third girl would be welcome too. I'm thirty-eight, time's getting a little tight . . . maybe it would be another pair of twins if we're lucky? My family always ran to them and so does Alleyne's. Uncomfortable but it saves time. If we live through this war, perhaps we should let the younger genera-

tion have the active tasks and settle down to teaching and policy all the time.

A herd of fawn-colored pronghorns with white bellies and rumps came from the south, pronking and stotting as they went—bouncing along like rubber balls or hopping straight up, apparently for the sheer joy of it, and she saw Alleyne grin as he watched. A few white-tailed deer wandered along the edge of the woods, darting away when they got within a few-score paces of the silent humans and finally realized predators were about; some feral alpacas grazed. A blaring sound in the sky made her look up and see a brace of massive snowy trumpeter swans going by. Other birds swept through northward towards the lakes that lay there, V-shapes of duck and geese and tern; a golden eagle cruised along the forest edge for a while, a seven-foot wingspan of savage majesty hoping to scare up something edible . . . which for that breed might be anything up to a pronghorn and certainly included the odd weakly lamb or fawn.

I do like the wilderness, she thought. *More than the tame lands. Though the forests of Mithrilwood are even more comely than this. Home is where your children are born.*

Then—

"That's them," she said, seconds after the two observers whistled the first sighting from their treetop perches— for detail her optics trumped their elevation.

Two groups of horsemen, riding along at a casual trot-canter-trot with remounts and pack beasts on leading reins, one coming from the east, the other from north and east.

"*Literally* six of one and half a dozen of the other," Alleyne said. "You're sure?"

"The blue scarves are the recognition signal, and

they're all wearing them. Either we're blown, or it's them."

It was possible they *had* been blown; this area had been part of the United States of Boise for over twenty years, though it was lightly governed, or had been until recently. It took only one traitor or a suspicious and conscientious officer making arrests and holding people's heads underwater until they talked, which everyone did eventually. She reached over her shoulder for an arrow and tied a bit of blue ribbon just below the head. Her man did likewise, and they rose and trotted out into the open. When they'd been standing for ten minutes each of them drew to the ear and shot skywards, and riders stood in the stirrups and waved back at them.

The Idahoans had a perfect right to be here on their home ranges, if anyone asked. They rode up boldly, and Astrid signed over her shoulder for the Sioux to come out beside the Dúnedain leaders. The two approaching parties traveled the last hundred yards side by side. One was commanded by a sixtyish man in rancher's leather and denim and linsey-woolsey with a Stetson on his head, and a Sheriff's star on his jacket. The other's leader was fifty-something, dressed in fine fringed buckskins with a bar of white paint across his eyes; there was as much gray as raven black in his long hair, which was bound at the rear of his head with a fan-shaped spray of eagle feathers. The rancher's troop had excellent horses of a nondescript quarter horse breed; the Indians rode striking-looking animals with almost metallic-golden forequarters and socks, fading to pale gray with patches on the rest of their bodies.

The rank and file of the cowboys and Indians—her lips quirked for a moment—contained surprisingly few men in their prime fighting years.

Teenagers old enough for work but too young for call-up and women, mostly, apart from the two leaders.

The tyrant in Boise had been reaching deep into his pool of potential fighters. Alleyne met her eyes and nodded very slightly.

And most of them Changelings; not just in fact, but technically, as in born after March 17, 1998. That's happening more and more and it's a bit of a shock. Counting my ohtar, the majority of this whole gathering are Changelings. I think more than half of all the people on earth may be Changelings now, or will be soon.

A few of the locals had leather breastplates or light mail shirts, and all had slung helmets modeled on those of the old American army to their saddle bows. Everyone wore a saber or the heavy curved blade called a shete, and had bow in saddle scabbard, shield and lariat hanging at their cruppers, quivers across their backs, the gear common to the whole interior range-and-mountain country from the Cascades far into the eastern plains. The Sheriff drew rein first; despite his age he looked tough as the tooled leather of his saddle, though it bore images of flowers and his face had only lines and crags. His eyes were as blue as hers, startling in his weathered face.

"Ms. Larsson," he said. "Long time no see. Though we enjoyed the letters."

"*Mae govannen,*" she replied, putting hand to heart and bowing slightly. "*Im gelir ceni ad lín, Arquen Woburn.* Well met, and I'm glad to see you again, Sheriff Woburn. But it's Astrid Loring, now; this is my husband, Alleyne Loring. Alleyne, Sheriff Robert Woburn. We met in the first Change Year, and a couple of times afterwards, though not lately."

"She and Mike Havel and the rest of their bunch saved our *ass* the first Change Year," Woburn said. "That one's still on the debit side of the books."

"Ah, yes, the affair of the soi-disant Duke Iron Rod," Alleyne said. "I've read about it in the chronicle Astrid kept."

"The Red Book of Larsdalen," she affirmed, with a nostalgic thrill at the thought.

Though the *Annals of the Westmen* was current, started when she and Eilir refounded the Dúnedain. And by then she'd been able to write it in Tengwar.

The other party reined in as well. The leader grinned at her and exchanged greetings, then explained over his shoulder.

"Astrid I know from way back. We owe her a couple of favors. Big ones."

To her: "Glad to see you got hitched. Any kids, by the way?"

"Two girls and a boy," Astrid said. "I've got some pictures . . . later. You, Eddie?"

"Five; three boys, two girls. Yeah, hopefully we'll have catching-up time."

He made a signal to his followers—given the number who were women, she couldn't say "his men"—and they dismounted and began to unload the packsaddles; Sheriff Woburn did likewise. The Indian went on, looking between the Sioux and her:

"So, who are these dudes? The message didn't say, which is fair enough, seeing as it might have been read by not-good people. I presume they ain't elves."

"Neither are we," Astrid said dryly. "We're Men, well,

People, of the West. These are John Red Leaf and Rick Three Bears, of the Oglalla and the Seven Council Fires of the Lakota *tunwan*."

Who are sort of like the Riders of Rohan in some ways. Hopefully they'll also come charging to the rescue.

"*Hau Kola*," they said, making the peace sign.

"Eddie Running Horse." He introduced himself and shook hands. "Of the Nez Perce. Or the *Nimi'ipuu* as we say."

"Meaning *The Real People*," Red Leaf said dryly. "Self-esteem's a wonderful thing . . . and isn't Running Horse a Sioux name?"

"Not when you say it in our language *or* in English. And *Sioux* means *rattlesnake*, doesn't it? Or *torturer*? Or maybe *movie Indian*."

"Well, fuck you too, Mr. I-will-fight-no-more-forever," Red Leaf said.

Alleyne looked very slightly alarmed to one who knew him as well as Astrid did; she caught his eye and shook her head a little.

I think they're—

Red Leaf and the Nez Perce burst out laughing.

. . . joking.

"Eddie Running Horse . . . Jesus, were you at the last Crow Fair in 'ninety-seven? Yeah, you were in the rodeo—I remember you."

"Christ, you never forget a face if you remember me from *that*."

"Nah, I couldn't tell your face from a prairie dog's ass."

"Not the first one to note the resemblance."

"But I never forget a *horse*. You were riding one that looks a hell of a lot like him."

He nodded towards the beautiful Appaloosa.

"Yup, he was Big Dog here's granddad's brother, but we bred some Akhal-Teke into the line right afterwards; got the first colts the year of the Change."

"Shiny."

"Yeah, it does give their coats that look, not to mention putting in more staying power. Say, I remember *you*."

"*You* never forget a face?"

"No, but I never forgot about hearing how this crazy Sioux named Red Leaf was dragging around a *Mongol* with a *yurt*, of all things. A *yurt* in the Tipi Capital of the World!"

"It's a ger. Yurt's what the Russians called them. We use a lot of them these days. Chinua—it means Red Wolf—showed us how, married my little sister too. How's things here for us 'skins?"

"Oh, not as good as I hear it is for you folks, but until just recently, not so bad. We got left alone most of the time. Trouble with the fucking *wasichu* as you snakes call 'em every now and then, but what can you do? It's a little late to say *There goes the neighborhood*."

"Nothing personal," he added to Astrid, as Sheriff Woburn glowered a little.

"I'm a Númenórean myself," Astrid pointed out. "House of Hador, probably."

And one of your Real People is as blond as I am, so there, she added to herself. *Honestly, it's not like any of us were half-Elven or anything you could get* really *huffy-stuffy about.*

Their followers and her *ohtar* had pitched camp; staking out horses on picket lines, sending working parties into the woods for deadfalls to use as firewood, and in the case of the locals unpacking food and setting to cooking dinner. That included steaks, fried potatoes, cowboy beans with garlic, bacon and onions, and frybread. Frybread with honey was one of her favorites, and after so long on cold trail rations it was all very welcome. As the evening fell the leaders leaned back against their saddles around a fire, sipping at chicory-root coffee improved with brandy. Sparks fled upward towards the bright stars as the wood cracked and popped, and a rhythmic *whoo-whoo-whoo-whoo-whoo-whoo-whoo* sounded in the forest just upslope, a great gray owl proclaiming its territory to the world and especially to any other owls listening, before it set out on the evening hunt to feed the new chicks.

"So," Eddie said, his hands busy loading a long-stemmed pipe. "OK, we still owe you one. We'll get Red Leaf and Three Bears through to Montana. Now that we're all supposed to be lovey-huggy with those Cutter maniacs, you can go through as Nez Perce trading horses or something."

"The Cutters don't have enough horses?" Alleyne asked, his officer's mind working at the implications.

Eddie Running Horse grinned. "Not like *our* horses. Plenty of rich Ranchers and those priest-whatevers like fancy stock, let me tell you."

He turned to the Sioux: "If pretending to be Real People doesn't offend your dignity."

"Bro, if it gets me back to Fox Woman and the kids alive, I'm all for it and I'll make like a goddamn Pawnee. Or paint my face white and pretend to be a street mime, for that matter."

His son made an inquiring sound. "Classical reference, I'll explain later," his father said, and then went on to the Nez Perce leader:

"Figure we could cut kitty-corner up into Drumheller and then go through the Dominions from there, it all being nice and flat along that way and not too far to their border with the Seven Council Fires."

"Lady Sandra has given our friends a laissez-passer," Astrid said.

At the uncomprehending looks, Alleyne amplified: "A diplomatic passport. Drumheller and Moose Jaw and Minnedosa have diplomatic relations with the Portland Protective Association; they'll give Red Leaf and his son help and transport."

"Doable," Running Horse said. "Horse traders, or maybe hunters or trappers . . . that would be the best cover story, and you could stay in the panhandle almost all the way there; it's a big country and not many people. With some good remounts, it wouldn't take long at all this time of year. Except that the patrols're checking a lot harder these days for draft dodgers, but you're old enough that won't be a problem and we could fix it up for your son here."

A grin. "Maybe he could pretend to be deaf and dumb; I notice he doesn't talk much anyway. Our good Sheriff Bob here could do an exemption certificate to explain why he's not pounding his ass on a saddle in the U.S. Cavalry for the holy cause of national reunification. Which, let me tell you, we weren't all that crazy about the *first* time."

"I could," Woburn said. "Not too often, but I've still got enough clout for an exemption. Though the way they're centralizing everything in Boise these days, God knows how long that'll last."

"Draft dodgers?" Alleyne said, a keen hunter's attention on his face. "There's discontent with the current ruler's policies, then?"

Running Horse laughed hollowly as he reached out to the fire and lit a pine splint from it:

"Discontent? Oh, no, no, *hell*, no. We all just *love* to die to make that buffalo-headed whistle-ass would-be emperor with a Julius Caesar complex down in Boise the fucking king of the world. If you don't believe me, just ask *him*, or read one of the posters plastered on every wall between Drumheller and Utah."

He lit the pipe, passed his palm over it, puffed and handed it to Astrid with a ceremonious two-handed gesture; she took a puff, fought not to cough at the fiery itch in her lungs and handed it on around the circle herself.

"Said Imperial Wannabe is also known as *Martin Thurston*," Eddie added sardonically. "Also known as General-President of the United States Martin Thurston, and according to rumor now Beloved-of-the-Prophet-Sethaz Martin Thurston. Jesus, his dad was slow enough about getting an election going, but at least he *did* eventually get around to it and he was pretty evenhanded even while he was using the Emergency Powers Act. Official line from Number One Son is that we'll have elections when the quote present emergency situation unquote is over. Which means sometime around the Fucking Fifth of Never, is my guess."

"Yup, that's about what I figured," Woburn said in his slow deep twanging voice. "Or if we do, they'll be 'elections' the way a gelding is a stallion."

I doubt anyone elected you two, Astrid thought. *Though I don't doubt you're popular enough. And anyone who doesn't like the way Alleyne and Eilir and John and I run the Rangers is perfectly welcome to leave.*

The Sheriff went on quietly: "My boy Tom died at

Wendell when we fought the Corwin . . . *maniacs* is a pretty good word, Ed."

"You should hear what our *tiwe-t* and *tiwata a-t*, our medicine people, say about them."

"And ours," Red Leaf put in.

"About the same's what the preachers say," Woburn said. "And the Mormons hate 'em like poison . . . Wendell, that was a fight that needed fighting; that and helping the Deseret folks. I wouldn't be having this here conversation if old General Larry Thurston were still alive."

"You knew him?" Astrid asked. "Personally, I mean."

If he had, it had been after she went through. Of course, a good deal could happen in twenty-five years. Thurston had been one more refugee trying to get out of metro Seattle then.

"Yeah. I worked with him when we joined up with Boise, which was relatively peaceful, back in Change Year Four. OK, he was always a serious hard-ass, but he was an honest man too, and he meant it about putting the country back together, as near as anyone could after the Change. Then suddenly after the battle at Wendell back two years ago the President was dead and his boy was running things."

"Which I recall you weren't altogether against," the Nez Perce chief said.

"Not at first. I knew Martin was smart. But then we were *allied* with the Prophet, who's all of a sudden supposed to be helping us restore America, and then we're fighting off in the west. And the story about Frederick Thurston being behind his father's death. Damned suspicious I said right off, you'll recall."

"Not too loudly," Eddie added.

"Nope. Lately things have happened to folks who got too loud about being unhappy. *Or* who say they don't think young Fred was to blame for his father's death, especially if it sounds like they had Martin in mind instead."

"Like, Fred Thurston is any better than his big brother?"

"*Much* better," Astrid said firmly. "And we have eyewitness testimony that it was Martin who killed his father. Finished him off after the Prophet's men wounded him, that is. And strong suggestive evidence that he let his father's command center be attacked by the Cutters in the hope that the President would be killed. In collusion with the Prophet."

Woburn nodded slowly. "Yeah. I can see that. And . . ." He hesitated. "That's what Mrs. Thurston thinks, too. Thinks that blond bitch he married put him up to it, as well. Not that he needed much persuasion, probably."

Eddie Running Horse sat upright. "You never mentioned *that*, Bob!"

The rancher-Sheriff chuckled dryly. "Well, now, what were we saying about what happened to folks who went around flapping their lips a lot, these days? Yeah, I know Cecile. And I know some other people who know her, people who live in Boise and can pass word along."

"Ah," Astrid said neutrally, feeling things moving in her head, like the Watcher at the Ford beneath the waters by Durin's Doors. "That is quite interesting, Sheriff."

"Poor lady, I sure don't envy her any, stuck in Boise with that son of hers, and two daughters to look after," Woburn said. "It'd take a hard man to harm his own kin, but if the rumors are right Martin's exactly that sort of hard man. Bad man, come to it."

"Perhaps something could be done about that," Astrid said, her eyes looking beyond the circle of fire for a while. "That would let young Frederick tell everyone the truth and hope to be believed, if his mother was backing him up."

"Well, I don't know," Woburn said, taking a final ceremonial puff on the pipe. "He's fallen in with some mighty strange company—this Artos fellow we hear tell of, and those knights-in-armor people and all."

"Hey, let me tell you about Rudi," Three Bears said, speaking up in the company of his elders for the first time. "That's what his friends, Fred Thurston included, were calling him when he showed up in *our* country. Then—"

Astrid smiled to herself as the highly colored tale of adventure and derring-do sounded. Even compared to the Histories it made a stirring epic; and her nieces were involved with it too, to the honor of the Dúnedain and her House.

"OK, that's impressive," Woburn said, and Eddie nodded. "But I'm still not sure . . . I don't want to see Idaho invaded."

"That's see *the United States* invaded, Bob," Eddie said. "And if you don't believe me—"

"Just ask Martin Thurston, yeah," Woburn said. "It's still our home, whatever it gets called."

He wrapped his hand in a kerchief to reach out and pour more chicory from the tin pot balanced on a stone at the edge of the fire. At his raised brows Astrid held out her own cup. He went on as he clunked the pot back on the fire:

"Still, fighting and killing and burning on our own land . . . and then what? Those weirdos building *castles* here?"

"No, that's not what we had in mind at all," Alleyne said smoothly. "We . . . we Rangers and the other free communities . . . fought the Portland Protective Association and beat them, ourselves."

More or less beat them, Astrid admitted to herself. *Beat them enough that they abandoned any ambitions to conquer the rest of us. And that may be as much due to Norman Arminger dying as anything else; they got less greedy without him to drive them on. Or more patient, perhaps. Certainly Sandra is. Saruman in a cotehardie, if you ask me.*

"They're just one power among many, and nobody's going to let them hand out fiefs," her husband went on. "But we do think it's time we stopped having wars among ourselves."

Astrid waved her cup. "Why should we fight each other? There's all the land and all the game and all the grazing any of us need or our children's children will need for a very long time. Trade will make us richer than stealing."

She signed and one of her *ohtar* handed her two small sealed bags of waxed paper, each exuding a faint rich scent.

"For example . . ."

She handed them to Woburn and Running Horse.

"The real bean?" Woburn said reverently.

"Jesus!" the Nez Perce chief whispered.

Astrid nodded. She'd never liked coffee all that much herself, despite Swedish and Danish ancestors, but she *did* love tea, and it had been a good day when the real leaf started trickling in through Astoria and Newport.

"We Rangers make our living guarding caravans and putting down bandits in peacetime, and believe me, the bandits enjoy the holiday when we're on war-duty. And this is the new world, the Changed world. We can't have a government that ties everything up in paper and forms anymore. The land is too *big*."

"Got a point there," Woburn said. "Still . . ."

"Wouldn't it be better for Boise to be part of something bigger, but still fully autonomous within its own borders?" Alleyne asked. "And for the ruler in Boise to leave the rest of Idaho to govern themselves in most things, rather than taking your young men and crops and horses for its wars? Especially if, umm, *Reunification* could come anyway."

"With a *King*?" Woburn asked, shaking his head.

"An *Ard Rí*, a High King. Who presides, but has only enough power to keep us from fighting each other and enforce a few clear rules. No costly standing armies to support, no armies of clerks telling everyone what to do, either."

"How does that work?" Woburn said. "I like the bit about the clerks. If you knew the forms and regulations they've brought in this past year—and there were enough before . . ."

"The High King has only what the founding laws and the member realms give him, what they are willing to levy on themselves in money or troops. There will be a Meeting of delegates from each people, to oversee things, as well, and a High King's court to decide disputes between them."

Eddie Running Horse nodded. "Sounds OK. I'm not dead set on Boise being the capital of whatever but it *would* be nice not to have to worry so much about the neighbors."

Woburn frowned. The talk flowed on late into the night. When she lay at last in her sleeping bag, Astrid cuddled her back up against Alleyne's and stared at the fading banked embers, glowing like red stars in the deep velvet blackness of a moonless night.

That poor lady, held captive in Boise by a murdering usurper, she thought. *Something has to be done about that. Eilir and I swore that oath to succor the defenseless . . .*

CHAPTER FIFTEEN

"So far, we haven't done much this year," General-President Thurston said.

They were using a third-floor chamber in a pre-Change building for the conference. It had glass walls on two sides, facing west and north; you could see the line of the—criminally inadequate—city wall along the bend of the Deschutes River that had given the city its name; he instinctively drew a mental picture of how it *should* have been done, the underground aqueduct to secure the water supply, the height of the wall, the wet moat and glacis. He knew that from there it followed two of the old roads in a right angle to the eastward, encompassing the old core of the city, and the visibility made his sense of frustration at the stalled campaign worse. The room also had the slightly dead feel that old buildings often did; you just couldn't get the ventilation to work properly and frequently, as here, the windows didn't open at all.

"We're not accomplishing anything," he said. "Not fast enough."

Not since that . . . that whatever it was. His mind shied

away from remembering it, and he forced it back. *Something . . . something like a flash of light . . . something about the Sun . . . anyway, it's put a crimp in your style.*

The Prophet of the Church Universal and Triumphant smiled. Martin Thurston blinked. There was something . . . *wrong* about the smile. Sethaz was a middling man, middling height and coloring and features; very fit but otherwise unremarkable, save for the tuft of brown chin-beard and stubble-shaven head that the higher echelons of the Church Universal and Triumphant affected. A little older than Martin Thurston, in his early thirties, but young enough to be more or less a Changeling.

And there's something wrong *about him.*

"You sense higher things, the touch of the Ascended Masters. Yet you are still blind to them."

As Martin stared, the ruler of Corwin went on, and the *wrongness* seemed to fade:

"We have taken Bend and all of central Oregon; and we have pushed the enemy out of the Palouse and confined their holdings along the middle Columbia to a narrow strip."

Martin nodded jerkily.

And I need him and he needs me. Which is the best reason for cooperation there ever was. But we're not taking any more castles by the . . . special means he had. That's why Dad never tried to break the PPA; they had too many of the damned things by the time we were organized enough to think about it. Storming one castle is expensive. *Fighting your way through country full of them is a nightmare, like dancing up to your knees in molasses.* "Yes," he said aloud. "We have. Unfortunately, that means we've taken a lot of thinly populated rangeland. We won't have mortally wounded the enemy until we cut them in half by cracking the line of the Columbia down to the sea, and we won't have disposed of them until we've overrun the western valleys. And we've lost more men than they have."

"We can afford it and they cannot." Sethaz shrugged. "The lifestreams of the fallen will be welcomed by the Masters."

There was a rattle in one corner of the room. He had a six-man squad from the Sixth Battalion here—just in case, and in full armor of hooped plates, with shield and *pilum*; tough young farmboys, smelling of sweat and leather and oiled metal. The rattle had been the men moving—not enough to notice, they were still rigidly braced—but enough to show their start of indignation. Martin Thurston was known to be a ruthless bastard, but he was also one who husbanded his men and hated to lose one without a measurable result.

Two centuries of infantry waited in the street outside. Sethaz might be an ally . . . *but I'm not crazy enough to actually trust him.*

"My intelligence indicates the Midwestern states are making preparations for an attack," the General-President said, tapping the files before him on the table. "We may not have as much time as we thought."

"They are preparing for war," Sethaz said equably. "But they are very far away. Also the Church Universal and Triumphant's territories are between them and Boise."

"And what about this Sword?" Martin asked. *Because that's what scares me.* "Every rebel and guerrilla is talking about it—"

Sethaz screamed.

For a moment Thurston simply stood staring at him. *He's gone mad*, he thought, and then they locked eyes.

The eyes *drew* at him, a whirling vortex. He could feel bits and pieces of his mind *shredding*, flying away, sucked in by the spinning nothingness. He was floating, falling, drawn down, deeper and deeper and something *waited* for him at the bottom of the darkness. Not-being. Not-anything. Waiting to un-make.

Martin Thurston screamed in agony, and then in something far worse, that made him shriek on the same rising-falling note as the Prophet.

Did you think that you had bargained with Me? a voice asked. ***No, you deceived yourself. I have no need to buy men. They give themselves to Me.***

FREE REPUBLIC OF RICHLAND
SHERIFFRY OF READSTOWN
(FORMERLY SOUTHWESTERN WISCONSIN)
MAY 10, CHANGE YEAR 25/2023 AD

"Not as nervous as you were last time, *meleth nín*," Mary Vogeler teased gently. "Even though it's just the two of us for now, instead of the great band."

"*Herves*, last time I wasn't sure whether big brother Ed was going to greet me like the prodigal son or kick me out like the proverbial polecat," Ingolf said, taking a deep breath of the clean moist air as the earth exhaled last night's rain. "Also we weren't married yet. It's calmed me down a lot and given me a more optimistic outlook on life."

And last time I'd been away for ten years. Now it's only months, and two of those . . . just went missing in an instant while we were on Nantucket. But I haven't been feeling homesick quite as hard either, and that's the truth. It's as if something inside has let go. Mary and I will have our own place someday, and in the meantime we're each other's home.

"Anyway, we're just going up to see about those troops."

It was spring instead of late autumn this time, too; the same season when he'd originally stormed out as a young man to begin his wandering years as a paid soldier and salvager.

Mary grinned. "*Anyway*, Rudi's giving you a last chance at a visit home while everyone else is stuck at the muddy junction of the Wisconsin and the Mississippi rivers, waiting for the barges. That's why he didn't ride with us, too. He wants you to have some time with your family before he arrives."

It may well be the last time you can be here, went unspoken between them. *Crossing the continent isn't something that many men have done once, let alone two or three times.*

They followed the dirt track north from a hamlet named Crawford, with forested ridges on either side crowding closer to the winding Kickapoo or opening out into a wider view. Mostly they traveled at an easy trot, the fastest pace a good horse could keep up for any distance. Every few miles they slowed to an ambling walk for ten or twenty minutes; that combination gave an average speed close to a man running. It didn't even make conversation too difficult, if you were used to it and traveled side by side. Right now the traffic was light enough for that, only an occasional buckboard or someone on foot pulling a handcart or in the saddle or a bicyclist now and then lurching along on a solid-tire makeshift.

"What I'm really worried about is Rudi," Ingolf said.

"I think we'd better get used to calling him Artos,"

Mary said; but she said it without the usual smile in her voice.

"Yah, OK, I'm worried about His Majesty Artos the First, High King of Montival, our liege-lord," Ingolf said. "Also my friend and brother-in-law Rudi Mackenzie. I'm worried about both of him."

"Why? He's coping very well. Look at the way he remembered you'll possibly never have a chance to visit Readstown again."

"That's the problem," Ingolf said; talking crystallized his thought, giving it form. "You'd need a general staff to do a lot of the stuff he's doing *all by himself.* Yah, he was always an impressive guy, but some of this . . . remembering every name in that pissant village at the mouth of the Wisconsin River? All the ones he heard *once* when we were through it for *one day* last year? I was born not two days' ride from it and *I* don't! You notice how he doesn't make *mistakes* anymore?"

"He never did make many."

"Now he never forgets anything, not even his spare bowstring. He never has to stop and figure things out anymore!"

Mary was subdued; when she spoke it was slowly.

"I asked him . . . I asked him a while ago if he wasn't making decisions too quickly. He said there just wasn't any point in pretending he had a choice. What did he *mean*? Is the Sword . . . is it taking him over?"

Ingolf shook his head; it was hard even to talk about this, as if there weren't the right words in the language.

"It's spooky, but I don't think so. It doesn't give you that creepy feeling the Cutters do. I think . . . this is just blue-sky . . . I think the Sword is too *smart*. Or makes him too smart."

"How can you be too smart?"

"If you *knew*, if you really *knew* what would happen when you made a decision . . . would you have any freedom left at all? There would be only one thing you *could* do."

"Oh," she said, and shivered. "I guess it's like the Elven-Rings; good, basically, but perilous to any but the strongest bearer."

For a moment he felt impatience that she was dragging the Histories into things again. Then he shrugged mentally. In fact—

"That's actually a good comparison . . . what Doc Pham, our doctor in Readstown—God, how could anyone know so many books?—he used to tutor me sometimes as well . . . what he used to call a *metaphor*."

She nodded; he knew without resenting it that she had a lot more book learning than he did, even if much of it was bizarre.

Though I'm better at lifting heavy weights . . . That's me: strong like an ox, sharp like a watermelon.

"Metaphors help you understand the world," she said. "Otherwise . . . otherwise it's just a mass of *things* without pattern. It doesn't mean anything. But you've got to be careful with them. They can make you see patterns that aren't there."

"Yah. Only the Sword seems to be a, a *metaphor* that's actually *there*. Not just a way to sling words together; it's a physical *object* you can touch, so the story is telling us instead of the other way 'round. Damn und hell, but that's scary."

Mary shivered, and he knew exactly how she felt.

"It's like the old legends about Gods becoming men, or animals talking. I mean, they're wonderful as stories and they show you the way things are underneath, but if you actually *met* one it would . . . would sort of *break* things. Not deliberately, not because it was bad and wanted to do that, but just by being too real for us."

Ingolf smiled grimly. He reached over and touched her eye patch with the thick calloused fingers of his right hand, very gently:

"We've both met men like that before. Only they were *bad*, as well as scary, if you know what I mean."

"*Oh*, yes." Then she brightened. "Most of the time, though, it's as if the Sword makes him *more* of what he was already."

Ingolf grinned. "Super-Rudi. Ye . . . Gods, that's a scary thought too!"

They laughed together, and then by unspoken mutual agreement brought themselves back to the moment. For a while after they left the village the landscape was mostly abandoned land used for summer grazing if at all; tall grass and thickets of raspberry bushes, goldenrod, and surging clumps of young elder and elm struggling with them and the saplings spreading out of the old woodlots. All were loud with birdsong as the migrants settled in and disputed their territories; flights of blue warblers chased cloud-formations of mayflies in melodious flocks.

He saw tracks and scat of elk, deer, feral cattle, swine and half a dozen others, but this road was traveled enough that animals were wary of men by daylight; they caught only a fleeting glimpse of what might have been a wolf or a very large coyote. And once, laughing, they steered their mounts around a defiant skunk standing with raised tail.

Mary was looking at the roadway too; much of it was post-Change, created by the traffic pounding the soil when the road by the river was washed out. Improvements later had mostly meant a little ditching, the odd brushup with a horse-drawn grader, reused culverts, and shoveling gravel into the worst wet spots when they threatened to swallow travelers or their horses whole.

"Is there normally so much traffic on this road?" she said.

"No," he said, noticing. "People usually float things up- and downriver; the Kickapoo's not big enough for real boats but canoes do fine most of the year and they can carry a fair bit. And mostly we swap around locally anyway."

By definition any area that had come through the first Change Years without utter collapse was self-sufficient in everything it really needed. Where trade had revived at all it was mostly in light high-value luxury goods, particularly here in the backwoods.

Which Readstown is, you betcha, even if we . . . they . . . don't like to admit it.

"Wagons and horsemen both," Mary said, looking down again. "Horsemen in column of fours, and trains of wagons. The troops we're supposed to be looking for."

"You've got a good eye."

She hit him on the shoulder; mostly theoretical when he was wearing a mail shirt and gambeson, but he cowered theatrically. Then he went on:

"Hmmm, looks like it was mostly a couple of weeks ago and then tapering off; it's real blurred by the rain. Well, we'll find out."

Now and then a Norway spruce or an old apple tree still valiantly showing a few flowers served to mark the site of an abandoned homestead. Once a ruin's glass shards glinted from the high ridge to the west, beneath the purple blaze of a rambling lilac.

"Why would anyone build up there?" Mary asked. "Well, easier to defend, I suppose . . ."

She stood in the stirrups for a moment and shaded her eye with a hand; the sun was a little past noon, and the air was just in that place between warm and cold where you hardly noticed it except as a stroking on the skin. Then she took out her monocular.

"That was a pretty big house, not just a lookout post. No defenses . . . and the roadway to it runs straight up the slope; there's an overgrown gully where it washed out. Strange."

"There's actually good farmland up on the ridges in places, you just can't see it from here," Ingolf said. "But *those* were built for the view."

He raised a hand at her stare: "I swear to God . . . by the Valar. Just so they could live there and look at the view. Which *is* pretty."

"The view?" Mary said. "They put a house on top of a slope that would kill a team climbing it just to look out the *window*?"

They both laughed and shook their heads; you could go crazy trying to understand why people did the things they did before the Change. Then they emerged into the settled lands closer to Readstown with startling suddenness, shaggy neo-wilderness on one side of a weathered board fence, close-cropped green pasture on the other and then a not-quite-town.

"This used to be called Gay's Mills," he said. "We're about an hour from home, from Readstown, now. If nobody's horse throws a shoe, that is."

Both riders relaxed at the signs of habitation . . . relaxed a little . . . and slid their recurve bows back into the saddle scabbards at their left knees and the arrows into their quivers on their backs. Gay's Mills was a cluster of farms and cottages these days, with a blacksmith's shop by the side of the road and a gristmill somewhere close; they could hear the bur of the millstones. The full-bearded smith looked up from shoeing a big hairy-footed draft beast and gave a brief wave of his hammer with his mouth full of nails before he bent back to his task.

Ingolf's horse, Boy, threw up his head and snorted as the wind brought the scent of his own kind; Mary's dappled Rochael ignored them and him. A barefoot pigtailed girl in a linsey-woolsey shift and a floppy hat three sizes too big for her dragged a barking mongrel back just before he was kicked into next week, then stood gaping at them with one dirty foot tucked behind her other knee. Mary smiled and leaned down with effortless grace to pat her head in passing. They headed through a gaggle of chickens that stopped pecking at the roadway and scattered in mindless panic, and out into open country again.

Shod hooves thudded on the soft rutted dirt or sparked on the odd rock or clattered against bits of asphalt that had survived a generation of flood and frost. Shete and longsword rattled and banged against stirrup-irons occasionally, but the loudest sounds were birdsong and wind in the trees. There were farms set back at the edge of the hills every half mile or so, but none very close.

He spent a moment just enjoying the day and the view. There weren't many pleasures greater than the feel of a good horse moving beneath you on a fine spring day, with the woman you loved riding at your side.

The apple and cherry orchards were in full blossom on the south-facing slopes, frothing in white like snowdrifts, or pink like cotton candy; he could remember the planting of many of them. The season was far enough along that when the road twisted close the breeze brought not only the blossoms' cool sweet scent but drifts of petals on a gust of wind, settling now and then in Mary's long yellow braid of hair, framed against the ridge beyond and the piled clouds catching the westering sun amid an endless blue like her eye.

And that's just about the prettiest thing I've ever seen, Ingolf thought. *Like this is just about the prettiest* country *I've ever seen. Of course, I'm prejudiced. The Willamette's great too, and a lot of what I've been through is* grand, *but this place has my heartroots in it. Always will, even if I never see it again.*

The Kickapoo Valley was part of what they'd called the Driftless area back in the day, which meant it hadn't been planed flat and buried by glacier-born silt like a lot of the Midwest. Instead it was a maze of valleys like this, separated by steep ridges and little plateaus, spreading like the pattern of veins in a leaf. That had helped keep out most of the waves of cityfolk desperate for food and shelter after the Change, that and distance and plenty of hard fighting. There had been enough food even that first year . . . *just* enough, despite the waste caused by disruption and ignorance of how to handle it without machines.

The steep slopes of the uplands were a fresh intense green now with the new leaves of sugar maple and basswood, oak and hickory, with the darker green of hemlock and white pine where the land dipped northward, now and then some dark red sandstone where the earth's bones showed, here and there the cream of flowering dogwood. There were willows and elm and cottonwood by the river, with dense clumps of Virginia bluebells and geraniums nodding beneath; trailing arbutus and purple-blue wood violet grew by the side of the road.

They rode past a crude statue carved from an oak stump, and Ingolf grinned at the mocking portrait of Richland's original Bossman; he'd done that himself as a teenager with a couple of friends, just when the man was on a visit, and it had been worth the hickory stick his father applied. Between forest and water were the fields, many plowed in curving strips along the lay of the land, planted with different crops to help hold the soil, a succession of greens lighter or darker or a first fine mist of tender shoots across smooth disk-harrowed brown earth. He looked at them with a countryman's eye, enjoying seeing them simply *for nice* as his folk said, but mostly for their promise:

"Just getting the corn planted," he said, inhaling the mealy-yeasty-musty smell of damp turned earth, as appetizing as fresh bread. "Not before time, either."

A woman in dungarees and a straw hat was driving a four-row grain drill along the contour not too far away, the twin heads of her team of bay geldings bobbing patiently ahead of her as they strode along. She had a crossbow in an upright holder beside the seat of the planter, but returned his wave in friendly wise.

"Bandits?" Mary asked, eyeing the weapon. "We're not all that far from the Wild Lands."

"Possible," Ingolf acknowledged; this *was* the edge of civilization, more or less. "Mostly for the hoof-rats, though, I'd guess."

"Hoof-rats?"

"Deer, whitetails."

"Ah, yes. They're a menace back home too."

He nodded, though he'd been too busy to hunt while

he was there in Montival—mostly too busy recovering from being wounded near to death by Cutter assassins. Deer were a crop-and-garden-devouring pest in most places, what with all the abandoned farmland providing exactly the sort of scrubby edge-country they liked. It had gotten a little better lately as closed-canopy forest spread.

"Though Aunt Astrid insists deer are noble creatures. Not to mention the staple of the Dúnedain diet."

"What do you think?"

"Hoof-rats," she said, and they both laughed. "But the wolves and bears and cougars and tigers seem to be catching up, finally."

"Which if you're trying to raise livestock—"

"—presents its own problems. On the other hand, tiger skin makes a very nice coat."

"More excitement getting it than I like."

Children with slings on bird-scaring detail pointed excitedly at the travelers; the school year ended when the fields dried out enough for work nowadays. One white-headed six-year-old ran beside them for a while with a gap-toothed grin. A man was driving a potato planter behind a four-horse hitch in another field, a clumsy-looking thing like a tapering bin on wheels, its center of gravity dangerously high and all covered in patches and rust. He ignored them; all his attention was on his horses and the set of levers and ropes that controlled the mechanism which opened the furrow, dropped in seed potatoes and covered them up in turn. This time Ingolf laughed aloud.

"What's funny, my heart?" Mary asked.

"That potato planter."

She looked, and blinked. "Not much different from

most, except that it's old and mostly metal. Looks pre-Change, nearly. There's a story attached?"

"Just a memory, really. Back when I was about ten . . . that must have been around Change Year Four . . . my dad and my brother Ed and a farmer named Fritz Vent-luka made that. Cut it down and made eight one-row machines from this huge-erific old-time thing that fifty horses couldn't pull, and we were short of horses then anyway. We didn't have to go out and plant the spuds by hand that spring, and everybody was happy about that! I helped . . . well, I stood around and handed wrenches and hacksaws and ran for stuff. When it was finished, Dad let me have my first drink of applejack. Mom gave him hell for it, but he tipped me a wink behind her back."

She reached over and put a hand on his shoulder. "I wish I could have met your father. And your mother."

Ingolf snorted, trying to imagine it. "Dad . . . Dad could be sort of . . . drastic about things. Never could take being crossed, and he was a hard man when he was angry, or when he'd had one too many. I think Mom would have liked you, but she wouldn't have shown it. God knows she tried riding roughshod over my sister-in-law Wanda often enough, though she was wild about the grandchildren."

He shook himself mentally and looked around again. Haying would be the next busy time, but it would be a few weeks at least before the timothy or alfalfa was high enough to bring the mowers out to cut. And there was always the eternal battle with the weeds.

"The oats are in, good, it's always best to get them planted by the middle of April around here, the shoots are just showing now, see? Winter wheat looks fine, plenty of tiller, no bare patches from winter-kill . . ."

"My love, could we be a little less agricultural?" Mary asked.

"Sorry, *melda*," he said with a grin; his Sindarin was still shaky, but he'd mastered the endearments.

He'd also been about to comment that the stock looked in good fettle too—white naked-looking sheared sheep with black faces grazing under the fruit trees with a shepherdess and her collie in attendance, many of them with a lamb at their heels, Angus cattle like square black blocks of flesh in the lower pastures, white-and-black or Jersey milkers. Sows grunted happily as they mowed down young alfalfa with swarms of pink-and-brown piglets tumbling around them.

Ingolf glanced aside at his wife and found her watching fondly as well, and grinned to himself. It was an odd person in today's world who didn't find beauty in a well-tilled landscape. Even non-farmers such as the Dúnedain Rangers.

"Sort of like the Shire," she said, echoing his thought. "The people it's our duty to protect."

"Us Rangers," he agreed.

Apparently you got to be one by being sponsored and also by being able to do a bunch of things. Since the *Hiril Dúnedain* was Mary's aunt he didn't anticipate too many problems getting on the rolls formally.

The fortified Farmers' homes and their attendant clusters of Refugee cottages and barns and tall silos that dotted the land faded away as they approached Readstown proper; this was the Sheriff's home-farm, worked from his own place. The state of the road said that traffic had been heavy lately, hoof and wheel both; he was surprised his elder brother hadn't had a few teams out grading and smoothing.

Then they turned directly northward, onto a stretch that had been asphalt in the old days and still was where it hadn't been patched with gravel; the river was far enough away to their left that it hadn't washed out this section during the periodic floods.

"Well, *troops are gathering* didn't turn out to be an exaggeration after all," Mary said. "That explains the road."

She looked over at the rows of white tents, the men and campfires and picketed horses that occupied a long stretch of pasture between the river and the buildings, running up to the big truck gardens to the north.

"About three, four hundred here, I'd say," she went on, with an expert's quick appraisal of numbers.

"Yah," Ingolf said and nodded agreement. "Maybe a few less, they've got a lot of gear with 'em. Or a few more if they're quartering some of them in the homes. Must be putting everyone's nerves on edge. And that's why Ed hasn't graded the road just lately. Usually we do it as soon as things dry out a bit in spring."

"No sense in doing it four times if he can wait for the troops to move out and do it once," Mary said.

"Ed's . . . not exactly miserly. But he's tight with things."

"So he should be," Mary said. "It's not like someone sending a beggar away hungry because they won't spare the scraps. What a lord has comes from his followers, after all. It's his duty to be careful with their goods and labor."

Ingolf opened his mouth, closed it again, and nodded. "Yah, I should have thought of that. Maybe I'm not as much over my mad at him as I thought."

Readstown had been a sprawled-out village of about four hundred people, remote and sleepy ever since its founding around a gristmill not long after white men first settled this land nearly two centuries ago. In the years that followed the Change it had shrunk to a much denser core around the Sheriff's house—what had become the Sheriff's house—for reasons ranging from warmth in winter to security against the bands of starving, desperate wanderers who'd gone roaming and reaving in the terrible years, and your odd sneak thief or highbinder or gangs of plain old-fashioned bandits later.

Not to mention various bigger fights over stock and who got the everybody-needs-'em Amish and stuff like that, before the Richland Bossmen knocked some heads together and kicked some butt to create our glorious Free Republic. People did what they had to do in the early days. Dad not least. But that's part of why he drank too much sometimes. To forget what he had to do.

He'd just turned five when the Change came; he could remember fear and cold and conversations among the adults that stopped when they noticed him. Now and then someone started acting very strangely, and usually you didn't see them again. Or they ended up like his aunt Alice, who'd been gently mad and given to sudden fits of tears as she sat at her workbench over a half-finished lute.

Of course, she got caught in Racine at that stupid folk-music festival thing. Never did say how she made it back home. Young as I was I remember her turning up. She was as skinny as anyone I've ever seen who didn't actually die.

"Looks tidier than it did in Dad's day. A bit more than when we were through last year. Ed keeps plugging away, I'll give him that."

It had been worth the labor to link the houses here together into defended courtyards, and later to shift or build more structures into the same complex; just before his father died he'd put up a round stone tower at one corner of the main house with a catapult on a turntable atop it, and sheathed the lower parts of all the buildings with fieldstone batten-walls as well. In the more recent years of peace some new cottages had been built out on their own, and the sawmill and gristmill, of course, and the regional school and the Lutheran and Catholic churches. A teenager he recognized was on mounted sentry-go a little farther up the road.

"Halt!" the boy said, raising a hand. "Who goes . . . Uncle Ingolf, by God! Und Aunt Mary! Yah hey dere! How's she goin'?"

"She's goin', Mark, and hi backatcha. You're looking pretty military," Ingolf said.

He was, for someone just turned seventeen and gangly with it. Tallish, six feet and a bit already, but still colt-built, with freckles against pale winter's skin and corn-tassel hair cut in the rather shaggy local ear-length style. A scattering of nearly invisible hairs on chin and upper lip suggested he was trying to cultivate a beard as well, and failing miserably. But he had a mail shirt with short sleeves on too, over the usual padded undergarment, a helmet that looked like a local blacksmith's copy of the sallets seen on Rudi's party last autumn, a shield and quiver on his back and bow in a saddle scabbard at his knee, along with shete, binoculars, bowie and tomahawk at his belt.

Equipped just like me, in fact, Ingolf thought with an amusement he kept off his face. *Except for the trumpet, and except that you can see everything came from the best armorer in Richland, or maybe even Des Moines. Plain, but no expense spared . . . no, that mail shirt's a bit big. Probably allowing him some growing room; those things* cost.

"So," he went on, "they've got you out meetin' und greeting?"

"I'm officer of the watch!" Mark said; his voice rose and cracked slightly, and a fiery blush ran over his fair skin.

Then he nodded at the tented encampment. "It's Ensign Mark Vogeler, First Richland Volunteer Cavalry, now. Nobody passes wit'out being recognized."

"Well, I sure hope you recognize me, nephew," Ingolf said, in lieu of anything more sensible. "Seeing as I put you on your first pony. Ummm . . . Where's Ed?"

"Dad's over to the house, out front, last I saw them, with Mom. Talking wit' a messenger from Richland Center. Uh, pass, friend!"

They legged their horses up to a canter for the last thousand yards.

"He reminds me of me." Ingolf chuckled when they were far enough away not to be overheard.

"He's cute. But then, so are you," Mary said.

She winked, then rubbed at her eye patch. "*Ai!* I'm still not used to the way that makes me *blind* for a moment."

Ed was looking harassed and talking to his wife, Wanda, and both of them were tossing instructions at people who came and went; he was also looking pretty much the way Ingolf suspected he himself would look in fifteen years or so, if his scalp started showing well above the forehead through thinning brown hair—that was on exhibit, as Ed Vogeler swept off his feedstore cap and crushed it in one big knobby fist and pulled in a thunderous curse—and if he let himself develop a beer gut. The thought made him suck in his own stomach a little as they swung down from their horses and handed the reins to a stablehand to be led away, though there currently wasn't an ounce of spare flesh in the two hundred pounds of muscle that covered his broad-shouldered, big-boned frame.

Not after the things I've done these last few years, almost none of which have involved sitting around knocking back the brewskis. Mind you, Wanda brews the best and runs a mean kitchen too.

"So you tell Bill Clements it's *his* job to get that fixed!" the Sheriff said to a wiry man in dusty leathers. "Uff da, try collecting any taxes if she goes and we get a flood!"

The courier nodded respectfully, swung into the saddle, and cantered off northward with two remounts behind him on a leading rein.

Then: "Ingolf!" Ed said, smiling, and they shook hands. "How's by youse?"

"Ingolf! Mary!"

Wanda hugged him, and then her; she was a motherly-looking blond woman in early middle age, wearing a kerchief around her hair today, and a set of overalls with garden dirt on the knees. And in Ingolf's considered opinion she was more than half the brains of the Sheriff Vogeler outfit, and three-quarters of the ability to judge people.

Besides being a first-rate manager. She ran the indoor part of the homeplace, which meant everything from the dairy's butter and cheese to carpet-making, and directing the labor of dozens. *But something's bothering her badly, underneath.*

"What's the Bossman done now?" Ingolf asked.

"It's dat . . . goddamned dam up at La Farge. I wish they'd never built it!"

"Pretty lake," Ingolf said, remembering trips there.

"Good fishing, too." He frowned at a memory. "Didn't Dad say they nearly *didn't* build it?"

"Finished just before the Change. Und now the intake tower's blocked and we're having a hell of a time getting it cleared."

The Sheriff crushed the billed cap again; it was pre-Change, a badge of rank, and he made himself relax with obvious effort.

"Glad to see you made it," he said gruffly.

"*Most* of us made it," Ingolf corrected, his tone grim. His eyes looked beyond the busy scene for a moment. "Most."

"Yah, we figured Pete wasn't coming back when he didn't show up after a couple of months. Seeing as he wasn't planning on going all the way east with you."

"Jackie? How's she taking it?"

"Hard, what would you expect? She moved back to her folks over in Forest Grove a couple of weeks ago, wit' da kids. But when a woman marries a man thirty years older, what can she expect?"

Wanda made a stifled gesture, as if she'd prevented herself from slapping her husband upside the head only by an act of will. Ingolf gave a silent *woof* of relief, even though it made him feel a little guilty; Pierre Walks Quiet had married one of the abundant widows and started a second family here after he drifted in from the North Woods early in the Change years, on the run from one of the grisly little massacres that had punctuated those times. He'd ended up as timber-runner and game manager for Ingolf's father, who had an eye for ability, and he'd taught woodcraft to the Sheriff's children too.

That his wife had moved out meant Ingolf wouldn't have to tell her and the children about the old Indian's death personally. Though there were far worse ways to go; he'd died with his face to an enemy worth fighting, knowing he'd won, and he'd gone quickly and without much pain. Nobody lived forever, and seventy-odd was a good long time these days.

"He died up in the north country," Ingolf said somberly. "On the Superior shore this side of Duluth, a few weeks after we left, fighting the Cutters and their local converts among the wild-men. And a couple of the Southsiders died too, and Odard later . . . long story."

And damn, I miss Odard. Which is crazy because I didn't like him much, or he me. He was too full of himself even after he'd gotten over some stuff and he was a lot fonder of being Heap Big Baron than he should have been, and he liked needling people too much, and thought he was smarter than he was, and . . . but he was a good man to have at your back. I wish we still had him.

Mary squeezed his hand; he knew she missed the Baron of Gervais too, although the Havel sisters had had a half-joking, half-serious running feud with him most of their lives. It was amazing how you could get to knowing what was in a woman's head if you were together long enough. He never had been before.

And I like it.

Ed nodded, and Wanda went around and pushed them all indoors.

"In! We don't talk out on the step wit' family, here, like you were road-people begging for a handout. We will sit like civilized folk, under a roof. Und I will get youse some lunch, you look hungry."

The main house seemed to be a bit crowded, probably the officers of the troops outside, who'd be of Farmer and Sheriff families and expected to put up with the local boss. People were rushing up and down the stairs with towels and bedding and rolled-up futons and blankets and pairs of boots. After the travelers had washed—the house had running water—the four of them settled in the breakfast room, which was cheerfully well lit through big windows that looked in on a courtyard, set with pine and maple furniture handmade by Readstown's own carpenters, with rag rugs on the floor before the empty swept fireplace and a few pictures and photographs on the walls. There was a faint smell of woodsmoke, inevitable in a building heated with stoves and hearths, and of dried wildflowers in jars on the mantel.

The courtyard was one Wanda used for her herb garden, some espaliered fruit trees against the walls and a selection of rosebushes, with flagstone paths and a few benches and some wrens and bluebirds squabbling around a feeder. That interior orientation was what allowed the big windows, though there were steel shutters with loopholes for shooting ready to be slammed home, and racks for crossbows and quivers of bolts. Mild scents of flowers and turned earth drifted in through the opened panes, and the trowel-work in the raised beds was as neat as a snake's scales. Wanda attended to that herself, saying she found it soothing. Right now several of her children were playing, tumbling over each other much like the puppies who were helping them at it. Though little Jenny was lying in a cradle, being still at the stick-everything-in-your-mouth stage.

"Let me guess about the troops," Ingolf said.

By then they'd been seated and a girl from the nearby kitchens came in with a tray of kielbasa and blutwurst and liverwurst and three types of cheese, rye and wheat bread, pickles and tall steins of turned maple-wood full of Wanda's foaming Schwarzbier.

"Thank you, Wilma," Wanda said with a smile, and promptly loaded plates. "You two missed lunch. Eat!"

Ingolf took a deep draught of the dark-colored beer, savoring the almost bitter flavor like coffee-and-chocolate, wiped foam off his mustache and beard with a napkin, and saw Mary still swallowing blissfully. There wasn't much conversation until they'd graduated to oatmeal cookies studded with walnuts and a big pot of chicory coffee with beet-sugar and cream on the side.

Ed ruffled the ears of a large nondescript dog that sat with its head in his lap, tail thumping the floor.

"The Bossman over in Richland is getting a volunteer force together?" Ingolf went on. "Not just Readstown? And that outside is our contingent?"

"Yah, cavalry only, all volunteers like you guessed, to join up with Iowa. We're figuring on three or four thousand all up, from what Richland Center tells me, say five or six regiments; the ones you saw are us, Forest Grove and Franklin, Ross, Viola, a couple of others. Another four thousand each from Fargo and Marshall. Everyone's pretty hot to trot about the Cutters, now that what happened in Dubuque has gotten around."

"Everyone?"

"Everyone who matters, and *everyone* in Iowa. All the Bossmen round about for sure, young Bill Clements here und Dan Rassmusen in Fargo and Greg Johanson in Marshall and Carl Mayer in Nebraska and Andy Hickock in Kirksville and even whatshisname, McIvery, down in Concordia—"

"What used to be Kansas and northern Missouri," Ingolf explained to Mary; she'd have seen old-world maps, but she wouldn't be familiar with the modern political boundaries.

"—so it's not just Iowa," Ed continued. "Having those lunatics knock off one of their own has the Bossmen all antsy, and I don't blame them wanting to put a stop to it either. The bastards tried to kill Tony Heasleroad's *family*, too. That's going off the reservation."

"Any more trouble since?"

"A bit. Assassinations, riots, Cutter agents stirring up the city rabble and hobos and such against the authorities; more of that in Iowa, but dey're the biggest anyway, hey? We've all agreed to outlaw the Cutters and send men, and the Sheriffs here in Richland voted to support the Bossman on it by t'ree to one. Iowa and Nebraska are kicking in the main army, especially the infantry and artillery and engineers, but everyone's sending cavalry. Figure they're going to need all they can get, up there on the high plains and in Montana."

"Yah hey, you betcha they will. That's how the Sioux kept running rings around us in the war . . . *that* war—"

The Sioux War had been his first serious conflict, when he'd left home as a volunteer in the force Richland sent to help Fargo and Marshall. Looking back, it had been educational, if also deeply stupid and pointless.

"—they could move faster. This is going to be on a different scale, though. And hopefully the Sioux will be on our side, or at least neutral."

Says Ingolf Vogeler aka Iron Bear, he thought, a little bemused. *Never thought I'd be a blood brother of the Lakota, after I spent all that time fighting them.*

"Yah," Ed said. "But since it's all volunteers and not a regular National Guard call-up . . ."

". . . it's also a complete cluster . . ." Ingolf paused and remembered Wanda was present. "Cluster-frack. Und who's you got bossing da troop I saw outside?"

Home a couple of hours und I start already talking da Deepest Cheesehead again, he thought, hearing himself begin to turn the "th" sounds to "d."

Though he'd never lost the flat hard vowels and hint of singsong in the years of his wandering. For that matter, unless memory was fooling him it had gotten a bit stronger here since he left.

Of course, everyone wants to sound like they've lived here forever. It's . . . what did Father Ignatius call it? The prestige dialect. If you can't be a Farmer, you can at least sound like one.

Ed went on: "Will Kohler's commanding, for now. Brevet National Guard rank of Major, got the Bossman to confirm dat."

Ingolf nodded; Will Kohler was about forty, the local drill instructor, and his father had held the job before him—and before the Change he'd run a martial arts club, and been in the old American military before *that.* As Sheriff, Ed Vogeler was in charge of the county's militia and maintained a force of Deputies, who were the closest thing to a standing military force the local government had as well as police and first-responders and much else, but Kohler handled most of the training and organization.

Then the wording his brother had used struck him and he spoke sharply:

"For now?"

"Ah . . ."

The Sheriff coughed. Wanda spoke:

"A lot of the people who have cavalry training and whose families can spare them in da working season are Farmers' sons, or even Sheriffs'. Und—"

"And Will Kohler isn't," Ingolf said. "Yah, yah. They'll

be young and full of beans, too. Average age under twenty-one and even dumber than I was then. What was it you said last autumn, Ed?"

His brother coughed again and looked at his wife. "Ah . . . at nineteen a man is *supposed* to think with his fists and his balls."

Wanda laughed ruefully, but the problem was serious. Here in rough-and-ready Richland where everyone put his hand to the work of the season class divisions weren't as strong as in wealthier and more sophisticated parts of the Midwest. But the division between Farmer and Refugee was there, and stronger in the younger generation.

With exceptions, of course.

Wanda's family had run a microbrewery in Madison, and had arrived in Readstown with a wagonload of tools and hop-seed pulled by some big draught horses; nobody thought it odd that she'd ended up marrying the Sheriff's eldest son. Others had had useful skills, been blacksmiths or carpenters or bowyers or whatever. Nor was William Kohler exactly a Refugee, even if his father was originally from Racine.

But he isn't from a local Farmer's family, either, Ingolf thought unhappily. *No feedstore cap in his closet.*

Talking to Mathilda and her friends had given him more tools to think about how it worked.

A lot of the volunteers are sons of . . . Matti'd say manor-holding knights and barons. That's what they are for all practical purposes, though they don't know it yet. And Will's just a paid soldier, a noncom. Except that he really knows what he's doing and they don't, and damn it that ought to count for more.

He caught Mary's eye. He could read what she thought, too, by now:

Since when does ought *mean that much?*

Ingolf sighed. "Yeah, if I hadn't been Dad's son, God knows I wouldn't have gotten a command right away in the Sioux War; and God also knows I was pretty useless until I learned by doing. So Will can't lick them into shape? I'm a bit surprised."

"Oh, he's kicked some of their sorry young asses," Ed said. "While I handled their folks. And the ones from right hereabouts know him. The worst of the rest left und the rest have learned, dey *are* volunteers. But they're not happy about it. That's why they need a Sheriff's son in charge."

Ingolf put his cookie and his coffee cup down abruptly. "Wait a minute, Ed! I'm working for Rudi . . . Artos . . . now! And *he's* as busy as a centipede in an ass-kicking contest, and it's getting worse. He can't spare me."

Ed nodded, smiling. "And this army we're all raising is going to be fighting the people who're after him!"

Ingolf sighed, and rubbed his hand over his short-cropped brown beard, feeling the tug as his calluses caught and wondering when the first gray hairs would show. His elder brother had plenty, and he was starting to sympathize with him as well. It felt odd, after so many years of being a resentful exile.

"And when's Rudi arriving? The whole bunch going to be with him?" the elder Vogeler went on.

"Ah . . . just him and just a flying visit. Time's pressing. And we've got about a battalion with us; call it five hundred."

Ed's brows went up. "More wild-men like the Southsiders? They've learned a lot, but dey're still sort of rough at da edges."

Ingolf shook his head. "No, no, there's civilization in

northern Maine. Farms und such, at least, couple of towns, a government. They've done pretty well."

"Yah, Yankees then."

"Ah . . . not exactly, Ed. Let's just say that since our family're squareheads, it's going to be sort of like meeting some real old stories."

The original Vogelers had been from Lower Saxony, though they'd married the usual local mixtures in the eighteen decades since; other varieties of Deutsch, plenty of Norski, some Polak and Czech, even Yankee and Irish.

Ed frowned. "Thought it was all Yankees and Frenchmen there in Maine."

"Dere's some Svenska, couple of places named New Sweden and Stockholm and such. Settled back in Civil War times, a little after we Vogelers arrived here in the Kickapoo country. But mostly it's . . . there was this guy named Erik, who started out in Massachusetts, and he . . . it's a long story, that's what it is. Five hundred good fighting men, though. Rudi has a gift for making strong friends."

He took out his pipe, and his brother filled his own and pushed over fragrant shredded tobacco in a container made from a section of polished curly maple, and a lighter. Mary ostentatiously coughed and looked revolted as he filled it, tamped it down with a horny thumb and spun the lighter's wheel and held the flame to the bowl.

Figure I don't indulge often enough for you to really get upset, darling, he thought.

There was no point in *saying* it, and the smoking habit had largely died out in Montival. Wisconsin had been tobacco-growing country before the Change, though, and had kept it up. In the old days they'd believed that smoking was bad for you, but there were so many other things that could, would and did kill you now that people didn't care. Mary simply disliked the smell and made no bones about it.

Not much use in pointing out that that guy Strider smoked a pipe, either, and Gandalf. And all the furry-foot brigade lit up at the drop of a match.

He wasn't afraid a pipe now and then would kill him. As far as he could tell, a lot of the old Americans had been quivering daisies who thought they'd live forever if only they were careful enough, as if life was worth living that way. Some of them had believed eating *butter* was bad for you, of all things.

"By the way, Ed, what's Mark doing all dressed up like he's off to da wars?" he said instead.

Mary's eye rolled. "Because he *is* off to the wars, *alae*, duh!"

"*Ensign* Vogeler of the First Volunteer Cavalry?" Ingolf asked incredulously. *Mark's his son, but . . .* "That's for real, he's not just dressing up until they leave?"

Wanda glared at her husband, and Ed puffed furiously on his pipe. They both had the look a long-married couple got who'd chased an argument around in circles long enough that they'd stopped, if only because biting each other on the buttocks was the sole way to continue.

Ed's tone was defensive: "Look, he *is* off to da wars. He threatened to run away und join up as a paid-soldier trooper somewhere if I didn't let him, and he meant it. What am I supposed to do wit' him, throw him in jail for da next six months? I don't have enough pull outside Richland to stop someone hiring him."

Ingolf opened his mouth to say *You betcha you should put his butt in jail and paddle it too* and closed it again; what Mark threatened was more or less what his uncle Ingolf had done after his grandfather died. Ingolf and Ed had spent six months butting heads before the call for volunteers to fight the Sioux came down from Richland, and he'd leapt at the chance.

"Yah," his brother went on, reading his hesitation; he wasn't stupid about people when he bothered to pay attention. "If I locked him up, he'd leave when he got out and never come back. A man has to know what he can do wit' his sons, and what he can't. Dad would push us too hard, sometimes."

I nearly didn't come back. Wouldn't have, except for the thing on Nantucket and the way that worked out; I'd have gone on being mad at you until I died, because it'd become a habit. And I'd never have seen Wanda again, or met my younger nieces or nephews, or remembered Mark as anything but a little kid.

He couldn't even tell the boy this war was an exercise in mutual stupidity like the fracas with the Sioux. He *could* say it was a stupid thing for a very young man to do when he had a perfectly good reason for staying home, but that was like saying that the world would be a better place if everyone followed the Golden Rule.

Which is true, but deeply fucking useless, because it's never going to happen.

"Ed . . . I'm not sure this is a great idea. Want me to try and talk Mark out of it?"

Ed sighed. "You can try, but he reminds me of you at that age. Or me. He's getting to da stage where your old man is so stupid the whole world can't bear it. Or anyone older if they cross him. Yelling didn't work, even Wanda crying didn't work for long, and he's too old to put over my knee."

"I hear you. Butting at everything like a young ram in the spring, eh?"

"Right. Und he'll be better off wit' you. Hell, he's not that much younger than *you* were when you pulled the same stunt."

"Two years. That's nothing for you or me now, but seventeen to nineteen's a big jump. He's got his growth but his bones haven't knit and he's not as strong as he'll be in two years, or as fast. He's just not damn-well *ready* yet but he *thinks* he is. It's dangerous enough when you are ready."

"No, he's not ready!" Wanda cut in. "Uff da! He's still a child."

Of course, he'll always be your firstborn baby boy, Wanda. Ingolf knew mothers thought that way. *But you're right. Just now he's a kid who thinks he's a man.*

"Yah yah, Wanda, OK!" Ed said desperately. "But he *will* run off if I don't let him go! Can *you* talk him out of it, woman? What'm I supposed to do, break his legs?"

Mutely she shook her head, and looked out the window at twelve-year-old Dave and Melly and young Ingolf and Jenny.

Ed sighed. "And I figure you can keep an eye on him, Ingolf. I'd appreciate it."

Ingolf felt his shoulders go tight, and his lips; he forced relaxation on himself, using a technique he'd picked up in Chenrezi Monastery, in the Valley of the Sun. It had been designed for more serious things, but it worked for this too.

"You don't know what you're talking about, Ed."

The older man bristled. "I've been in fights, some of them before you had hair on your . . . chin! I know—"

"You've been in fights, Ed. Yah, in Dad's day, the upstream raid at Cashton, and against the road-people. You did well in them too. You've seen men die, had them try their best to kill you, killed a few yourself."

For a moment Edward Vogeler glanced down at the table and turned the bowl of his pipe between his big knobby hands, looking at somewhere far away from this pleasant homey room.

"Oh, yah," he said quietly. "Damn und hell, yah."

Ingolf nodded, not really in agreement. "What you haven't been in is a *war*. Not the same thing. This is going to be a *big* war; it's already gone on for years out west. There's going to be real *battles*, and against real soldiers, in real gear with real weapons, not starving city-folk with baseball bats and kitchen knives, or even some raggedy-ass woods rats with hunting bows and bowies. They'll be fighting to kill, not to steal a flitch of bacon and a pie, or run off a horse, or just to get in out of the cold."

"OK," Ed said. "You *do* know about dat stuff. So you can—"

"I'll be doing my *job*. I can't be Mark's bodyguard. I couldn't keep him safe even if I *was* his bodyguard. I can't even keep *her* safe—"

He pointed at Mary. She nodded soberly and touched her eye patch, and said flatly:

"I can't keep *him* safe either."

Ingolf nodded: "A stray arrow, a catapult ball or a bolt coming in from a thousand yards away, or some weasel bastard of a paid soldier who's *forgotten* more about using a shete than any seventeen-year-old kid can know and sees Mark between him and safety, or—"

He saw Wanda wincing more deeply with every sentence, and dropped the litany. It was probably worse because she knew he wasn't pulling up possibilities out of his imagination. Every one he'd mentioned was something he'd *seen*, and she could hear it in his voice.

"Damn und hell, men die in every big army camp I've ever seen just because they get caught in front of a bolting mule team hauling a wagon full of hardtack or some shit like that! I don't want Mark hurt, and I don't want you hating me, Ed; we did that long enough. I especially don't want Wanda hating me. Or me hating myself, come to it."

He could see his brother fighting down anger; Wanda brushed fiercely at her eyes with the back of her hand. Ed puffed at his pipe, waited a moment, puffed again, then spoke with careful softness:

"That's all God's truth," he said, and crossed himself for emphasis. "But, Ingolf, I *can't stop him*. I tell myself it's a good thing he gets some military experience for when he's Sheriff, und all that shit, but it's what's going to happen. Please . . . I know you can't keep him *safe*, but I know he'll be safer with you than he would bolting and getting into some half-hard bunch where nobody knows his ass from Adam or gives a damn about him. Please, little brother?"

Ingolf closed his eyes and put his hand across them for an instant. "OK. I'll do my best. But I don't promise you anything, understand?"

Rudi, get here fast, would you?

CHAPTER SIXTEEN

"**H**e's dead?"

Artos nodded.

"Yes, he is, Otter. In a battle with the Cutters."

Jake sunna Jake's woman had taken that beast's name for her own here, while she'd stayed the winter. She was groomed now, her brown hair sleek, and wearing a Richlander-style woolen dress and good shoes with a silver Triple Moon pendant around her neck. It was as if she'd never squatted barefoot in rags and half-cured rabbit skins; he could tell she'd been looking forward to impressing her man. Now her eyes rolled up and she started to buckle; Samantha, the Vogelers' housekeeper, caught her by one arm. A low wail escaped her lips, not too loud but continuous.

Artos waited for a single hopeless moment; he didn't know her well enough to embrace her, and—

Then he drew the Sword sheath and all and held it between them with his hand just below the guard. That put the antler-embraced crystal of the Sword's pommel between their eyes, so that they saw each other through it. The Southsider woman staggered, her dark face losing the rubbery slackness that had washed over it. After a moment tears trickled from the corners of her eyes, but the stare remained steady. It was his own face he could feel going white, as if spikes of ice had been driven into his chest and would never let go.

Dying must be like this. Or losing something that is beyond bearing.

"He was a brave man and died well, face to the foe," Artos said, after a moment that seemed to stretch forever, and put a hand on her shoulder. "You and your children will always have my protection, as my own kin, for he was my brother. You shall be lady of Dun Jake. Now go and keen him, as I did."

Tuk and Samul, the dead man's half brothers and nearidentical save that one was dark brown and the other pale-fair, moved to support her. Artos staggered as they left, his hand fumbling a little as he slid the scabbard back into the sword-throg that hung from his belt on three buckled straps. On the second try he managed it, and saw how shocked Mathilda's face was.

To be sure, I'm not clumsy for the most part, he thought. Aloud:

"It's all right, *mo chroi*, my heart. I'm . . . I'm not hurt in body."

He leaned against a tree, and took long deep breaths. In, hold, out . . . as he'd been taught, the body helped govern the mind and spirit, for they were one. In, hold, out . . .

"What did you *do*, Rudi, you idiot!" she said, hugging him fiercely.

That helped as well. Another deep breath, and:

"I ate her grief." A quirk of the mouth. "Or some of it, at least. The first blow of loss. Swear you'll outlive me, my heart . . . or no, perhaps I'd be cruel to ask that of you, for I've never felt any single thing half so bitter. Not broken bones or cut flesh or fear of death."

The pain receded a little as he spoke, but he sensed it would never be entirely gone. He'd grieved for Jake himself after the fight on the ice, as for a loyal friend and comrade.

"But this is entirely different," he said, hearing his own voice shake.

As he straightened he fought for an awareness of the day, the noon sun overhead and its warmth on his bonnet and the plaid across his shoulders, Mathilda's solid comfort and the clean scent of her hair, somewhere a horse neighing, somewhere a girl singing "Barbara Allen" and a spinning wheel moaning with a rising-falling note. The life of Readstown and the First Volunteer Cavalry was going on. As Jake's woman and the sons she had made with him did; life was the answer to life, and death and loss were part of that never-ending story.

Know joy, there in the Summerlands, Jake sunna Jake. I wish you'd lived, and that we'd been friends all a long life-time, and sat together to feel the sun on our aching bones and watch our great-grandchildren draw their first bows. But that wasn't your fate. Or mine either, and I know that for a fact. I wish I didn't *know what I'm condemning Matti to, and that is also a fact.*

"You ate her grief?" Mathilda said, a little white about the lips. "That's . . . that's *terrible*, Rudi!"

"It is," he agreed hoarsely. "But a grief shared is lessened, just as a joy shared is doubled. And Jake came with us because I asked him. I was his chief; isn't it for me to comfort his darlings, just as it is to see to their welfare? If the Sword lets me do that more directly than words alone can accomplish, why, that's a mixed blessing but still a blessing."

Mathilda held her silence, but he could feel her radiating skepticism. He shrugged; the work of the day wasn't going to wait on his feelings, or hers for that matter.

"Let's to it."

Ingolf and Will Kohler were waiting for him in the flat meadow where the First was camped; Ed Vogeler too, and his son, and Wanda and some of her household workers not far off setting up trestle tables. A fair scattering of families—siblings, parents, lovers, or simple spectators—were waiting there beyond the weathered board fence. They weren't that far from the complex of interlinked and outlying buildings that made up Readstown, after all. Nor were these Richlanders much given to formality, even in war.

"Let's see them put through their paces, then," he said when he was near the little party of commanders.

Kohler nodded at him in friendly wise; they'd met and sparred—literally—on the quest's passage through this land last fall. He was a blocky muscular man a few years older than Ingolf, about four inches shorter than Artos' six-two, but nearly as broad in the shoulders and with a swordsman's thick wrists. His dark yellow hair was cropped rather shorter than the Readstown custom, and he'd have been handsome save for the fact that the tip of his nose was missing. Unlike most local men he was clean-shaven as well, which showed a chin like a lump of granite.

"Colonel Vogeler?" he asked formally, looking to Ingolf to confirm the order.

"Carry on, Major," Ingolf said.

"Ensign, sound *fall in*," Kohler said.

Mark Vogeler put his trumpet to his lips and blew the call. There was a concerted rush from the tents towards the horse-lines and a grabbing of saddles and tack. Of course they'd been expecting this, but nevertheless they were all standing in ranks by the heads of their mounts and ready to ride in a fairly commendable five minutes or so. All equipped as Ingolf's young nephew was, and as was common for cavalry in this part of the world; they didn't have heavy horse, though every fourth man had a light lance as well as bow and blade. The gear was approximately uniform, differing mainly in that some had scale-mail shirts rather than chain-mail ones, but the clothes were not; most were roughly practical, the sort of thing a man wore for a hunting trip, but he saw one pair of tight red trousers with gold piping on the seams, and several horsehair crests on helms, and plenty of tooled leather on saddles and tack and gear.

"Set them to it."

The volunteers formed into columns of fours and rode a circuit, leaping obstacles of fence-poles and bales of hay; for a wonder, nobody fell off. Then they gave a show of arms, shooting into plank-and-braided-straw targets with their saddle bows at the gallop, slicing tossed apples with their shetes, picking tent pegs out of the ground with the points of spears. They concluded by forming into two groups and charging each other. That ended up in a melee, and several *did* finish on the ground clutching sore heads or minor wounds; three had to be carried off and wouldn't be going on campaign anytime this year. Then they drew up for inspection again, and he went over them one more time when they'd been dismissed to their tents.

"More discipline than most rancher levies back home," Mathilda observed quietly.

"Yes, my heart, but that's like saying *drier than the Pacific* or *uglier than meadows of camas in spring*.

"Well, gentlemen," he said briskly, when their troop-leaders were in front of him.

They straightened with their helmets tucked under their left arms; from the looks out of the corner of their eyes they'd heard something of him, and the Sword drew glances as well. That and the effort of following his Mackenzie lilt made them pay close attention. Mathilda got a few glances as well, in her titanium hauberk and coif and sallet, with the long shield slung across her back blazoned with the Lidless Eye.

"First, let me say what I like. Your troopers are strong and fit, they seem to ride well and have some idea of how to handle their weapons individually. They also have *some* idea of drill and maneuver; though how well they'll remember it in a real engagement remains to be seen. And they're fully equipped. Their gear is excellent, of its kind. So are their horses."

Smiles were beginning to break out; the troop-leaders weren't much older than their men, and from what Ingolf had said they'd been chosen for birth and cockerel pride and willingness to take on the burdens of the office more than anything else. He made a chopping gesture.

"Oh, and one more thing: I've no doubt whatsoever that they're mostly brave as lions. With that I have exhausted the tale of their military virtues, so I have. They're raw. Green as new spring grass dribbling down a sheep's arse. The brave stupid ones will die, and the unlucky. The brave, lucky and clever ones may survive long enough to learn enough to be useful."

He turned to Ingolf and Kohler. "Speaking of gear, there's too much by about half."

"Oh, criminy, *yah*," the Readstown drill instructor said. "And believe me, we've been combing it out for a week already."

Artos nodded. "Essentials only, discard the rest, no more than one two-wheel cart for every twenty men. No camp followers, and no servants. They can do their own chores. And lose the plumes and brightwork, and brown all the metal that's been polished, the sorrowful waste of it. I don't want anything that draws the eye. These aren't knights who do nothing but charge. I want them able to scout and skirmish as well, and for that visibility is a drawback. Understood?"

Kohler grinned like something you came across in a wood. At night when you least wanted to, and after hearing several howls.

"Your Majesty, I understand you *perfectly*. I think we're going to get along just *fine*. I'll have 'em upside right by sundown."

"Good. Dismissed, then."

Raising his voice slightly: "Say your good-byes; we leave at dawn tomorrow and I expect to be at the landing before noon rolls around again."

The meeting broke up; a band with a tuba and accordion was warming up near the tables, and the friends-and-relatives crowd began to mingle with the young volunteers peacocking in their brand-new gear. A long banner went up between two poles: *Readstown Sends Her Best.*

Artos looked them over. The youngsters were eager, their younger siblings and the contemporaries stuck at home with the endless round of chores openly envious.

The older men here to see sons and younger brothers off were more somber and many headed for the racks of barrels that held beer and cider and applejack and whiskey; they'd seen the elephant themselves, mostly. In the years after the Change, or in the case of a few in distant lands before it, with weapons entirely different but dangers much the same. The younger women were flirting and laughing with the warriors and ignoring the burning glares of those not going.

Feast the fighting-men, dance and sing and send them off to war with kisses on their lips, Artos thought.

Their mothers and elder sisters tried for gaiety but their eyes were full of worry. They had seen their men ride out to fight before; they knew this was no game, and that there was no room for glory in the grave.

For the moment they all avoided Artos, still jittery from the rough side of his tongue. The battered brown-bearded face of his brother-in-law grinned.

"That'll teach 'em. They think they're hot shit and they're half right."

"It's to be hoped they'll learn."

"You really want to take 'em along? We could pick up a battalion in Iowa, probably, and it would save a little time."

"It's only a little time. They'll do; and nothing we could get in Iowa would be much more experienced. The longer you've got them under your eye, the better. Plus they know *you*, and your family, and me to some extent. Very few in Iowa saw much of us."

"Fargo and Marshall have more combat-trained troops, and they're on our route."

"But I'm even more of a stranger there than in Iowa; they're not going to give me men because I look so dash-

ing in my kilt, to be sure. And there's good material in
these young men if they can be hammered a wee bit . . .
Colonel. Do you have time for that with all the rest you'll
have to do?"

"No, but I have time enough for Major Kohler here to
use me as a scarecrow and boogeyman, hey? Good commanding officer, bad-assed second-in-command. It
should work."

"My thoughts exactly. The boats will be waiting and
we should be in Dubuque before the end of the week and
Des Moines not long after. A crowded journey, to be
sure."

Then he turned his eye on Mark Vogeler. The young
man's smile died at the cold blue-green gaze; the expression on Mathilda's face was just as bleak.

"You wish to enlist in this enterprise?" Artos said.

"Uh . . . yessir, Your Majesty."

"So."

Artos looked him up and down, ignoring his flush.
The boy's father suppressed a smile, and his mother
looked up and then away again, helping to remove the
cloths that covered trays of food and stacks of wooden
plates. She was well within earshot . . . but also a wise
lady and concerned for her son.

"Now listen to me, boy. Ingolf is my comrade by
shared peril and hardship, and my brother by marriage;
your family is kin to mine through that. Also your father
is my host and benefactor, and so we are tied by bonds of
guest-friendship and honor and alliance."

A pause, and then he barked: "*And that is why I
haven't sent you back to play soldiers with a stick behind the
barn.*"

The youngster flushed more deeply, until his fair freckled skin was beet-red, but he kept his stiff brace. Artos hid his approval; controlling your temper was hardest at that age, just as that was the time when it was hardest for a male to think of anything but girls, or calculate a risk without insane disregard for reason and probability. He undid his sword belt and handed it to Mathilda, along with his bonnet, and unpinned his plaid from the brooch of silver knotwork at his shoulder. The warm spring breeze cuffed at his long copper-gold hair, but he had a headband to confine it. Apart from that he wore only his shirt and kilt, knee-hose and shoes.

"Can you obey orders, boyo?"

A stiff nod. "Sir, yessir!"

"Good. Here's one. Kill me—or do your best."

Blank bewilderment met him. "You're in armor and you have a blade by your side and a shield ready for your arm. Do your best to kill me, boy, or I swear I'll paddle your backside with the flat of your shete here in front of all who know you until you run bawling for your momma."

Slowly Mark slid the blade out of its sheath, and the round shield with its brown surface broken by an orange wedge onto his left arm and then up under his eyes. He was frowning a little now, really thinking; Artos allowed himself a slight nod. The shete came up into the overhead point-forward-and-down position these easterners favored. It was the type of weapon you'd find horsemen using from the Rockies as far east as civilization went, based on the old tool whose worn-down name it had taken, but lengthened and slightly curved, sharpened all along the outer edge and a few inches back from the point on the other.

Like most this had a circular disk-shaped guard and

the hilt was canted against the curve of the blade; the whole thing had a look as if the agricultural tool side of its ancestry had had a brief fling with the sort of Chinese *dao*-saber found in the ruins of martial arts stores. At least in the mind of the smith who made it. The weapon was of fine steel, and sharpened to a good working edge too. Young Mark would be as tall as his uncle or father someday, and was nearly there now; that meant thirty inches of sharp steel in his hand already had an uncomfortably long reach.

He frowned again, moved his feet to set himself, and then cut backhand and forehand hard and fast. Air whistled around the steel.

Obeying orders, at least; he's not pulling it, Artos thought, as he swayed his torso aside and let the cuts sail by, moving without apparent haste and his hands clasped behind his back. *That would have killed me, right enough.*

The boy stumbled as the blade met air; then he recovered with an unconscious snarl and thrust directly for Artos' breast in an extended lunge.

Smack!

The calloused palms of the Mackenzie's large, shapely hands slapped together on the flat of the blade at its broadest section, just behind the point. The Readstown lad stood goggling for an instant, and Artos shoved his hands sharply forward with a flicking motion. The brass pommel of the shete smacked into Mark's face.

"My dothse!" he cried in a pained voice, clapping his hand to the organ.

Blood leaked between his fingers. Artos heard his mother give a gasp, and his father and uncle what sounded like smothered chortles. He dropped the youngster's shete, bounced the hilt off his foot to flick it head-high and snatched it out of the air. Almost in the same instant he dropped and pivoted on his left foot, his right shin raking out horizontally. It took the boy across the back of the knees, hard. He flipped into the air under the impact and landed on his shoulders and neck and head, driven stunning hard by the leverage and the forty-pound weight of mail shirt and shield. The breath went out of him in a bubbling wheeze, and again when Artos' boot slammed down on the shield and pinned his arm against his chest under it. The stamp wasn't hard enough to crack bone, but it was painful.

The shete moved in a graceful curve and dimpled the skin under Mark's chin, where the Midwestern-style mail shirt gave no protection. The young man grew very still, despite the blood running down over his nose and upper lip and sticking to his pathetic attempt at a mustache.

"Now, think on this; a man in a pleated skirt just took away the sword of your armored self, killed you with it twice . . . and stamped the life out of you into the bargain. What's the lesson of this?"

"Dat I'm not's gud's you," the boy wheezed, holding his nose and glaring.

Artos withdrew his foot and the blade. "No, it's that you're not good enough to be a fighting-man, not yet. There are ten thousand men and more, and more than a few women—one of them your uncle's wife—who could have done the same, or at least killed you in a more straightforward fashion. Up, boy!"

Mark stood and braced his shoulders back. Artos grinned.

"You're no coward, at least. But guts without brains are soon spilled to be meat for coyotes and crows, lad. Understood?"

A quick nod, and Artos went on:

"So if you're to be worth your food in my army, it's as what my Bearkiller relatives call a military apprentice. I'm making you your uncle's aide. That means you carry his messages, do his errands, pitch his tent, care for his gear—and your own—currycomb his horses, make up the fire and cook the rations and whatever else he can find for you to do, the which may include emptying the honey-bucket. You do it with your mouth shut, your eyes and ears open to fill your empty head, and willingly. If he tells you to run like a rabbit or jump like a frog, you do that. Is that clear?"

"Yeth, thir!"

Artos leaned closer; the smile went out of his face, and one knuckle prodded painfully into the teenager's sore chest.

"And at the *first* sign of insubordination, the first whine, the first complaint, the first stupid buck-in-spring prank to prove what a big brave bold man you are, I will send you back home in your drawers, tied to a donkey with your face towards its rump."

He leaned closer still. "And don't smile, because that's the truth of it and I swear it so by my mother's head and by all the Gods and by the oath of my people. Do you think I'm jokin', boyo?"

"No, thir!"

"Understood?"

"Yeth, *thir!*"

"Good." He relaxed and offered the shete hilt-first, spinning it so the blade lay along his forearm. "Go see to that nose. It's not broken, eh?"

"I doan dink so, thir."

"Scoot then, lad! And as long as you remember your promise, we'll all get along fine."

He turned away and let his grin grow; Ingolf returned it. Ed Vogeler waited until his son was out of earshot—barely—before bellowing laughter.

"Some things a father can't do. Thanks, Rudi. It's a load off my mind."

"I took some of the piss and vinegar out of him, Ed. And he could grow into a fighting-man to match the best. But he's young yet, and I can't put him in a barrel made of steel plate—"

A nod. "Ingolf explained that, und in goddamned detail. I still feel better about it."

"Men are weird," Mathilda said with feeling, and Wanda nodded emphatically.

"But . . . I feel better too," she said to Ingolf and Artos.

Her assistants finished removing the covers, and the civilians—and the troops, once they'd gotten out of their gear and freshened up—crowded around.

Mary came up. "Enjoy it while you can, boys," she muttered, as she took a plate. "It's hardtack and stewed mule soon enough."

"Exactly what I plan to do," Artos said.

Now that the focus of work was gone he felt that cold emptiness in his middle again; one way to fill it was with food. Body and spirit were one. You could work from the one to the other. He loaded his plate with slices of cured ham, cold roast beef, pickles, dabs of mustard and horseradish, chicken, potato salad, spring greens, rye bread with butter, pumpernickel and white loaf, and half a dozen kinds of cheese, and added a mug of a dark bitter beer. The dried-apple and cherry pies and pastries tempted him back again.

"How are they?" he asked his half sister. "Otter in particular and the Southsiders in general."

Ritva was off ahead of them all; as much to avoid Hrolf Homersson, he suspected, as because scouting was her specialty.

"Otter's asleep. I got her to take some lettuce-cake tea. I talked things over with Samantha—"

Who was the Vogelers' housekeeper, and unofficially and semi-clandestinely a priestess of the Old Religion, which had a small presence here. It wasn't identical to what Mackenzies practiced, nor yet to the eccentric Dúnedain version, but there was a basic similarity. He'd put the Southsider civilians in her charge when he left for the east. It was more easeful for Mathilda if Mary dealt with her, rather than him.

"—and they've learned a lot. The Vogelers helped by getting them put out to live with people who knew crafts, and they learned a lot by just doing the work of the season, too. Plus she was running a Moon School for them."

"They can follow along later, when the war is won," Artos said.

Or stay here and make a life, if we die instead, went unspoken between them.

CHAPTER SEVENTEEN

When I was just a young warrior and at most tanist to Mother, I went on a quest for a magic sword and saw wonders and terrors, Artos thought. *Now I'm to be a High King, and I spend most of my time in meetings. Meetings! So much for glory.*

Mathilda seemed to read his thoughts. She leaned over and whispered in his ear:

"Mother *likes* meetings. She even likes reading and annotating reports."

Artos stifled a groan, and took a glass off a passing tray held by a servant in archaic white coat and black bow tie. It was corn whiskey with water and, evidence of wealth and high civilization, ice.

Good of its kind, he thought, as the half-sweet, half-sour liquid bit at his tongue and slid down his throat. *But by each and every face of the Lord and Lady, there's a whole long list of things I'd rather be doing!*

He had Mathilda with him here in the big pavilion-style tent, with its drowsy-making scent of warm canvas. She was colorful and majestic in her cotehardie and wimple with its net of gold and rubies; she and black-robed

Father Ignatius were present as advisors. Ingolf and Mary were off elsewhere being invaluable, seeing that things didn't go to wrack and ruin in his absence. Ritva was present partly as Rudi's follower, but also because she was the niece of the Lady of the Rangers, with the seven stars and tree on her doublet; Fred because of whose son he was, proud in the old-fashioned green dress uniform of Boise's army, Virginia on his arm in the copper-riveted blue denim jeans, tooled boots and belt, white cotton shirt and silk neckerchief of a western Rancher. They were all looking a little grim, and hiding it well. Their mission would be much helped or hindered by what took place here.

Bjarni was King of Norrheim, of course, and so a sovereign ally, hiding his awe at the sheer size of Des Moines under a stiff dignity, and carefully refraining from mentioning the number of folk in his homeland when he spoke to local panjandrums. John Red Leaf and Rick Three Bears were in full ceremonial fig, including a sweeping bonnet of eagle feathers for the elder Sioux; he looked years older than Rudi remembered him, but that was probably largely exhaustion. Even his son, a man of Artos' own age and reared in the saddle, was keeping going by main effort and sheer will.

Red Leaf has come a long way, and very fast, to get here in time. Especially when he had to spend days talking to his own people's governing Council as well. That drains a man almost as much as twelve hours in the saddle, though in a different way.

"I'm going to sleep for a week when this is over," he muttered to Artos. "And getting the folks back home to agree to this was even harder than the traveling."

Artos nodded. *I wish we'd had more time to talk, but*

time is the one thing we lack here. I felt like I was dawdling all the way to Readstown, but we couldn't go any faster. Fortunately we've better prospects for speed from now on . . .

"Though we're getting closer to the enemy, as well," he murmured.

Mathilda's brows went up; she'd found time to pluck them. "I thought you said the Sword blocked their vision of you?"

"The vision of their adepts," Artos said quietly. "It does nothing whatsoever to hinder plain mortal spies using the eyes in their heads and passing messages to men riding horses back westward. We're not going through their territory this time, but we will be skirting it."

The Bossmen of the Midwestern realms were here too, or in the case of distant Concordia and Kirksville their heirs were, accompanied by senior advisors; the young men looked serious with their burden of responsibility. Abel Heuisink and Kate Heasleroad represented Iowa, the richest and most populous and powerful nation on the continent. The man was in his sixties but trim and erect, with only a fringe of cropped white hair around a bald dome and clear eyes bright blue in a seamed, tanned face. He wore the usual formal blue bib overalls and billed cap of a Hawkeye landed gentleman; Kate, the Regent, was a little younger than Mathilda, a tall willowy brunette, and dressed in an imitation of her cotehardie. The two young women had become good friends during the quest's brief, eventful stay in Iowa last year; Mathilda's political instincts had been instrumental in helping Kate secure her infant son's position when her husband was killed by the Cutters. She had also been rather taken with Mathilda's little talks on the virtues of hereditary monarchy. Which was what Iowa already *had* been before they arrived, her first Bossman being the sort of proverbial lucky adventurer who founded a dynasty, but without much of the terminology, techniques or attitudes that made it work smoothly.

And Ingolf and I were helpful in reconciling the Heuisinks to the arrangement, despite their being leaders of the opposition, and for making Abel Chancellor to cement the alliance. I will not *be informing her that Dalan and Graber are with us! I'm glad to see they haven't fallen out again . . . but a foreign foe will have that effect. The which the both of them know very well.*

Abel Heuisink whispered to Kate, and she cleared her throat. An attendant rang a bell, and the aides and assistants stepped back. The principals gathered around a table shaped like an elongated oval and sat—or at least everyone but Artos did. There were startled looks at the Iowans as he went to the position at the head of the table, and more as he drew the scabbarded Sword from the frog at his belt and laid it on the polished maple before his place.

He'd dressed for the occasion in the ceremonial version of Mackenzie gear that he'd left here in Des Moines last year; a fine tartan kilt and knee-hose with the little sgian dubh tucked into it, polished brogans, tight green Montrose jacket with its double row of silver buttons and froth of lace at cuffs and throat, and the long plaid caught at the shoulder with a knotwork brooch and a tasseled fringe on its ankle-length trail. A broad black leather belt with a massive worked buckle cinched his waist and held his badger-fur sporran at the front and the dirk on his left hip, and a spray of raven feathers rose from the Triple Moon clasp on his tam-o'-shanter.

With his six foot two of narrow-waisted, broad-

shouldered, long-limbed height he made a striking figure;
the more with the jewel-cut handsomeness of his cleft-
chinned face, framed by the red-gold of his hair and given
gravity beyond his years by the scars. He paused for a
moment to let everyone look—a King had to be something of an actor as well—then inclined his head a little to
the bewildered dignitaries. Dress and titles had altered
less here in the Midwest than elsewhere, though that was
changing. He gave a silent plea to Brigid for wisdom, to
Ogma of the Honey Tongue for the skill to express it,
and to the Mother of this earth with her gift of sover-
eignty for permission to speak. Then he began:

"In the name of the Divine by all the names we call
Them, be welcome, friends and allies. I am Artos, High
King in Montival in the west; on the old maps, that would
be Oregon and Washington and British Columbia, for a
start. The government of the great Provisional Republic
of Iowa has asked me to preside at this meeting."

There was a low murmur as rulers leaned back to listen
to the whispers of their advisors. He let it die, and continued with a slight bleak smile.

"With me you see those"—*some of those, but let's not
complicate matters*—"who accompanied me to Nantucket. There we found the source of the Change, and
were granted visions . . . and the Sword of the Lady."

The looks were dubious, until he laid his hand on the
hilt. Then there was a . . .

Shock, he thought. *Yet there's nothing physical, and no
one could swear that anything happened at all.*

. . . followed by a deep quietness. *Awe,* he thought,
and perhaps some fear, as well as confusion in plenty.

"We are gathered here to meet the menace of Corwin's black evil, of the Prophet Sethaz and the Church

Universal and Triumphant," he went on. "And his ally in Boise. With me are many who have suffered from that evil, and who can bring their strength to oppose it as well. Not least—"

His eyes flicked aside, and Fred rose, standing at parade rest with a face that might have been carved from dark polished wood.

"—Frederick Thurston."

Another murmur, and he raised a hand for silence as Fred sat again.

"Yes, the son of General-President Lawrence Thurston, and his rightful heir. Unlike the murdering parricide and usurper who currently holds that city and realm, who conspired with the Prophet to kill his own father."

Some of the Bossmen glanced at one another, or whispered eagerly with their advisors. Others sat with faces that might have been cast metal. None looked particularly surprised. Nobody who took or held power in these times needed to have a map drawn to show them where *that* could lead. He nodded to acknowledge it and went on:

"Now, you'll be wondering what I bring to this alliance that mighty Iowa gives me precedence here—besides a fancy Sword and a strange costume, that is."

A few flickering smiles. He nodded gravely and went on:

"I bring forty thousand men to the field in the High West. And more from other parts of my realm."

The Bossmen of northern Fargo and Marshall had been giving Red Leaf an occasional hard look. Now the lord of Fargo spoke.

Dan Rassmusen, Artos reminded himself. *Thin, a bit older than Ingolf, and a dangerous man if I've ever seen one. He fought the Sioux as a general for his older brother, and succeeded to the bossmanship four years ago in a neat little coup after the brother died, according to Matti . . . who is never wrong on such matters. Ignatius thinks him a capable man, but bad.*

"Where, exactly, is Montival, Mr. Mackenzie? Yah, I'd like to know where these troops are coming from, also exactly."

He was whipcord and sinew, with cropped yellow hair, a short beard showing the first silver threads and cold gray eyes. Two fingers were missing from his left hand. Judging from his glares at the Sioux, Artos suspected he knew *exactly* who'd removed them.

The Mackenzie met the northerner's gaze for a moment. "Well, my lord Bossman, what concerns the two of us is where the eastern border of Montival runs, does it not? For my realm stretches from there to the Pacific shores. And for that . . . well, better to show than tell."

He drew the Sword. This time the *shock* was definite and palpable, if still nothing that a camera or the machines of the old world would have recorded. The Fargo Bossman looked at it, winced a little, and then forced his eyes back to the gleaming length that seemed to draw in the sunlight from outside the pavilion's shadow until it blazed like the sun itself. Beads of sweat appeared on his tanned brow, and he was visibly compelling his breath to a slow even rhythm.

"What the *hell* . . ." he muttered.

His hands clenched on the arms of his chair, and he was far from the only one. Somewhere a dry sob sounded, under a chorus of gasps.

Artos took four steps backward, reversed the Sword and thrust it downward. Eyes widened as it sank ten inches into the fitted oakwood planks of the pavilion's floor with no more effort or sound than it would have made piercing so much water. Red Leaf rose, levering himself up against the arms of his chair with a slight grunt; he was fit for a man his age, but he was also well into his middle years, and he'd been pushing himself very hard indeed. Then he came to face Artos across the Sword, looking directly into his eyes.

"Hope I'm doing the right thing," he muttered. "Hope I talked everyone into doing the right thing."

Then he sank to his knees. His calloused hands reached out and clasped the antler-embraced crystal pommel of the Sword, and his eyes went wide in amazement.

"Damn," he whispered. "And I didn't think anything weirder than the Change could happen."

Artos reached out and laid his hands around the Indian's. For a moment he felt a wrenching disorientation, as if he were Red Leaf rather than himself, and staring at himself; then he was:

A man in a breechclout who raced his horse up a stretch of grass, shaking his Henry rifle over his head, shrieking Hoon! Hoon! *in savage exultation as the blue-clad troopers fell before the warriors who swarmed about.*

A man creeping on hands and knees through tall grass towards a herd of buffalo with spear-thrower in hand and dart clenched between his teeth.

A man who stood and lifted a hand in respect as the mammoth blundered belly-deep into the tundra bog and his tribesmen closed in around its wounded majesty.

A man who drew a flint knife and sang the high wailing chant of his death-song as the sabertooth flattened its ears and slunk closer . . .

And he knew what Red Leaf saw, what the Sioux chief *was* for instants that rang by like lifetimes:

A tall rangy man in buckskins with a flintlock in the crook of his arm, striding westward through a forest whose trees were like cathedral pillars.

A man raven-haired and high-cheeked, a hunter gliding beneath black pines on skis whose toes kicked up powder that glittered like diamonds.

A man blond and cold-eyed, dressed in mail sark and boar-crested helm, who leapt from the bow of a war-boat grounded by a burning village with a sword in his hand and a grin like a hunting wolf.

A man naked but for patterns in blue woad, his lime-dyed hair wild around his face as he ran out along the pole of the chariot between the galloping horses, shaking his spear and screaming defiance at the advancing legion beneath its eagle standard . . .

More, for both of them. Men plowing and planting and building, hunting and herding, fighting and falling, men looking on a woman's face with sudden astonished wonder, men leading children out beneath the night sky to name the stars for them, dancing joy-drunk in worship of their Gods or weeping in despair, singing as they brought in their harvest or starving in years of black disaster, men laughing, sobbing, dying. Back, back, until two who had the look of close kin stood dressed in hooded leather parkas and leggings by the shores of a lake that one day others would name Baikal. They embraced and spoke, and the words of a tongue long dead when the pyramids rose echoed down twice ten millennia:

"All the kindly spirits go with you, my brother."

"All the kindly spirits stay with you, my brother."

One man stood and watched with the tears trickling down his bearded face as the other turned to lead the sundered half of their clan eastward towards the rising sun—

Artos' eyes blinked, and it had all passed in an instant. His voice was steady as he spoke:

"*Whapa Sa*, Red Leaf of the Oglalla and the Lakota nation, in whose name do you speak?"

The Sioux had only a few seconds more to collect himself; Artos nodded very slightly in respect for his wit and strength of will as he mastered his confusion at the sudden vision:

"I am Red Leaf of the Kiyuska *tiyospaye* of the Oglalla and the Lakota *tunwan*, and I speak for the Seven Council Fires of my people by their free consent."

"What oath do the Seven Council Fires swear to me? And what shall I swear to them?"

"The Seven Council Fires offer their allegiance to the High King of Montival, their aid and advice in peace and the service of their riders in war. In return they ask good lordship and fair justice as with his other subjects, that they may hold their lands forever untroubled by any enemies and live by their own law and custom, under the protection of the High King's Sword. So long as he keeps faith with us, and his heirs after him, we will keep faith with him and them; this we swear by the spirits of our ancestors, by the Earth beneath us and the Sky above, and all the *Wakháŋ Tháŋka* and by our own honor."

Artos' rich baritone filled the pavilion:

"And this oath do I hear, and swear in turn: I, Artos, son of Michael, son of Juniper; son of Bear, son of Raven, and High King in Montival. I swear that while they keep faith with me, in my realm the people of the Seven Council Fires shall hold their lands freely forever, and their own laws and Gods. None shall trouble them, or settle within their boundaries without their leave which they may give or withhold by sovereign right according to their own custom. This right I shall defend with all my strength against all men, failing not while I live; and also to them I shall give good lordship and fair justice as my subjects, respecting all right and law. I swear this oath by all spirits of Earth and Sky, of Water and Fire; by the Lord and Lady and by the Sword that They have given me, forged in the World beyond the world. May they and the Sword witness it. To this oath I bind my successors in the line of my blood forever, until the sky fall and crush us, or the sea rise and drown us, or the world end. So mote it be."

A flash seemed to run through his flesh, and he was conscious for an instant of every vein in his body, every nerve, until it seemed he could see the very coiled matrix at the heart of each cell. Then it passed, and Red Leaf rose and put a hand on his shoulder. He returned the gesture, and the Sioux spoke quietly:

"You realize you're going to have to spend six months touring around the *makol* repeating that with bells, whistles, *chanunpa* pipes and sweetgrass as soon as this war's over, don't you, kilt-boy . . . I mean, Your Majesty."

"That I will, and enjoy most of it. But let's win the war first; time's a-wastin'."

He drew the Sword from the planks and sheathed it, conscious of a collective exhalation of breath from everyone within sight. This time he sat in the chair at the head of the table, adjusting his plaid as he did.

"Most of you gentlemen and ladies know the capabilities of the Sioux. Who have just, as you saw, joined themselves to the High Kingdom of Montival. Whose eastern border you now know, Bossman Rassmusen."

The lord of Fargo looked as if he'd bitten into a very green apple. "We never accepted that border as final after—"

Artos held up a hand palm out to keep Red Leaf and

his son from interrupting, which they were obviously boiling ready to do:

"You signed a treaty with the Seven Council Fires . . . which now means with *me* . . . and the border was about what it had been before the fighting started, was it not? I will see to it that the Lakota don't trouble you, and the border will be open for trade. Do you have any objection to that?"

The man looked as if he most assuredly did, but he shook his head. Artos went on:

"Now, I won't presume to comment on the military strategy of the campaign here, beyond the most general terms; you shall advance west, my forces—"

About which I know absolutely bugger-all, but let's not become bogged down in details, for all love.

"—move to the east and we crush the enemy between us. Sure, and it would be foolish to try for more; under modern conditions the distances are just too large for close coordination. I shall lead in the west, the great Provisional Republic shall lead here in the east."

He inclined his head towards Kate Heasleroad, and she returned the gesture with regal calm; Abel Heuisink was fighting down a grin.

"One point I do wish to make. The territories controlled by our enemies are part of the High Kingdom of Montival, and even if they don't know it the dwellers are my subjects, albeit some are in arms against me. This war is against the Cutter cult, and the regime of Martin Thurston. It is *not* . . . and I would like to repeat that, *not* . . . against the lands or peoples they hold in subjection. I know that wars kill people and break things, nor can a great and numerous host act like so many pilgrims to a holy shrine. War means fighting, and fighting means killing and destruction. But I *will* have pledges that there will be no unpunished killings of civilians, or arson or rape; that in short there will be no wanton destruction or plunder beyond military necessity. These are my people."

Abel Heuisink spoke: "I might add that Iowa fully agrees with our ally on *that* point. We want to beat armies, overthrow the men who've threatened us, and go home, not get locked up fighting peoples."

"We are avenging my husband, the father of my son, and securing all our lands and peoples against an enemy who have shown themselves to be utterly unscrupulous and insatiable," Kate Heasleroad added. "Iowa has no territorial ambitions in this conflict."

Artos nodded. *Which means nobody else should get big eyes either*, he thought. *And I will not have to start my reign with too many of my new subjects cursing my name.*

Aloud he went on: "And even purely from a military point of view, keep in mind that not everyone will fight for the Prophet or the Boise usurper . . . but that *anyone* will fight for their home and family."

There was general agreement, if a little grudging in some cases. Rassmusen spoke again:

"Just one thing more . . . Your Majesty." The tone was absolutely polite, but Artos thought he detected more than a little irony. "Just how do we in Fargo . . . and Marshall, and Nebraska . . . know we're not fighting to replace one threat on our borders with another? It's easy enough for Richland and Iowa and Kirksville to talk; we stand between them and the High Plains and have since the Change. The Sioux gave us a lot of trouble even with this Corwin cult causing problems to their west and distracting them, and obviously they'd be even more of a menace with you and, ah, Montival behind them."

"Security . . ." Artos grinned disarmingly. "Apart from my word, that is?"

His voice was calmly friendly, but the Fargo Bossman was a man of broad experience. He looked a little alarmed, and his pale eyes flicked to the Sword again.

"Nobody doubts your word, Your Majesty. But you're not immortal. Men die, and not always of old age. Policies change too. Geography doesn't. Suddenly I've got a neighbor that's over a thousand miles wide, instead of a couple of hundred, and I'm concerned about *my* grandchildren."

Artos nodded; that *was* a point. "To my word, you'll have to add common sense. Montival has, will have when this war is won—"

If this war is won, but let's be cheerful in public:

"—no more people than Iowa, or only slightly more. Dwelling sparsely in a land many, many times larger; and we have all of old California to the south of us when we need ground for expansion, as you Midwesterners have the empty parts of the Mississippi valley and the lands east of the river."

"In the long term, though, your great-grandson, say, might get big eyes."

Artos shrugged. "The Prophet Sethaz has big eyes *right now*, the creature; and Boise aspires to reunite the whole continent."

"Yah, yah, but—well, you have a point."

"The point being that a hypothetical threat in seventy years is no match for a very real one right now," Father Ignatius observed dryly. "As a wise man said, in the long run we're all dead. Sufficient unto the day is the evil thereof."

Artos nodded. "Montival's center of gravity lies very

far to the west, west of Corwin. Defending the Lakota territories we could do, at great cost and effort; fighting east of there would be a nightmare, against foes at least as strong defending their own homes and with their source of reinforcement and supply close to hand. As you said, lord Bossman, geography doesn't change. Geography in the form of soil and rainfall dictate that the High Plains will be thinly peopled, and will have mountains between them and the lands of the Pacific coast. Montival will be loose-knit by necessity, as well as inclination, and the Sioux territories will be a buffer. Now, to business."

The Chancellor cleared his throat, looked at Kate Heasleroad, and spoke:

"Iowa will contribute fifteen thousand cavalry, thirty-five thousand infantry, a hundred batteries of field artillery, and engineers, support troops and siege train in proportion," he said. "They're already mobilized. We're also prepared to supply rations, fodder and replacement horses for the other contingents while they're in the field."

Generous, Artos thought. *Though they can afford it.*

He felt more than saw Matti nod slightly beside him. She scribbled on her pad and tilted it so that he could see without being too obvious about it:

And it establishes Iowa as primus inter pares *here. Worth it for the long-term effect on the balance of power from their point of view. If they convince everyone of how strong they are, they won't have to fight to prove it. It'll show off the advantages of their central location, too. Abel and Kate want Iowa to be the power that settles disputes and holds the scales, but they don't want to take anyone over.*

Kate nodded at her Chancellor's words. "I might add that the Dominions to our north, all three of them, have agreed to declare war on Corwin *provided* that *we* all do so."

"Right away?" the Bossman of Marshall said.

"No, but just as soon as our forces actually take the field and cross the border, so that they can't be left swinging in the breeze."

"About time the Canuks got their thumbs out," someone muttered. "Sometimes I think that *they* think we're hardly better than the Cutters."

"I don't insist they love or trust us as long as they're *with* us," Kate went on. "And for their own good solid self-interested reasons."

Mathilda beamed at her, proud and fond, and Artos blinked a moment as he saw Sandra Arminger's face peering out through hers. They said that you should get to know a woman's mother before you married her, because she was your fate in twenty years, but . . .

Kate went on: "And I can't answer as to how many troops that means, but it does secure our northern flank and it can't hurt."

There was a murmur of approval. Bill Clements of Richland cleared his throat and spoke:

"Richland, Marshall and Fargo will each contribute a brigade of four thousand cavalry, and their support services and horse artillery. The troops are already moving, and we can discuss command responsibility when they get here."

And I'm glad that's Kate and Abel's job and none of mine, Artos thought.

Mathilda scribbled again:

Clements is happy that the younger brother of one of his Sheriffs is your brother-in-law. It gives him a link to Montival, which means he has an ally on the other side of Fargo

*and Marshall, which both outweigh Richland badly. They've
never actually fought but it's come close, and Richland has
had a border war with that smaller realm, Ellsworth I think
it's called. That's why they're not here.*

He nodded. Carl Mayer of Nebraska rose in turn.
"We'll kick in twenty thousand men, half mounted. Concordia and Kirksville will put theirs under our command;
five thousand more total. Twenty-five thousand men.
We're already working on reconditioning the railways,
have been for months now. We can push them across
Wyoming to the Rockies as soon as the troops can protect
the working parties."

Artos heard Bjarni grunt slightly, as if someone had
punched him in the gut and he was hiding the impact.
The number of *soldiers* promised here was more than the
whole of his people, men and women and children together, and these rulers were casually talking of campaigns across distances nearly as great as those between
Iowa and Maine. In the abstract, he sympathized; he'd
been stunned by the dense populations here when he
came through last year as well.

Bjarni was probably asking himself why he'd bothered
to bring his little battalion at all . . . and then reflecting
that it was for honor's sake, and also because while Syfrid
of the Hrossings was here, back home the new kingdom
was being consolidated by his wife and his uncle Ranulf,
who was also commander of his *hird*, his guardsmen. Not
to mention the prestige he'd bring back, and the loyalty
and tales of the men of all the Norrheimer tribes who'd
have fought and fared so widely under his command.

*Though the most remarkable thing of all about the Mid-
west is that even with all these people hereabouts, still they till
but a fraction of the land, and it so fine and fertile—only a*

tenth even here in Iowa where there was no famine and there are as many folk now as there were in the year of the Change. Still less is put to use elsewhere, where things were so much worse in the terrible years.

He'd seen that when he'd come through last year, and again this spring; each farm in Iowa with its farmhouse-manor and dependent Vaki village was an island of fields and tended pastures, surrounded by lush vastness going back to tallgrass prairie hardly used at all, or to burgeoning marshland. That tiny share of the land produced such abundance that even the poor and lowly ate their fill here every day as well, albeit it might be corn bread and fatback rather than steak and asparagus.

Yet before the Change it was cultivated fields to the horizon everywhere around here, and every inch of this lovely black soil under the plow, and each farm worked by a single family. To say three hundred million is one thing; to see the soil that fed that host in the ancient world, and with so little human labor, is another altogether!

Regent Catherine Heasleroad took the salute of the march-past gravely, proud in her not-quite-Montival-style court dress on the bunting-draped stand. Her right hand was over her heart as the last of the regiments went by with an earthquake rumble of boots and a ripple of pikes, a flutter of banners and barks of *Eyes right!* Behind her a nursemaid held her son, who was quiet enough with the wide-eyed curiosity of a dry and well-fed infant.

Not bad, Artos thought as he considered the troops. *They've been at work.*

It was a warm bright day, humid as it often was hereabouts, and there were plenty of red faces in the ranks going past, but nobody looked out of condition or ready to faint. The recruits had been big hard-muscled young farm laborers for the most part before they were called to war, well used to outdoor labor and handling stock.

And the gear is certainly splendid.

Half the footmen carried sixteen-foot pikes; they'd been converted to the knockdown Montivallan model, so much easier to handle on the march. The rest had crossbows with built-in cranks, and prods made from old automobile leaf-springs. That wasn't much different from the way many went to war in Montival, but here every man had half armor; steel back-and-breasts, tassets to protect the thighs, greaves and vambraces and mail sleeves. The smell of coal smoke seeped out of Des Moines, and it was stronger still within the ferroconcrete ramparts of the city wall, where the foundries and forges and workshops were; their capacity to turn out equipment in mass and quickly was astonishing.

As if to punctuate the thought, a train came in sight from one of the gates, pulled by sixteen pairs of big brown oxen leaning into their yokes and keeping the trek-chain tight. The rail-wagons behind were heaped high with fresh-cast round shot in boxes, neatly marked as six, twelve or twenty-four pounds weight; more crates held four-foot catapult bolts, or bundles of the smaller forged-steel type that could be thrown to create bee-swarms, or bundles of arrows. The Iowan Bossmen had built up their armories with paranoid persistence. Even the bicycles resting in endless rows beside the tents were more than half of post-Change manufacture. That meant they were heavier and cruder than the ancient world's models, but they were perfectly functional for the brawny plowboys who made up the army.

Most of the horsemen were light cavalry, bow-and-shete troops much like Ingolf's Richlanders save for details. There were experimental units of lancers armed cap-a-pie on barded mounts, but those had been put together since the party from Montival came by last year and described the PPA's chivalry. He didn't have much confidence in them. It took a long time to make a man-at-arms who could fight knight-fashion, and training his horses was nearly as much time and trouble.

Their field artillery is fearsome, though, and there's the Dagda's own lot of it. Plus the combat engineers, the railroad battalions, the medical corps, the signalers . . . all very formidable. Corwin has awakened a sleeping giant here, one they might have lulled to harmless drowsiness for many years yet if they hadn't been so heedless in their pursuit of me.

A cold certainty filled him; that compared to the threat of the Sword, even *this* army was as nothing. That was why the Prophet Sethaz had been willing to let all the threads of his intrigues here tangle and break in an effort to kill Artos before he reached Nantucket.

The which he did not do, though not for lack of trying. And now I come for you, ill-wreaker, and on that day you perish. There's a time for mercy, and a time when mercy to the guilty is cruelty to the innocent.

"You've whipped them into shape," he said to the Iowan rulers. "Much better than they were last year, I think."

Abel Heuisink shrugged. "We've all been working hard. It's doing Iowa good to have something to do *together*, come to that. We spent far too many years bickering with each other."

Artos smiled wryly at what it was politic to leave unsaid. Thomas Heasleroad, the first Bossman of Iowa and the father of Kate's late unlamented husband, had seized power in a coup during the confusion right after the Change and ruled with an iron fist. He'd been a tyrant's tyrant very much in the mode of Mathilda's father back home, if less given to picturesque trappings. Perhaps nothing else could have brought this land through so undamaged; granted that Iowa had been fantastically rich in food, still it had taken swift, ruthless action by a man with a clear vision and a willingness to smash all opposition in blood to make the transition without famine and plague.

Certainly even here in the Midwest nobody else had so little damage; most lost their bigger cities and a chunk of the countryside near them.

Unfortunately such a man didn't turn from lion to lamb when the crisis was past, nor cease to play games of intimidation and divide-and-rule, nor had he raised his son Anthony to be any better. The second Heasleroad had won Kate's love, but then he was the father of her infant son. Everyone else had regarded him with loathing tempered by fear of the State Patrol—which meant Secret Police; even those who backed him for reasons of realpolitik and self-interest had detested him as a man. His martyred memory was much more popular as a symbol of Iowa's affronted pride than the living ruler had ever been.

"It's a pity that unity here requires a war," Artos said tactfully. "But on the other hand, we've no *choice* but to fight that war, so you might as well get some lasting gain from it along the way, eh?"

And how many likely lads will be down in the dirt with a spearhead through their guts before it's over? How many homesteads burnt, livestock slaughtered, tools broken, how many children going cold and hungry? The Gods made men so that they fight now and then, but . . . it's not so much those like me I mind. I'm a warrior by trade, and I chose to take up the sword—and the Sword. It's my own choice, and one I make again every day. The most of those who die will be levied by their lords, dragged from the plow willy-nilly, or just caught in the passing of the armies. So we'd best get it over with as quick as we can, and with as little damage as may be.

Abel nodded; Kate sighed, then did the same. He suspected that they were thinking much the same thoughts, and he felt better for it. Some of the Bossmen he'd met . . . well, you didn't get to choose your allies any more than you did your relatives; he was going to end up with Sandra Arminger as his mother-in-law, for example. And even more disturbing, the ghost of Norman Arminger as his *father*-in-law.

Leading a band into battle, my blade in my hand and my chances no better than theirs, that was one thing. This moving armies like pieces on a chessboard is another, and one far less to my liking. But some men take to it as if it were a bowl of nuts and berries and cream.

The camp stretched out around them—endless rows of tents in a half dozen styles, picket-lines and horse corrals, more rows of wagons with their draught poles neatly aligned, pyramids of boxes and barrels of hardtack and beans and salt pork and spare gear stacked twenty feet high . . .

And men. Swarming, marching, heaving loads onto and off of carts and railcars from the half-dozen newly laid spur lines, bicycling as individuals and in squads and companies and battalions. Out on the open ground that in peacetime served as pasture for the herds of Des Moines and cleared ground for the murder-machines on the city wall, more columns and blocks drilled, the sun sparking off armor and honed metal. Lines of crossbow-men advanced, knelt, fired their weapons in a series of deep sharp *tung* sounds and worked the cranks. Forests of pikes crossed, countermarched, lifted and fell to the calls of bugle and drum . . .

The army of the League of Des Moines was enough to make the hair bristle up under your bonnet. Artos kept a calm front, but he had been staggered by its size as well. In all, more than sixty thousand men were camped here already. He mentioned that, and Abel shrugged.

"Plus what the Sioux can kick in. Though technically the Lakota are *your* men, now, Rudi . . . Artos."

"Twelve thousand men," Red Leaf said. "That's as much as we can spare and still cover our frontier. But they're the best light cavalry anywhere, and mostly combat-experienced."

Unlike your plowboys and the Farmer and Sheriff scions went unspoken.

"We can help you with supply; extra bows, arrows, mail shirts, helmets, and things like horseshoes," Kate put in helpfully, topping him neatly.

Red Leaf nodded. "I gotta say, though, this is impres-sive. Just the *numbers.* I haven't seen this many people all together since the Change, and that's just the army, not the city. *That's* just ff . . . damn amazing."

"It's not full mobilization," Heuisink said, jerking his head at the camp. "If we called up all the militia, we could field somewhere over a hundred thousand. More if we had time to train the Unorganized National Guard reserve. We've got a program in hand to give everyone *some* training but that's for the future. Then if we really had to we could raise a quarter million. That's not counting any allies. Iowa's the biggest dog in the pack but we're only about a quarter to a third of the total population of the Midwest . . . nobody knows exactly, we're the only people who do a real census."

For an instant Red Leaf looked as though he'd swallowed something sour. Artos nodded soberly. Sandra Arminger had a mania for collecting numbers—statistics, they'd called it in the ancient world—and the Dúnedain Rangers had sent explorers very far afield; both estimated that there were between fifteen and twenty million human beings between what had been Guatemala and the high Arctic, halfway through the third decade of the Change Years. Around half of them lived in Iowa and its immediate neighbors; over a tenth in Iowa alone. A rough rule of thumb was that a well-organized farming community could put a tenth of its total numbers into the field in time of war; more if the war was short and close to home.

Potentially the Midwestern bossmandoms could raise a *million* troops.

"But this is about as many as we can reliably feed out west, providing we get the railways repaired," Heuisink said. "I have to admit the Nebraskans have been working hard at that and they're well organized for once, and we've been helping. Even so, after a certain point the horses pulling grain eat everything they started out with. That point comes later on steel rails than it does on roads, but eventually you get there anyway."

That admission made the Sioux look a *little* less unhappy, but not much. If you had an enemy who could shrug off the loss of whole armies as great as any you could field, and simply replace them with new ones just as large, the end of any struggle became rather predictable. Artos remembered things he'd read and that Sir Nigel had told him about Rome.

"Now it's time for the State banquet," Kate said firmly.

Mathilda laughed at the look on Artos' face. "Enjoy it while you can, darling," she said. "We're going to be traveling very fast indeed as soon as they get those tread-mill railcarts for the horses ready."

"Hippomotives," Abel said and looked at him. "Which will be by day after tomorrow, the engineers say. I'm a little puzzled why you're taking any troops. It'd be faster still if you and your friends just went hell-for-leather, and you said you need to get back as soon as possible."

"Partly to make it more difficult to overrun us with a raiding party, and even more the politics, my friend," Artos said. *The which Matti advised me on.* "They're expecting me, back home. Me and the Sword of the Lady."

He touched the crystal pommel.

"And they'll be glad to hear of the mighty host you've raised to their aid. But a mighty host a thousand miles away is one thing, and soldiers there to see and smell another; a sampling will be . . . reassuring, so it will. And I'm making sure that word gets there quickly enough."

"I'm not altogether certain it's appropriate to start a whacking great war by stuffing yourself and listening to music, much less speeches," Artos said.

The banquet was in the throne room of the Bossman's palace in Des Moines—that wasn't precisely what they called it, but it was what they meant. A great dome soared above in a fantasy of rare woods and columns, and the floor tiles of colored marbles swept in a circle around an oculus in the middle of the chamber, itself edged with a railing of gilt brass and wrought iron. The banquet tables were arranged in a larger ring around the oculus, and the Regent's seat was back to the throne at the base of the great staircase that swept upward between two tall bronze statues of robed maidens holding lanterns.

Those glowed as the gas flames heated their incandescent mantles. The scent gave a faint tang beneath the odors of the roast suckling pigs, glazed hams, turkeys, barons of beef or buffalo or elk, lamb and veal, platters of smoked sturgeon, potatoes whipped with cream and scallions and garlic or scalloped or *au gratin*, tender asparagus, salads of greens and nuts and bloodred tomatoes, hot breads and a dozen more dishes. More lights of the same sort flared and hissed on the huge cut-crystal chandeliers above, and a spendthrift extravagance of fine beeswax candles burned on the tables, glittering on glassware and polished silver and gold and fine cloth. All the wealth and power of Iowa were here, the Sheriffs and richer Farmers, the National Guard generals and the industrialists of the city.

Most of the younger women were in local imitations of the cotehardie Mathilda had introduced and Kate taken up last year, a blaze of brilliant color and jeweled bands around gauzy, elaborately folded wimples and wrists and waists. A rather smaller proportion of the young men were in parti-colored hose and doublet and houppelandes with trailing dagged sleeves, but there was a fair number nonetheless. The sight gave him a moment's sorrow for Odard. Matti glanced at him and he touched her hand, knowing she shared it; the young Baron of Gervais had delighted in that peacock display. Some of them looked as if they'd plundered the same books the PPA and its Society ancestors had referenced, with a wild disregard for mixing periods.

"At least Mother keeps the Associates to the fourteenth century, mostly," she sighed.

"Little did you know what you did when you entranced Kate with your tales of court at Portland and Castle Todenangst," he said to her. "I hear they've taken to tournaments, too."

Matti grinned. "I never really did like the cotehardie. At least I don't have to wear one here in *summer*."

The older folk stuck to dresses and the bib overalls that were gentleman's garb here, or even to the archaic suit and tie, though the greenish formal uniforms of the Iowa National Guard were common as well.

Servants in bow ties and white jackets swept away the last of the food and set out delicate desserts of pastries and ice cream, and the priceless rarity of coffee only slightly stretched with chicory. Artos sighed within; now would come the speeches. Iowans loved after-dinner speakers even more than Associates or the Faculty Senate down in Corvallis, if that were possible. You could tell none of them made offerings to Ogma the Honey-Tongued or Brigid, who was the patroness of eloquence and rhetoric, either. Mackenzies loved argument and debate, but at least they mostly did it well.

"Get used to this, Rudi," Mathilda said. "A King's life has a *lot* of ceremony."

He sighed openly. "You know, acushla, there's many a thing I want to *do* as High King, starting with winning this war but not ending there. Things that need doing, and I think I can do them well—more of them with you to back me, and our friends. But it bewilders and amazes me that so many wish to have such a job *as* a job. I'd rather work in a sawmill. I'd sleep better and my digestion wouldn't suffer, so it wouldn't."

Mathilda chuckled and began to reply. Then she stiffened, staring at the side of a towering silver basket full of colorful fruits. Her hand darted out and seized a porcelain coffeepot and whipped it over her shoulder.

"*Assassins!*" she screamed, in the same instant—not in fear, but at maximum volume to cut through the buzz of white noise.

A real scream sounded . . .

Artos rose and turned before the first syllables were out of Matti's mouth, pushing off with one foot against a table leg and swaying his torso aside. A nine-inch curved blade flashed by, brushing his ear with cold fire; he wasn't sure whether it had been aimed at him or Mathilda, but he was sure that the bow tie and white tuxedo coat weren't the man's real uniform. Not that it mattered, and half the killer's face was covered in scalding-hot coffee. The bladed palm of his own left hand whipped down into the shoulder of the assassin's knife arm, striking with a dull axlike sound as bone and cartilage snapped. In the same instant his knee pistoned up into the man's crotch. He was wearing a cup beneath his trousers, but that still brought a shrill shriek.

Artos turned instantly, leaving the first assailant. Mathilda was handicapped by the cotehardie, but in seconds she had the man efficiently facedown on the table with his functional arm in a paralysis hold and his own kill-dagger pricking behind one ear. He heaved and screamed in rage despite the agony until she reversed the weapon and rapped him behind one ear with scientific precision.

Artos had his own problems. The whole head table was dissolving into a chaos of screams and flashing knives.

Mary and Ingolf were back to back in front of Abel

Heuisink, who was clutching at a spreading red stain on his side and stamping at something out of sight on the floor as if on a scorpion. Ingolf had another of the false waiters by the wrist and had disarmed him by the straight-forward method of squeezing and twisting until the bones broke with a tooth-grating crackle, while he used the captive arm to whip the man forward into a crunch-ing head butt. He could see Virginia Thurston, née Kane, taking down another with a spectacular leaping kick with one hand braced on the table; she'd insisted on wearing the gold-riveted blue jeans that were formal wear in her native Wyoming.

Fred was nearly as fast, but he'd been delayed by snatching at a saber hilt that wasn't there. Iowa was a civilized realm, where men didn't carry swords or fighting-knives to a state dinner. Father Ignatius was on his feet, one hand wrenching the rope belt of his black robe free; from the way it whipped through the air as he sidled in front of Mathilda the knot at the end had a lead core. Artos snatched a cover off a plate and dove to his right towards the Regent of Iowa with desperate speed, thrusting it out like a buckler between her and the Cutter. The dagger there clanged against the antique silver, but that left him draped across the table and off balance.

Kate Heasleroad was as helpless as he, sprawled back-ward and pinned by the royal clothing, but she scrabbled and kicked furiously, and the heavy skirt took the first stab of the dagger. Artos scissored his legs and came erect in time to catch the man under the jaw with the heel of his palm. He wasn't set for the full bone-shattering power the blow could deliver, but it jarred through his arm and shoved the smaller man back on his heels. He was vaguely conscious that Bjarni had closed with the only other assassin, taking a stab in the belly that the mail vest under his shirt turned, then grabbing him in a bear hug and squeezing, squeezing . . .

The last man was back on the balls of his feet, knife held out and point down with his thumb on the pommel, an expert's grip that could stab or back-slash with rattle-snake speed. Artos stripped the little sgian dubh out of his knee-sock. Perhaps thirty seconds had passed since Mathilda saw the first man's reflection in the silver before her and saved them all, and the guards were closing in at last—there weren't as many of them in the throne room as there had been in mad Anthony Heasleroad's day.

There was the briefest pause as the knife-man's eyes locked on his.

"Don't do it, man," Artos said. "Surrender and I'll pledge your life."

The blue gaze narrowed, and the knife-point began to move. Artos looked into the face of desperate courage, and killed it.

Then he stepped back, and the mail-clad guards rushed in. Ignatius straightened and spoke, steady and controlled but loud:

"Everyone, please remain calm. Don't try to leave, everyone must be questioned."

The cool good sense cut through the room; most of the guests weren't sure what had happened anyway, except that it was bad. Kate Heasleroad stepped forward with her eyes flashing:

"*Captain Dietrich!*" she snapped.

The commander of the State Patrol stepped forward in his turn; he was a young man with a clipped blond mustache. Turnover in the security corps had been rapid after last year's change of regime, not to mention that the head of his service had died in the turmoil.

"Ma'am?" he said, standing ramrod straight and obviously wishing his vital functions would cease.

"Chancellor Heuisink is wounded. Get a physician. And take control of the surviving assassins. I want a *full* debriefing by no later than tomorrow. Interrogate them. *Break* them, do you understand me?"

And last year she was a gentle, shy, retiring girl, Artos thought, as his breathing slowed. He exchanged a glance with Mathilda, his wry smile saying, *Well, you helped her hatch* as plain as words, then spoke:

"I think the Sword could help with that, Lady Regent, and make the process swifter and less bloody all 'round."

Many hours later he buried his head in the curve of Mathilda's neck; they were alone at last. She stroked his hair, careful the bandage over his ear.

"I'm tired of this, Matti," he said. "It's been years now; fighting and running, now them running and still more fighting. I'm tired of seeing brave men die; tired of killing them. I want to make us a home, and wake up beside you every day, and take our children on visits to their grandmothers. I want it to *stop*."

"My poor darling—"

CHAPTER EIGHTEEN

"I feel like a bug on a plate," Ritva Havel muttered.

She pushed steadily at the pedals and looked out the windows at the landscape of the big-sky country, with the rush of the wind thuttering under the rattle and whine of the wheels and gears. This railcar held three rows of three operators pumping away with their feet, but apart from the motive power it didn't have much in common with the makeshifts the questers had cobbled together back in Norrheim. The streamlined sheath was made mostly of salvaged aluminum with some modern laminated ash in the frame, and the operators all lay back to pedal in recliner seats padded with sheepskins. Windows all around were from pre-Change automobiles, complete with the cranks for raising and lowering.

She opened one a little more, letting the warm air play over her sweaty face. It was worth the tiny bit of extra drag. The prairie wasn't entirely flat anymore; this part had a gentle roll to it, and there was the slightest almost-seen trace of blue-white along the western horizon, just starting to hint at mountains. The grass was about calf-high and still bronze-green as spring faded towards summer, starred with pink shooting star and windflower, the blue of larkspur and beardtongue, white fairy bells, yellow balsamroot, until parts of it were like a glowing carpet in Stardell Hall. The odd tree was usually an aspen, except where a shallow draw wound eastward and brought water closer to the surface to support cottonwoods and wolf willow. The dry thundery-ozone smell of a high-plains summer day was a clean, welcome contrast to the slightly rancid canola-oil lubricant and the inevitable sweat and metal inside the cab.

They were making a steady twenty miles an hour for hour after hour, and could have done better save for the limitations of the main party plodding along behind them at the pace horses on a treadmill could achieve, which was quicker than they could do with their hooves on the ground but less than humans pushing pedals. Even at that almost supernatural speed, well over a hundred miles each and every day, the endless grasslands seemed to *crawl* by.

"I'm a bug on a plate and soon the fork's going to come down on me," she went on, quoting her half brother.

It was even worse coming east on horseback, of course; that didn't just seem to take forever, it nearly did. Months and months. And I miss the way Mary and I did everything together before she got married. I miss all of them, being off on my own like this. I even miss Hrolf. Was I stupid to break up with him? No, that was the right thing to do. Spending my life with him . . . the thought just didn't appeal, and he wanted that, but it's getting . . . Oh, by Manwë, I'm not even twenty-three yet! Plenty of time, provided I don't get killed. I'm just envious of Mary for getting a good one.

"Fork, or flyswatter," she added.

Her escorts were native plainsmen and had grown up in places more or less like this; she could sense their incomprehension at her feeling of being lost in all this space. The trooper beside her did say:

"Yeah, I get the same feeling sometimes. I'm from up north near Rycroft in the Peace River country, myself. Way north, right up to our frontier with the Dene tribes. It's hills and woods there as well as prairies, and there's the river and lakes, and then there's the forests on the border that go north forever. But it's not so fine and warm as this, eh?"

Constable Ian Kovalevsky seemed to be a nice enough young man, around her age but seeming a little younger. His intentions were obvious; but then men were like that, and occasionally it was pleasant or only mildly irritating. And he looked quite dashing in his mail-lined red serge jacket, midnight blue breeches with yellow stripes down the seams and high brown boots; he had close-cropped ash-blond hair, slightly tilted gray eyes and a snub nose.

"You redcoats seem to do most of the same things here we Dúnedain do in Montival," she said.

The Dúnedain didn't have much contact with the Dominions. The only route that didn't go through the PPA territories—where memories of the War of the Eye ensured that Rangers were grudgingly tolerated at best—went through the United States of Boise. Which hadn't been friendly even before the war; and farther east was Corwin. She'd been mildly surprised to find that though Minnedosa, Moose Jaw and Drumheller were all independent they also all helped support this autonomous warrior band whose mark was the red serge coat, and let it operate throughout their lands.

Well, that's one of the great things about traveling—you see strange lands and their ways and customs. Otherwise we'd have stayed in Larsdalen and gotten on the A-list and married other A-listers and grown roots like turnips. A trip to Corvallis for some shopping would be a big deal we'd hash over for weeks. Shudder!

He nodded. "Well, we keep the peace, help out isolated settlements, track down robbers. And fight when we have to. It's worthwhile work. And it gets you out of the hoose—"

He pronounced the word as if it rhymed with *moose.*

"—oot and aboot, all over, and people are mostly glad to see you. And the Force has its own ranches to raise our horses, and salvage operations and workshops to make our gear, so we do some of that work too."

A snort came from behind her, where the corporal in charge of the detachment sat at his own pedals. The common troopers were called *constables,* which sounded a bit odd to a Montivallan ear. That was a title of rank in the Association territories, and a rather exalted one; the commander of the PPA's armies was a Grand Constable.

"And you don't have to spend the summers pushing a plow on your daddy's farm and the winters freezing your ass off and worrying about the Dene, Kovalevsky," the noncom said.

"I ran a trapline in winter," the constable said mildly, and added: "Corporal."

A thought occurred to her. "This land here is *warm?*"

It certainly was right now, but she remembered winters in the high plains around Bend, east of the Cascades. This was much farther north and a lot farther from the moderating influence of the ocean . . .

"Well, it's warmer than the Peace River! In winter,

particularly. They get these Chinook winds and it can melt all the snow even in February; it's lousy country for cross-country skiing here. Anyway, things get a lot less flat just a little way west. We're nearly into the foothills. That's very pretty country."

"It'll be a change," she said. "I like mountains to look at but they're a bit of a pain when you're in a hurry."

More miles flowed by, with only an occasional rough patch to rattle their teeth; once a pack of wolves, or mostly-wolves from the floppy ears and parti-colored coats of a few, looked up from their feast on something that might have been alpaca or antelope. Then they dipped their heads again to rip at the carcass. The Drumhellers had kept up their rail net, more or less, at least to the point of patching and filling now and then, but—

"Not much through traffic?" she asked.

"We cleared the line a while ago," the corporal said. "Emergency Powers Act. Usually there's a fair bit on this stretch—coal from Lethbridge or Crowsnest, wool going north, timber and flax and salvage goods coming south and east, that sort of thing. All horse-drawn except for the mails, and some passengers who can afford pedal-carts."

An hour later they slowed to let a herd of buffalo cross ahead of them, several thousand head with the light brown calves running among their massive, darkly shaggy elders, and a little after that a herd of mustangs paced the car for a while, their manes and tails flying. Very occasionally they passed herds of cattle or beefalo, sheep or llamas, with a party of mounted cowboys riding guard and a chuck wagon following along behind each band.

Then the evidence of men grew stronger; a brace of canvas-tilt wagons and a party of horsemen rattling down a dirt track and waving their Stetsons in greeting, a quartet of mowing machines cutting wild hay, watering-points with their tall windmills spinning to pump from the well beneath. Then a small dam across a stream, and a long narrow stretch of irrigated land planted to wheat and alfalfa, truck and orchards, with trees around the little lake that watered it. A ruined, burnt-out house and barns stood near the shore, long abandoned and stripped of anything useful down to the chimney bricks, though the extensive corrals were still in use. Much closer to the tracks and just north of them was a complex of modern rammed-earth buildings on a low rise—

A low rise being the only type of rise they have *around here,* she thought sardonically.

It was big for a village but too small for a town, and surrounded by a wall, not very high but thick and of the same hard material, topped with a timber fighting platform and with towers at its corners and beside the south-facing gate. The blocky rammed-earth structures were two stories high on fieldstone footings, and the whitewash that covered them glowed in the sun against the red-brown tile of their low-pitched roofs. Smoke rose from the chimneys there, and a bell began to ring as the railcar came into sight; a flashing glint from the gatehouse was probably a mounted telescope. Outside the wall and south of the gatehouse was a long low warehouse right by the rails.

She recognized the bulky angular look of the *pisé de terre* construction, damp earth hammered down in layers between temporary timber forms that were then moved on to let the mixture cure to a consistency like coarse friable rock. It was popular in the drier interior parts of Montival too, cheap and easy to make since it didn't need expensive materials or much skilled labor, fireproof, lasting forever if well maintained, and excellent insulation against the heat of summer, the cold of winter, and the arrows of neighbors. Also familiar was a flag flying from a staff on one corner tower; not the actual design but the practice of using the cattle brand as a house banner in ranching country, rather the way nobles of the Association used their coats of arms.

"That's the Anchor Bar Seven ranch headquarters," the corporal said. "We've been on their land for three hours now. The flag's not at half-mast, either; Old Man McGillvery must still be hanging on."

Evidently *headquarters* was the local term for *homeplace*; she'd noticed that the dialect here was crisper and more formal-sounding than the ranchland speech of eastern Montival, more like what they spoke in Corvallis but with a subtly odd elongation of the vowels and occasional strange bits of vocabulary. A rustling of paper from behind her showed he was consulting a map.

"The ranch-house there got burned out not long after the Change—people from Calgary—but they drove some of 'em off and set the rest to rebuilding it the way you see."

"It looks like they expected more trouble. That's more protection than most ranchers' homeplaces have in Montival."

She could hear his shrug before he continued: "Those were hard times, ma'am. We had a couple of big cities, too big to survive, and no mountains between them and the rest of us."

And he's old enough to remember some of it—nearly forty but not quite, I'd say, about Aunt Astrid's age give or take. He'd have been in his early teens. Things weren't nearly as bad here as in some places, but bad enough.

"We're not all that far from the old U.S. border with Montana here either," he continued. "There's been a trickle of refugees from the Cutters for nearly twenty years; some good people, but some not, and some just desperate. And we've had some pretty big skirmishes with the Prophet's loonies. Not real war before now, but there've been raids."

"And the odd bunch of horse-thieves from the Sioux territories," Ian observed.

"Nothing serious; they just think stealing horses is a fun rough sport, like we do hockey."

"Serious enough if they lift your hair while they're lifting your stock, Corporal."

"And that's why we hang them by the neck if we catch them at it, Kovalevsky."

"Hell, Corporal, you've got a really hard-nosed attitude to a roughing penalty."

Everyone laughed, and the corporal went on to her: "Do you want to stop here for the day, ma'am?"

Ritva sighed and looked upward in thought, tempted. The ranch was a major one, and the homeplace would have a lot of free space kept for riders who slept out with the herds except in the cold season. It would probably be a chance to eat decent food and sleep in a bed, and certainly one to do minor repairs and have a bath or at least a shower.

And to get my sore butt out of these seats.

Riding hurt too eventually—there was an old joke about a book entitled *Twenty Years in the Saddle, by Major Assburns*—but she was *used* to that, having ridden at least a little nearly every day since she was four. They'd come over a thousand miles in a week and it was beginning to feel as if she'd bounced all that way with her coccyx dragging on the deteriorating roadbed of the railroads of three bossmandoms and as many Dominions. The temptation didn't last long. From the sun it was about an hour past noon, and the letters from home piled up at the railhead had all sounded anxious in the extreme, if you knew how to read between the lines. Mathilda's had made her go white, when she decoded them.

Far too early to stop and no time to waste now that we don't have to coddle the horses as much, she thought. *Granted when you're going across a continent you have to remember* more haste less speed, *but we can't dawdle even one day*. She went on aloud:

"Just for a few minutes to exchange news. We should get in at least another three or four hours today and that's sixty or seventy miles."

"You're the boss-lady," the corporal said; his superiors were cooperating nicely and the redcoat Force evidently had splendid discipline. "Pity. They do some really good ribs with red sauce here. Squad . . . rest easy!"

The railcar was on a barely perceptible upward slope. It coasted to a halt just before the long warehouse-style structure that flanked the right-of-way, and the noncom threw the brake lever to keep them from sliding backward. Silence swept in and the endless space stretched to the world's edges. The wind's sough around the car was the loudest sound, that and the endless *hshshshshshshshs* of the rippling grass and the ringing bell from the ranch. They all popped their doors and got out to stretch; Ritva joined in the knee bends and twists, then got her sheathed sword out of the rack and slid it back into the frog on her belt with a habit as automatic as breathing. It wasn't much cooler, but the fresh wind made her feel as if it was.

Almost as soon as they stopped, a party rode out of the

homeplace gates and along the rutted dirt road that led from there to the railway. There were fourteen saddles followed by a light two-wheel cart pulled by a single horse, and her brows rose a little as she examined the riders, especially the ten who looked like soldiers. Part of their equipment was just cowboy working gear—lariats, belt-knives, curved swords, round shields blazoned with the Anchor Bar Seven's brand, quivers and recurve bows. But the warriors in the party were in mail hauberks as well, knee-length and split to the waist before and behind rather than the lighter, shorter versions common in ranch country, and helmets with horse-tail plumes, and steel forearm guards. They also all carried real lances at rest in tubular scabbards behind their right elbows, ten-foot weapons with pennants attached below the point. Their horses were a bit taller than the common quarter horse pattern as well.

"Is that gear usual?" she said.

Ian Kovalevsky spoke helpfully: "It's what the Force uses for a stand-up fight. Most of the Ranchers train some of their men to use it as well."

The corporal was grimmer: "Getting it out between maneuvers means the McGillverys are expecting trouble, taking men away from the herds this time of year. It's when they put the stock out towards the edges of the property, now that calving and lambing and branding and shearing are over. And you can't push cows in that stuff; it's too heavy."

The Rancher was a lean, fit-looking man in his thirties, black-haired and clean-shaven, with bright blue eyes and the ageless weathered and lined face born of a life outdoors in dry harsh summers and winters harder yet. The somewhat younger woman beside him with the auburn braids and the lovely palomino horse was probably his wife, to judge by the family resemblance in the boy and girl in their early teens riding behind. All four were in costly copper-riveted blue denim jeans, even more expensive cotton shirts and printed silk neckerchiefs, with broad Stetsons on their heads. The lancers spread out, mostly facing south.

"Damn it, Dudley," the man began as he dismounted, then noticed her.

His horse stood stock-still, as if the dropped reins were tied to a post, and so did those of the others; he looked her over, evidently not recognizing the crowned tree and seven stars on her green jerkin.

"Ah . . ."

The noncom made an introductory gesture. "Ma'am, this is Avery McGillvery of the Anchor Bar Seven ranch, Captain in the South Alberta Light Horse Regiment, Member of the Legislative Assembly and Justice of the Peace. Mrs. Naomi McGillvery . . . Dirk and Amy McGillvery, their eldest. Sir, we're escort for, ah, the lady here—"

Ritva removed her hat—it was a peaked Montero, the type Robin Hood was usually shown wearing, and had a peacock feather tucked into the band—and bowed slightly with her right hand on her heart and her left on the hilt of her longsword.

"*Mae govannen, brannon, hiril,*" she said. "Well-met, lord, lady. May a star shine on the hour of our meeting. I'm Ritva Havel, a *roquen* of the Dúnedain Rangers."

Since Aunt Astrid just promoted us from ohtar *by long-distance mail. Well deserved, if I do say so myself. It's nice the Dominions are being so cooperative.*

"*Roquen* means 'knight.' I'm from Montival in the far west. No, I'm not an Associate of the PPA, either. It's a long story. We Dúnedain fought the PPA as well in the old days."

And I know Drumheller had a nasty little indecisive war over the Peace River country with the Association before they split it between them, so I'd better make that clear. My, how the Armingers managed to make enemies! Matti isn't like that, but it's going to give her problems all her life.

She smiled benevolently and shook hands as the Rancher and his family struggled to take that in; or rather the parents did, and the children looked intrigued. There had probably been rumors about the Dúnedain here at least, but news took strange forms when it traveled far. Then she handed over her letters of introduction; from the governments of Iowa, Fargo, and Marshall, and from the Dominions as well. They had an impressive set of signatures and seals, and the border-lord gave her a brief nod as he returned them.

The "all possible assistance" they asked for carried an unspoken corollary: *don't ask questions*, and he didn't.

"Please, don't let me interrupt," she completed. "Since I'm just passing through."

The commander of her escort cleared his throat. "How's the old man, sir?"

A flicker of pain passed across the Rancher's face.

"He's failing," he said, and nodded brusquely as the newcomers all murmured condolences. "Another stroke, Doctor Nirasha thinks. Well, seventy-five's *old*, and that's all there is to it."

"Sorry to hear that, sir. He helped this area through the Change very well indeed. Any unusual activity along the border?"

"No," the master of the Anchor Bar Seven said slowly. "Not a solitary peep."

"Ah," the corporal said noncommittally.

The Rancher nodded unhappily, showing he wasn't a novice either, then went on more briskly:

"All right, Dudley, where's my coal? It's a week overdue, and we're about to start burning cowflops and buffalo chips like a bunch of Cutter savages in Montana! Not that the blacksmith is going to get much use out of *those*."

"And I had some sheet music on order from Lethbridge, Corporal Dudley," the young girl said.

Her mother gave her a quelling look before she added: "And the spring shipment of linens and . . . well, what's happening? Do we have to go back to doing *everything* ourselves?"

The noncom cleared his throat. "Priority traffic on the line, Mr. McGillvery, Mrs. McGillvery."

"War," the Rancher said, with something not quite a sigh. "It's really going to happen, eh? I always thought we'd have to do something about the Prophet eventually. Premier Mah did send down a Warning notice to all the local spreads, which is why I have some of my men on active duty. They mean it this time? I always thought Emily spooked too easily. That's why I didn't vote for her."

"I don't think she does, and I *did* vote for her," his wife said forthrightly.

"The Commissioner and the Commander of K Division are pretty sure, sir, and I understand Premier Mah concurs. And Premier Szakacs and Premier Wuthrich back east too. The Yanks are serious about settling Corwin once and for all and we're going to help."

"God knows they've given us reason over the years."

"That they have, sir. Incidentally, A and B troops of the Force are moving into this area sometime soon to screen the border while we mobilize. Moose Jaw and

Minnedosa are calling up the first-line battalions of their militia regiments too. It'll take them longer than it will Drumheller, of course."

The man looked grim, his wife anxious, and the children a little excited.

"I've stepped up our patrols, and pulled in some of the line camps," he said. "Damn, but that's going to waste grazing. Not that we're short, but there's the principle of the thing. Live like you'll die tomorrow, but manage your grass like you'll live forever."

Then his glance turned pawky. "And meanwhile we're short on everything we don't make ourselves, so do the right thing, Dudley, and *get me that coal*. If there's going to be trouble, I'll need it more than ever."

"Sir, I'm sorry, but the Force is in charge of setting priorities and the line's been cleared for military traffic. As a matter of fact, there's a big contingent of the foreign troops coming through right behind us."

"Yanks?" the Rancher asked.

Ritva cut in: "Some of them, but they're led by my brother, Artos. Artos the First, High King of Montival. And they'll be buying supplies. With Iowa's money, good coined gold."

That brought a sudden silence, and when the Rancher started arguing again it was in a much less sulky mood. While they spoke the two women who'd been driving the light cart pulled up and got out a picnic lunch that included beer, fresh bread, the promised barbecued beef ribs and an actual *green salad* with lettuce and tomatoes and spring onions and celery and radishes dressed with oil and vinegar. Ritva felt her stomach growling at the sight and smell; it seemed to remember far too much trail food, and winter fare at that. She chatted with the children as she ate; they had both read the Histories, though they'd thought them mere tales.

Ritva spoke regretfully as the railcar pulled out:

"They seem like very nice people, and extremely hospitable."

Corporal Dudley grunted. "Nice enough, ma'am. Avery McGillvery's no fool, but he gets to acting like a bit of a little tin god sometimes, the way a lot of the big Ranchers do down here in Palliser's Triangle. He doesn't meet anyone who can tell him 'no' from one month to the next, except his wife, and he starts thinking the Force is just another set of his ranch hands."

"He's right about part of it, though, Corporal," Ian said. "They *do* carry a lot of the national-security weight down here. This is the dangerous border, now that the knights-and-castle freaks—sorry, ma'am—"

"No sorry needed, Ian. My father died fighting the Association. He killed Norman Arminger, in fact."

"Oh, sorry about that, ah . . . well, now that the PPA have learned to keep on their side of the old BC border."

"Which is why the Anchor Bar Seven and the other border ranches get tax exemptions and subsidies on their military equipment," his corporal said.

The map crackled again: "And why *we* spend so much time around here, too. Let's see, it's about sixty miles to Bone Creek. That's the last place with enough good water before we turn north for Crowsnest Pass. We can make it by about four and scout it out, and the main body will be in by sundown."

Ritva nodded; they were making a loop southward before they approached the pass. Threading the steep route through the mountains would be the difficult part; once they were over the Rockies they'd be in the

Okanogan country, Association territory and part of Montival now.

Say what you like about the Spider of the Silver Tower and Lady Death, and Count Renfrew for that matter, they'll have everything organized to rush us south fast. By the Valar and Maiar, it will be good to see Montival again!

The ground grew more rolling, and the railroad crossed a few gullies or small rivers. Sometimes that was on the pre-Change embankments or bridges. Once or twice it was on more recently built and more flimsy timber trestles that made them sway and rattle alarmingly as the railcar shot across.

Something teased at her as they slowed down to take one of those. Nothing she could have put a name to, nothing heard, something *felt*. They were the advance party, after all.

Who scouts for the scouts? she thought.

Her father had used an expression, *Polish Mine Detector*, for the people he put on point—she could just barely remember him laughing about it when he'd come back from that duty himself, and not understanding at the time.

And . . . All right, Aunt Astrid, Uncle Alleyne and Aunt Eilir and Uncle John, a Ranger is supposed to pay attention to everything. What is it that's nagging at me? Relax, take deep breaths, feel your legs moving, empty your mind . . .

"Do the birds usually shut up this time of day around here?" she asked suddenly.

Until a few minutes ago there had been yellow-breasted meadowlarks chattering and singing, bluebirds swooping after grasshoppers, and dozens more. Even the occasional red-tailed hawk or falcon or eagle only made them scatter for a little while. Also there had been more than a few prairie dogs, waddling about or sitting in the entrances of their burrows going *eeek-eeek-eeek* at the passing humans and their machinery. Now there was silence save for the ticking of insects.

"No, they don't," Corporal Dudley said suddenly, throwing her a respectful look. Then: "Squad, rest easy!"

The vehicle coasted to a halt. "I think it's maybe *too* quiet," Ritva murmured, and suppressed an inappropriate giggle as most of the redcoats nodded solemnly.

There were hatches on the roof of the railcar. She opened the one above her seat and got out her binoculars, and so did Corporal Dudley. There was nothing but the rolling swells of the prairie, though through the glasses the Rockies were definitely visible now.

"No game, either," she said. "Nothing moving but the bugs and those ravens over by that ravine."

Minutes ticked by. Kovalevsky jittered a little, but he was the youngest of his band; the others had stayed quiet after checking their fighting gear. Ritva smiled and glanced down at him, then quoted a training mantra of John Hordle's:

"Who dares, wins. Who gets the wind up and buggers about like a headless pillock, loses. Know when to wait, know when to kick them in the goolies, and you'll be the one telling lies over your beer."

Corporal Dudley looked at her again. "You really aren't just somebody's relative, are you, ma'am?"

"No," Ritva said flatly. "No, I'm not."

Normally she'd have embroidered on the theme, but the sense of something *wrong* was building instead of fading. From the way his head swiveled back and forth with the binoculars, so was the corporal's.

"I think we should turn the railcar around," Ritva said after a longer wait. "Just in case."

"My thought exact—"

The first horsemen came out of the ravine ahead of them before the word ended; evidently they'd decided that their prey wasn't going to walk into the parlor. Corporal Dudley shifted in midsyllable.

"—*squad reverse railcar!*"

The eight scarlet-clad men and one woman in gray-green flung themselves out of the vehicle and at the handgrips built into its sides. Ritva grunted as the weight came on her arms and back and the corrugated metal bit into her palms; there was a trick to throwing your whole body into an effort like this, like drawing a bow. The same lightweight construction that made the railcar fast also made it possible to lift, if you worked carefully and in coordination. They did, feet churning to avoid tripping on the rusty rail or splintered, obtruding ties where gravel had washed away.

Clung.

The flanged wheels came down on the pitted steel of the rails again.

"Hup!"

The redcoats threw their shoulders against the open doors of the car and pushed to get it going; a fractional second later so did she. It was a good idea, overcoming the inertia faster than they could have by pedaling alone. In a few seconds they were moving it at a pounding run.

"Middle seats in . . . *now!*" the corporal barked. "Outer seats in . . . *now!*"

She hadn't practiced this maneuver the way the men of the Force had, but she was a Ranger, and she'd spent endless hours climbing and tumbling and doing gymnastics. Her body thumped down in the left front seat beside Constable Kovalevsky about the same time as the others, though it took her an instant longer to get the soles of her elf-boots on the pedals. They were all pumping hard in unison, and then the corporal's voice barked as speed built:

"Shift gears . . . *now*. And shift gears . . . *now*. And shift gears . . . *now!*"

The sound of the wheels built to a thrumming whine, interspersed by the *clickity-clack* as they crossed the joints. Her eyes went to the mirror outside the window.

The helpful little *objects in the rearview mirror are closer than they appear* printed on the convex surface was deeply unwelcome, because the onrushing horsemen were far, far closer than was comfortable in any case. More and more of them were pouring up out of the ravine as she watched as well, laboring over the steep lip or traveling north and south for shallower exits, then crowding back until they formed a reverse crescent behind the railcar. Was it her imagination, or could she already feel the earth shaking beneath the impact of hundreds of hooves?

"A thousand yards and gaining," she said.

Corporal Dudley grunted agreement; he had a mirror too. "The lightest men on the fastest horses," he said. "They're getting strung out."

She hadn't had time to be afraid before; you didn't, when you were scrambling to meet an emergency, or fighting. Now she was just running away, and she found her breath coming faster than the exertion would justify. She slowed it by a practiced effort of will; if you made yourself act brave, you were. That was what being brave *meant*. She'd met a few people—all of them men, which didn't surprise her—who really didn't feel fear. Every single one had been a dangerous lunatic, useful mainly to stop spears or arrows which might otherwise have hit a real human being.

Hrolf Homersson, for example, she thought snidely.

"Still gaining," she said, in a dry matter-of-fact tone.

"They will for a while," Dudley said in a bass version of the same tone, and she nodded.

A horse could gallop at over thirty-five miles an hour for about as long as a man could run at top speed, allowing for condition and feeding. A quarter horse could hit fifty or a little more for very short sprints. Bicycles had far more endurance but they weren't as fast in a dash, though the lower rolling friction on steel and the low-drag housing of the railcar and the fact that they were going slightly downhill helped; this was a courier and mail vehicle and built for speed.

We'll either get to the Anchor Bar Seven homeplace before they catch up with us, or we won't . . .

There wasn't any point in talking; they needed all their wind. The harsh sound of their deep breathing dominated the interior. Her eyes flicked to the speedometer, which thankfully was in miles and not the other system they sometimes used here. Thirty-two miles per hour and rising slightly, as fast as she'd ever gone for any length of time except in a glider. A trestle went by rattling beneath them, and she managed a wheeze of excitement as she looked in the mirror and saw the horsemen check as they guided their horses into the dry creek-bed it spanned and then up again. That slowed them, but less than trying to pick their way over the ties. Then she cursed silently as the rails stretched into a long shallow curve ahead; the pursuers cut across the cord and regained the lost ground.

Eight hundred yards now between them and the foremost spray, with the rest stretching back to the original hiding place.

"Christ, there's hundreds of them. Maybe thousands," Corporal Dudley said.

"That's why . . . the birds and animals . . . were so quiet," she said, timing the words to her breath. "They hid very well . . . but there were so many of them . . . it spooked the wildlife."

No more talk for a while. She caught glances going up to the ceiling; their shields were all in racks there, forming a second roof beneath the outer shell of the vehicle. The Force used one much like the Dúnedain model she carried, a shallow convex disk about a yard across, made of birch plywood covered in bullhide and then with thin sheet steel. It was much better protection than the body of the railcar, but there were gaps between the shields.

Corporal Dudley began to turn the crank of a siren mounted beside him; its horn was flush with the exterior of the car. The sound built, an earsplitting rising-falling wail that drove into the ears like ice picks. The homeplace would hear that long before they arrived. Workers outside the walls would hear it and head home too, or ride for safety if they couldn't. Ritva looked at the speedometer again; thirty-five miles an hour, more than a horse could maintain for any distance but less than it could do in a flat-out rush. The interior of the railcar was thick with panting and rank sweat; it ran stinging into her eyes. Then she glanced back to the mirror, and bit back a curse.

Four hundred yards.

That large a group was bound to have some very light men—no women, not in a Cutter war band—riding without anything but their clothes and weapons on very fast horses. As she watched, one of them stood in the stirrups and bent his recurve, aiming high for a long-distance shot.

"In your dreams, maybe, fool," the corporal hissed. "It's a bow, not a catapult."

The arrow disappeared from the mirror's view, but her mind's eye could see it, arching up, hesitating at the peak, turning and rushing downward. A little bit of trivia from an early lesson back at Larsdalen came to her, from the schooldays before she and Mary got bored and exasperated past bearing with Mother and moved out to Mithrilwood to become Rangers. It might even be from before Father died in his duel with Norman Arminger at the end of the War of the Eye; the facts came with a feeling of sleepy boredom and warmth and the smell of chalk.

An arrow shot upward at forty-five degrees hit the ground going at seventy percent of its initial speed. Some part of her mind did a quick calculation:

Say two hundred feet per second when it leaves the string, so that's a hundred and forty feet per second when it hits you *and does nasty things.*

The shaft reappeared as a blurred streak across the mirror for a fractional second, and then again quivering in the dirt as it fell away behind the speeding vehicle. The man who'd shot it had lost some ground while he did; now he was hunched forward in the saddle, beating his horse on the rump with the bow stave and probably screaming curses. They wouldn't make that mistake again.

Twenty, twenty-five minutes since we sprung their ambush—they can't keep this up much longer. Their horses must be foaming out their lungs, she thought. *We'll be in sight and hearing of the ranch in about another seven minutes. Or I'll be dead.*

Being captured would be worse, of course. Even with ordinary bandits, and infinitely more so with Cutters, but there were ways to avoid being taken alive. Usually. If you didn't lose your nerve. There were ways to stop yourself thinking, too: she used one, focusing tightly on the feel of the burning muscles in her legs, *push* and *push* and *push*—

The pursuers were much closer now, a long dark column rising and falling with the roll of the land behind them; even over the wail of the siren the dull rumble of the hooves was loud. Three hundred yards, extreme effective range for longbowmen in still air. Most saddle bows didn't shoot quite as far. Closer, closer . . .

This time a dozen of them rose in the saddle at the same time, probably to someone's order or signal. The tiny figures in the mirror seemed to writhe in unison, drawing long and then jerking backward as recoil made them sway. The Change had changed a good many things, but not the equal and opposite reaction when you threw something away fast and hard.

"For what we are about to receive—" Corporal Dudley began.

A rising whistle even through the whine of gears and the song of steel on steel from the wheels beneath them. The sound of arrows striking in dirt or railroad ties or banging off the rails was lost, but not the *shink-thack!* of one punching through the thin sheet aluminum of the roof and hammering into the more resistant surface of a shield.

"—may the Lord make us truly thankful—*shit*!"

Ritva craned her neck around as far as she could without interrupting the rhythm of her feet on the pedals. A sharp-pointed bodkin head stood out three inches from the felt on the inner surface of the shield over Dudley's head, just where it would have gone through his forearm if he'd had it in the loops. That was one of the many unpleasant things about being shot at with arrows from powerful war-bows; they were very hard to stop short of your own precious irreplaceable body. The light mail lining the redcoats' jackets or her green leather tunic was fair protection against cuts and of some use against stabs, but it was only marginally better than cloth when it came to a hard-driven arrow with an armor-piercing head.

The railcar swayed with its speed. She tore her eyes away from the mirror, since there was literally nothing she could do about that. The buildings of the Anchor Bar Seven homeplace and their protective wall were visible now, dot-tiny in the distance but growing; they'd certainly have heard the siren, and everyone outside the walls would be running pell-mell for the gates, if they had a good emergency drill. Her impression of Avery McGillvery was that they'd have one, and practice it frequently.

"All right, squad!" Corporal Dudley bellowed. "We were tasked with getting the lady through, so she's the mission priority. She goes out first and the rest of us follow, and if she's wounded *she* gets carried but you leave anyone else—no, *don't* argue, ma'am. Get ready—*shit*!"

This time six arrows hit the railcar's roof: *shink-thack! shink-thack! shink-thack! shink-thack! shink-thack!* and then one that ended in a nasty wet sound, *shink-thwack!* as it missed the shields and struck flesh. There was a short, high-pitched shriek. She took a look behind; the man next to the corporal had one through his left arm between elbow and shoulder, and his face was contorted in pain. He was still pedaling, though, and he gasped out:

"Leave it! It's plugging the hole! Just cut it off on both sides Jesus Christ fuck *shitshitshit!*"

That's a brave man, she thought soberly. *And he can't run fast with that. It's a death sentence.*

Another volley, and something hit her hard between the shoulders; there wasn't any pain or the unmistakable feeling of split flesh, so the back of the seat must have held it. The siding and warehouse were getting closer and closer; now she could see people streaming in the gate of the ranch headquarters, on foot and horseback; and she thought others were forcing their way *out*.

I certainly hope they are! she thought, and called aloud:

"We should halt just beyond the warehouse building. It'll give us a little cover for a couple of seconds."

"Right, we'll do it that way. *Good!*"

That accompanied a glance in the mirror. She looked in hers; the foremost Cutters were falling away, their horses shaking their heads and crabbing or just slowing down despite spur and riding crop. One simply keeled over, hopefully pinning and mangling its rider's leg in the process. Even at this distance she could see how the poor beasts were foaming and heaving; they were being ridden to death. And behind them was the whole mass of the attacking force, coming on at a hand gallop, parting to pass the exhausted front-runners—not quite as fast, but that pace was something a horse could keep up much longer. They'd be within range in ten or fifteen minutes if the railcar kept going, and then there would be *hundreds* of them shooting. These were plainsmen, born to the saddle and the bow, and the chances of surviving that storm of shafts were somewhere between *bloody nothing and bugger-all*, as Uncle John would have put it.

What a pity. Just another few hundred yards' start, and

we could have run their horses' hearts out and pulled away from them and gone straight back to Artos and the rest!

Though there were an uncomfortable *number* of the Cutters, enough to outweigh the nine-hundred-odd in the main party. The warehouse flashed by, and everyone lifted their feet. There was a screech and rooster-tails of sparks and lurching momentum threw her forward as Corporal Dudley hit the brake and then there was no time for anything but *moving*.

Dart upright, hit the door latch, and snatch her shield out of the holder above with her right hand on the leather sling strap. Duck her head through that and pull it tight even as she turned and shouldered the door open, with her helmet rattling where it was hooked and strapped to the shield. Left hand stripping the longsword out of the rack, leave the bow and quiver, a bit of a momentary pang because it was a *good* bow and she was used to shooting it. Feet on the ground—blessed flow of clean air after the stuffy fetor of the car into her lungs and out into her limbs as extra strength—*praise to the Valar*—and out with her feet on hard ground covered in scrubby grass and brown ruts dried like iron and old cowflops and horse dung. The long low-slung warehouse was to her left, and the track to the gate was ahead of her. The corporal released the brakes again, and the redcoats gave the vehicle one last push, so it coasted off downhill, slow but gathering speed.

Meanwhile she ran. Long strides, arms pumping with the sword scabbard in one hand, shield rattling on her back, making her chest swell with a deep quick rhythm. Not shallow panting, and *willing* that no stitch should cut into her side.

I'm probably going to die now. This is about the way I

always expected it to happen. Better than typhus or a breech birth. Just not so soon, *maybe! By the pits of Thangorodrim and the Mace of Morgoth, my story isn't finished yet! Or maybe it's* Rudi's *story and he's about to lose his sister which is a terrible tragedy that will show how noble his grief is to everyone hearing the bards singing his epic—*

Now she *could* hear the rumble of the oncoming host. Hear it and feel it through the ground when her bounding feet touched down. And a crashing bark, underneath a growling as of wolves when they closed in after a chase:

"Cut! Cut! *Cut!*"

Ritva could tell the redcoats were right behind her, a double rank of them—except the wounded man, and she felt a stab of shame that she'd never even learned his name. She'd flashed by him where he was crouched behind a watering-trough/hitching-rail combination, with his sword out and his shield hanging over his useless shoulder and his kettle helmet askew on his head—it looked like a steel version of what her mother had called a lemon-squeezer—getting ready to do what he could to slow down a couple of thousand men.

Run, woman, run. You have to deserve *that.*

The enemy had checked as the railcar went behind the warehouse, from their perspective, and then coasted out into view again. *Someone* must have suspected what had happened, but they were moving too fast to stop without a clear sign, and the whole clot at the head of their rush went past the warehouse after the moving target, shooting as fast as they could draw and loose and take the curve without going over. Probably it was superstition as well; their religion hated any but the simplest machinery.

It was the *next* clump who saw the small figures running down the road towards the gates of the Anchor Bar

Seven's homeplace, and even they couldn't be absolutely sure that it was the ones they were chasing, instead of a clerk and his helpers caught stacking bales of wool or hides or barrels of tallow in the warehouse when the alarm went off. The ranch's big bell was ringing frantically, too. A quick glance told her that a clump of fifty or so Cutters had peeled off after them with more behind; they had a standard at their head, a rayed golden sun for the Church Universal and Triumphant, with six horsetails hanging from a crossbar beneath. Their horses . . .

Started out reasonably well but they were ridden hard and put away wet even before they chased us for miles. They're blown, they won't be any real use for a day or two. But even a blown horse is faster than a human, until it falls over.

There *were* men coming out of the ranch gates. About thirty of them, all armed and mounted, some of them in the heavier lancer gear she'd seen earlier. They spread out in two neat ranks and came on at a gallop, shooting over her head—which meant the Cutters would be in range soon, if not already. Then they were past her in spurts of dust and clods of dirt and glimpses of set faces and sabers and honed lanceheads. She *certainly* wasn't going to look back now. Arrows began falling around her, but not nearly as many as she'd feared; the enemy were distracted by the counterattack and the gates began to loom ahead. There was a deep dry ditch all around the wall—that was probably where the earth for the structures had come from—and it was filled with sharpened angle-iron and rusty barbed wire, and there was a bridge over it to the gate.

There's no gate! her mind gibbered. *It's not just open; it's gone. They must have had it down to repair it—*

Even that didn't make her pause in her sprint, and then she realized that it had a gate, just not one with the usual outward-swinging twin doors. Instead the whole thing slid out of a slit in one side of the wall along a strip of metal laid in the roadway, and then into a matching opening on the other side. It was something new to her, but it certainly looked strong.

Best of all, it's still open *for us!* she thought.

Dry air sobbed into aching lungs and the ground shocked up through foot and ankle and shin. The Rancher would have been justified in closing it; after all, his first responsibility was to his own. That wasn't just a fort held by a garrison, it was where his family and those of his followers lived, including their children. It was *home*.

Behind them there was a series of hard *thud* sounds as lances struck home in bodies, a sudden burring roar, the hard cracking sound of blades on shields, the discordant ringing of steel on steel, and the screams of men and horses in rage and pain. The little party from the ranch was grossly outnumbered by the Cutter force as a whole, but not by the vanguard directly behind the fugitives. And their horses were fresh and their ranks compact. The noise faded quickly, and hooves sounded behind her as the Anchor Bar Seven men turned and raced for home. They'd knocked the pursuers back on their heels, at least.

"Grab on!" a man yelled, as a horse came level with her.

Her right hand snatched at the stirrup leather and closed on it. The quarter horse's acceleration almost snatched it away again, but she held on and used the horse's momentum to add to her own, bounding along faster than she could have run herself. The squat towers flanking the gate were close now; something went *tung* on one of them, and a four-foot dart flashed by just over her head and a horse screamed briefly, louder than any human but just as piteous. Two arrows hit her shield from behind, *tak! tak!*, like blows with a hammer, but the points didn't go through and strike her jerkin. The other horsemen were all around her, and redcoats among them running as she was.

Then right ahead of her Ian Kovalevsky gave a cry and loosed the stirrup leather he held and fell, an arrow pinning his coattail to his trousers and another through his upper shoulder. Ritva let go too, throwing herself forward so quickly that she caught him before he'd finished hitting the ground. A deep-knee squat and his body was over her back in a fireman's carry, and she wheezed upright. He wasn't a big man, no taller than her five-nine, but he was *heavy*, thirty pounds more than her at least. She blanked her mind and *pushed*, and she was running forward with horses buffeting her on all sides and a series of faint screams in her ears from the wounded man she carried. Then just in the gateway something hit her in the leg.

She sprawled, pulling at the redcoat across her back so he wouldn't land wrong and drive the arrows deeper. She stared downward numbly; there was an arrow in *her*, through her left calf, and blood leaking from where it transfixed her boot. Then the pain started, and she ground her teeth and gave a muted sound like a teakettle boiling. More horses trampled around her, and then someone grabbed her under the arms to pull her backward; the press of bodies and men and horses was blocking the gate, and unless it was cleared the enemy would get in. The pull dragged the flight-feathers of the arrow against the ground, working it in the wound, and she screamed in earnest then.

Others were screaming, men screaming but not in pain. Raw terror, somehow harder to listen to. She looked up and saw the long blackened muzzle of a steel tube protruding from a horizontal slit in the right gate-tower, and behind it the flicker of movement as men heaved at a pivot-pump. That shocked her into silence despite the agony, as the amber stream of liquid arched out to play over the dense-packed mass of men and horses where the Cutters had halted. They shrieked as the stream splashed into their bearded faces; she could smell the sharp kitchen-and-laboratory scent of canola and coal-oil and wood alcohol mixed with quicklime and powdered aluminum and dissolved rubber.

Her eyes met one man's, as blue as hers, wide and staring as napalm dripped from his face in thick liquid strings. Then the flame began, running down the arching stream in a flicker of blue and crimson almost too fast to see, and the whole area it had soaked went up with a *WHUMP* and a pillow of hot air struck her, making her skin prickle and the little hairs in her nose start to shrivel. The gate swung across the scene before she could force her staring eyes to close, sliding home with a rumble and *chunk* and a clunking sound that was some sort of locking mechanism going in.

Even with the solid metal-shod baulk in the way, the screams were loud, for a single instant. Two middle-aged women in shapeless pants and shirts with red-cross armbands added dragged Kovalevsky facedown onto a stretcher, grabbed it and bore it away at a staggering run. Two more started to reach for her.

"No!" Ritva said, then managed a firmer "*No!*"

She pulled her holdout knife out of her right boot, took a deep breath, gripped the arrow by the fletching and cut.

"Naeg!" she swore with a yelp.

The pain was like white fire, icy and burning at the same time, shooting up her leg towards her groin and almost making her bladder release. Whoever had fashioned the arrow had used nicely seasoned red ash, and it was dry and tough. Doggedly she cut the fletching side, gripped the part behind the head, took a deep breath and screamed as she pulled it out:

"Naeg! Rhaich! Naeg-naeg-naeg! Ai, ai!"

Her breath came faster as she pulled off the boot and tight-bandaged it, and gummy saliva filled her mouth until she spat to clear it. Corporal Dudley put a hand under her arm as she fumbled the knife back into the sheath.

"Let's get you to the infirmary, ma'am," he said, half shouting through the racket. A hesitation. "That was a brave thing to do for Kovalevsky. You shouldn't have done it, but it was brave."

"To Morgoth with the infirmary. Get me up on the wall!"

She stood and put weight on the leg. It wasn't as bad as she expected, only enough to make her break out in a muck-sweat, cold and gelid. At his look she snapped hoarsely:

"I can't run away and I can't dance a lavolta, but I can still stand and fight—and if we don't hold the wall, we're all going to die anyway. I'd rather die fighting."

"Point."

"Get me up there."

"Let's go."

He put her left arm over his shoulders and they moved a little like a three-legged race at a Bearkiller Gunpowder Day celebration. Everyone in the little settlement was pouring from the houses and the clear space inside the walls up onto the fighting platform, or at least everyone of either sex over the age of thirteen who didn't have some absolute duty elsewhere; all of them were carrying weapons, and many were struggling into bits and pieces of gear, helmets or mail shirts. The stairs were an integral part of the thick rammed-earth walls, the risers surfaced with planks but without rails or guards, and fairly narrow. Ritva and Corporal Dudley toiled up one with the four surviving unwounded or walking-wounded redcoats running interference for them.

The hoarding atop the wall had a thick sloping roof facing outward, a chest-high solid timber wall with slits for firing arrows, and it overhung the wall by about a yard so that trapdoors could be opened and things dropped or thrown directly down. It was the same principle that castles and city walls in Montival used, except that even with the ditch this wall wasn't nearly as high. There were piles of rocks, racks of spears, and quivers of arrows and crossbow bolts ready for use. People were going around with burning splits to light gas-fed jets for heating pots of boiling water and oil; evidently the Anchor Bar Seven homeplace had a methane-digester system.

Ritva propped herself against the parapet and looked out, carefully avoiding the hideous knot of dead and not-quite-dead men and animals in front of the gates, although she couldn't help smelling the greasy black smoke that poured off it. The Cutters were still arriving, and her eyes went wide at the numbers. A catapult cut loose from a tower, and a twelve-pound ball of cast iron snapped out. The targets were far enough away to dodge it, but some of them shook their fists or weapons—probably cursing the impious device, since their faith abominated the complex gearing involved.

"Couple of thousand," Corporal Dudley said. "Ma'am, they take you really *seriously*, don't they?"

He sounded more admiring than not. "It's my big brother they're really after," she said. "And yes, they *do* take him very seriously indeed."

"I guess we didn't travel faster than the news after all."

The alarm bell stopped; she was suddenly conscious of it because of its absence. Ritva looked over her shoulder and saw that it hung in the tower of a squat-looking church . . . not that there was much alternative to "squat" when you used *pisé* as building material. Instead a column of bright red smoke rose from the same square height, shooting into the air and bending gently eastward with the prevailing wind. The sky was still clear and blue—she blinked a little to realize it was only about three in the afternoon—and it would be visible for a *long* way.

"Like the beacons from Nardol to Dîn in the Histories," she murmured to herself.

"It's a long way to the next ranch," the redcoat said. "They were big around here even before the Change because it's dry, and the ones that survived took over the land of those that didn't. Old Man Keith McGillvery was Rancher here then . . . manager, at least, and nobody was going to go to Toronto to look up the stockholders when he claimed the property."

Ritva nodded absently; she was watching the Cutters swarming around the warehouse and the corrals down by the little lake the dam made.

I've actually been to Toronto and I don't think anyone's going to be showing up with a title deed, she thought mordantly. *Except ghosts. Though right now it wouldn't be worth much anyway.*

Avery McGillvery himself came by, in war-gear with

some of his armored retainers in tow; he and his wife greeted people by name, she smiling and nodding and he slapping backs cheerfully and telling them how they'd slaughter the invaders under the wall. He gave Ritva a quick nod as well as he went by, and she put her hand to her heart and bowed slightly. Corporal Dudley saluted.

He's doing this as a lord should, she thought. *Keeping his people in good heart by example. His father must have known the way of it, to have come through the Change so well.*

The idea that someone could own land without being there to hold and defend it was another pre-Change mystery; maybe Dudley was old enough to understand it, but she wasn't, not really, not down in the heart. Then she noticed the roof of the warehouse by the railway collapse in a cloud of dust, with dozens of lariats strung to saddle horns pulling at it.

"They're making ladders," she said, as she unclipped the helmet from her shield, stuffed her hat into a pocket and set it on her head. "Tearing out the beams and boards for it there, and from those corrals. And fascines to throw in the ditch, and some mantlets."

"Jesus, you're right, ma'am. They're going to assault. Oh, *that's* going to cost them quite a butcher's bill."

They glanced at each other: *But not as much as it'll cost us*, went unspoken between them.

Counting the redcoats, and one walking-wounded Ritva Havel, the Anchor Bar Seven had perhaps a hundred and fifty fighters to man the walls, and too many of them for comfort were teenagers just big enough to work the crank of a crossbow, or women.

That wasn't necessarily bad; she considered herself well above average as fighters went, and she'd killed enough men to prove it. On the other hand she was also about five inches taller and thirty pounds heavier than the average woman, nearly all of the weight flat straplike muscle. That made her as tall as most men and stronger than some. Also she was very fast indeed, plus she and Mary had been brought up in the households of warrior nobles with the very best training provided from toddlerhood on. The women she saw on the wall here looked like they were housewives and weavers and cheesemakers and such mostly; doubtless brave when fighting for their homes and families, but only sketchily trained in their off-hours and smaller, weaker and lighter than virtually any Cutter they'd face.

Probably a lot of the menfolk were out with the herds where they could do little good, and had been too far away to get back in time. Coming back *now* would just mean throwing themselves away against that horde, though they probably would anyway.

This is a . . . a very, very unpleasant situation. We really must find a way to say we are so fucked *in the Noble Tongue.*

"The wall will be a big advantage," she said, and Corporal Dudley nodded.

She could read his thought: *True as far as it goes.*

More and more of the Cutters were dismounting, sending their horses to the rear and loading themselves down with extra quivers and bundles of arrows. Pack beasts with more stood behind, and other groups had long ladders knocked together out of beams with fence boards nailed or lashed across them. Ritva put weight on her wounded leg, and hissed as she fastened the chin-cup of her open-face sallet helm. The calf would bear her weight, but only if she didn't have to use it much or for long.

"The leg works, sorta. Though we Rangers usually prefer sneaking around to this sort of fighting," she added.

"So do I," the corporal said dryly. "If you mean prefer it to *being trapped* and *vastly outnumbered*."

"Don't think of it as being outnumbered," she said, forcing a smile and ignoring the dryness of her mouth. "Think of it—"

"—as having a very target-rich environment, yes, ma'am, we tell that one too."

He passed her a dipper of water from one of the pottery jugs that hung at intervals; it was cool with evaporation through the coarse earthenware. She drank gratefully, handed it back with a nod of thanks and spoke aloud:

"Could someone get me a bow?" she asked. "Medium weight. Heavy side of medium."

The word ran along the parapet, and the weapon was passed down. It was a common-or-garden four-foot recurve, an imitation of pre-Change hunting weapons but with a heavier draw. Honestly made, a sandwich glued together of sinew, a central layer of yew wood and springy horn; the riser was of mountain maple with a fitted handgrip and arrow-rest through the center. She drew it experimentally, into the full deep C-shape; heavy for her, ninety to a hundred pounds, but not impossible. Then she took a seven-foot spear out of a rack and propped it nearby point down beside her shield against the timber rampart; she wanted a weapon with a bit of reach, at least to start with.

There was a pause, most of an hour; she spent the time reciting training mantras and whistling softly and remembering things and trying to ignore her leg. Leaning against the parapet she even managed to doze for a few minutes, though she jerked awake again immediately from a dream of wolverines tearing at her calf. The Cutters were closer then, and starting to look more organized.

I wonder what our section of the Halls of Mandos is like? she thought. *Do we just wait there to come back, or what? That sounds boring, unless it's just a kenning for the rest of the Summerlands. The Histories aren't clear except that we're Sundered from the elves, but then, I've never met any elves so that's no hardship, really. Are there sort of news bulletins, so you can find out how things turned out back here? Or scrying crystals, like a palantír?*

Then the enemy started to move forward. They were chanting too, the onomatopoeic war cry of the CUT, starting as a rumble and then growing into a growling blurred chorus as they lashed themselves into a frenzy:

"Cut . . . Cut . . . *Cut! Cut! Cut! CUT! CUT!*"

"I don't think they'll stop," Corporal Dudley said quietly. "There aren't enough of us to kill enough of them to sicken the rest."

His men were bunched around them. A little down the rampart a girl three or four years younger than Ritva was whimpering slightly without being conscious of it, but she was also propping up a heavy crossbow, ready to shoot through a firing-slit. A younger brother with the same carroty hair and freckles was struggling behind her to load another, doggedly working the lever to cock it ready to hand forward.

"CUT! CUT! CUT!"

The enemy began to run forward to get through the killing ground, masses of them, their leather and undyed wool dark against the tawny green grass but their faces showing lighter under helmets or hats. Here and there a mail shirt showed gray and gleaming with oil, or more often a breastplate of molded hide with steel strips riveted on, but most had only their leather jackets and shields.

"Attacking all 'round," Corporal Dudley said. "So we can't shift men to meet them."

Every catapult cut loose, six of them, one for each tower, with a series of heavy *tung* sounds. This time the round shot couldn't miss; the figures were still doll-tiny, but her mind sketched in what happened when the hard, hard metal hit and bounced and twisted through the ranks. Again and again as fast as the crews could cock and load, they were aiming for the mantlets, improvised shields on wheels taken from farm carts. Those were covering the men with the ladders and fascines.

Then the artillery crews switched to clay pots full of napalm that wobbled as they flew and trailed black smoke from the sheaths of burning rag rope wound around them. Bright streaks of yellow flame blossomed where they struck. One hit a mantlet and sprayed through every gap in the crude carpentry, and men ran out from behind it with their clothes and hair on fire, rolling screaming on the ground in a futile attempt to put out the clinging death. A few of their comrades paused to give them the mercy-stroke.

"*Shoot!*" someone shouted on the wall; she thought it was the Rancher, Avery McGillvery.

The extra height meant they had the range on the attackers, and everyone cut loose; the hard *snap* of bowstrings mingling with the deeper note of crossbows. Some part of her that wasn't focused to a single diamond point of concentration on drawing and shooting until her shoulders burned noted that they were splitting around the approaches to the gate. Even that mass of savage faith wasn't going to face the flamethrower's arc again. Probably some of them were thinking of what they'd do to the crew of it when they got their hands on them.

"*Look*—" someone began to shout, as snarling horn-signals went through the Cutter force.

Half the onrushing horde stopped, alternate blocks—or clumps, for they were in no formal order, but close enough. Afternoon sunlight sparkled along their ranks as they raised their bows, blinking off the points of the arrows like starlight glimmering on the sea. An odd whispery creaking sounded, the noise of many, many powerful composite bows being drawn to the ear by as many brawny arms.

"—*out!*" the cry finished, and nearly everyone ducked away from the firing-slits.

The shout was almost drowned by the whistling rush of air. Ritva turned with her left shoulder against the thick planks and forced herself not to close her eyes in a futile attempt to deny what was rushing at her. This was worthy of a Mackenzie arrowstorm; bowmen could pack together much closer on foot than as mounted archers. Seconds after the strings snapped out their unmusical note the first shafts hit the wood of the fighting platform. Then the mass arrived, a drumming roar like massive hail on a roof, going on and on, more flicking through the fighting slits and down into the settlement. Trying to shoot back at once would have been suicide.

"This is what my father called trying to fight projectiles with targets!" she shouted, and thought Corporal Dudley grinned even then.

Thunk as they sank into the timbers or the thick planks and she could feel it through her shoulder like a trembling vibration over and over again. *Pock* for the ones that fell a little short and hit the *pisé* wall beneath her feet, some sticking and others bouncing off with little divots of the rocklike material knocked free. *Hsss* as hundreds more went by overhead, arching down into the space inside the wall, and more and more cracking on the tile roof or arching over it.

Cries of pain came as the unlucky or incautious fell; one white-bearded man not too far away staggered backward with an arrow through his face and fell over the rail and down the inside of the wall. Then the storm slackened as the attackers fired individually rather than in massed volleys; those were rancher levies out there for the most part, not professionals.

Haven't seen the Sword of the Prophet, she thought; their reddish-brown armor was unmistakable. *Don't miss them, but that means they're probably all out west trying to kill my family.*

Ritva took a deep breath and stepped to the arrow-slit and shot and shot and shot, then ducked back. Beside her the girl with the red braids was shooting too, handing her crossbow behind her, taking the next from her brother, squinting down the sights and wincing as the butt thumped against her shoulder.

"Here, Anne!" he cried, just barely audible through the surf-roar of noise, shrill and high. "Get 'em, Annie, get 'em!"

Another shout ran around the parapet: "Shoot the storming parties! Leave the archers, shoot the ones coming at us!"

Good advice, she thought, and shot three times again.

An arrow came through the slit and just missed her as she ducked back, close enough that she could feel the wind of its passage on the sweat-wet skin just below her ear. Men fell out there, many, she needn't pick individual targets, just shoot into the brown. They had their shields up, but at this range they likely wouldn't stop an arrow; some of them were holding up improvised siege shields made of planks from the fences and buildings. One of those fell as she shot, a man taking an arrow through the toes and staggering aside hopping; two more hit him and he fell limply. Ladders and fascines dropped, then came on again as hale men snatched them up and rushed forward with the others over the bodies of their dead and wounded. The catapults were shooting steady as metronomes, blasting tracks through the dense mass of men.

Then the storm of arrow fire lifted; the attackers were getting close enough that they endangered their own men. They were at the ditch, throwing the bundles of brushwood and bales of hay into it. Others butted the long poles that had been warehouse or barn rafters and let them topple forward. Hundreds of knotted lariats snaked towards the parapet, each topped with a barbed steel hook. Defenders hacked or pried at them, and used spearpoints or forked poles to push at the ladders. Many fell back, but myriad hands raised them again. Ritva leaned over the edge for a second and shot directly down at no more than five yards distance.

Two women near her walked forward with a big jar held between them, cloth wrapped around the handles. The contents smoked and seethed; a third woman unbolted and lifted a trapdoor. The first pair lifted and poured in careful unison. The boiling tallow poured in a translucent torrent, and war cries turned to shrieks below. Others were doing the same, or lifting the traps and throwing javelins and rocks downward.

Ritva shot once more and then dropped the bow and

stooped for her shield. As she rose she saw a face appear over the parapet, grinning in a rictus around the knife held in his teeth; a steel hook was deep-sunk in the timber to hold the rope he climbed. The women with the pot took a step and jerked the ceramic container forward. A double cupful of hot tallow was left in the bottom; the Cutter had just enough time to jerk a hand up before his eyes and begin to fall backward before it hit.

"*Thanks!*" she shouted, though they probably couldn't hear her.

Then she snatched up the spear and shrieked the Dúnedain war cry:

"*Lacho Calad! Drego Morn!*"

She thrust through the firing slit, stabbing blind towards where the rope must be hanging. The point met something solid but soft; there was a bubbling shriek that faded away as the weight jerked off the point. Then she tried to pry the rope hook out of the timber, jamming the point beneath it and working back with all her weight and both hands. It started to yield, and then something hit her very hard in the shoulder. She staggered and then started to fall as her injured leg buckled. A light flashed in the corner of her eye.

Blackness.

CHAPTER NINETEEN

Artos looked through a slit to the car ahead of him and grinned. Garbh was sitting on the roof of it, her mouth open and her tongue and ears flapping and fur rippling in the breeze of their passage, a look of exultant pleasure on her face and her tail beating hard on the curved plywood.

Edain followed his gaze and grinned. "Looks happy," he said.

"Looks like a thirsty man on a hot day who's just for the first time discovered there's such a thing as beer in the world, drawn cool from a jug kept hanging in a well," Artos said.

The horses were considerably less happy about their mode of travel, particularly Epona, which was why she was here with a whole car to herself. She crowded against him again; it was for reassurance, not with any intent to harm . . . but when a seventeen-hand, twelve-hundred-pound animal pressed up against you, with an unyielding surface waiting behind, harm could result.

"Stop that!" he scolded, slapping her on the shoulder. "You great pouting baby of a creature, mind your manners! You're a middle-aged horse and a mother, for Her sake!"

She sighed—it was a sound in proportion to her deep chest—and turned her neck to nuzzle him, her grassy-musky smell as familiar as the straw-horse-piss-and-dung scent of the bedding beneath them. That was part of the fabric of life from his earliest memories.

Make it stop and let me out! was as plain as words in her nicker.

He stroked her nose and made soothing noises, reflecting that he'd never been in a traveling stable before either, but that it was probably much harder for her. It might have been better if the compartment was completely dark, cutting off a view of the countryside passing by as fast as Epona could have covered it at a round canter, but you could see the prairie through the boards that made the walls.

Each of the trains in the convoy that bore his force had four cars; the forward hippomotive where eight horses walked on inclined treadmills to drive the wheels through gearing; two more each holding eight resting horses—each was big enough to take about forty men, at a crowded pinch—and a fourth bearing copious spare parts for the temperamental mechanism and fodder for the animals. It was a very fast way to transport horses, since with teams spelling each other you could average a hundred and forty or fifty miles a day even allowing for the frequent infuriating breakdowns. That was five times what horses could do on their hooves for any length of time.

Unfortunately it really wasn't a practical method to transport anything *but* horses given the coddling the mechanisms needed; the beasts were slower but much more efficient pulling cargo along the rails on their own feet. His troops were pedaling along themselves, and having no problem keeping pace with the horse-powered vehicles. The whole thing depended on having water and fodder available at close intervals too, since the horses were mostly hauling horses.

Artos felt the fabric of the wagon jerk a little. He looked around; it was Mathilda, with a worried frown on her face. She'd dropped off one of the cars ahead, and jumped up to snatch the handholds.

"The Canuk commander wants you to see something, Rudi," she said through the boards. "I don't think it's good news."

"Is it ever?" he sighed. "I've been feeling . . . prickly myself. As if lines of might-be were gathering here."

He could feel the hippomotive slow; a set of whistle signals spread down the long awkward chain that stretched for miles across the prairie. Epona snorted and stamped in approval, assuming this meant a break to drink and graze and roll. The train of cars lurched and then ground to a halt as the brakemen threw their wheels with a squeal of steel on steel. Artos and Edain opened the door just enough to let themselves out, ignored the great black horse's indignation and trotted forward through the rustling prairie grass.

The human-pedaled railcars were stopped nose-to-tail ahead of this, the first of the hippomotives; their doors were open and men peering out curiously, but discipline held them within. His staff—which was to say his friends—were waiting for him, along with the commander of the redcoat escort.

"There," Inspector James Rollins said. He was about Ingolf's age and height, and similarly brown-bearded and blue-eyed, but slimmer. "It's gotten higher since I called the halt."

He took the offered binoculars and looked. The plume of smoke was distant, but it was visibly rising. And it was absolutely *red*, in a way normal smoke rarely was, probably with something added to the fire to make the message clearer.

"That's the Anchor Bar Seven Ranch, all right," Rollins said. "And that's the *under attack by superior force, help urgent* signal. It's a strong Ranch headquarters—"

By which he means fort *or* stronghold *or* castle, *I would say,* Artos thought absently. He'd seen enough of them in this trip.

"—one of the strongest southern ranches, with a well-trained militia company. And the McGillverys don't scream at the sight of a mouse. They wouldn't use that just because of a minor border raid."

Artos tapped a thumb on his chin, an old habit with him. His right palm caressed the hilt of the Sword, a new one.

"Could the Cutters have sent an army over the frontier without your knowing it? It's not far, no more than three days' ride, and unfortunately they're probably aware of your impending declaration of war against them, the black sorrow and misfortune."

Rollins shook his head. "Not an army. A big raiding party, possibly, especially if they didn't really plan on getting most of it back; a thousand to two thousand men, absolute tops. The smoke will be visible to riders on every neighboring property, and they'll have the news to the militia HQ and the Force soon."

"Reinforcements to this ranch?"

Rollins nodded. "And blocking forces to the border.

We've had raids before, it's often more effective to try and catch them as they retreat with the stock they lift."

"But this is not just a raid," Artos said gently. "It's a war, and they're here to kill, not to steal cattle merely. They're after me; and failing that, destroying this ranch would tear a hole in your southern boundary that could not quickly be put right."

The redcoat nodded jerkily. Artos stood for a long moment. Father Ignatius cleared his throat.

"We could retreat faster than they can pursue, until reinforcements arrive," he pointed out, his voice carefully neutral. "They may well outnumber us, and their aim is definitely to attack *you*, Your Majesty."

Rollins nodded unwillingly, though obviously every fiber of his body longed to rush to the rescue; he knew that war meant hard choices. The warrior-monk continued:

"Undoubtedly they had intelligence of our route. As I understand it, their mundane means for that work as well as ever. And if they harm you, we are no better off than we were when this war began."

Artos smiled, but the negative gesture he used was brusque; he knew that the argument had to be made, but he very much doubted Ignatius either thought he'd listen to it or really believed it himself.

"I'm not likely to do well in this war if I refuse to engage whenever the enemy has more numbers," he pointed out. "Also we have the advantage of a fortress to serve as anvil to our hammer—while it holds out, the which it may not do for long unless helped."

And to be sure Ritva is there, probably. It would be a world less merry with her off to the Summerlands. And I would dislike to see that branch of my blood father's line cut off.

Mary had carefully said nothing about her twin. Everyone on both sides was someone's brother, sister, husband, father; a King had to keep that firmly in mind, whatever his own feelings were, if he was to keep faith with his subjects.

"And besides," he went on easily, "there's the using of the lovely gifts my mother-in-law-to-be has sent."

Messages and light cargo had been passing over the border with Drumheller since that realm decided to commit itself some months ago, even before the snows melted in the passes, for which he had Sandra Arminger to thank, and Abbot-Bishop Dmwoski. Besides letters, they'd found several boxed suits of plate complete waiting for them as they advanced, neatly tailored to their measurements and made of the most refractory alloy steels modern armories could work. It was the sort of gift only a monarch could make at such short notice, and a rich one at that.

Say what you like about Sandra, she's not petty.

Ingolf spoke over his shoulder to his nephew; Mark went running to alert the Richlander cavalry regiment.

"Now this will be a careful matter of timing," Artos said. "The problem being that it takes so long to get the horses off the hippomotive-drawn trains and deployed."

He looked behind him at the long, long line of vehicles on the rails. In point of fact they'd be helpless as sheep in a pen if they were attacked thus, and the riders not much less so than the horses. Which meant he had to get them down and deployed at a considerable distance from the enemy, while the Norrheimer foot could spring out of their pedal-carts and be ready in instants.

Ingolf caught his eye, and he nodded curtly; their minds were running on the same track. It was the only one available in this situation, if you knew your work.

"Major Kohler, get them deployed," his brother-in-law said. "Company columns of march. Extra quivers slung to the bow-cases. Tell the troop-leaders to prepare for a meeting engagement."

"Inspector Rollins, the map," Artos said.

Kohler took off at a run, bawling orders as he went; presumably the men would be waiting already, with Ensign Vogeler's warning. Artos bent over the paper, though he didn't need it himself. He'd always had a good eye for terrain, and now he could *see*, as if hovering over it on hawk wings. But physical images were still the best way to explain to others. He could trace them on the map with his finger, and to his mind's eye they became *real*.

"Father Ignatius, you'll take both field artillery batteries with the footmen, under Bjarni's overall command. Edain, you'll command the foot-archers, our war band and the Norrheimers both; Bjarni, you'll be in charge until I arrive, but I'd advise listening carefully to both of them—and then making your decisions. Here's what we'll do—"

When he'd finished, the fleece-lined sacks with the leaders' plate-armor were open at their feet, and attendants were stripping off their clothes. Then they helped them into the black padded undergarments, with mail insets at vulnerable points like the underarms and grommet-laces for fastening to the armor. The steel carapaces went on swiftly as they spoke.

Bjarni's plain Norrheimer hauberk was a lot less trouble to don; he shrugged into it and grinned at Artos' plan.

"This is like the story of the sheep, the cabbage and the wolf, and how the man had to get them across the river in a canoe," he said cheerfully. "Still, the landwights and the High One willing, we can do it if Wyrd will have it so. You don't want me to reinforce the burg?"

"No; you could make it too strong to storm, but then the enemy will just ride away and hover about, making a nuisance of themselves and delaying us, the creatures. The railroad is too vulnerable and we can't do without it, we don't have the *time*. It's squashing them like a roach under a boot I'd be doing, not swatting them aside like a buzzing fly that comes back to drive you mad."

Bjarni nodded wholehearted agreement; there were reasons his folk had named him *Ironrede*, hard-counsel.

"It's not too complex, at least," he said. "The timing will be tricky, but then it always is, eh?"

Not a word on how he and his will all die if I don't manage the other part properly, Artos thought. *I didn't misjudge this man's quality.*

Mathilda handed him his sallet; Sandra—or more likely Tiphaine d'Ath or someone in her service—had had the new one also scored and inlaid in niello in imitation of Raven's plumage. The black feather crests over each ear rustled as he settled it on his head, buckled the chin-cup and flicked the visor up and down; with the plate suit's bevoir covering his neck and chin, that left no gap for a point to use. He bent, twisted and stood again. The suit's joints worked with marvelous fluidity, as if they moved on jewel bearings like a fine watch; the articulated lames that made up the back and breast gave him nearly as much flexibility as mail, with far better protection. It was a bit lighter, too, though even hotter than chain links since there was no movement of air through it.

"Now go," Artos said. "Your Gods go with you."

Bjarni turned and trotted over to his railcar, gave a

brief explanation to the chiefs of his tribal contingents, and then they were off again.

Artos spoke quietly to Mathilda, in the moment when they could be private: "If I fall, *you* must take up the Sword, *mo chroi*."

She went a little white with shock, but when she spoke her voice was quiet and controlled: "Have you *seen* something?"

"No," he said, and shook his head. "If anything, victory is likely, and myself surviving it. But it's not *certain*. An arrow at the wrong time . . . and if that happens, *you must take the Sword*. It would be . . . hard, for you. It's made for me and my descendants. But I've never known you to shirk a task because it was hard; not even when you were a prisoner, in the War of the Eye, and you and I washed dishes together!"

She stared at him for a moment, then ducked her head. "Your Majesty," she said.

His mouth quirked. "You needn't be quite so formal as *that*, acushla." More seriously: "I wouldn't demand this of the Princess Mathilda as my vassal. That would be stretching a lord's authority too far. I ask it of my friend."

A brief pressure of the hand: "Of course, Rudi."

The First Richland Volunteer Cavalry fell in with commendable speed. Artos made a stirrup of his hands for Mathilda to mount, lifting her and the armor without much effort. Then he went to one knee for an instant, taking up a clod of dirt and touching it to his lips, the warrior's acknowledgment of mortality.

He rose and murmured with his head against Epona's saddle. "Lady Morrigú-Badb-Macha, hear me. Great Threefold Queen, Red Hag, Crow Goddess, Dark

Mother, She who is terrible in majesty amid the clash of spears. On Your earth will the blood be spilled; to Your black-wing host I dedicate the harvest of the unplowed field whose crop is the skulls of men. Be with me now, and know that when my time comes I will go willingly to You, joyful, as to a bridal feast."

Then he put his hand on the high cantle of Epona's war-saddle and took a skipping step and swung up. Someone handed him his lance, and he rested the butt in the ring on his stirrup. Beside him, Ingolf grumbled:

"Yah yah, the armor *fits*, but I'm less mobile than the rest of my command," he fretted. "Bad practice. A single unit should have uniform equipment."

Artos grinned. "Your function is to command, not dash about shooting your bow," he said. "And that gear will let you shed most arrows."

Which is what's bothering you—the desire to share more of your men's risks, he thought. *Commendable, to be sure, but I'm not going to let you deprive me of such a man as yourself to soothe your feelings, brother-in-law.*

"*I* have no objection at all," Mary said beside him.

"This is fascinating," Fred Thurston said, looking down at his own suit. "I don't think a sword could hurt you at all in this stuff . . . except *your* Sword, of course, Rudi."

"Not unless you lie still and let someone stab you in the face," his wife, Virginia, said. "But this much iron-mongery cramps my style and I'm not used to having the stirrup leathers so long. Feel like I'm standin' up, not in the saddle at all. Still, I got this awful feeling we're going to need every advantage we can get."

Rollins and his forty redcoat lancers fell in around him. The red serge jackets were still visible, beneath the knee-length hauberks and plate vambraces and greaves. Their helmets were odd, a blunt serrated cone in the center with a flat brim around it, and hinged cheek-pieces; more or less a kettle helm, such as many of Ingolf's country-men preferred, but also like a metal hat. Their round shields bore a buffalo's head face-on, topped with a crown that bore a cross and the French motto *Maintiens le Droit*.

"'Uphold the Right,'" Artos said. "Fitting! And the gear was mostly copied from the PPA's style, eh? Or what they used ten or fifteen years ago."

"When we were fighting the Association for the Peace River," Rollins said. "And it's proved useful elsewhere. Though from what you and your horse are wearing, we've fallen behind the times."

"Not necessarily. This is specialized equipment. Imagine five thousand men-at-arms in plate on barded horses."

The redcoat whistled silently. "That would hit like a sledgehammer on an egg!"

"Sure and it would . . . does, in fact. But imagine them lumbering across these plains, with horse-archers stinging like wasps and running away faster than the knights could pursue. What you've got there is a good compromise, and you can still shoot from the saddle as well."

The horsemen were all ready to advance now, de-ployed columns of fours with Artos and the redcoats on the right and the First Richland on his left. He pulled on the guige strap that held his shield across his back, then ran his arm through the loops. A brief alarm, and then forty more Anchor Bar Seven cowboys joined them; they'd been gathering for a doomed attack of their own, and their relief at seeing a substantial force was palpable.

Artos tipped his lance to the west, and the pennant flapped in the breeze.

"Forward," he said.

Bjarni Ironrede pointed his red-running sword downward. "Plant the standard!" he barked. "Shield-wall, shield-wall! Positions!"

The raven banner's butt-spike was rammed into the hard prairie dirt, and a hundred warriors formed up to either side of it, their big round shields overlapping with a hard clattering rattle of ironbound birch. Those in the second, third and fourth ranks stood ready behind them. That gave everyone the place they'd need; then they relaxed for a moment, leaned on their pair of spears, many pushing up their helmets and taking a drink from their canteens as the foe drew off. They didn't stop just out of bow-range, either; as soon as they weren't masked by the Norrheimer force the catapults on the walls opened up on them, bolts and round shot hissing by overhead and driving them a thousand yards away.

Bjarni took a drink himself, the warm stale water flowing blissfully down his throat; this climate sucked the water out of a man's body, he found, and it was turning into a warm day, with scarcely a cloud in the sky. His breathing slowed after the mad dash from the railcars and the brief savage fight; running in armor took almost as much out of you as battle. He was rank with sweat beneath his mail, but that was a familiar enough experience for a warrior and a farmer both.

The bowmen were to their left in a double rank—what Edain Samkinsson called a *harrow* formation. Everyone was facing south and a little east, which put the afternoon sun over their right shoulders and in the foe's eyes. To their right and behind them was the burg, and most particularly the gate guarded by the flamethrower, the firedrake's breath whose ugly work lay twisted and blackened and smoking still before it. Ladders and leather ropes dropped from the ramparts as he glanced that way, pushed and pried away.

The Christian mass-priest Ignatius was getting the eight light field-catapults set up in front, spreading the trails, testing the elevating and traverse screws, hooking the armored hoses to the pumps and the hydraulic jacks that cocked the springs. A priest, but a man too, and a dangerous one for all he was so quiet. Dangerous with his hands, more so with his head.

"Good," Bjarni grunted. "This is a solid position, with the fort at our backs. We can hold this ground."

The endless horizons here still made him feel nervous and out of place, but the iron-copper stink of blood and the dung smell of cut-open bodies were wholly familiar—for that matter, it was not altogether different from the autumn hog-butchering time. Syfrid came up beside him, with his son Halldor bearing his white-horse flag; the Norrheimers were formed up about two hundred yards from the walled burg of the local chief. That had been his own inclination, reinforced by messages born by runners let out by the little postern gate in the nearest tower.

The godhi *here has his wits about him*, he thought. *And there are many enemy dead around the walls. The Cutters are brave men, killers, but they're tired and they're confused. They've been hit from different directions, distracted with a new task before they could finish the first. This can work. Thor, lend me your might!*

"Are these the Cutters that are supposed to be so fearsome?" the lanky chief of the Hrossings said contemptuously.

He kicked a body aside and leaned on the haft of his ax. Many of the men had shoved enemy fallen aside with their feet as well, to make for better footing. Most Norrheimer helmets had a nasal bar; Syfrid's had a triangular mask instead, with large holes cut for the eyes; it gave him the look of a predatory bird, and the twin horse-tail plumes that rose from either side of its peak added to his height. His teeth showed yellow-white through his thick brown beard.

"They were as awkward as hogs on river-ice," he went on; the blade of his bearded ax was wet, and there was a shiny line on his helm where a shete had grazed it. "Not much more work than slaughtering-time after the first frost, Lord King."

"We caught them mostly by surprise," Bjarni said; he'd been using his ears as they came west. "And they fight on horseback by preference, with the bow; they dismounted to storm this burg, not to stand shield-to-shield with us. I'd not care to be caught out here on the plains without horsemen of our own, or a burg to retreat to."

He glanced left. "*And* plenty of good bowmen," he added.

They were mostly his men, but they'd been selected by Edain the Archer from among the many volunteers and he'd seen to their gear and had been bully-damning them into constant practice all through their journey. Privately the Norrheimer king was impressed by how much they'd improved and more than a little awed by how even the best of them still fell far short of the master-bowman's skills.

The man is like Ullr come down among us, he thought.

*He's called the Archer and is the best of these Mackenzies . . .
but their battle line must be fearsome if they can produce a
man like that. And he knows every trick to make arrows
count for more in battle, too. I wish he were my handfast
man, and not Artos'. Some like to hoard gold or weapons or
horses, but what a King should covet is* men. *Good* men *can
always get you gold and gear and stock.*

"Here they come," said Syfrid, who'd kept his eyes
fixed on the enemy; he crouched a little, shifting his ax to
a one-handed grip and bringing up his shield.

"Come and kiss this!" he shouted at the enemy, and
flourished his war-ax; then he turned, bent a little, and
slapped it on his buttocks in derision.

"Are they supposed to kiss your ax or your arse?"
Bjarni said, and everyone within hearing laughed.

This time the enemy had all had a chance to get
mounted; their chiefs had called back their storming parties from around the wall, and they broke forward in two
compact bodies from either side of the wrecked building
by the rail line. They charged straight towards his men,
and already he could see them rising in their saddles and
drawing.

"*Shield-wall!*" Bjarni shouted, and his signalers repeated it by horn-call.

The snarling dunt of the ox-horn trumpets brayed beneath the gathering thunder of hooves. The shields of the
rear ranks came rattling up, overlapping like a shingled
roof or a dragon's scales, with the warriors' spears making
the spikes of a porcupine. Bjarni nodded even as he raised
his own; they were notably faster and crisper at it than
they'd been when they left Norrheim.

And then the artillery cut loose; eight *tung-crack!*
sounds as the heavy springs released and the throwing

arms smacked into the padded stops. The weapons were Iowan-made, light six-pounders; they called them *scorpions* after a deadly stinging insect of the far southern deserts. His own folk used catapults mainly on ships, and sometimes to defend towns. Bjarni had wondered whether they and their horse-teams were worth the bother of dragging along in the field. Now he watched the fist-sized iron balls smash into the enemy, traveling so fast that their passage was a blur until they struck. Again and again, gruesome tangles where they'd aimed low to set the shot bounding through the thicket of horses' legs.

We must have this art in Norrheim too, some part of Bjarni thought. *We can't afford ignorance, as if we were wild-men. We won't be isolated forever.*

And then the crews crouched under their own shields as arrows arched up in a mist like rising threads. He could hear a piercing whistle, and the shafts seemed to fly faster as they approached. He ducked his head and held the shield higher.

"Draw . . . wholly together . . . let the gray geese fly . . . *shoot!*" came Edain's bellow.

Shafts began to arch out in return in pulsing volleys. Just then the first flight from the Cutters struck the shield-burg like a stream of gravel striking an old sheet-metal barn, but one that did not stop. Bjarni grunted in surprise at the force of the impacts against his shield; as he watched, four gleaming points showed through the tough birch plywood and sheet steel and the felt covering on the inside. The metal boss over the grip kept his hand safe, but he could hear men cursing or screaming as points went home. More banged into shields, bent or snapped or glanced off hauberks and helms, but there was no way to strike back and even good mail wouldn't stop them all.

No way to strike back here, he thought. *Not for us. But the archers—*

The enemy were slanting away sharply from Edain's command, with piles of horses and men kicking or crawling or lying still in front of them . . . but some of the bowmen were down too. They couldn't hold shields up and shoot at the same time, and mostly they had less armor.

Still, horses are bigger targets than men.

Then the Cutters were looping away and shooting over the rumps of their horses, ready to turn in a circle and come back to peck at their foes once more. The field-pieces began to speak again as the crews scrambled to their machines; they outranged the saddle bows by two or three times.

"The bastards can shoot," Syfrid said, looking at his shield; there were seven or eight arrows standing in it, and some of them had punched through a handspan or more. "If they could do that to us over and over again—"

Bjarni used the hilt of his sword to hammer the points back out of his own shield, then a sweep of the blade to cut the shafts on the other side.

"They won't," he said stoutly.

He glanced eastward down the long curved length of the railroad where the railcars stood with their doors open like the wings of birds. Artos was there, invisible behind the swell and drop of the land, waiting for precisely the right moment to appear and strike.

Not waiting too long, I hope!

"Deploy them in double-rank line," Artos said.

Epona paced forward, treading the hard ground of the

dry prairie beneath her hooves. The sun was four hours past noon, moving to a point where it would be in their eyes, but not too low yet on this long summer's day. Tiny white grasshoppers spurted ahead of the hooves of the horses; the ironshod feet made a drumhead of the soil, a low muffled rumbling at this steady pace, and a plume of dust rose and drifted behind them. The visor of the sallet acted like the brim of a hat while it was slid up along the smooth low dome of the flared helmet, and the land rolled in green-tawny waves ahead of them.

"Two-deep is pretty thin," Ingolf observed.

"There are more of them than of us, even with Bjarni tying some down," Artos said. "I don't want them to flank us. Your Richland heroes are a little green for a maneuver as complex as refusing a flank in the middle of a moving cavalry engagement. And I don't want them piling up and colliding when they try."

Ingolf's mouth twisted in agreement. "But they'll do fine in a straight-up charge."

"That they will. There are old soldiers, and bold soldiers—"

"—but few old, bold soldiers," Ingolf finished.

"Also it will avoid getting into a long arrow duel."

Ingolf nodded again. His countrymen here were mostly from the landed classes, who had the leisure to practice with horse and shete and saddle bow. The Cutters didn't just practice; they would be men who rode to earn their living on the open range, long hours every day. And who shot from the saddle every day too, to fill the cookpot or to protect their herds or just because there was nothing else to do while you were herding but shoot at thrown targets or bushes or cowpats or prairie dogs, except stare up the south end of a northbound cow. Their rulers had been at war for most of the past generation, too; they would all have fought before.

"We'll do better if we get stuck in hand-to-hand," the Readstown man pointed out.

"Also true."

The youngsters all had good mail shirts and steel helmets, and they were better drilled than the enemy. The Sword of the Prophet had discipline, and their standing army, but the Ranchers and their men fought more like a swarm of bees. A shirt of light mail wasn't all that much of an advantage against arrows. It was a very considerable one in a hand-to-hand fight with blades.

Montana is poor in metals and rich in men; no great cities before the Change and plenty of rangeland. When the old world fell, the folk were mostly able to escape, but there are few of the great steel towers for salvage.

The Church Universal and Triumphant's hostility to all outsiders and its bans on many types of machine hadn't helped, either.

Ingolf nodded, raised a hand in salute and turned his horse. Mary followed him, though she paused to say:

"The hand of the Valar over you, brother."

"The Crow Goddess spread Her wings over you, sister," he replied. "And may She be with Ritva, too."

"So mote it be."

Ensign Vogeler's brass trumpet blew a call, and the First Richland shook themselves out from column into two lines staggered so that each man had a clear view ahead, moving smoothly on horses who knew the trumpet calls as well as their riders. Men and mounts looked harder and leaner than they'd been at home, but the humans were just as cockerel-confident. The redcoat commander gave them a pawky glance and angled over beside Artos.

"First battle?" he said.

"For most of them. Ingolf has experience and to spare, and his second-in-command fought the Sioux in Marshall and Fargo. A few others."

"They'll be brave, then," Rollins said sardonically. "Fool's courage."

"Which works as well as any other; a man's first charge may be the best he ever has in him. Now, we'll be the pivot on which the door turns. We'll need to keep your men well in hand."

The older man looked slightly offended. "We're the *Force*," he said. "Your Majesty."

"That's what I'm counting on and why I'm using you here, Inspector," Artos pointed out, and grinned.

Mathilda rode behind him and to his left—his sword side, which meant that she could use her shield to cover him in a melee.

"You know how to get him going, don't you?" she said softly as the redcoat reined aside to lead his men.

"It's part of a King's trade," he said, then turned his head. "Eh, Fred?"

The younger Thurston nodded. "That's not quite how Dad put it, but it amounts to the same thing." A frown. "I don't know if I can do it."

"Yes, you can," Artos and Virginia said simultaneously; she bit back a snort of laughter.

"And you'll have your opportunity soon enough," he said.

The dark handsome young face turned southward and west. "We're not far from the border," he said. "The old Idaho border. Red Leaf said there was news about my mother and my sisters."

"They're safe enough," Artos said.

Which is probably *true. Even a bad man will love his mother or his younger sisters, more often than not. My judgment of your brother Martin was that he was ambitious beyond reason, and ruthless as a stoat, but not the sort who lacks all human connection. And Virginia is giving you a very worried look. She doesn't know or love* them; *she loves* you *and she loves the prospect of vengeance on those who killed her father and took her family's ranch.*

"Now let's cut a way for them to freedom, eh? And to a payment on an account the Cutters owe the whole world."

The pillar of red smoke had grown as they approached. Now they came over the last rise of land and saw the Anchor Bar Seven homeplace laid out before them. Ahead the strip of cultivated fields, to the right the dam and lake, and then beyond that the walled headquarters on its not-quite-hill. It was toy-tiny in the distance, and the figures of the men who fought beneath the walls were like ants, but he *knew*. Knew where each was, the pitch of the land, the range of the weapons on the towers. Things that *might be* played out in his mind, each turning on the pivot of his decisions like the throwing-arm of a trebuchet. They were many, but the thread of his actions led through them like a vein of gold in quartz.

And it is the best course, he thought, shivering a little internally. *Not a certain one, because the world is not made so that anything is certain, but the closest to certainty and near enough for King's work.*

"Here they come again!" Syfrid said harshly.

The enemy were forming up, just beyond catapult range. The ground between them and the Norrheimers was littered with dead men and dead horses, or some of both not quite dead; every time they came across the killing ground to within bow-range of the men of the shield-wall the catapults Ignatius commanded reaped them, and then the engines from the towers, and then Edain's bowmen.

"They're paying," Bjarni observed.

"So are we," Syfrid said. "We've lost thirty men, and more wounded, and all we are is *bait*. We haven't landed a blow since we chased them away from the wall."

"Not bait," Bjarni said. "We're the plug that keeps them back. They could overrun the bowmen if we weren't here. Horses won't run onto a spearpoint, or ram into a shield-wall."

Syfrid jerked his head backward. "Within that burg they couldn't touch us and we could massacre them if they tried to storm the wall."

"They'd be all over us if we tried to retreat, like flies on a midden. Besides, Artos needs us here," Bjarni said. "They've lost five to our one, maybe more, and more of their horses. They weaken themselves, like a man trying to butt through a locked door with his face. While we're here they don't think of anything else."

Syfrid nodded grudgingly. "As a man will with a bit of gristle stuck between his teeth and driving him mad. But if your blood brother Artos doesn't come soon they'll gnaw us down and swallow us."

"He'll come," Bjarni said. "And we'll die the day the Three Spinners cut the thread of our lives; not a day sooner, not a day later."

Syfrid's face stiffened a little; that was an implied rebuke. Then they had more pressing work. Bjarni frowned as he watched the mass of horsemen approach. They were packed closer together, the formation a bit deeper and wider. And they were picking up speed, not holding to a hand gallop but coming flat-out. All the ones with any body armor were in the front, the men of rank . . .

"They're not going to shoot us up and retreat, they're trying to overrun us. Something's changed. They want, they *need*, to finish us quickly."

He glanced eastward. Was that a twinkle of sun on steel, above a distant black line?

"Yes!" he said. Then he filled his lungs and shouted:

"Our brave comrades are here, they'll strike the enemy soon! Hold fast, Norrheimer men! This time we can greet them with spears and welcome them with swords. Hold fast! Thor with us!"

"Ho La, Odhinn!"

A growl went up with a baying eagerness in it; his men were tired of being pecked at from beyond their own reach. A ratcheting clatter began as spearshafts and the flats of swords and axes were hammered on the shields, building up into a drumming thunder of defiance and anger as men stamped and roared. The catapults shot; only five were manned now, for want of crews. The beating of the hooves filled the earth, and the ground to their front was a solid mass of riders. The first flights of arrows were rising from the bowmen to his left, and then every man in the enemy host rose in the stirrups. The Norrheimer shields came up, but this time more men fell as shafts punched through, or flicked through the gaps.

"*Close up, close up,* Niðhöggr *bite your balls!*" he heard a voice rasping. "*Close up when a man falls, don't leave a gap!*"

"*Ready, ready,*" Bjarni called.

He crouched with the shield-rim right up under his

eyes, grunting a little as the shafts went *thock-thock-thock-thock* and hammered him back against his braced right leg. Two more broke off his helmet, hurting like blows with a sword, and another banged at an oblique angle into the mail over his right shoulder, breaking several of the links but not penetrating the stiff linen padding beneath. The ground was shaking beneath him, thousands of hooves hammering through it. A few men around him were wide-eyed; more were mouthing curses or calling on their Gods or just baring their teeth and screaming hatred and rage. The arrowstorm slackened as Cutters began slapping their bows back into the scabbards and drawing their shetes, a long rippling glitter along the enemy line, a flexing as they slid their shields onto their arms.

"CUT! CUT! CUT!"

Bjarni rose and held his sword up, sucked the hot dusty stinking air into his lungs:

"Now!" he screamed, and slashed the blade downward towards the foe.

The shields came down from overhead and every man behind the front rank threw a spear. The heavy weapons weren't really made for that, but the target was close, close. Three hundred punched into the mass of horsemen, and they staggered. The front rank of Norrheimers crouched, butting the ends of their spears into the dirt as if they faced so many bears or boars, and the charge struck like wagonloads of anvils. Horses reared and struck out at the shields with their hooves, and Norrheimers shouted and stabbed at their faces and chests and guts, holding up their shields to stop blows as the riders hammered at them from above.

"Kill them! Kill the swine! Don't prick their pimples, *kill!"*

Near Bjarni a horse took a spear in the belly and went mad, bounding forward in a great leap, then falling screaming like a woman in childbirth, thrashing blindly. That did what no spurs could; it broke the shield-wall as the half-ton beast collapsed forward onto men and kicked about. Instantly a wedge of horsemen were thrusting into the gap. Bjarni threw himself forward; the first of them was a man with a thong-bound yellow beard beneath a scarred contorted face. He had a mail shirt and a helmet of leather covered in metal plates and topped with a horsehair plume dyed scarlet, and he dodged a spear and leaned far over and slashed with terrible skill. A man spun away with half his face sheared off, screaming in a spray of blood.

The wounded man rammed into the Norrheimer king, broke Bjarni's forward rush and left him staggering, his shield swinging wide in an instinctive try for balance. His *hirdmenn* threw themselves forward to cover him with reckless abandon, but more Cutters were pushing through behind the chief in the plumed helmet. The blade went up, fluid and sure.

Then the fixed snarl behind it turned to a gaping scream. Syfrid was there, his shield slung over his back and his ax in both hands, extended in the follow-through to the blow that had hacked the Cutter's thigh open and chopped through the bone, with a spray of blood following the blade in a curve that seemed to hang in the air like a trail of scarlet light behind a torch.

Bjarni was back on his feet; a guardsman put his shield against his back to help him.

"*Behind you, Syfrid!*" he shouted.

*   *   *

Now they don't know whether to shit or go blind, Artos thought grimly.

He took a deep breath of the thundery air, smelling of endless grass like a giant haymow, and horse and sweat and oiled metal and leather. His men were sweeping in from eastward now, between the railway line and the little lake where the ruins of the pre-Change ranch-house lay, a long rippling line of armor and the plunging heads of horses. They rode up the long shallow rise from the tilled fields towards the modern settlement, jumping the little irrigation ditches without effort or splashing through them in wings of spray. There was a huge clot of Cutters hung up at the Norrheimer front, and his lips skinned back in what might have been a smile.

A *moving* horse under close control was a weapon in itself and one of terrible power, besides what its rider could do. In a melee, the saddle of a frightened *stalled* horse was like trying to fight while sitting in a chair—a skittish chair that jerked you around at short, unpredictable intervals. The Norrheimers were breaking their ranks and wading into the Cutters, spear and sword, ax and hamstringing seax-knife, giving more than they received. Their archers had closed up and were shooting into the enemy's rear, steady careful aimed shots.

Artos blew a *hufff* of relief. He couldn't see it at this range, but that close control meant Edain was still alive, as surely as a glimpse of the oak-colored curls would have. Every time you took a pot to the well, there was a certain chance of it breaking, and he didn't want to be the one to ride to Dun Fairfax with *that* news. Plus Edain was his closest friend, Mathilda aside.

And he's my strong right arm, with the strength of the good brown earth that bore him.

The rest of the Cutters were turning to meet the new threat, all of them that could break away; they had the sun behind them, an advantage since it meant his men were staring straight into it. He'd always been good at calculating numbers quickly, but now he *knew*. Eight hundred twenty-six, more than half of what they had left. More than he had, but not impossibly more; they were good riders, but their horses looked tired. His eyes flicked over the battlefield and then he saw the light pedal-cart that Ritva had taken ahead on the scout with Rollins' men, abandoned a hundred yards eastward of the wrecked warehouse. It was empty, the doors wide open, and feathered with arrows until it bristled like a porcupine. His mind sketched distances.

Possibly, he thought. *Possibly. Or possibly she's dead, though I see no bodies. Poor Ritva, it was always like a game to her, even when the stakes were life and death, the which she knew full well. They say our father was like that; that there was always a bit of a grinning boy on a dare in him, even at the end when he knew he was dying.*

The trumpet brayed again, and the First Richland moved up from a trot to a canter; they would all switch to a gallop when they were closer, to get the horses to the target without being blown. Epona responded automatically, and he glanced over his shoulder.

Then he blinked. Virginia Thurston still had her visor up, and . . .

I've always known she hated the Cutters. He'd seen her *scalp* one of her neighbors who'd gone over to them, on the border of the Powder River country last year. *I didn't suspect quite* how much *she hated them, though.*

Though all the Powers knew they deserved it, the sight of her white staring face was still a little disconcerting. She had her bow in her hands and an arrow on the string, not being trained to the lance. He looked around again, and the Cutters were much nearer; the two forces were coming together with the shocking combined speed horsemen had in open country.

"It *was* a complex plan," he admitted to himself with another mirthless grin. "But sure, it was complex in *conception*, not execution. It's simple enough the now. There they are, and we bash them. Time to kill."

Filling his lungs: "Sound *charge!*"

Rollins' trumpeter sounded it, and it went down the line.

Then he used the edge of his shield to knock down his visor, and the bright world narrowed to a slit.

"Morrigú!" he called, then screamed on a rising note that built to a banshee shriek: "*Morrigú!*"

The arrows lifted from the oncoming Cutters, and the Richlanders and redcoats shot back. Behind him Virginia was screaming wordless hate as she drew and loosed, and Fred called: "*Ho La, Odhinn!*"

The long lifting stride of the great mare was like floating, like flying. The arrows came down with a whistling rush, and he brought his kite-shaped four-foot shield up and let the lance incline down. Shafts went *thunk* into the shield, skipped and broke and glanced from his armor with sounds like a metalsmith's hammer striking, and felt like that too, but it was nothing. A few broke off Epona's barding, and she bugled shrill defiance.

Behind the raven visor his teeth pulled back from his lips; the men ahead would kill him if they could, and he intended to return the favor. Swelling speed, dust, the huge bellows sound of Epona's lungs working, strings of slobber from her mouth spattering her barding and his armored legs. The lancehead came down; the others to his right followed in a rippling wave. He rode lightly, picking his man, some Montana Rancher with the rayed sun of the CUT painted on his steel-strapped leather breastplate.

The man brought his shield up, but the light leather targe barely slowed the point of the lance. The Cutter's body flexed like a flicked whip as the lancehead punched through him and blood burst out of his nose and wide-open mouth. Impact shocked Artos back against the tall cantle of the war-saddle and the lance cracked across.

He threw away the stub and swept out the Sword.

Shock.

The world seemed to slow for an instant, sounds deepening. Arrows moved past him, and he could see how they twirled as they flew. Cold fire ran through him, and he screamed in what might be agony or joy beyond bearing, and he could feel his connection to everything that was. Raven wings beat behind him, vast, implacable, fanning the fires that consumed worlds. He was those fires, the twisting transmuting light at the heart of exploding suns, the primal blaze that set the universe alight and made the very fabric of things. Time rushed past him, and he rent the substance of eternity as time itself rent apart cheap cloth. Behind him new life would rise.

This is how it is to wield the lightning, some lost fragment of selfhood knew. *This is what it is to be a God, a lord of sky and storm and war!*

He screamed again as the *ríastrad* took him and the Dark Mother's mantle covered his eyes. He danced among veils of stars and galaxies, and the substance of his being flung outward. A tug at his hand, and a man's arm flew upward; a backhand cut and ruin flopped away.

Epona slammed into a lighter horse shoulder to shoulder, and the beast flipped backward to land on its wailing rider. Men hammered and stabbed at him, but shield and armor protected him like Her wings. He struck and struck, and struck and struck, killing with each blow. An ax twisted the metal of his visor, and he ripped it off with an impatient sweep of his shield-hand and cast it aside. He was wholly of the moment, and the observer at the still and hidden heart of things, the pivot on which the worlds turned.

Men saw his face, and the hardened fighters of the CUT screamed and threw themselves aside and fled. A few drove their own blades into their throats before he could reach them.

Sword and man and horse were one.

And that One was Death.

"Rudi!"

A voice was calling him, beneath the long slow sonorous song that was the dance of Time running from glowing Creation to the flaming Rebirth. The Sword struck, struck—

"Rudi! Come back! Now!"

Light and darkness blew through him. He was a man who rode a horse, and—

"I am the smile of the Mother and the grin of the Wolf, the dancer and the Dance! I am light, and lust, and power, and love, and hate! *I—am—Artos!*"

"Rudi, please, please don't leave me!"

Shock.

He gasped, mouth struggling to suck in air to a body burning its substance with supernal speed. A wave of weakness, as he stared at Mathilda's white tear-streaked face. He blinked, and then screamed again as he collapsed back into himself, as if the universe crammed itself into a grain of sand. Time resumed.

The battlefield had fallen still, except for the sounds of agony in the background. Men were staring at him; some had thrown themselves down and beat their faces against the earth, or hammered at their own temples with their fists. Many wept.

"I . . . I'm me, Matti. Thank you."

The bulk of the Cutters were still in front of him, though a spray were already in full flight southward. He rode out towards them; Epona reared and milled the air, shrilling a challenge, then came down again, pawing the earth with one hoof. He thrust the Sword towards the sky.

"*Hear me!*" he called into the echoing silence. "This is no mere war of men for land or power. Your lords have sold you to demons who are the enemies of humankind, and of Life and Mind itself; their victory would be your own eternal defeat. If you stand here, every one of you will die. Run, and some will see their homes again; not many, but some. Tell your people what I have told you, I, Artos, High King of Montival, who am the Sword of the Lady. *Go!*"

He never knew what followed in the next few minutes. When he came to himself he was standing and Mathilda had her arm around his waist, holding something to his lips. He drank, choked on the strong almost tasteless vodka, drank again. The Sword was sheathed again; it never needed to be cleaned or sharpened.

"God, that was scary," Ingolf said slowly.

"You don't know the half of it," Artos said. "From the inside, it was far worse."

"Ah . . . you want a pursuit? Our horses are fresher, we could probably catch a lot of them."

Artos shook his head. "No. No need to lose men in little scrimmages, and it'll be dark soon."

"I hate to see so many get away."

Artos' hand touched the pommel of the Sword, and he spoke with the certainty of a man saying the rain would come when the clouds rolled in black:

"I told them the truth. Not one in ten of them will cross the border alive."

He looked around. The after-battle tasks had resumed, and folk were pouring out of the gates; a few score of the enemy were captives, not counting their wounded. The Drumhellers were giving those first aid, rather than the mercy-stroke, though of course they tended their own hurt first . . . and the strangers who'd come to rescue them. Bjarni's men had taken the gravest losses, but most of them were still on their feet. He gave Mathilda's arm a squeeze, more symbol than anything else when they were both in full plate, but symbols were important— more important than anything else, he was finding.

Then he walked over to where the Norrheimer flag stood. Bjarni was there, looking downward at something . . .

Syfrid of the Hrossings, Artos thought.

Lying on his back, mouth still a little open and his great ax in one outflung hand, two arrows through the mail on his chest. Lanky Halldor Syfridsson glared across his father's body at Bjarni.

"*Wyrd bithful araed,*" the Norrheimer king said. "Fate is that which cannot be turned aside."

"Now my father is dead," the younger man said, a tear streaking his blood-spattered face. "As you wished!"

The redbeard shook his head; blood clotted the close-cropped whiskers as well. It pooled on the ground around them, and the flies buzzed hundredfold.

"No, by almighty Thor and Forseti who hears oaths! Your father was not my friend, but he was my father's man, a worthy *godhi* and a strong warrior, brave and cunning, and we fought side by side."

"He should have been King!"

"He would have made a good one, but that was not his Wyrd. We were rivals, yes. So the Gods made men: to contend with each other for power and place, as they made bulls or stallions to be rivals to lead the herd. Yet I did not wish him dead."

"So you say!"

The Hrossings and Bjornings bristled at each other, and the men of other tribes looked alarmed; that was perilously close to calling Bjarni a liar. Artos stepped forward and pulled the sheathed Sword from its frow.

"Hold!" he said, and held it pommel up between them. "*Look*. Look and see the truth of each other's hearts!"

They did, their eyes meeting through the crystal. Artos felt a humming, a meeting and merging. Bjarni's face went pale. The long horselike countenance of the younger Norrheimer seemed to waver. Then it firmed as he clenched his jaw.

"I have wronged you, lord. I say it. Accept me as your handfast man!"

"I will. It's right to grieve for a father, but this day Syfrid feasts with the heroes in Valhöll. He waits your coming, and your sons, and the sons of your sons."

Halldor went to one knee, and Artos stepped back smiling very slightly. He and his party faded away, to leave the Norrheimers to settle their own affairs. A man in a long mail hauberk rode up and slid from the saddle with the ease of one who'd lived on horseback.

"Mr. Mackenzie?" he said, extending a hand. "I'm Avery McGillvery, the Rancher here. Many thanks! Your sister gave us *just* enough warning—she's in our infirmary, resting."

"Ah, and that's good news!" Artos said. He felt something inside him thaw.

"And then you showed up just in time. They'd have been over the wall in another ten minutes."

Inspector Rollins came up, grinning as well. "A and B troops are nearly here," he said. "Another four hundred men."

"So, the Force is with us!" Artos said.

The Rancher and the Inspector laughed. Artos and his party looked at them in surprise.

CHAPTER TWENTY

Ritva opened her eyes and winced as pain speared into both. A hand was under her head, and held a glass of water to her lips; it was well water, cold and good, and she swallowed it and let her head fall back. A light shone in both her eyes, candle-flame reflected from a mirror in a little box. She was in some sort of big open room, a long whitewashed rectangle with a high ceiling of beams and planks, a school or a church or something of that order. There was a slight smell of blood, and a stronger one of medicines and antiseptic.

"Hi, sis! It's the day after the battle, if you need to know. We're visiting the wounded. You count, sorta."

Mary was grinning down at her—a few scratches on her face and hands, bruises, the white mark a helmet's padding made across your forehead. Her eye patch had a new silk ribbon, and her hair was back in a neat fighting braid, and she was in formal Dúnedain black with the crowned tree and seven stars on her sleeveless doeskin jerkin. She held up a helmet, a plain sallet which after a moment Ritva recognized as her own; it had a crack in the crown and Mary stuck the tip of her little finger through it.

"You keep getting banged up like this, people will be able to tell us apart!" she said, wiggling the finger again.

They smiled at each other wordlessly. Rudi's face moved into view. "And how are you feeling?"

Ritva made a mental effort—her head ached and he was a little blurry around the edges—and switched to English.

"I feel," she said, "as if someone shot me in the leg and the shoulder and then hit me over the head with an ax. But you ought to see the shape *he's* in."

"Worse than yours, though you'll have to stay here for a bit and heal. They're good people, and much taken with you."

A groan came from the bed beside her. She looked over; it was Ian Kovalevsky, and the doctor was changing the dressing on his buttock. Rudi chuckled, and for a moment he was the brother she'd known all her life.

"Now *there's* an unfortunate," he said.

"Why?" Ritva asked. "It's an honorable wound and no worse than mine."

Kovalevsky groaned again, and the doctor—she was a short slim middle-aged woman in a green tunic and cap and trousers, brown-skinned and gray-haired, with a bird's fine-boned grace—said in a pleasant chirping sing-song accent: "Shut up, babyish boy. There are many more injured than you, oh yes indeed."

Two younger women helped her, dressed in outfits of the same color and cut and sporting the same stetho-scopes around their necks: they were obviously her daughters, and equally obviously their father had been someone who looked more like the Constable.

"It's not the pain," the young redcoat said.

Rudi laughed. "No. It's the thought of being . . . what's your name, lad?"

"Kovalevsky, sir."

"Being *Half-Ass Kovalevsky* or something of the sort for the rest of his mortal days."

"They wouldn't . . ." Ritva started, then thought; she knew young men, including Dúnedain. "They would. Even his friends."

"Especially his friends," Artos amplified, and the injured man nodded mournfully into his pillow.

"And how am I supposed to show off the scars?" he asked. "*Moon* everyone?"

"Men," Ritva and Mary said simultaneously.

The doctor and her helpers pronounced the same curse in almost the same breath. Ritva's brother laughed—heartlessly, she thought—as the young man hid his head in the pillow.

"And my sister, Dr. . . ."

"Dr. Padmi Nirasha," the woman said, and then looked surprised and pleased as he pressed his palms together before his face and bowed slightly.

"The leg and shoulder wounds are muscle damage and need only time and perhaps some physiotherapy to heal properly, given her excellent physical condition. The blood loss was not too serious, so we used only saline drip. I have disinfected and debrided. There was a concussion also. That is never to be taken lightly, no, no. But recovery is progressing. Strict bed rest for at least the rest of the week is indicated."

"That's good to hear," another voice said; Avery McGillvery. "Your warning saved us, Ms. Havel."

"And she should be allowed to rest," the doctor said

tartly. "Even by a tyrant and oppressor such as yourself, Rancher, if I, a mere captive put to hard labor may say so."

He grinned at her. "Going to burn the place down again, Padmi?"

"I think of it every day! Now remove your large carcass out, and leave my patients in peace!"

Ritva felt her eyelids fluttering; she *was* very tired. Rudi held his arms up and spread, palms skyward, and Mary joined in the gesture. They both chanted softly as she drifted away:

"*Come to me, Lord and Lady*
Heal this body, heal this soul;
Come to me, Lord and Lady
Mind and body shall be whole!
Beast of the burning sunlight
Sear this wound that pain may cease;
Mistress of the silver moonlight
Hold us fast and bring us peace!"

Father Ignatius and Mathilda waited for him outside the schoolhouse-turned-infirmary. He nodded at them and they relaxed in relief; they and the Rancher strolled out the gate. People were busy with repairs; the bodies were all gone, and the dead horses, but flies still buzzed over the places where blood had soaked the soil, and the faint smell was unmistakable. A group of Cutter prisoners was working over near the wrecked warehouse, helping put back what they'd destroyed. A tent town had sprung up on the banks of the little lake to house the troops; the Norrheimers, the First Richland, and the newly arrived redcoat bands. Cowboys were driving in herds to the complex of corrals, to be slaughtered for the feast to come, and neighbors had arrived as well with help and supplies.

Artos looked at the faces of those they passed. He'd seen the like before; there was sorrow for those who'd lost kin and friends, but the relief and joy outweighed it. They knew what a Cutter victory would have meant. There were always costs to a fight when you won, but fighting and losing was far worse. This wasn't the first time these people had been on the receiving end of a raid, and they knew how the world worked.

The Rancher seemed to be searching for words: "So, Mr. Mackenzie . . . your family is Scottish?"

Artos glanced down at his kilt, recognizing a conversational icebreaker:

"My mother's mother was Irish; from *Oileán Acla*, Achill Island. And she married an American named Mackenzie who was Scots mainly, with some German and a wee bit of Cherokee and traces of this and that. My blood father was half Finn, with the rest split between Swedish and Anishinabe . . . Ojibwa. My foster father's English."

"Scots and English, myself . . . a little Ukrainian and Blackfoot."

Artos offered a harmless question in turn. "What was that about your excellent doctor indulging in arson?"

A short snort of laughter, and the Rancher waved a hand towards the ruins of the old house by the lake.

"She was part of . . . with, at least . . . the gang that did that. People from Calgary, summer of the first Change Year. Not really bad, most of them, just hungry and desperate, trying to take a place where they could feed themselves. My father broke the gang up, but he let some stay if they could work for their keep, and a lot of 'em turned out pretty good; they and their kids are half the people on the Anchor Bar Seven now. Padmi spent a month or so shoveling and pounding earth before she'd tell anyone she was a doctor. She still claims it's forced labor and she'll burn the place over our heads someday. I don't know if it *started* as a joke, but . . ."

Artos laughed; it was a better ending to the story than most from those times.

"It's sorry I am that you've taken damage and loss from my coming, and yourself so hospitable and helpful," he said bluntly. "I can't bring back the dead or heal the injured, but I can compensate for material losses."

"I haven't taken damage from you, Mr. Mackenzie; you and your sister saved us. My people and I have taken loss and damage from the *Cutters*. No need for payments."

"Ah, well, you should be knowing that it's Iowa's money, and none of my own. And Iowa has more money than is good for them, or at least for their neighbors, so you'd be doing a good deed by taking it. A little financial letting of blood to correct the humors."

"Oh, in *that* case . . ." he said, and they both chuckled. Then grimly: "And this isn't the first time we've fought the Cutters, though it's the worst so far."

"Ah, now that's what we need to speak of."

"Well . . . I'm not the Premier."

Father Ignatius bowed his tonsured head. "No, Captain McGillvery, but you *are* a man of great influence here, most prominent of the Ranchers in the southern portion of this Dominion. They will listen carefully to you, and your government will listen in turn to them all. And we have no time to spend in consultations with Premier Mah in Drumheller. We know that she has agreed to declare war on the Cutters, but not how vigorously she will prosecute it."

"My mother . . . the Lady Regent Sandra of the Portland Protective Association . . . told me that Premier Mah was very able, but a little too cautious sometimes," Mathilda added. "Too inclined to hedge her bets."

Artos could see *Oh*, that *Princess Mathilda* run through McGillvery's mind. Here in Drumheller they had to have dealings with the PPA; not particularly friendly ones, though there hadn't been war beyond the odd border scuffle since Norman Arminger had died. That meant they knew at least a little of what went on farther south in the rest of Montival as well. Mt. Angel had daughter houses here, and the Order of the Shield of St. Benedict was well thought of.

"Well, for what it's worth, Mr. Mackenzie, I'm in favor of settling Corwin's hash once and for all."

"That's the immediate task," Artos said. "Though I've a horrible suspicion that it will be but a battle in a longer war."

"Of course . . . what exactly do you intend to do with Montana *after* you get rid of the Cutters? After we all do, that is. If it's left alone it'll be chaos, then bandits and anarchy, or warlords. But Drumheller certainly doesn't want to annex it. Enough of those people have ended up here anyway."

"Our plan is to incorporate it in the High Kingdom of Montival, for precisely those reasons."

"Er, that'll cause . . . concerns."

"It's my thought we should speak a little of how the High Kingdom and the Dominion had best arrange their affairs both during the war and after it. For we'll have a border to your southward, as well, should things go well."

"You're not inviting us to join, I hope?" McGillvery said. "The, um, High Kingdom, that is."

Artos grinned. "No. Though I'd not turn you down did you wish to. Yet I don't anticipate you will. You've a well-governed and not-so-little realm here. All you really want of your neighbors is peace, and perhaps trade, eh?"

The man nodded in relief, and the discussion between the four of them was brisk. It turned into something like a procession, as McGillvery toured the camps of the various contingents, formally inviting them to the victory feast—most of which would be conducted in the open or under tents, but officers and a select few others were bidden within the Anchor Bar Seven's homeplace walls. That in turn led to a few impromptu speeches by commanders to their men:

"And I know what great fighters you are," Bjarni went on to *his* assembled band, standing on a massive barrel that gurgled hopefully with good Canuk ale. "You showed it yesterday, against these Cutter swine who're supposed to be so fierce."

A roar of approval greeted him. His men hadn't packed fancy clothes along, though they were combed and trimmed and had their arm-rings on. The bearded faces looked up into the torchlight, cheerful with the expectation of the feast—particularly at the prospect of unlimited fat, tender young beef. Cow-beasts were mostly working oxen or for dairy back in Norrheim, where they had to be fed in barns on hay and grain and roots five months of the year. They weren't slaughtered until they were good for nothing else, except on special occasions or when a chief was feeling lavish.

And McGillvery's looking a little apprehensive. They are a wee bit rough in appearance, I will grant.

"But I also know what a bunch of drunken, brawling, rutting horn-dog arslings you turn into the moment someone waves the bung from a barrel under your noses," the Norrheimer said flatteringly.

That brought laughter; he cut it off with a motion of his hand.

"Drink your fill and eat your fill, gamble and arm-wrestle and sing, boast and have riddle-games and swap lies with your friends and our allies," he went on. "But remember that we're guests here, with a guest's obliga-tions. If you misbehave it touches the kingdom's honor and my own. No fights, or at least no steel. And keep your hands off any woman who isn't willing—and if you're in doubt, she's not. Any who disgrace us I'll send to the High One with a rope and a spear! Now go enjoy yourselves, and have a taste of Valhöll, for you earned it!"

Artos smiled and turned to his own smaller war band. His close companions didn't need any such advice, but the Southsiders and Norrheimers picked up along the way might. Customs and standards differed.

"It's proud I am of you, my hearts, every man and every woman, for you've been all that a lord might wish in his companions," he said. "But my friend Bjarni's ad-vice is good. Do remember that looking too often into the bottle is not an excuse for violations of hospitality. Also remember, those of you who haven't seen Montival yet, that if a man forces a woman, we Mackenzies bury him—alive—at a crossroads with a spear in the dirt above his coffin, to turn aside the wrath of the Mother and ap-pease the Earth Powers."

"Ah . . . you actually do that?" McGillvery said, as they walked on.

"Such a stuffy death," Ignatius murmured, which Mathilda seemed to find amusing for some reason.

"To be sure, we do," Artos said. "You hang men, in the same circumstances, I believe."

"Well . . . yes, these days we do. My father says they just put them in a prison in the old days."

"Odd." Artos shrugged. "Very odd, to make honest folk pay to support the wicked."

McGillvery shrugged as well. "Didn't even make them work, according to the old man," he said.

The Rancher was about a decade older than the Mackenzie, which meant his first real memories were of the years just after the Change. Those had been times with even less room for waste than nowadays.

All was nearly ready for the feast when a scout rode in and hauled his lathered horse to a halt before the Rancher; the beast's sweat smelled musky-strong in the cooling evening air, and its eyes rolled white against shadow.

"Sioux, sir, a big bunch of 'em heading this way. They've got a peace flag up, though."

McGillvery looked alarmed, and Artos grinned as he spoke:

"I think I know who those are."

At the Rancher's questioning look, he went on: "You may remember that I said few of the enemy would cross the border into the CUT's territories alive?"

McGillvery whistled softly. "You do like to arrange things neatly, don't you, Mr. Mackenzie?"

"I find it saves trouble," Artos said gravely.

"I'll go tell them to put a few more head on the grills," the Rancher said. "Not the first time the Lakota have ever eaten Anchor Bar Seven beef, but it's probably the first time I've *given* them any. And I'd better warn everyone. Wouldn't want any misunderstandings."

Ignatius and Mathilda sent him odd looks as well; the

more so when the Sioux war-party rode up a little later, just as the sun was finally slipping below the western horizon. The civilians and the various forces made a broad corridor for them; there were around three hundred, with many horses driven behind them, and fresh scalps on their shields or spears or belts. They all wore light shirts of good riveted mail, and two scorpions bounced along at the rear with their packhorses, Iowan-made like the armor. As Red Leaf had said, when it rained soup a sensible man took off his hat and replaced it with a bucket.

Their leader reined in and raised a hand in the peace sign; he had red paint striped with black on his forehead, eagle quills at the back of his steel cap, strings of hollow bone cylinders across his chest, and his long brown braids were bound in quillwork and fur thongs.

"*Hau, Rudi,*" he said as he slid from his horse like a seal from a rock. "Father," to Ignatius. And: "*Hau, wigopa,*" to Mathilda; which meant *hiya, pretty girl*, more or less. It was brotherly . . . also more or less.

"*Hau, blotáhu ka,*" Artos said, as they touched fists; it meant *Greetings, war-chief.*

Then he continued in the same tongue: "*I see it has been a good day, a day when the Sun shone on the hawk and on the quarry. The knives and arrowheads of your brave ones are red; you have taken many horses, many scalps.*"

"No shit, Sherlo—" Rick Mat'o Yamni—Three Bears—began boastfully; then he did a sudden double take that set his braids swinging.

"What the *hell*? Since when did you speak Lakota, Rudi?"

Artos shrugged. "Rudi didn't. Artos the First"—he touched the hilt of the Sword—"apparently does. It's a bit like having a wackin' great library in your head, I find.

Among other things. Though it's hard to organize it without drowning in knowledge. Things . . . *appear* when I need them. Well, the Lakota are to be part of the High Kingdom, so the High King should speak their language, eh?"

"*Shee*," Rick said, and shook his head.

"Let me show you where you can camp," Artos said. "And let's see to your wounded . . . and there's a big blowout planned, to which you're all invited."

The young Sioux leader cocked a hazel eye at him. It had a tint of green in it in certain lights; his mother was called *Sungila Win*, Fox Woman, from the color of her hair. His tone was dry as he asked:

"You sure about that invitation? 'Cause I headed up here real quick when my great-uncle—"

"The *pejula wacasa*?"

"Yeah, the scary old dude who did your adoption ceremony . . . anyway, he told me the Spirit People said I'd better make tracks this way quick, and then stick to you like glue for the rest of this war, if I wanted things to turn out right. So I picked up a lot of these guys near the border and they, ah, know their way around here."

Mathilda snorted laughter. "Now why, why, *why* would that be, Rick?"

Three Bears looked at her with a crooked smile. "Oh, some of 'em might have come up here to ride around in the dark a little one time or another, maybe stumble across a few horses and cattle . . ."

". . . and steal them," Mathilda finished.

"Did I say steal?" He cocked an eye at Father Ignatius, who was quietly telling his rosary. "Wouldn't want to shock the good Father here."

The warrior-monk smiled. "My son, I do not shock as

easily as you apparently think. Also I am a soldier and a ruler's advisor, as well as a priest and a monk. And I doubt you need fear that memories of old misdeeds will make you unwelcome tonight. Your riding in with . . . ah, concrete evidence of finishing off most of the raiders who attacked this place put . . . how shall I express this . . . the cherry on the cake for most of the people here."

Artos chuckled. "Rick, my friend, as High King I officially know nothing of such things. I will not promise these good people that I will stop the Lakota from lifting horses—"

"Even with that Sword, Rudi, you wouldn't have a prayer. You might as well promise to make rain fall *up*."

"That's one reason. Another . . . have you ever heard of the *Táin Bó Cúailnge?*"

"No . . . wait a minute, wasn't that some sort of ancient Irish thing about a big cattle raid?"

"That it is, and a fine rollicking story to boot. It's also an illustration of why it would ill behoove a Gael to be too sanctimonious about a passion for other people's livestock. However, I will do nothing whatsoever to stop the Drumhellers from punishing any light-fingered souls they find on their own land absconding with their sheep. Just as I would ignore any protests they made about you dealing with any of their folk you found prowling about your herds."

"Oh, not *sheep*. Never sheep. Have you ever tried to make sheep run fast?"

"A point. And there is this; if such persons were to kill anyone in the course of . . . riding around in the dark, shall we say . . . the Drumhellers may hang them, and *I* will most certainly hang them myself if they make it back to Montival, for the sake of peace between the realms. Exactly as I would insist, on pain of war, that they hang any of their own who did the same to you."

"Oh. Oh, well, I can see that, sorta."

"I'm going back to the ranch," Mathilda said. "Father, would you come with me? I want to confess and be communicated before the feast starts, if it's not too much trouble."

"No trouble at all, my daughter," Ignatius said. His face lit with an impish smile. "Your confessions are rarely very traumatic, you know, my child."

"Alas," Artos said and winked at her; she blushed.

"I'll stay with Rick for a bit," he said. "See you in a little while, acushla."

Pitching camp for the Sioux was simply a matter of finding a suitable stretch of prairie, picketing their horses, bringing in a water-cart from the ranch wells, and unrolling their sleeping bags. That done, they trooped down to the lake to wash and began primping for the celebrations, with horseplay and joking about the cooking smells beginning to waft from the barbecue pits. It was well into the long summer twilight by then, when two men walked up to Artos.

Three Bears looked at them casually, then cursed and reached for his shete. Dalan flinched, and Graber put an arm around his shoulders.

Artos laid a hand on Three Bears' where it rested on the hilt of his blade.

"Quietly, my friend, quietly. You'll find these men somewhat changed."

"They threatened my family, on our own land!" the young Sioux leader snarled, pointing at Graber. "He threatened to kill my whole clan, down to the youngest children!"

"And tried his best to kill me and mine, if you'll recall," Artos said. "And tried more than once, so he did, and did kill some who were dear to me. Hear them out, for my sake, my friend. And for the world's."

Grudgingly, inch by inch, the younger man relaxed. "OK. This better be good, *Major* Graber. And the High Seeker . . ."

Rick Three Bears was extremely angry, but he was also intelligent and perceptive.

"Is that really him? It's his face but the . . . the *look*'s all wrong. He doesn't stand or move like that guy, or any of them."

"It is him and it isn't," Artos said. "It's the boy he was before the Church Universal and Triumphant took hold of him. Before the . . . *things* . . . that they miscall their Ascended Masters got their claws into his mind."

"What happened to him?"

"*This* happened to him," Artos said grimly, touching the Sword. "It . . . undid that part of his life. And while the man you met deserved to die, this lad has done none of the man's deeds. Instead he's trapped inside that man's body, with all his best years stolen from him."

"Oh," Rick Three Bears said, and shivered slightly. "Oh, man, those CUT guys are just . . . they're just not *right*."

Graber nodded to him, then addressed Artos: "My lord, I told you that I had come to believe that the masters of the Church have . . . have betrayed we who served them. I now believe . . . believe that I must turn against them. Go among my own people and try to tell them the truth. I have come to ask your permission for this."

The man's face was still a thing carved from granite slabs, but it had a sheen of sweat now, far more than the mild summer evening could account for. He would know, better than most, what that would mean if he failed; and failure was almost certain.

"You *can't* believe him!" Three Bears said.

"Graber," Artos said carefully. "I know you're telling the truth. No man can lie to me now and be believed. But you served the lords of Corwin for a very long time. The Prophet himself put you on my track. You are . . . marked. And vulnerable to them."

Bobby Dalan nodded eagerly. "Yes, sir. That's why I had Major Graber come to you. You can touch him with the Sword like you did me, and then he'll be safe!"

Safe from anything but inconceivably prolonged torture and death, Artos thought.

Graber met his eyes. "If you would, my lord," he whispered. "If it can be done without destroying my memories and purpose."

Artos stood silent for a long moment, looking up into the darkening sky; the first stars were glimmering above the distant eastern horizon, and the moon shone silver.

I did not ask to be a judge of men's souls.

"I know a little more of the Sword now than I did on Nantucket," he said at last. "It is the Sword of the Lady, and therefore the Sword of *Truth*. I can use it to . . . to cleanse your mind, Graber, and to establish barriers there. But that means that *you* must confront yourself. Everything that you have been and done, and how those you served were woven into it. You will not lose your years, as Dalan did; but you *will see them*."

"Please, my lord," Graber asked.

There was no point in delay. With a single swift movement he drew the Sword. Three Bears gasped and blinked as it caught the moonlight in its not-steel, but Dalan

smiled with an innocent joy. Artos flipped his grip so that
he was holding the hilt with the blade pointing down and
the pommel above his thumb, then pressed it against the
other man's forehead.

Shock.

A whirling through his own mind, a moment of piercing grief, of *sorrow.* Then Graber was on his knees, panting and pressing his clenched fists to his temples.

"No, no, *I didn't know,* no—"

The mumbling went on and on, until Artos feared the
man was mad; the smell of his sweat was heavy and sour.
Dalan whimpered and wrung his hands. Then bit by bit
Graber gained mastery of himself, staggered erect, braced
his shoulders back. He looked to have aged five or ten
years in as many minutes, but it was an age like sun-dried
jerky or tough rawhide thongs. Whatever else the lords he
served had taught him, he had learned a merciless control
that Artos could not help but respect. Dalan came beside
him, offering a shoulder as a son might, and the older
man rested a hand on it.

"Why—" Graber croaked. "Why did you wait until
now? I am free, I am *free.* That was as bitter as death but
it *freed* me. I see . . . I see now. I see it all."

Tears ran down the hard weathered face, without the
man being really aware of them. Artos sheathed the
Sword and considered for a moment, his hand on the
pommel.

"Because . . ." he said, then began again. "Because I
could not do it until you had walked a certain distance
along that path yourself, of your own will and choosing
and through your own wrestling in the silence within
your head. To use the Sword before you had done that
would only have broken your mind. A very wise man said

to me once that none of us could know what a devil was, or what a devil he himself might be, until he had conquered the devil in himself, and that by hard work. I think you know, now."

"I . . . it was as if all my life I was living in a story, and then I awoke. And until I did I lived as in an evil dream."

"That's what compulsion does. No man can be free, be really himself, unless he makes himself so. Then the Sword could help you. The Lady heals, but She doesn't enchain; and not even She can make an evil as if it had never been. Now you must make such atonement as you can."

"Thank you, lord," Graber said thickly. His face hardened into the bronze mask Artos was familiar with. "I will. Though my life would be no payment, it is still all I have."

But he is different, as a spear is different when it's aimed in a new direction.

"I think I understand. *Now* I understand. Yes, I must do this. Though I die, I must."

Dalan nodded. "And he's safe, now. The bad things can't get into his head *anymore.*"

"Indeed they can't," Artos said grimly. "But their arrows and swords and red-hot irons can."

Graber managed to smile. "*That* never frightened me, lord."

"Rick," Artos said, turning a little to the Sioux warchief. "Could you help me with this?"

The whites showed all around Three Bears' pupils, but he nodded jerkily.

"OK, Rudi. We got plenty of guys who don't *look* all that Lakota, whatever their spirits are. We could make these two up like they were ours, and send them back with some of our walking wounded in the next couple of days, so they'd be in position to slip across the border. I know the guy to handle it, too."

He called and talked to the man, who responded in a quick mixture of English and Lakota that Artos would have had trouble following a year ago. When his follower had led Graber and Dalan away he shook himself and shivered again. His finger wobbled a bit as if he didn't dare point directly at the sheathed Sword.

"Man, oh, man, that is one fucking *scary* Wakháŋ artifact you got there!"

"My friend, you don't know the half of it."

Three Bears fumbled at his belt, rolled a cigarette, and touched it to the flame of a flint-and-steel lighter. He drew and handed it to Artos.

"You sure you can handle it?" he said.

Artos let the smoke out through his nostrils; for once it wasn't just something to be endured for ceremony's sake.

"No, I'm not sure," he said, handing the little burning cylinder back. "Not at all. But I have to do it anyway!"

"Better you than me, dude."

"And don't I wish it was anyone but me! There's one thing I *am* sure of."

"Which is?"

"That as soon as I can I'm going to put this"—he slapped the hilt of the Sword—"in an honored place on the wall, and not touch it unless driven by sheer stark necessity. It's dangerous, that it is; more dangerous to my enemies, which is why I bear it, but . . . it's too *real* for the world, I think. It threatens to break the fabric of things just by *being*, and unravel the story of our lives, as if it were an anchor of cast crucible steel dropped into a world made of gossamer. And we the butterflies among the threads, so."

"Dude, watch me shudder."

He did, and drew on the cigarette until the ember underlit his high-cheeked, proud-nosed face.

"I'm just glad you're on our side."

"Frankly, so am I. And now I suggest we eat, drink and be merry. For tomorrow—"

"We ride like hell with hemorrhoids, yeah. I better tell my boys not to get too deep into the firewater and forget they're guests."

"There's a fair bit of that advice going around tonight, I think." Artos laughed. "And much-needed."

His own gaze went westward, towards the high peaks his mind's eye knew were there. What was happening beyond the Rockies now? Then he shook his head, and turned towards the lanterns that burned bright all along the walls of the Anchor Bar Seven. Mathilda would be waiting.

He smiled at the thought, and stepped out more quickly.

CHAPTER TWENTY-ONE

Crowsnest Pass
(Border, Dominion of Drumheller/
High Kingdom of Montival

(formerly Border of Alberta and
British Columbia)
June 7, Change Year 25/2023 AD

"Home," Mathilda breathed.

"Home," Artos said, then laughed and shouted: "*Home!*"

He stood in the stirrups, and Epona reared beneath him. The Sword flashed free—

Shock.

The moment stretched, and he *saw*.

Mounted warriors fought on a grassy plain that rolled upward towards forested mountains, their swords glinting in the bright sunlight. A white road lined with poplars smoked dust as a long train of wagons passed, leaving the powder heavy on the fresh green leaves of the trees and the yellowing grain behind. A couple made love in a haymow beneath the roof of a barn whose rafters were carved in sinuous running knotwork. A big dog and a five-year-old wearing nothing but a kilt and his own gold curls stamped and romped gleefully along the edge of a pond and ducks avalanched into the sky. A man with silvery stubble on his cheeks crouched in a dark stinking alley and clutched a bottle, whispering a name as he sobbed and rocked. A woman squinted as she leaned into the tiller of a gaff-rigged fishing boat; dolphins broached from the whitecapped waves around her as she called sharply: *Haul away and sheet her home!* A smith took a piece from the coals between his tongs and considered its white-red glow as he reached for his hammer. A tiger woke in a den on the slopes of a snow-topped mountain and lifted its head from huge paws, yawning, stretching until its claws slid free, its red tongue curling over ivory daggers . . .

"Rudi, where were you?" Mathilda asked, her face anxious.

He looked at the blade and smiled at her; he blinked against what he recognized with astonishment were tears.

"I was . . . *everywhere.* Everywhere in this land of ours, Matti, acushla, and I was the folk and the trees and the beasts and the land itself. Oh, and it's beautiful, our Montival, a land fit for Gods and giants and heroes!"

"I hope we can make it a good land to live in," she said soberly, still darting a cautious glance at the Sword. "For just plain people."

"It's not all bad, what the Sword does," he said gently. "And we shall do just that, so."

Then he laughed again as he sheathed it. "And right now, we're riding up to Castle Corbec. We're *home*, Matti, the two of us, and summer is coming, and the harvest of our hopes."

Mountains lifted all around them, thickly forested with lodgepole pine and Douglas fir and clumps of aspen. Hills rolled down to the road bright with green grass, and a cool wind blew from the naked granite teeth of the heights, clean and scented with conifer-sap; snow glittered on the higher peaks. In the near distance a herd of elk took fright and leapt over the remains of a ruined fence, heading higher into the hills. Then they came over a rise, and the border fort was before them.

To the right of the roadway was a long blue lake that lapped against cliffs northward, and to the left the land rose rapidly. Ahead the highway crossed an arm of the water on a pre-Change bridge at one narrow spot where the flood turned emerald-green. Castle Corbec reared on a hill just before it, faced in hard pale mountain stone over its concrete and baring fangs of crenellation at heaven with water on two sides and a moat around; southward a waterfall brawled down a mountainside, thread-tiny in the distance.

"Looking as if it had been there forever and not just fifteen years, so it does," he said.

Twin round towers with pointed roofs flanked the gatehouse, and flying from the spike atop one was . . .

"Arra, *that's* even quicker work," Artos said.

It was the green-silver-blue flag of Montival, the crowned mountain and the Sword, in pride of place above the other banners.

"That's my mom," Mathilda said proudly. "Bet you there's thousands more like it all over the kingdom now, and not just in Association territory."

"*The kingdom*. It's starting to seem real to me, and there's no escaping it. We dreamed a new name for a new country, and by the time we return everyone's accepted it!"

"They were afraid," she said, with the cool certainty that made you remember she was her mother's daughter. "And frightened people grasp at things. They're more ready to change."

He looked back. The troops followed in a long column twisting eastward and downslope; lanceheads and spears glittered, and bright banners flew, but most of the colors were dark—leather, oiled gray mail, green or gray cloth or undyed linsey-woolsey, only here or there a glimpse of scarlet and blue and gold. Edain rose with a clod of earth crumbling between his fingers, and Garbh sniffed curiously at it. Most of his close companions were looking upward at the banners as well.

"It's not just like riding up the lane to Dun Fairfax in the Clan's territory," Edain said, grinning. "But then again, it's not entirely unlike, either, is it not, Chief? Though I'd give a good deal to see my family now, that I would."

"Not entirely unlike, no. And I suspect there's a few gathered to welcome us."

A party was waiting for him under a pavilion not far from the gates. His breath came quicker as they approached, and he turned aside from the main road. A quick twitch of two fingers brought Mark Vogeler to his side.

"My compliments to Colonel Vogeler and Inspector . . ."

No, he's promoted in time of war, when his redcoats become warriors rather than keepers of the peace.

". . . General Rollins, I should say. The men are to camp on the open ground before the castle gates and picket the horses by the lake; there's firewood and hearths prepared and food and fodder will be sent out. We're expected."

"Yessir!"

The young man had acquired a scar on his chin in the fight at the Anchor Bar Seven, but still had that reckless smile. He thundered away, and for a moment Artos could be Rudi Mackenzie again. He pressed his legs to Epona's flanks, and she wheeled and went up the little lane with gravel spurting from beneath her hooves, his plaid fluttering in the wind. Yes, a slight figure with gray-streaked red hair dressed in saffron-dyed long tunic and wrapped arsaid. The Lady Regent near her, and many another.

Epona reared again, and he laughed joyously. Then he slid to the ground . . .

And the whole assembly went to their knees. He stopped, shocked. Mathilda was beside him, and he could hear the chiding in her voice as she murmured, though it was warm and fond:

"You're the *High King*, Rudi! What did you expect, a slap on the back and a mug of ale?"

"Rise, my friends," he said.

They did, and his blue-green-gray eyes met his mother's tear-brimming leaf-green ones.

She looks older, he thought. *More than two years older.* Then: *Anwyn's hounds take protocol!*

With a roar he snatched her up as she rose, whirling her slight weight around and up in a circle.

"*Mo ghaol, mo ghràdh, is m'fheudail thu, mo mhacan àlainn ceutach thu!*" she called, between laughter and sobs. "My love, my dear, my treasure, my fair and beautiful son! *Céad mile fáilte!* A hundred thousand welcomes, my son!"

A few looked shocked at the informality when he'd put her down and kissed her on the forehead; more were smiling at him.

"My friends," he called, his arm around her shoulders. "I've returned. *We* have returned; and there's much to do, a war to win, a kingdom to forge. But for a brief while, let us be men and women who've returned to their kin after long absence and even more worry and care. Yet one thing first."

He squeezed his mother's shoulders and released her, then turned to Mathilda. Their eyes locked, and he went down on one knee. Her hands went between his.

"Mathilda, we can have the great ceremonies later and the grand occasions. But will you wed me, heart of my heart, *anamchara*, and be my love and my other self, and I yours? This very day, on the soil of our own land, and with our good friend and comrade Father Ignatius to speak the words for us and our kin and friends to witness?"

"*Yes!*"

That did not surprise him, though he could feel his heart leap at it.

Behind her, though, Sandra Arminger put her hands to her face and wept tears of relief and joy, and *that* shocked him even in his moment of happiness. He'd known her since he was ten, and he didn't think she'd ever made such a public display of emotion in all that time.

Sam Aylward looked at his son for a long silent moment as the nobles passed by towards the castle drawbridge; the square face that was so much like his, older now by more than two years but still so young, so young . . .

Full-grown now, though, the Englishman thought. *Got a few scars there, and on his 'ands, that I can see. Twenty-one, by God! Just a hair taller nor me; and a hair thinner, maybe, the very last of the puppyfat gone. Looks 'ard enough to spit bullets; looks like I did when I yomped me way to Mt. Tumblehome. And if I were meeting him for the first time, knowing nothing, I'd say to meself: Samkin, be careful with this one, for he wouldn't start a fight but he might be the one to end it.*

The younger Aylward had his Scots bonnet in his hand; he started to twist it between his fingers, and then forced himself to stop, took a deep breath and spoke:

"Well, Da . . . well, I'm back."

Samkin Aylward reached out and rested a hand on his son's shoulder, squeezing a little. Garbh butted her head under his other hand, and he ruffled her ears absently.

"That you are; your mother sends her love, and your sisters, and they'll be glad to see you when you can be spared. And you've gone a long way to get back 'ere, eh?"

He nodded a little, looking at the taut quick strength of his son that made him feel every one of his sixty-six years.

"You'll do, lad. You'll do."

They exchanged a quick fierce embrace. He turned his eyes to the tall honey-haired girl who walked beside Edain.

Bit of all right, that. Looks strong for her weight, too; this one's seen the elephant. And sensible, I'd say from first impressions. No nonsense there.

She met his eyes with respect but pridefully, blue eyes searching pale gray. He let his slight smile grow to a grin.

"You'd be Asgerd Karlsdottir, then, lass?"

"Yes, Master Aylward."

"Welcome to the Aylward Asylum for Bedlam Boys, then. It's the women who keep the wits."

She hesitated, then seemed to realize what he meant and ducked her head in acknowledgment.

"What does the collar mean?" she said after an instant.

"This?" He touched the thin torc of twisted gold

around his neck; he was so used to it that he didn't notice it unless reminded. "That Oi'm handfasted . . . married, most say. Could Oi see that bow?"

Surprised, she handed it over. He drew it—about eighty pounds, very respectable for a woman and more than he was really comfortable with himself these days— and looked down the length of it before he returned it to her. It was very much as he'd have done it, if he was working with hickory rather than yew; that was a good second-best for a bowyer, tough and springy.

"Well, all the time Oi spent teaching this gurt gallybagger wasn't wasted. No, not wasted at all. Come on, lad."

He led them a little south, well past the road leading to the castle gate. A tented camp lay by the water's side amid scattered pines, looking across the emerald lake to the rock and scree of the mountainside; little three-man tents, grouped in threes themselves around common campfires, with each set of three in a triangle to make nine in all. Racks of bicycles were propped near them, and some light carts rigged so that they could be pulled by two horses or fitted with a frame for four bicycles. Kilted figures sat working on their gear and talking, or stood to shoot at man-shaped targets of folded straw mats and poles scattered out several hundred yards eastward. Arrowheads flashed in the afternoon sunlight, and the pale blur of gray-goose feathers.

"Mackenzies!" Edain said happily.

"Yus," his father replied. "The High King's Archers. All volunteers, mostly young, and a wild lot. But good shots and good at fieldcraft, every one of them, and at least fair with a blade."

"Who's in charge of 'em?" Edain asked wistfully. "I'm bullyragging the ones the chief . . . the High King . . .

picked up along the way. Fast learners and hard fighters, but not bowmen born like us."

"This lot're under Aylward the Archer," he said casually, then laughed at the younger man's double take. "Yes, you. Oi'm not 'im, not anymore, so that leaves you, which stands to reason."

He nodded down towards the camp. "Think you can 'andle 'em?"

Edain's gray eyes narrowed, and his mouth drew into a line as he thought for a moment and then nodded slowly.

"Sure and I can," he said; his accent had acquired more of Rudi Mackenzie's lilt in the past two years. "I don't see why not. There's been a good deal of news about the place, concerning our little walk in the woods, I'd be thinking?"

"News whenever a letter made it 'ome. And songs, stories and tales, each one wilder than the last and more each passing month," his father replied. "And while they're mostly about Rudi and the Princess, you're mentioned in many. Young Fiorbhinn's been making a few of them!"

His mouth quirked and Edain chuckled; Lady Juniper's youngest had all her mother's music and magic, but not nearly as much hard-learned common sense as yet.

Mind, in wartime people need dreams more than ever.

"Ah, well, that will all help, a wee bit," Edain said shrewdly, nodding. "And I'll just tuck the Southsiders and Norrheimers who swore to the High King in with 'em, too; they've had a chance to get to know me, and they'll want everyone else following orders as well."

Sam Aylward hid a sudden fierce surge of pride. *A thousand years of farmers and fighters,* he thought. *And this one's an Aylward with the best of them.*

Asgerd caught his eye and glanced away swiftly, hiding a smile herself; he had the uncomfortable feeling that she'd read his mind.

No, no fool she. And best not to let the lad get too cocky, he thought, and went on aloud:

"You'll be glad to 'ear Eithne's not among them. She's handfasted to Artan Jackson over to Dun Carmody . . ."

"Artan the leatherworker? Big fella, missing half his left ear, Elk sept?"

"Roit. And she's just delivered of twins."

Edain blew out his cheeks in a soundless *whoosh* of relief. Asgerd cocked an eye at him, and he shrugged and grinned sheepishly.

"You'd be an odd young man if you hadn't been interested in women before you met me," she said dryly. "But now that you *have* . . ."

"And there's a fair number 'ere you 'ave met." He put two fingers to his lips and gave a piercing whistle. *"Oi! Dickie! Front and center!"*

"Me brother," Edain said aside to Asgerd. "Three years younger than me, three years and a bit . . . by Maponos of the Youths, he'll be near eighteen now! Eighteen come this Lughnasadh!"

"Time doesn't stop while you're on a journey," Asgerd agreed.

Then she glanced eastward. Sam thought she was thinking of *her* home, clear the other side of the continent, and one she'd probably never see again.

"Fetch the rest, lass," Edain said to Asgerd. "Best they meet their new comrades. You can make Dick's acquaintance later." A grin: "Though I'd wish you to meet Ma and the sisters before me lout of a brother!"

She nodded and trotted off. A man came bounding up

the low slope, moving with a springy elastic step despite the weight of brigantine, sword and dirk and buckler, slung longbow and the war-quiver of forty-eight arrows and knocked down swine-feather over his shoulder. The green leather surface of the torso-armor carried the new arms of Montival's High King, the crowned mountain and Sword, rather than the Moon and Antlers of the Clan Mackenzie.

The face above the mail collar was high-cheeked and snub-nosed, blue-eyed and pale apart from the half that was summer freckles; his long hair was rust-colored, falling down his back in a queue bound with a spare bowstring, and a sparse scattering of lighter hairs showed he was trying to grow a mustache and failing miserably. An enormous grin showed square white teeth. He was lanky, but an inch or so above Edain's five-nine, and his chest and arms showed the effects of thousands of hours of practice with the bow since the age of six as well as a countryman's labors.

"Edain!" he shouted. "A hundred thousand welcomes, brother!"

"Dick!" Edain called back. "This pup's grown teeth, by the Gods!"

They fell on each other in what was half an embrace and half a bearlike wrestling match; Garbh growled dubiously, then caught the younger man's scent, froze as her memory worked, and began leaping about happily herself. It ended with Dick's head clasped under Edain's left arm while his right rubbed knuckles vigorously on his brother's head until they were both roaring with laughter.

"Ah, Dick, it's good to see you again, by each and every one of Them, from the Lord and Lady down to the house-hob," Edain gasped, releasing him.

"And you too, even if you were the bloody noogie champion of Dun Fairfax."

Then Edain went on more soberly: "So, it's the High King's sworn man you'd be?"

"What else, for an Aylward?" Dick said.

"What else indeed," Edain said.

He stepped forward and embraced him once more. "That's from your brother, then."

Then he cuffed the younger man across the side of the head, a *clap* of calloused hand on bone.

"*Ow!* Boggarts bugger you, what was *that* for?" Dick said, rubbing at his ear; the blow hadn't been enough to really hurt, but it hadn't been a love-pat either.

"*That* was from your bow-captain; the bow-captain of the High King's Archers. Found your sept totem yet, Dick?"

"Wolf, of course. Came to me plain as daylight while I slept in the forest. Sounded like Da, that he did."

"He did for me too, but it's a bit of a surprise, it is. I was thinkin' it would be Coyote, or maybe Raven or Fox."

Edain pointed his index finger in his brother's face. "I know how you love your daft jokes, Dickie. But this is serious business, so we'll not be havin' any of that. I've thrashed you before, and I can do it again if you need your face put in the midden. Understood? You're a grown man now, and I'll be treating you as such."

The younger Aylward brother straightened pridefully. "Understood, bow-captain!"

"Good. Fall them all in, then."

He grinned again, slapped his fist to his brigandine and bounded off.

Sam spoke casually: "Would you loike me to tell 'em you're in charge?"

"By Lugh of the Many Skills, no, Da!" Edain said briskly. "How could I ever get a fair grip on them then? They have to learn to listen to *me*."

His father nodded, hiding his smile once more. Then the younger man went on, looking over his shoulder.

"Ah, good."

A column of troops came trotting up forty strong with a jingle and clank of gear, Asgerd at their head. He ran an experienced eye over them. About two-thirds were dressed and equipped in the Clan's style, brigandine and bow and shortsword and buckler, right down to the kilts. Far more of them were dark-skinned than you'd find in a Mackenzie dun, but any single one of them could have been dropped in without exciting much comment. Most of the Clan or their parents had started out as farm and small-town folk in western Oregon, but a fair scattering had come from the cities and a few from everywhere under the sun.

Including England! Sam thought wryly. *Those would be the Southsiders he spoke of.*

The rest were in trousers and jackets, with bigger round shields slung over their quivers and longer swords at their belts; a few had axes across their backs, carried in loops beside their quivers.

Must be that place in Maine where they're all fair mad for the Viking bit, Sam mused, then felt his kilt brush his knees. *Well, who am Oi to speak, so to speak, eh?*

One huge man with a forked braided beard carried a gruesome ax–war-hammer combination, and looked able to use it. A big thickset woman with extremely cold dark eyes nodded to Sam Aylward in mutual recognition, and he pursed his lips at the way she moved. Built like a brick on legs but very fast with it; fast and heavy was rare and dangerous.

"Follow me," Edain said curtly.

And they do, no arguing, Sam thought as he strolled in their wake. *Oi did a proper man's work raising this'un, bugger me blind if Oi didn't!*

The hundred and twenty Mackenzie archers had turned out and were waiting—not standing at any rigid attention, many leaning on their unstrung bow staves, but in good order. About a quarter were women, and a good half hadn't been in the First Levy when his son left that April day two years ago, and few of them were older than Edain. He nodded to a few friends, and then stood before them with his thumbs hooked into his sword belt. He spoke in a carrying voice, not shouting and not excited, but hard and clear.

"I am Edain Aylward Mackenzie, called Aylward the Archer; the totem of my sept is Wolf."

Then, suddenly punching his fist skyward: "Hail to Artos, High King of Montival. Hail, Artos! *Artos and Montival!*"

A moment's surprised silence, then a roar from every throat; to his surprise Sam found himself shouting too:

"Artos! Artos!"

When silence had fallen again, Edain went on: "So you'd be the High King's sworn archers?"

"Aye!" someone shouted, and the others took it up.

"Then I'm to command you. For three reasons, each good and sufficient: I can outshoot any of you, I've more time in the High King's fighting tail than any of you . . . and third's the charm, the High King wishes it so. Any questions?"

Silence, and he went on: "These behind me have been with the High King longer than you, as well. With him through battle and ambush and long hard journeying.

That makes them your comrades, and you'll all be treating each other as such. We're all going to be like brothers and sisters or I will kick your arse so hard your teeth will march out like Bearkiller pikemen on parade. Is all that clear, *mo seanfhaiseanta bithiúnaigh féin*?"

"Aye!" his very own old-fashioned cutthroats replied.

"Can't hear you."

"Aye!"

"Better. Now here's your first orders. There's to be a handfasting this night—"

Ignatius looked around the Sacristia of Castle Corbec's church, the vesting room behind the altar. He smiled a little at the familiar scents of wax candles and the metal and cloth of the cruets, ciborium, chalice, paten, the altar linens, the vessels of the Holy Oils; they were like old friends, greeting him after long absence. Candlelight glittered on the golden thread of the vestments waiting on their T-shaped stands. Then he stood as Abbot-Bishop Dmwoski entered the room.

"Most Reverend Father," he said, bowing to kiss the older man's ring, then standing at the Order of the Shield's version of parade rest. "I give thanks to God that we meet again."

The words were conventional, and his face remained calm, but he could not keep all emotion out of the tone.

"At ease. I also thank God," Dmwoski said, and after a slight pause: "My son."

They both looked down for a moment in silent prayer, their hands folded in the sleeves of their habits.

"Or perhaps I should say *my lord Chancellor*," the older man said, with a slight smile.

Ignatius felt himself flushing a little. "My acceptance

of the office was of course conditional on your approval, Most Reverend Father."

Dmwoski chuckled. "Which you have."

"I confess . . . I am not altogether sure that I should have accepted. Apart from doubts as to my capacity, we are enjoined to avoid *the near occasions of sin*. This will be a post of great power, and hence, of great temptation."

The Abbot-Bishop shrugged. "You swore poverty, chastity, and obedience; my command is that you accept this position, which means that it fulfills obedience rather than violating it. Even the Cardinal-Archbishop in Portland agrees that having a cleric in such a post will be most advantageous to the Church. I do not think that you will be tempted by riches, or that chastity will become harder for you in a high office. Power, though—power itself can be a temptation. But then again, so can anything else in this fallen world."

Ignatius bowed his head. "I can only try my best and throw myself on God's loving mercy," he said quietly.

"And He has blessed you, my son. You have brilliantly fulfilled the mission I assigned to you so long ago," Dmwoski said warmly. "I have made many errors in my life, but that, I think, was not one of them. I do not doubt that you will fulfill future missions as well."

His square face was more lined than Ignatius remembered, and his fringe of white hair would never need to be tonsured again. He'd begun to stoop a little, noticeable in a frame that had always had a soldierly erectness, but the eyes were still very shrewd, calm and blue and penetrating beneath the tufted eyebrows.

"Fulfilled it and more besides," he went on. "Our brethren have been greatly heartened by your reports in this time of war and trial."

The older man shook his head slowly and turned to look at Ignatius' sword, hung on the rack beside the door. It was of fine steel but plain and in an equally plain black-leather scabbard, an Order-issue cross-hilted long-sword a little under a yard in the blade, with the Raven and Cross on the fishtail pommel. The elder cleric reached one hand out and almost touched the double-lobe grip.

"I have seen our High King's Sword," Dmwoski said. "And it is, mmmm, most impressive. Terrifying, even. But this . . . *she* touched it?"

"Yes, Father. The hilt, and my forehead. And . . . it was cold, the air was thin there on the mountain above the high white valley, and there was light, so much light, and . . . no, it is impossible to describe completely. Words themselves break and crumble beneath the strain."

Dmwoski nodded and sank to his knees before the cross-shape, taking his crucifix between his hands and bowing his head. Ignatius followed suit, remembering the feeling of being *illuminated*.

"It was astonishing," he said softly after a moment. "I saw myself more clearly at that instant than ever before in my life, and the weight and stain of sin and error I saw in me and woven through me should have been enough to break my mind. Yet there was a . . . how can I say it . . . such a *tenderness* in her regard, a fire within her greater than suns, which yet warmed and comforted while it burned, as if it flamed away the dross but left me un-harmed. I knew my own failings, and wept for the shame of it. But I saw what *she* saw in me as well. I saw what I *could* be, what God had made and meant me to be, and knew what I must strive to be every hour of my life there-after."

Dmwoski surprised him by chuckling. "Brother of the

Order, have I ever told you why I am so glad to be a son of the Church, rather than a Protestant? Or a Jew or Muslim, for that matter."

"Ah . . . because ours are the true doctrines in accordance with the truths set out in Scripture, by the *magisterium* of the Church, and by reason? And of course that ours are the forms of worship most pleasing to God the Father, Son and Holy Ghost?" Ignatius said.

It wasn't a question which had ever occurred to him. *Perhaps because I was a man grown, albeit a young man, before I ever really spoke at length with anyone who was not a follower of Holy Mother Church? Things were otherwise before the Change.*

"Of course," the Abbot-Bishop said. "But the reason *I* find most comforting is that we have the bright legions of the Saints and the mercy of the Blessed Virgin to intercede for us before the terrible majesty of the Godhead."

"It was . . . terrible enough, Father. Not frightening in the way a physical danger might be, of course, but terrible as a storm or a sunset is. To see a soul that was human, so very human, but truly filled with the divine Light, freed from sin and soaring to heights I could not imagine or grasp."

"You have been granted a very great honor, my son," Dmwoski said meditatively. "One such as few men have known. Yet as you say, a frightening one as well. The higher a man rises, the lower he can fall. The Adversary himself was once closest of all created things to God, and so closest to Him in knowledge and power and virtue."

"I can only strive to be worthy," Ignatius said; the words were grave, but he felt himself smile at the memory of that mixture of awe and joy. "Worthy to be the Knight of the Immaculata."

"Inspiring that a knight-brother of the Shield of St. Benedict was chosen," Dmwoski said. "And especially to the younger members of our Order. Their faith was strong before, but it *burns* now. Which is of course the purpose of miracles; they show a possibility."

"And my report of the events on Nantucket?" Ignatius added. "I have eagerly awaited your thoughts on the matter, Most Reverend Father. It was far less . . . *straightforward* is not the correct word, but I confess I am at a loss for a better one."

Dmwoski sighed ruefully. "Now there, my son, you have touched on mysteries too deep for this hard head of mine. Reports have been dispatched to the Curia in Badia and I have requested that they be brought to the immediate attention of the Holy Father and the Church's most learned theologians. But to be granted the experience of the Beatific Vision *as well as* a call to her service from the very Mother of God . . . it is almost excessive!"

"A glimpse of the Beatific Vision, yes. Or as much of it as my limited perceptions could grasp; a . . . a metaphor, perhaps. But . . ." Ignatius said, and signed himself, then touched his fingers to his forehead. "But *you* were most definitely the voice I heard and the person I saw. Yet . . . you assured me that you were still alive; that what I beheld was not bound by Time, for it was already partly in Eternity. Most Reverend Father, I assure you it is beyond *my* comprehension as well."

"How could it not be beyond our comprehension?" Dmwoski laughed. "Are we not servants and celebrants of a Mystery? I confess to both fear and longing at your description; but those are the emotions that the contemplation of Eternity is *supposed* to arouse. Only when it is achieved can joy be unmixed, and as I grow closer to the end of my days the longing grows stronger. Yet I have work to do first; and hopefully a long life of effort and struggle awaits *you*, Brother."

"And there is the matter of the marriage," Ignatius said, as they signed themselves, rose and sat on the hard wooden stools. "I am troubled by that as well. Torn between joy and doubt."

He smiled. "And it is so *good* to have someone to turn to, someone older and wiser than I to share my thoughts and advise me! If I had to say what most comforted *me* about being part of the body of the Church, Father, it is that I need not always face these matters alone. If the service of God is perfect freedom, then the service of His Church is a great comfort."

Dmwoski's brows went up. "The marriage has been long contemplated. Contemplated since they were children, I suspect, by their mothers. At the very least since the end of the War of the Eye, possibly earlier."

"Most Reverend Father, the Immaculata *herself* entrusted the Princess to my care. And I have come to feel for her as a person, as I might a beloved younger sister; I have learned to admire her intelligence, her courage, her earnest desire to do right, and her devotion to Holy Church. Not to mention her cheerfulness through all our trials and dangers and—harder for one of her birth—the hardships and inconveniences."

Dmwoski nodded. "A remarkable young woman. But why do you feel the marriage is questionable? She has no vocation for the life of a religious; and therefore she should marry. Even as a private citizen, much less a monarch with the fate of a dynasty in her blood. We are not all called to make the same sacrifices or to carry the same Cross."

"But . . . no, you are right. Though she is very devout. My principal concern as her confessor and spiritual counselor has been to warn her against the danger of scrupulosity."

Dmwoski chuckled. "I am not surprised. That is the besetting temptation of pious youngsters, and pious young women in particular. That her duties will lie in the secular sphere should help her guard against it. Yet her destiny is a throne; and so she must marry for reasons of state, and there is only one obvious choice. The High King—"

"Yes, our High King is a fine man, one worthy of her, as few could be. A man of almost intimidating qualities, in fact: a true hero, but no man of blood by his own choice either, not hungry for power in itself, and a good and loyal friend as well. And I think God has made him His instrument against the Cutters. Also the two of them love each other deeply. But he is pagan."

A grave inclination of the head. "Do you think marriage to him will shake her faith?" Dmwoski said. "For that would indeed be reason to oppose it, regardless of consequence."

Ignatius paused. "No . . . no, not that. She loves him, but she loves God with equal passion."

"Then I do not think we need fear excessively. Mixed marriages are permissible under canon law, and have been for some time, my son—unlike some ordinances of the late pre-Change era, those were *not* rescinded by the Third Council."

"If she is blessed with children, which God grant—"

"We must insist that they be taught the Faith, certainly."

"His Majesty has agreed to that. You can guess his reservations, I think."

"That his unspoken intent is that they be exposed to *his* faith as well, and decide for themselves when they come of age whether to follow the Church's teachings or the so-called Old Religion? That would accord with Mackenzie custom. They are tolerant, if anything tolerant to a fault."

"Yes. He remarked, in fact, that his mother had been raised a Catholic, and laughed good-naturedly at my silence. It is important to remember that his physical talents are matched by a very keen mind, Father."

Dmwoski spread gnarled, battered hands. "I do not think we can legitimately object, then. Particularly when this marriage is so essential to the defense of the Church against the CUT's heresy and diabolism. Remember to take a long perspective on these matters, my son; we are bidden to be as wise as serpents and as gentle as doves."

"Yet the Immaculata called me a *miles* of Christ, Most Reverend Father."

Dmwoski chuckled indulgently. "And a soldier of Christ must learn His virtues as well! You are still a young man, and the desire to beat down opposition to God's will with hammer blows burns hot in you. Yet Holy Mother Church has won many battles by persistence, by endurance, by humility and above all by *patience*. She is wise with years, and knows how to bide her time."

"My heart tells me that much good will come from this union, yet . . . perhaps much of the good will take generations to unfold. Well, we serve the Church Militant, not the Church Triumphant. Not yet."

He smiled wryly as he went on: "I think that it will also make the two people concerned very happy indeed. I feared that would cloud my judgment, Father, for they are both very dear to me."

"Then you are once more privileged, my son, for you will be able to give them deep and abiding joy through your service as a priest in sanctifying their union."

"God is good," Ignatius said, crossing himself again.

Dmwoski laughed wholeheartedly at the slightly dubious tone.

"Yes, He is!" he said, and shook an admonishing finger. "So you need not fear He is . . . ah . . . *setting you up.* Lugh might; but Lugh is a fable."

Ignatius flushed and nodded. "I have been much among pagans, Father."

"And now you will marry one to a Catholic princess!" Dmwoski said, smiling. More soberly: "May I help you with your vestments?"

"I would be honored."

Ignatius drew a deep breath and took the amice from the elderly cleric's hands. He donned it, and murmured:

"Place, O Lord, on my head the helmet of Salvation, that so armed I may resist the assaults of the Adversary—"

"And to think I wanted something quiet and private," Artos grumbled. "I thought we could have it here, so remote and peaceful . . ."

Matti smiled, but there was a quaver in her voice. "Nothing we do can ever be very private," she said. "The nearest I ever got to private was Dun Juniper . . . and that wasn't very."

Their mothers had swung into operation almost the moment he'd spoken and Mathilda answered. They'd even found time to have the inner walls of the keep garlanded with fir boughs and bright wildflowers; the high castle ramparts left a soft shadowed darkness amid the scent of pine, but dozens of torches cast a ruddy light, and the sun painted the high snowpeaks a like crimson. There was a fair crowd, as well; his stepfather, Sir Nigel, was here, and Eric Larsson of the Bearkillers, and at least one or two from most of the other realms that made up the new-minted Montival. Even a McClintock from the far south, looking a bit hairy and disheveled in the Great Kilt they affected. At least that meant the enemy had been held short of the Columbia Gorge; from what he'd heard they were trying to hammer it down and cut Montival in two.

"Rudi, let's *enjoy* this? Please?" Mathilda asked.

He took a deep breath, then grinned. "Acushla, how could I not?"

Now he stood in his best kilt and Montrose jacket, with lace at his throat and cuffs; Sandra had had a white-cream-and-pearl cotehardie ready for her daughter . . . which didn't surprise him at all. A crown of meadow-sweet whose flowers matched it encircled her cascade of unbound brown hair, its delicate almond scent strong. Castle Corbec was a major border fortress, and the chapel could seat several hundred. It was finished in the same pale rock as the exterior, but the walls were a lacy framework for the glowing stained-glass windows. The inner keep courtyard where it stood was paved in the same stone; its confines were handsome but rather bare apart from the church and the afternoon's improvised additions, since this was a Crown fortress garrisoned by the Regent's troops, not a fief with a resident lord and his family.

Sir Nigel Loring came up; he was in the same high-festival Mackenzie costume as Artos, small and trim and alert in his early seventies. His eyes were blue and a little watery—legacy of a battle injury before the Change—and his voice had the softly clipped gentry accents he'd learned from the grandmother who'd raised him after he'd been orphaned in infancy. *She'd* been born well over a century ago, and had been a debutante when Edward VII held Britain's throne. Artos' mind felt jittery, as if it was skipping from thought to thought like a drop of oil on a griddle; some part of it wondered what that stern dame would have thought if she could have seen her grandson now, and thought for a moment of how *her* grandmother had seen Napoleon depart for Elba.

Only three lifetimes. And now the fire-and-steel wonders of those centuries have risen and vanished in their turn and once more the world moves to the pace of the horse and the plowman.

"Mathilda, you look absolutely ravishing," Sir Nigel said, bowing over her hand with courtly grace. "This is all improvised, but your mother thinks it would be appropriate if I gave you away. I hope you concur, because you certainly have the last word in the matter."

"I'd love that, Sir Nigel," she said warmly; they'd gotten along well during her stays at Dun Juniper in the years after the War of the Eye. "You've always been like a second father to me. And now you *will* be one."

"Stepfather-in-law, at least, my dear girl," he said. "And it will be good practice for the state ceremonies later. Though Maude and Fiorbhinn will never forgive you for marrying without them present."

Which was true in a sense, Artos knew; both his mother's children with Sir Nigel would be livid.

Though they'll forgive me, and they love Mathilda dearly. Who could not? Well, some, but they show their lack of taste and wit thereby.

"We'll be having at *least* two other wedding ceremonies, Father," Artos said.

"Affirmations and commemorations," Mathilda said. "This *is* the marriage."

Artos nodded, though to Mackenzie sensibilities that was a distinction without a difference. Clan custom and law held that it was the public declaration of intent and then living together that made a handfasting; the ceremonies simply bore witness to it and asked blessings and luck of the Powers on the new family. He knew Christians thought that the ceremony *was* the marriage, though.

"One at Dun Juniper, and one at Castle Todenangst. And Eilir is here, at least," he said aloud.

"I can assure that that will make things worse with your younger sisters, not better, my boy," he said dryly. "And now take yourself off to the church to await your fate in fear and trembling, and you, young lady, go to your bridesmaids—they're either that, or a troop of light cavalry, and a most formidable one."

Artos took a deep breath, squeezed Mathilda's hand, and did so. Edain was deep in talk with the under-captains of the King's Archers, and flashed him a smile and a thumbs-up as he passed. The rest were busy sprucing up their gear; most of them had flowers tucked behind their ears.

They have something planned, then.

That worried him a little, thinking of some of the high jinks that went on at a Mackenzie handfasting.

But Edain's a steady man. He'll keep them in hand.

A crowd of male friends came with him to the church gates: Ingolf, Fred, Bjarni, a half dozen more including those he hadn't seen since he left; Alleyne Loring and John Hordle of the Dúnedain for starters. Michael Havel

Jr. was there from Larsdalen—though *not*, he noted, his mother, Signe.

"Mike!" Artos said, grinning as they exchanged a hand-to-forearm grip.

The younger man had grown a good deal since Artos had last seen him, several months before he left for Nantucket; he was past seventeen now, and nearly Artos' height. And their family resemblance was much stronger. That was most apparent in the face, a high-cheeked, square-jawed handsomeness that they'd taken from the Bear Lord, their common father. Signe's heritage showed in the corn-yellow hair and bright blue eyes. He'd acquired a couple of scars on his face and hands since the questers left too. Then Artos saw the small burn-mark between the other's brows, made with the touch of a red-hot iron; it was the mark of the A-list, the Bearkiller equivalent of knighthood, and nobody got it for any reason whatsoever except proved merit.

"You're young for that, boyo!" he said admiringly.

"Ah—" he said, flushing. Then he rallied: "Well, you got *yours* from Raven when you were only ten!"

His cousin Will Larsson grinned beside him; they were of an age and height, but the son of Signe's brother had skin the color of light rye toast. He also had the A-list brand.

"We got the combat exemption," he said proudly. "Fighting at Pendleton, we got caught up in a complete ratfuck during the retreat."

"And fought like heroes, I have no doubt."

"*Everyone* was a hero there. Unfortunately so were the enemy!"

Artos did a few quick introductions. The men who'd stayed in Montival looked curiously at the questers, and met the same regard. Artos smiled to himself at the quick careful appraisals that went back and forth, and the nods of cautious respect.

Eric Larsson of the Bearkillers was among them, Signe Havel's twin brother and her war-commander; a big scarred blond man in formal Bearkiller denim, a brown so dark it was almost black. He was called *Steel-Fist* these days. Seeing the gleaming prosthethic where his left hand had been was a vivid reminder that life had gone on here too in the last years . . . and that a lot of it had been war. Right now he grinned and nudged Artos with an elbow; he could tell the Bearkiller was bursting with military news and plans, but he'd put them aside for the moment. His son Will whispered in his ear, and then they *both* grinned at Artos.

"You're looking a little peaked all of a sudden, Your Majesty," Eric said, amused. "Pale and interesting and elfin. Or maybe just so goddamned frightened you're about to puke."

"Perish the thought! Artos the First is unmoved. But Rudi Mackenzie, now . . ." He put his hand to his stomach. "Right now *he's* feeling nervous, and that's a fact. I've walked towards a shield-wall full of spears and angry strangers with less apprehension."

"Your dad said the same thing when he and Signe got hitched. Of course, he was marrying *Signe*, which was enough to frighten the shit out of anyone, even then before she became such a goddamned she-dragon."

Artos laughed: "A fluttering in the gut, perhaps a little wobbling in the knees. Hard to imagine Mike Havel feeling such, but I certainly do!"

They all nodded; the married men among them with rueful understanding. Eric's good hand slipped inside his

jacket with its black-on-black braid-work and snarling red
bear's-head badge. It came out with a silver flask that
gave off a welcome flowery scent when he twisted off the
cap. Artos took a quick swig, and then another; sweet fire
ran down his throat. It was Larsdalen brandy, and well
aged in oak.

"Arra, those grapes did not die in vain," he said.
"Many thanks. Too much of this is weakness, but a little
can be strength."

"And that's our cue," Ingolf said, as organ music
pealed out.

It came through tall doors whose wooden panels were
carved with a rather gruesome depiction of the martyr-
dom of St. Sebastian, in which the archers looked suspiciously like Mackenzies; it had probably been done before
the War of the Eye. They all racked their swords in the
vestibule just inside it, and Eric's son looked curiously at
the Sword, whistling softly under his breath.

It's odd how reactions vary, Artos thought. *It makes
some fear, gives others exaltation, and then again some can
only see a sword . . . at least when it's sheathed and I'm not
holding it.*

"You don't mind letting it out of your sight?" he asked
Artos, frowning a little.

"I do, Bill," he replied to the dark young man. "But
because it makes *me* nervous to be without it, so; that's a
side effect of the thing. Not for any fear of what might
happen to *it*; a little fear of what might happen to anyone
who tried to touch it, rather."

Within, the church was a little like being inside a jewel
box, with the evening sun sparkling through the great
arches and rondels of stained glass, and the candles high
above twinkling in rings of stars amid drifts of blue

incense-smoke. The Catholics touched their fingers to the holy water and signed themselves with the Cross, and the women covered their heads as well; Artos and the others of the Old Religion made a reverence towards the altar, and the great Rood on the wall behind. Another, and deeper, to the blue-robed figure of the Virgin in the side chapel; she was shown crowned, with the form of a dove hovering above her head in a burst of radiance. The painting was a little stiff, partly because the limner had been trying for a fourteenth-century style, and more so because this was a remote provincial keep far from the Regent's art schools.

But there's Power there, Artos thought. *I can feel it, as real as I might in a* nemed. *Sure it is that They have many faces. All the shapes the Divine shows us are true; and none are all the Truth.*

His stomach fluttered again as he took his place at the head of the main aisle of the church, just below the steps to the altar and the carved waist-high wooden screen. The rest of his party took their seats, save for his grooms-men, Ingolf and Fred, at his elbow.

"It's really happening," he muttered under his breath. "Sure and I wanted it so badly for so long, and now I'm restraining an impulse to show a pair of heels and run screaming into the mountains looking for a cave to hide in, resident bears or no."

There was a little cold sweat on his forehead all of a sudden. Fred and Ingolf were close behind him, which was some comfort. His mother was in the front pew, which was more. She caught his eye, then slowly and de-liberately winked. He thought her hand moved under a fold of her arsaid; either in the Invoking pentagram, or a simple thumbs-up.

And suddenly I feel better. By the Ever-Changing One, but it's good to be home and among my kin once more!

"Time," Ingolf whispered; he'd been raised Catholic and was familiar with the service.

Father Ignatius came out of the Sacristia, bright in his white and gold and crimson vestments, and the folk in the pews rose to their feet. The organ thundered again, and Artos turned to watch Mathilda pace through the door, with Mary and Virginia garlanded as her bridesmaids and matrons of honor. She put her arm through Sir Nigel's and continued up the stretch of red carpet, smiling gravely, holding her bouquet in gloved hands. A light gauze veil covered her flower-circled hair and shadowed her face.

She is so beautiful, Artos thought. *Enough to make a man ache, and not just in the obvious places.*

Not conventionally pretty; her features were bold and a little irregular and her face long—she took after her father in looks, as in her height. But there was a glow to her that went beyond mere youth and health, and her light brown eyes were wells where thoughts moved like golden-scaled fish in the depths. He saw himself reflected in them, and knew she saw herself in his.

And though we have known each other so long, my breath comes fast at the sight of her. With a cool shock: *The Goddess is here, here and now. So Maiden becomes Mother, and the Son becomes the Lover. We too are part of all that is.*

The music died, and they took the steps to the altar. Ignatius smiled at them; Artos almost thought that *he* winked a little too. Then he raised his hands and spoke:

" 'Dearly beloved, we are gathered together here in the sight of God to join together this man and this woman in holy Matrimony; which is an honorable estate, instituted of God in Paradise . . .' "

The words and gestures went on. At last Ignatius took Artos' right hand in his own, and Mathilda's from Sir Nigel's, and laid them in each other's. He felt the strong slim calloused fingers of her sword-hand grip his as his smiling stepfather stepped back to join his mother.

"Say after me: *I, Rudi Artos Mackenzie—*" the priest began, and Artos echoed him.

". . . *and thereunto I plight thee my troth*," he finished, his strong clear voice filling the church.

Mathilda's answered it: "*I, Mathilda Christine Arminger, take thee, Rudi Artos Mackenzie, to be my wedded husband, to have and to hold from this day forward, for better for worse, for richer or poorer, in sickness and in health, to be bonny and buxom at bed and at board, to love and to cherish, till death us depart, according to God's holy ordinance; and thereunto I plight thee my troth.*"

For a moment Artos knew sickening fear; the whole matter of the rings was suddenly gone from his mind, as if it had stuttered and missed a step. Then Ingolf and Mary each stepped forward with the golden bands on small satin cushions. Ignatius extended his hands over them and raised his voice:

"*Bless these Rings, O merciful Lord, that those who wear them, that give and receive them, may be ever faithful to one another, remain in Your peace, and live and grow old together in Your love, under their own vine and fig tree, and seeing their children's children. Amen.*"

The priest's voice was strong and well trained, but for a long moment Artos lost the thread of it, simply looking into her smile. Then she squeezed his hand again, and he heard:

". . . *thereto have given and pledged their troth each to the other, and have declared the same by giving and receiv-*

ing of a Ring, and by joining of hands; I pronounce there-
fore that they be Man and Wife together, in the Name of the
Father, and of the Son, and of the Holy Spirit. Amen."

He took a long deep breath of delight, hearing Ignatius add under his breath: *"Bless you, my children."*

"Wife," he said softly to Mathilda.

"Husband," she replied.

"It's not a formal part of a Catholic ceremony," Ignatius said, "but you may kiss the bride."

He lifted the veil and did. Her lips were soft and sweet,
but the arms that went around him were strong. The
scent of her mingled with the flowers in her hair and
made him dizzy, as if the great stone mass of the church
were tilting slowly.

"And there is a time and place for everything, my
son!" Ignatius said, with suppressed laughter in his voice.

Mathilda was flushed and laughing herself as she drew
away. Mary stepped closer, elegant in Dúnedain formal
black and piratical with her eye patch, and handed
Mathilda the bouquet.

"Give everyone a chance to get out, so you can throw
it, Matti," she said. Then she smiled. "Sister."

Mathilda blinked in surprise. "We are now, aren't we?"
she said, delight still bubbling in her voice.

The great doors spread wide, and they walked towards
them. Mathilda's eyes went wide as well, as the pipers of
the High King's Archers sounded off on either side of the
portals; the sound was stunning-huge, magnified by the
high walls that surrounded the keep of Castle Corbec,
and the superb acoustics of the church.

"Edain, I'm going to *skin* you!" Artos muttered.

Then he saw his mother grinning, and knew the Archer hadn't been alone in it. These weren't the sweet

uilleann instruments usually played at a handfasting either, since nobody had thought to bring those from the Clan's territory in a time of battle and tumult; they were the *píob mhór*, the great war-pipes, and from the sudden rattling roar beneath the savage drone someone had dragged a Lambeg along as well. The ranks of the High King's Archers stood without, with their bows raised to make an arch.

At least they're not playing "The Ravens' Pibroch" or "Hecate's Wolves Their Howl," he thought; it was a march, his own mother's "My Heart Sees Green Hills in the Mist."

There was no choice but to pace forward to the stately rhythm. Mathilda's hand tightened on his, and he could see she was fighting not to smile. Then as they crossed the threshold—someone had the minimal tact to wait until they were off the consecrated ground—Mary snatched a besom from a girl behind her and laid it before them with a sweeping gesture.

Oh, well, Artos thought, and caught Mathilda up in his arms.

"*Over the broom and into new life!*" his clansfolk shouted, as he stepped over it.

He kissed Mathilda again, and then the Mackenzies stormed forward, cheering. The men among them grabbed him and tossed him up and bore him overhead on their upthrust arms, and the women did likewise for Mathilda. Then they began to dance, two lines curling around each other *deosil* and *tuathal* to the music of pipe and drum, faster and faster until both the newlyweds were tossing and whirling like boats on a stormy sea. At last they stopped, threw both upward with a great shout, and then set them on their feet. The pair staggered together, arms around each other's shoulders.

"Well, at least they didn't strip us naked, carry us upstairs and throw us into bed," Artos said in Mathilda's ear.

She blushed—exactly that wasn't uncommon at a Clan wedding—and they straightened as the bagpipes fell silent.

Voices rang out instead, and somewhere a flute, both high and sweet. He recognized his mother's soprano, still effortless on the higher notes, and then saw his nearest kin standing about her, with his elder half sister Eilir swaying and Signing the lyrics as the others sang:

> "Fly we on o'er hill and dale
> Spruces guard our faery tale
> Hemlock branches bless and say
> Upon my lovely's wedding day
> Joy on thy fair handfasting day!"

Juniper stepped forward and sang:

> "Tide will roll and bridge stand fast
> Eagles watch and breezes pass
> Ebb and flow whilst ravens play
> Upon my fair son's wedding day
> Joy on thy fair handfasting day!"

Then Mary and Eilir took the forward place:

> "Upon my fair brother's wedding day
> Joy on thy fair handfasting day!"

Juniper herself brought him the plate with the fruitcake, though Sandra was beside her.

"Made with my own hands," the Mackenzie chieftain-ness said.

"I threw in some currants," Sandra added. "Really, it's all right, dear. I checked; this isn't a pagan rite. Well, no more than Christmas. And it *will* make the Mackenzies happy."

"I'm not worried," Mathilda said. "I'm—" She checked and cuffed at her eyes. "I'm almost crying, and I don't know why."

Artos pulled the sgian dubh out of his knee-hose and cut the round cake. There was another cheer as he and Mathilda each fed the other a bite. He leaned close in the course of it.

"Only a little longer to wait."

"Rudi . . ." she said two hours later.

"Yes, my darling one?"

"I . . . um, could you leave the Sword outside?"

"I can deny you nothing."

The castellan of Corbec had given up his private quarters in the South Tower with every evidence of willingness at the bridal feast.

Mind you, with Sandra here so would I, in his position!

Those quarters were a suite of rooms just below the machicolations of the tower. Edain and a squad of his King's Archers were a floor below, and had cheerfully promised to pitch anyone who came up the spiral stair-case right back down again, or out an arrow-slit and into the lake. The stairs gave directly onto a semicircular space, and the doors leading to the individual rooms opened off that. Artos drew the Sword—

Shock.

Gentle this time, distant, like a chiming of bells and the scent of mulled wine.

—and thrust it into the floor before the entrance to the sleeping quarters. The surface was granite tiles on concrete beams, but the blade sank in a double handspan and stood quivering.

"I think that will ensure us all the privacy we need," he said.

"You're showing off!"

"To be sure. And when better?"

Corbec was at nearly five thousand feet, and the nights were chill. A crackling pine-scented fire was burning in a big tiled hearth in the bedchamber, and it was pleasantly warm, smelling of blossoms and clean linen. There were wildflowers on the tables and headboards and in the arched windows, pale yellow and bright gold, blue and purple and crimson—saxifrage, mountain jasmine and penstemon and more. Artos could sense Mathilda's nervousness, and he crossed to the table and poured them both a glass of white wine from the bottle that rested in its silver ewer full of snow.

"*Anamchara* mine, we've waited this long, a little more won't hurt. It's not as if we had to show a bloody sheet!"

She surprised him by laughing. "Oh, we couldn't." At his raised brow: "I've been riding astride all my *life*, Rudi! Mom asked the doctor and she said it was all gone by the time I was thirteen."

He joined in the chuckle. "But you are nervous, my darling. I can tell, you know!"

"I'm—"

She sat down, looked at her hands, spoke in a small voice. "I'm afraid I won't be any, ummm, any good at this, Rudi. And I really want to be."

Artos sat beside her and put an arm around her shoulders and kissed the sleek brown hair over her ear. "Now, acushla, I'm going to betray one of the Men's Mysteries to you."

She made a small inquiring noise, and he went on: "And that mystery is that while for a woman it can be good or bad, well . . . for a man, unless he's ill or very drunk, it can only be good or better. So let's start with good, and get better with practice, shall we? Years and years of practice!"

She laughed and punched his shoulder, and suddenly they were kissing . . .

EPILOGUE

Edain Aylward Mackenzie looked up from where he was about to throw the dice onto the inside of the buckler lying on the floor. There shouldn't be any noise—the ceiling above this ready-room was tall, and good and thick to boot—but suddenly there was, beyond the subdued buzz of voices and the hoot of the night wind around Castle Corbec's towers.

"Quiet!" he said

The conversations died instantly. Men and women froze where they were, sitting at the tables or leaning against walls between the racks for spears and bills. Some reached for weapons, and then froze at his upraised hands.

The sound grew, faint and haunting, like the bridle-bells of the Fair Folk heard through trees on a moonless night. Then it rose to a peal like a silver carillon, and white light flooded down the stairwell. The skin at the back of his neck crawled a little in awe, and he heard whispered prayers and saw signs made.

"The jewel in the Sword. It must be as bright as the Sun itself," he whispered, and then it died away.